Gramsci in Love

T0288506

Gramsci in Love

Andrew Pearmain

TOP HAT BOOKS

Winchester, UK
Washington, USA

First published by Top Hat Books, 2015
Top Hat Books is an imprint of John Hunt Publishing Ltd., Laurel House, Station Approach,
Alresford, Hants, SO24 9JH, UK
office1@jhpbooks.net
www.johnhuntpublishing.com

For distributor details and how to order please visit the 'Ordering' section on our website.

Text copyright: Andrew Pearmain 2014

ISBN: 978 1 78279 811 8
Library of Congress Control Number: 2014949215

All rights reserved. Except for brief quotations in critical articles or reviews, no part of this book may be reproduced in any manner without prior written permission from the publishers.

The rights of Andrew Pearmain as author have been asserted in accordance with the Copyright, Designs and Patents Act 1988.

A CIP catalogue record for this book is available from the British Library.

Design: Stuart Davies

Printed in the USA by Edwards Brothers Malloy

We operate a distinctive and ethical publishing philosophy in all areas of our business, from our global network of authors to production and worldwide distribution.

"I have rejected every opportunity for polemics, and resisted every temptation, strong though this might be, to string together pieces of inaccurate, distorted or simply speculative evidence offered by sensationalists, often with a simple passion for scandal."
Paolo Spriano, Antonio Gramsci and the Party: The Prison Years

"The Italian author would not write a biographical novel without cramming it with tiresome rhetoric... They represent serious matters as if they were shop queue chatter... As a result, these biographies get written by foreigners."
Antonio Gramsci, 1930

Part One: Three Sisters

"From Russia, swarming through the whole world, came men and women who had been formed in ruthless battle, who had but one aim in life, who drew their breath from danger... None of us had, in the bourgeois sense of the word, any personal existence. We changed our names, our posting and our work at the Party's need. We had just enough to live on without real material discomfort, and we were not interested in making money, or following a career, or producing a literary heritage, or leaving a name behind us. We were interested solely in the difficult business of reaching Socialism." Victor Serge, Memoirs of a Revolutionary

"For a very long time I believed that it was absolutely, fatally impossible that I should ever be loved." Antonio Gramsci, 1923

"The buttons on your collar, the colour of your hair, I think I see you everywhere..." Paul Buchanan, 'Mid Air', CD 2012

Serebranyi Bor Sanatorium, Moscow 1922

He sat looking out over fields of spindly silver birch trees and rough scrub, dissected by winding streams and straighter cuts which he imagined served the purposes of irrigation or drainage. They were too narrow for navigation or transportation. The landscape was gently flourishing in late spring bloom. The silver birches were in full new leaf, the scrub was topped by heavy waving clusters of seed, and the streams flowed freely towards the river running through the distant village.

For the moment it presented a scene of easy vigour, full of itself, like a fat smiling peasant. Later in the season, he presumed, it would all dry and wither. With the sudden plunge in temperature and air pressure which heralded the vicious Russian winter, it would hurriedly shed leaves and stalks and viscosity. Everyone talked about it – "When winter comes..." – as if it punctuated the rest of the year. The trees and scrub would withdraw into their roots for earthy warmth, and the streams thicken and start to freeze over. By late November the ice would be thick enough to skate on.

Or so he imagined, from what he'd heard about the deep prolonged cold this far north, or for that matter about the alien pursuit of ice skating. It was nearly three thousand kilometres from his native temperate Sardinia; five hundred less from his adopted northern Italian city of Turin, where he had spent most of the last ten years. The winters could be hard enough in northern Italy, especially if you had inadequate clothing and nourishment – as he had for many of those years – but he was younger then, and the Italian sun was never too far away.

Here in Russia, even in late spring and early summer, the sun always seemed to be smaller and lower and paler, and somehow more timid, as though it was afraid of getting too close. It was hardly surprising that everyone he met, from the highest official to the lowest orderly, seemed to have cold hands. Russia had that effect, keeping you at a distance, chilling your bones. A troubling thought emerged from within his steady contemplation of the vista: would he still be here at Serebranyi Bor at the onset of hard Russian winter? *My goodness, I really can't afford to be out of circulation that long.* He was bundled up in layers of heavy blankets against the early evening chill. The attendants had insisted on wrapping him up tightly in his wicker chair, on top of the thick pyjamas and dressing gown he had been issued a week earlier when he had arrived at the sanatorium on the outskirts of Moscow. He had at first resisted their ministrations, in the sunny warmth of the late May afternoon, in his still rudimentary Russian – "I'll be fine without, I'll be fine..." – but they had fussily persisted. "Comrade Gramsci, you will catch cold! On top of everything else..."

He detected in their concern for his welfare a deeper concern that they might be called to account for it. As the two burly men tucked the tasselled edges around and underneath him, he pushed against their big strong cold hands for some room to move and breathe. For all his best efforts at self-restraint and politeness, a gasp of exasperation escaped his lips and noticeably moderated their touch. He hated this feeling of swaddled confinement, having spent so much of his childhood bound and restricted, his parents' vain attempt to cure his deformities and straighten him out. This had included strapping him into a kind of corset with rings on it, suspended for hours on end from the kitchen ceiling. The treatment was somehow supposed to dispel the emerging hump on the right side of his back. He could remember slowly twirling, looking down on the bustling assembled family of mother and father and six other young children, like a strange insect or bird or some kind of contraption for drying clothes.

He was glad of the blankets now. They would allow him to defer by at least half an hour the long slow trudge in his Soviet issue slippers back to his gloomy room on the ground floor at the back of the palatial old building. His room reflected, he reckoned, his relatively lowly status in the Communist International as a recently arrived delegate from a minor party. The Bolsheviks might be building a new world of liberty, equality and fraternity, assuming the mantle of the French Revolution as the driving force of history, but that didn't mean they were quite so free, equal and fraternal just yet.

As Marx had always insisted, the material reality of socialism would be based on what had gone before: all those long aching bloody centuries of oppression, exploitation and misery. The explosive power of capitalism created massive inequalities in wealth and status, heaped on top of the rigid stratifications of feudalism, so that every individual was allotted their place in the stultifying social hierarchy. It took concerted collective action by masses of people over many years, guided by the best strategic brains of the age, to break it apart and reorder things.

And as the Russians themselves had been painfully discovering, in the years of civil war and famine and their faltering two-steps-forward-one-step-back construction of the new socialist economy, you couldn't just do away with the old unequal ways by decree or even fire-power. This was a society busily, ferociously, bravely remaking itself, but there was still a long way to go, lives to be led in the meantime, and it all had to be done on the basis of what had gone before. Hegemony was a many-layered, multi-dimensional structure, more of a process really, always shifting and changing, like some kind of geological substratum infused with primordial gases and liquids.

Perhaps it was best to think of it as a living organism, already rearranged and patched together by previous generations. It could only be taken apart and reconstructed one or at best several pieces at a time, and with great care and skill because every element was separately alive, throbbing and twitching, discomfiting every other. It would always be difficult, and you could never be sure what you would end up with, especially here in Russia, with its primitive society and state, and still largely feudal economy.

He had heard Lenin himself say so to the Comintern just a couple of weeks ago: "It is a terrible misfortune that the honour of beginning the first Socialist revolution should have fallen to the most backward people in Europe." The dictatorship of the proletariat required patience and cunning and compromise, no less than the dictatorship of the bourgeoisie that preceded it. Were the Russians up to it, with their millions of illiterate peasants barely out of serfdom, tiny urban proletariat and even tinier intelligentsia? How to build a new world on such a narrow base?

The great and glorious October Revolution was only a tentative first step. A clarion cry around the world, no doubt, but always exceptional. Hadn't he inadvertently said so at the time, in an article headed "The Revolution *Against* Capital"? He meant it as a tribute to Bolshevik decisiveness, in contrast to the plodding reformism of the Second International, all those old men waiting around for change rather than making it happen. But ever since then he had been chided by comrades – for the most part playfully – for his anti-Marxist "voluntarist" heresy. Five years older now, and with first-hand experience of Russian conditions, he could see their point.

The Soviets' isolation proved there was no substitute for the hard graft of political change in the Western European heartland of industrial and finance capitalism. There the revolution would be much more difficult and protracted, and couldn't be rushed unless you wanted to provoke reactionary backlash. The continuities of history were just as important, and in their own dumb way constructive, as its ruptures. You had to work with the grain as well as occasionally hack into it, respect reality as you tried to reshape it, recognise the material you had been given by history to work with. That required careful research, rigorous analysis, and always the desperate mental struggle to understand concrete historical reality. As he thought this through, feeling the pull of his writing desk back in his gloomy room, the fingers of his right hand tapped steadily on the wooden arm of his wicker chair, like a carpenter making guide marks with his chisel.

This building, an old Tsarist summer palace converted into a hospital for the new revolutionary proletarian elite of the Communist International, was proof of all this. As were the obsequious manners and behaviours of the doctors, nurses and attendants who – it seemed to him – had swapped one set of masters for another as easily as they changed their white coats for clean ones. The fact that they addressed the new lot as "comrade" instead of "sir" was progress of sorts, but they were still unquestionably and unquestioningly subordinate. They might be serving a higher and nobler ideal, the cause of world proletarian revolution, but they were still undoubtedly serving.

* * *

Antonio Gramsci had come to Russia from Turin as late spring turned to high summer, departing on 26th May 1922, for the Fourth Congress of the Communist International scheduled to begin in November after many months of intense preparation. He travelled with fellow *Partito Comunista d'Italia* members and Comintern delegates Amadeo Bordiga (the new party's first leader) and Antonio Graziadei. They took a circuitous route into Russia via Latvia, stopping off along the way in Berlin, where Gramsci called on his old university professor and intellectual mentor Umberto Cosmo, now a diplomat at the Italian embassy. They finally arrived in Moscow on 2nd June, a whole week after setting out, exhausted and (in Gramsci's case) seriously ill.

They had left Italy in a state of turmoil whose outcome was as yet utterly unclear. It was already beginning to feel like a historical tipping-point, the very last of the "red years" of revolutionary agitation following the war, and the very first of the black years of counter-revolutionary Fascism. The surge of reaction began in the countryside, breaking strikes and occupations and besieging whole towns and villages with military precision, spreading north and south through the Italian peninsula like fire in a cornfield. Thousands of disgruntled soldiers – Gramsci's own younger brother Mario amongst them – had come back from a war they were supposed to have won but which felt more like a defeat, and set about exacting revenge on their fellow countrymen, guided by the rabble of histrionic, sneering, ex-socialist intellectuals and disaffected provincial gentry around Benito Mussolini.

It was nasty enough at the beginning, with widespread organised violence and even murders, wrecking and burning of the offices and halls of the left wing parties, trade unions and labour centres, peasant leagues and food cooperatives, and the quashing of whatever counter-strikes the scattered and fractious Italian left could muster in their own defence. But the full institutional horror of Fascism had yet to be revealed and turned into a matter of totalitarian state policy. For now, all that was immediately apparent was the paramilitary violence of the *fasci di combattimento,* founded in Milan in March 1919 but now active across the country.

At this stage it was widely considered a passing fad, the slow winding-down of one world war rather than the beginnings of another, even among its most immediate victims and implacable opponents on the communist and socialist left. They told themselves it was just a bunch of brutish thugs running around the country causing mayhem in the political vacuum created by the war, another local example of the rag-bag reaction of the unemployed, ill-disciplined, demobilised and traumatised soldiers making trouble in most European countries, allied with marginal, opportunist elements of the old ruling class.

There had always been plenty of that in the Italian

countryside, hired hoodlums brought in by the big, largely absentee landowners to beat the peasants into line and make sure they voted the right way in elections. In substantive terms, Fascism was little different to what had gone before, "a natural and predictable stage of development in the capitalistic order", as the Second Congress of the *Partito Comunista d'Italia* resolved in February 1922. Its leader, Amadeo Bordiga, had called it "…merely a change in the governmental team of the bourgeoisie".

What's more, the comrades said amongst themselves, if Fascism had the effect of sweeping away much of the old corrupt liberal parliamentary circus of long-time Prime Minister Giovanni Giolitti, so much the better. The purgative "revolution" Mussolini proclaimed as his objective would destroy the ceremonial trappings and niceties of Giolitti's *Italietta* ("little Italy"). Getting rid of the bourgeois-democratic sham of pluralism, freedom of association and the press, the legal protection of the individual from the state, etcetera – the respectable veneer over the harsh realities of capitalism – would leave the way clear for a properly proletarian revolution and a socialist state on the Soviet model.

If Antonio Gramsci had any suspicions in the summer of 1922 that his ex-Socialist comrade and fellow journalist Benito Mussolini's movement would prove a more durable phenomenon, he kept them largely to himself for now. The very suggestion would undermine the whole notion of the historical inevitability of proletarian dictatorship and international socialism. History could not possibly stop halfway or go backwards, could it? And after all, confined by chronic illness and nervous exhaustion to this Russian sanatorium for the foreseeable future, thousands of kilometres away from the violence and upheaval in Italy, he was in no position to do anything about it.

Grigoriy Zinoviev himself, President of the Communist

International, had noticed how frail and tired the new Italian delegate was at the opening meeting of the Comintern in Moscow, and wondered whether he might be suffering from nervous exhaustion, or neurasthenia, like so many others in these years of upheaval. Gramsci had been elected as the Italian representative on the Comintern's Executive Committee, known by the suitably modern and polyglot acronym of *Ispolcom*, and as a member of its smaller Presidium. Afterwards Zinoviev suggested a recuperative spell in the sanatorium at Serebranyi Bor, so called because it was set in a wood of silver birch trees.

"We pride ourselves," he said, in his oddly clipped and surprisingly quiet voice, his diffidence accentuated by his deployment of cumbersome Italian for the benefit of this new arrival, "on the quality of our care. Our doctors and clinics lead the world in the treatment of neurasthenia. We consider it a distinctly modern illness, symbol and product of the progress of civilisation."

They were walking at some pace down a corridor between meetings. Gramsci found it hard to keep up. He also found it hard to equate Zinoviev's global reputation for terror with the clean-shaven, pale, slightly puffy face looking down and sideways at him from the mop of curly black hair atop his slender round-shouldered frame. There was little of Lenin's resolution; rather, a somewhat brittle affectation of confidence and authority.

"Of course neurasthenia is especially prevalent here, with widespread physical and mental fatigue from two revolutions, the civil war, capitalist blockades and famine, and the massive epidemics that followed. We might have expected it to ease with the prosperity of the New Economic Policy, but if anything it's getting worse. The latest manifestation is a wave of suicides among young men worried about sexual dysfunction as a consequence of excessive masturbation."

Zinoviev stopped abruptly for a moment of contemplation,

his fingertips playing with the little tassels of silk cord he wore instead of a tie. Gramsci took advantage of the halt to regain his breath. Then just as abruptly Zinoviev carried on walking and talking.

"But whereas in the west, nervous illnesses are confined to brain-workers from the so-called advanced races and upper classes, here in the Soviet Union we find them all across the population. In fact we regard it as a sign of growing equality and of upward social mobility, so we have given it the clinical name of "Soviet nervousness", *iznoshennost'* or *utomlenie* in Russian. I assure you, Comrade Gramsci, there is no shame or stigma attached to it. Widespread neurasthenia is emblematic of the Soviet condition, what you might call a badge of honour. In fact it is especially prevalent amongst active Communist Party members and Red Army veterans..."

Zinoviev's motives in sending Gramsci off to the sanatorium may not have been entirely medical or altruistic. The Italian party was in a mess, small and fractious and divided, implacably sectarian to any other political party and even towards itself. There were already several distinct factions, barely a year after its foundation, and they were based on sharp political, personal and regional differences. It seemed unlikely that its right and left wings, with various smaller less clearly defined groupings between and amongst them, could stay together for long, let alone organise a revolution. The party's temper was, as Zinoviev had noted during the *Ispolcom* discussion of prospects in Italy, "somewhat fissiparous..." To this its leader Bordiga responded, sitting bolt upright in his chair and thrusting an arrow-straight forefinger towards the ceiling, "Yes indeed, Comrade President, nothing clears the air like a good split!"

Lenin had derided this fiery bombast in *Left Wing Communism: an Infantile Disorder*. In their own histrionic way, the *Partito Comunista d'Italia* – born from a highly unsatisfactory breakaway from the much bigger and longer established if ideologically muddled Italian Socialist Party – were just as bad as the Americans, whom Lenin privately referred to as "that rabble of polyglot squabblers" made up mostly of recent immigrants and refugees, or the "vegetarian cranks, shrieking suffragists and permanently enraged Celts" of the tiny and ineffectual British party. None of them seemed to occupy any permanent, secure or central place in their own national politics. Hadn't Lenin also been heard to remark, when introduced to the "Red Yankee" John Reed, author of *Ten Days That Shook the World,* "My goodness, an *American* American..."? None of them measured up to the Russians, the Germans or even the eastern Europeans. The Italians were just another of those "artificial parties", called into being by the distant glowing beacon of the October Revolution but with no real historical or social roots in their own societies.

Or so went the latest gossip around the corridors, parlours and communal kitchens of the expropriated hotels, mansions and palaces where the Comintern installed its foreign members and functionaries. Packing the Italian representative, this funny little hunchback with a squeaky voice and an earnest manner, off to Serebranyi Bor for a while might suit everyone. Zinoviev and his colleagues at the top of the Comintern had more promising revolutionary prospects in other countries to consider. Rested and restored, the Italian might have something worthwhile to contribute to their debates and declarations. He was the editor and founder of the journal *L'Ordine Nuovo* after all, which Lenin had singled out for praise at the Second Comintern Congress in 1920 as the only source of communist good sense in Italy.

Gramsci's physical symptoms – convulsive trembling and what he himself later described as "ferocious-looking" fits, when his hands and arms jerked uncontrollably and his fingers took on the shape of talons – were cause enough for major comradely concern. He told the Comintern doctor who attended to him when he had collapsed at a meeting, that he felt cold shivers and then tightness in his chest, "…as if the heart were being grasped inside a hand, or a supple octopus was fastening its tentacles around it." Inside half an hour of initial observation, his temperature fluctuated between 96 and 100, several degrees either side of the normal 98.6. In the Moscow mid-summer heat, even in a high-ceilinged room with the curtains closed and the windows wide open, he was bathed in sweat; as much from anxiety about what was happening as from fever, with just a little bit of embarrassment at disrupting the proceedings like this. He could see the alarm in the eyes of the huddle of people gathered around him. *They know I'm Sardinian,* he thought to himself. *Maybe they think I'm about to knife someone!*

He was feeling better now at the sanatorium, this wild-haired hunchbacked brigand, even if only from the effects of good and regular meals, enforced rest and (for him, a lifelong insomniac) relatively sound and undisturbed sleep. It had been at least two days since he'd had one of the splitting and pounding and utterly debilitating headaches which had blighted his adult life. The new glasses, prescribed for him by the sanatorium's eye-doctor and manufactured at the recently nationalised and re-opened lens factory in Moscow, were certainly helping. After all these years of thinking and theorising, reading and writing, debating and speech-making, he finally had the time and nervous energy to devote to matters of feeling and sensation; even to his own personal appearance, which he had neglected out of shame or simple disregard.

He had even started to grow a moustache. At the ripe old age of 31 he thought it was about time. All the Russians wore beards or moustaches. *When in Rome,* he thought, combing through the thickening stubble on his upper lip after his morning wash and shave, *or rather Moscow...* He had also begun to remember his dreams, previously a jumble of nonsense and occasional terror shrugged off within moments of waking, and to record the most notable. In the latest he had been amongst a group of people who were all hovering around ten centimetres above the ground, quite upright and interacting as if it were the most ordinary thing in the world. No matter how hard he tried, he could not emulate them, but remained resolutely earthbound. Now what on earth – or rather, ten centimetres above it – could that signify?

Sitting here now, on the sunny terrace of the sanatorium, he even allowed himself the luxury of natural observation, for almost the first time he could remember since he was a boy in Sardinia. Then, he had gone off tracking porcupines and foxes around nearby orchards and fields, and brought home tortoises, falcons and larks to raise with his friend Luciano, the village chemist's son. Now, from out of this very different terrain, he saw cranes slowly rise, apparently straight up from the water, and circle gracefully around the tips of birch trees until they came flapping slowly to rest on the bank of another stream or cutting.

He watched swallows or martens – he could never, to his continuing frustration, tell the difference, though he knew that both slept high on the wing – wheel and dive in busy aerial ballets and somehow miraculously avoid crashing into each other or the trees. *They must operate in a different dimension of time,* he thought, *like flies or children.* A large bee, drawn to the vivid colours of his top blanket, buzzed around his lap in search of pollen. It brought to mind an old Sardinian folk-rhyme:

"Mister Bee in his stripy jumper, all puffed up in his self-importance,

Busier as the morning lengthens, dozier as the afternoon shortens.

My goodness, he thought, *I must be getting better if I can summon up a memory like that.*

* * *

"Good evening, Comrade Schucht. How are you?"

"Very well, Comrade Gramsci, though my doctors might not agree..."

He leant closer to her and whispered conspiratorially. "And what would they know?"

Evgenia Schucht, middle in age of the five Schucht sisters, giggled back at this funny little Italian's irreverence. It had been quite some time since she'd had much to laugh about, or been able to practice her conversational Italian, acquired during her family's sojourn in Rome. She still spoke the language fluently and, as Comrade Gramsci had complimented her when they had been placed together at dinner, "beautifully, Comrade, beautifully". Amongst all the coughed and barked and mumbled Russian, the lithe swooping poetry of the Italian language offered a very welcome change, as well as an impenetrable code between the two of them against the prying ears which in this place never seemed far away.

Evgenia was confined to a creaking wheelchair, on account of a "nervous debility" which had induced partial paralysis of the legs and kept her bedridden since 1919. None of the doctors at the Schucht family home in Ivanovo Voznesensk, at the specialist institute in Moscow or here at the sanatorium had yet been able to diagnose the cause in anything other than the vaguest terms. It might have something to do with her service in the Red Army rifle corps during the civil war, and the lasting effects of shell shock from exposure to battle. But – they mumbled amongst each other, always within her strained hearing – how common was that amongst women? Female nervous breakdowns tended to take a rather different course, and derive from other, more interior traumas. *Yes,* she'd thought to herself as she surveyed the white-coated and turbaned ranks of male doctors, *you always have been mystified by our insides...*

And, in truth, Evgenia's military service had mostly involved riding across and around endless steppe in search of elusive White Army enemies, in stuttering fuel-starved trains and then on scrawny horseback when they thought their quarry might be near. She confessed to her most trusted doctor that she had only engaged in battle on a couple of occasions, that they amounted to little more than skirmishes (the so-called "Second Battle of Kharkhiv") with fleeing bands of mercenaries and bandits, and that she had otherwise been kept in reserve for offensive charges that were never ordered or required.

She added, in some kind of mitigation, that she had proved herself an outstanding marksman during battalion target practice. But again she had to admit that when they had live rounds to use she was competing against ever rawer recruits. And at other times, when ammunition was scarce, the battalion commander had judged their accuracy from the steadiness with which they held their rifles while pretending to shoot. This callow bespectacled youth from the university town of Kazan was intimidated by her haughty manner and, she implied, romantically attracted to her, so his judgement was, "shall we say, Comrade Doctor, somewhat suspect..."

Even more speculatively, the doctors noticed that her paralysis had followed soon after her acceptance into membership of the Communist Party of the Soviet Union, under Lenin's personal sponsorship. Could there be some kind of psychological connection? A fear of disappointing her father Apollon, an old-time Bolshevik, perhaps? Or, through the psychic mechanism of transference, her newly adoptive "father" Lenin? "Well, perhaps..." she had responded when this hypothesis was first advanced, then, "Don't be ridiculous!" when she thought about it.

Apollon might be a fearsome orator and disputant in public, but at home with his lively daughters and solitary son and watchful wife, he was quiet and collaborative and, as Evgenia had realised in infancy, readily susceptible to feminine charm and manipulation. As a follower of Rousseau, he was always inclined to leave these "noble savages" to their own devices, rather than subject them to the traditional bourgeois "stern mouldings" of his Teutonic forebears.

And while Lenin might have signed her membership application form, this was at the behest of his wife Krupskaya, who knew the Schuchts rather better than her eminent husband, and whom Evgenia had briefly served as personal secretary at the Commissariat of Public Education. It was a small momentary favour for an old comrade, a scribble of a pen amongst a huge daily batch of state papers. Evgenia had only ever met the great man when she was a small child, and their families were part of the small itinerant band of obscure anti-Tsarist intellectuals going in and out of exile across the vast Russian landmass and the more congenial sanctuaries of Western Europe. Since then, she had had to make do with her father's reports and anecdotes. Lenin certainly had nothing to do with the paralysis in her legs. So her "nervous debility" went unexplained and unattributed.

At the Serebranyi Bor sanatorium, rather lower down the hierarchy of Soviet medical science than the prestigious Moscow clinics, the junior doctors assigned to "nervous disorders" like hers tended to look for less obviously experiential causes. These all – Evgenia thought to herself – came down to her and her "weaknesses", as if her paralysis were somehow her fault, or even choice. She had heard the word "psychosomatic" bandied about more than once at their bedside consultations, and knew enough of the latest fashionable medical theory to understand that this meant they thought she was making her illness up. The latest label they were trying to attach to her was "acquired invalidism", coined by the shining red star of the new Soviet psychiatry, Dr. I.V. Gannushkin.

A young doctor had stood before her in his long white overall and turban and run down a check-list of symptoms which he said would help this latest attempt to establish the "scientific basis of your condition, Comrade Schucht... Do you feel apathetic, unable to work or relate to your surroundings, and lost to society?"

"Er, I'm not sure... After four years in here, wouldn't anyone?"

"Do you feel uncertainty in yourself and your abilities?"

"Sometimes..."

"Would you say you are completely dissatisfied with your life, with no chance of future happiness?"

"Well, I'm not sure I'd go that far..."

This new label of "acquired invalidism" was some improvement on "hysteria" no doubt, but when it came down to it weren't they all just pseudo-scientific terms for madness? And if that's what they thought, why didn't they just come right out with it? Have done with the nonsense, and pack her off to that other enclosed part of the hospital behind a particularly imposing row of silver birch trees, the unnamed and unnumbered "secure ward" which "rest cure" patients like herself and Comrade Gramsci frequently talked about in hushed and conspiratorially disparaging tones. A number of discarded "companions" and errant children of senior Comintern figures were reportedly housed there, alongside the raving lunatics and irremediable cretins from Tsarist times.

It was all just too ludicrous. She was perfectly sane, lucid and emotionally continent. And why would she, who had loved to run around the family gardens in Geneva, Montpelier and Rome, and challenge her sisters to private races which she knew she would win, feign paralysis? Her legs would simply not move properly. It was up to the doctors to figure out why, and do something with their probes and blades, tinctures and poultices to set her back upright and mobile again. It was them, not her, who seemed to be stuck in some kind of mental paralysis.

* * *

She had tried explaining all this to Comrade Gramsci during their first meeting over dinner, but had noticed his tender blue-grey eyes cloud over with that attitude of sceptical reserve she seemed to provoke in every man she ever encountered, medical or lay. It was almost as if, she had concluded with a nod of acknowledgement towards those fashionable psychoanalytical theories she so resented when applied to her, they were afraid of getting stuck to or even inside her. She could see them withdraw into themselves after five minutes' exploratory conversation, like snails back into their shells, shrivelling under her insistence (and yes, she fully understood the sexual analogies). This in turn provoked an impulse in her to shake them by the shoulders and shout, "Why won't you believe me?"

She had stopped short of trying this on Comrade Gramsci. She would return to her theme of medical incompetence later, when she felt more confident of the little Italian's sympathy. For now she diverted this delightful conversation back onto safer ground, something about the wholesome but stodgy food they were being presented with. She relished the sound and feel – almost a scent or a taste – of the Italian words, like pastilles in her mouth: *alimentari terribili! O per un pomodoro fresco! Per amor del cielo...* She should be satisfied, she told herself, with the therapeutic benefits of his company, and the sweet conspiracy of their necessarily private dialogue; not to mention – and indeed, she barely dared mention it to herself – the possibilities of blossoming romance as they got to know each other better.

They compared families and noted their stark contrasts. Hers was a cosmopolitan, multi-lingual bevy of five wandering daughters and a solitary son, poor put-upon baby Victor. This large brood was loosely overseen by their mother Julia Grigor'evna, and supported by their father Apollon Alexandrovich's substantial inheritance from illustrious and enterprising forebears. The Schucht fortune was wearing a bit thin these days, in the aftermath of war and revolution, but it still just about kept the large family going, topped up by whatever extras the girls and Victor could bring home.

As German Catholics fleeing persecution during the Reformation in the early 1700s, the Schuchts had been received at the court of Catherine the Great and absorbed into the Russian aristocracy. Apollon's grandfather had owned a watch factory in Petersburg. His father Alexander was a cavalry major who was killed fighting the Turks in 1878, and buried with great military honours in Constantinople. Alexander's wife Ottilija, Apollon's mother, was the daughter of Franz Xaver Winterhalter, a court portrait painter who had received commissions from most of the European monarchies.

Under the pre-revolutionary Tsarist order, Apollon was formally designated a noble of the Byelorussian city of Mogilev, and followed his father into the Imperial cavalry. However, in the 1880s he was drawn towards revolutionary ideas, and dropped out of military school to undertake musical training at the piano and in composition. Apollon was also widely read and a capable author and critic, fluent in Russian, German, French and Italian. In 1885 he married his wife Julia, the daughter of a prominent Ukrainian-Jewish lawyer in Petersburg, Grigorij Girschfeld. Her brother Osip was a fellow student of Lenin at the University of Kazan.

Under Russian law Julia had to convert to Orthodox Christianity in order to marry Apollon. In 1887, the young couple were involved in *Narodnaya Volya* ("People's Will"), alongside Lenin's older brother Alexander Ulyanov, and were swept up in a wave of arrests following a failed attempt on the life of Tsar Alexander III. Ulyanov was sentenced to death, and hanged with three other conspirators a month after turning twenty one, the basic hurt which sparked his younger brother's revolutionary career. But because Apollon had repudiated the "revolutionary terrorism" of the Narodniks and argued against the assassination attempt, he received the lesser sentence of exile to Tomsk in Siberia. The Schuchts' first three daughters were born there in quick succession, Nadina in 1885, Tatiana in 1887, and Evgenia in 1889.

After several years of relatively comfortable exile in Siberia, the Schuchts were allowed to move south to the rather less harsh climate of Samara, where they became friends of the progressive Regional Governor. There they met up again with Lenin, who had also been exiled with his family and acted as godfather to the Schuchts' fourth daughter Anna. In 1894 the Schuchts moved to Geneva in Switzerland, where Julia was born in 1896. She came to be known within the family by the Russian diminutive "Julka", partly to distinguish her from her mother, Julia Grigor'evna, and partly because she was the youngest daughter. Finally, Victor was born in 1899. In 1904 the family moved to Montpelier in France, then to Rome in 1908. Along the way the children absorbed Apollon's passion for music and literature, and Julia's for natural science and philology. All of them excelled at music or science. Between them they were able to play duets and quartets, expertly led by Apollon at the piano. As "The Schuchts" they could draw sizeable gatherings to their recitals.

"It's an unusual family name," Gramsci observed.

Yes, she explained, it was a Russified version of the German Schacht, but they could count so many other birthplaces and nationalities amongst their identities that they were probably best considered just European, or even stateless. They had been, she confessed with some hint of embarrassment, part of that curious *fin-de-siecle,* supra-national diaspora of mid-European intellectuals and fading aristocrats who thought of themselves as the political and cultural vanguard of modernity, but might more accurately be described as a shifting *milieu* of the self-dislocated.

"All over the place, in every sense..."

"What Marx called rootless cosmopolitans..." he said.

"Precisely!"

"Even though he could be said to be one himself... Jewish too..."

"Well..."

In the great yawning late nineteenth century historical chasm opening up between revolution and reaction, these people could have gone either way, afloat on the raging sea of class conflict over the spoils of industrial capitalism and rapacious imperialism. The Schuchts had made their choice early on, pursuing Apollon's chosen destiny of international communism. Their internal exile in Siberia and Samara under the Tsar was almost fashionable at the time, and now conveyed enormous retrospective prestige. But even there they had managed to avoid the poverty and degradation of the local, mostly poor peasant population, and live comfortably if never prosperously. They had never really bothered putting down permanent roots anywhere, beyond stylistic affectations and vague nostalgic yearnings: for their relatively prolonged and pleasurable stay in Rome in particular.

"Ah, whereabouts in Rome?" asked Gramsci, seeking to establish links with his own very much more limited travels and sojourns. Evgenia rattled off a couple of addresses in districts he had never visited or in one case even heard of. Then she returned to her account.

The family had felt settled in Rome, insofar as they ever settled anywhere, for some nine years in all, the first six of them in the pre-war golden era of old Europe. They all remembered those Roman years in the full colour of bright sunlight and new green foliage. That was when they acquired their facility in Italian and *amore di tutte le cose italiane*, and where Apollon took on his one and only regular job, teaching Russian to officers at the Ministry of War. In the autumn of 1913 the sisters began their own independent travels, to Warsaw, Switzerland, and finally for Evgenia, her sisters Anna and Julka and their mother Julia, to Moscow.

The rest of the family joined them there in 1917, just in time for the later phases of the Soviet revolution. Apollon was not closely involved in the October Revolution, but assisted in the nationalisation of the banks shortly afterwards. In 1919, at the height of the Civil War, he helped to oversee the education and rehabilitation of prisoners-of-war and refugees. Now, in 1922, the

Schuchts had settled in the textile town of Ivanovo Voznesensk, a substantial settlement of 100,000 people with its own music school and museum, 250 kilometres north east of Moscow. They were heavily involved in the Bolsheviks' political struggles, most notably against the "petty bourgeois" Socialist Revolutionaries who had been making trouble in the town's mills and factories.

Apart, that is, from Tatiana, who had stayed in Italy to pursue a medical career and pretty much lost touch. The last they had heard of her, from a family friend in Rome, was that Tanya was working at the Policlinico Umberto, nursing children with malaria. Nadina had died in childbirth in late 1918, during the giddy pell-mell of the Civil War, somewhere in Southern Russia. These, Evgenia concluded, were the only clouds on the family horizon. Unless they heard otherwise, they had to assume that Tanya, "a fully grown woman after all", was fine. The other Schuchts could now enjoy some stability and security, as the momentum of revolution slowed and the new Soviet Union settled into something resembling a normal society. With their father's political record of early revolutionary agitation and exile now an asset rather than a burden, they could also begin reaping the rewards of their impeccable Bolshevik credentials.

Gramsci struggled to keep up with Evgenia's breathless account of the Schucht family fortunes. He could scarcely believe that people had ever been able to move so freely around Europe – especially in these times of sealed borders and naval blockades – acquiring cultures, languages and identities as easily as rented accommodation or a new suit of clothes. From what Evgenia said, the Schuchts seemed to live in a shiny bubble of glamour, comfort and adventure that floated free across the continent, blessing ordinary mortals like him with their dazzling, temporary presence. Only the apparent disappearance, for years at a time and for largely unexplained reasons, of one or other of the sisters cast any shadow on this cosseted existence. It was also not entirely clear to him how the Schuchts had managed to live relatively well for so long with very little earned income beyond Apollon's dwindling inheritance, but perhaps this was one of those Bohemian-aristocratic mysteries with which European economic history is littered.

He summed up his own family history in a few sentences. His was a large gang of four brothers and three sisters brought up in the village of Ghilarza on the impoverished Italian island of Sardinia, up in the mosquito-ridden hills and well away from the cooling sea breezes and the capital Cagliari. It was, "I assure you, Comrade Schucht, a long way from anywhere you might have been or even heard of!" They were descended from Greek-Albanian exiles, which explained their unusual surname, "spelt G-R-A-M-S-C-I but pronounced with the soft Italian –c," not the hard Slavic –k sound he had got wearily used to correcting on every new encounter here in Russia.

"Well yes, Comrade *Gramshi*," Evgenia responded. "I had assumed that!"

There was something not wholly convincing in her assurance, but that may just be her manner, or something to do with her Italian, which was (he reminded himself) just one among a clutch of languages and not necessarily her first or most natural. With a resigned sigh he went on." But then my name gets muddled up in all manner of unlikely ways: Gramasci, Granusci, Gramisci, Granisci, even Garamascon, with every bizarre intermediate stage you can think of. I now spell it out as a matter of routine, and try to explain that it's simply the two common parts – Gram as in the measurement of weight, and the common ending 'sci' – put together, but they never seem to grasp it..."

Apart from him and his brother Gennaro, who had both moved to Cagliari then over the sea to Turin to study and work, his parents, brothers and sisters and various cousins had rarely left Ghilarza where most of them were born. Even those who had served in the war, his younger brothers Mario and Carlo, had returned to the area when it was over. It was all very different, he observed, from the cultivated and much-travelled Schucht family.

"And yet here we are together, *Compagna Evgenia,* as our very different trajectories converge. Turbulent times..."

Just how much meaning did his words carry, Evgenia wondered, and what should she make of his remarks on this first encounter? Did he, she could not help wondering towards the end of this lovely introductory Italian conversation at the sanatorium dinner table, propose to take matters further? Perhaps, perhaps not... For all the reckless post-revolutionary upheaval in the Soviet Union and beyond – with insurrection in the air in Germany and Hungary and lingering hopes for a rapid transition to proletarian dictatorship in Italy, and newly formed communist parties popping up all over the world proclaiming themselves the local subsidiary of Lenin's heroic Bolsheviks – personal relationships amongst communists still moved with a stiff, stately formality.

This was partly because of lack of time and opportunity, when there were so many other bigger and more important objectives to pursue and tasks to perform, but also because of a principled obligation to traditional proletarian norms. The freethinkers and free lovers of the *demi-monde,* the soft underbelly of the transnational intellectual vanguard, might feel able or even politically committed to indulge their carnal urges and desires, to fritter away their time on idealistic speculation and romantic delusions, but they were cranks and dilettantes, wallowing in their decadence and aimlessness, and in most cases coming to a thoroughly bad end.

And serve them right, Evgenia would think to herself when she heard or read of the downfall and disgrace of the latest paragon of vice. This included a number of prominent communists, accused of "irregular habits and questionable lifestyles", demoted or even expelled for their improprieties. Proper communists felt obliged to set an example and avoid causing offence to the workers whose upright morals and respectable values were being elevated and codified into a new global order. Communists must be serious, skilled, disciplined, responsible people, who could inspire confidence in their ability to manage society and the economy successfully, especially in this epoch of scientific progress, industrial productivism, technically proficient management and post-revolutionary reconstruction.

* * *

Though they were both temporarily out of the struggle, finding time alone at Serebranyi Bor was quite a challenge for Antonio and Evgenia. She was still for much of the time bed-ridden, incapable of little more than cursory reading of a novel or newspaper, or short bursts of faltering embroidery with her aching fingers and shaking hands. In her first year at the sanatorium she had contracted tuberculosis, and though she recovered surprisingly quickly it could always flare up again in bouts of coughing and breathlessness. The doctors said this was another reason for her to rest, and though they didn't spell it out, to keep away from other vulnerable patients.

She was left alone in her room for long hours of supposedly recuperative rest, between increasingly chivvying attempts to get her to her feet and walk. She began to call herself, in her own sardonic mental or muttered running commentary, "Lazarus." On several occasions she experienced half-waking dreams where a Bolshevik Christ would be standing at her door urging her to "take up thy bed and walk, comrade..." She told her doctor about these dreams, but his only response was to wonder whether the Christ-figure, "beneath the crown of thorns and the full head of hair", was in fact her father, or even Comrade Lenin?

"Ach..." she replied, exasperated, and resolved to keep her dreams to herself in future. Most of Antonio's days, while ostensibly resting and recuperating, were spent undergoing various "treatments" for his own ill-defined diagnosis of "nervous exhaustion". These usually involved extremes of heat and cold, sometimes both together, as in ice-packs and hot water bottles applied alternately or simultaneously to particular parts of his body; or the excruciating Russian "banya" ritual where he was confined to a scalding hot steam room then plunged into an icy cold bath, then back round all over again. The treatments themselves frequently prompted the muscular spasms which heralded the onset of another fit. They'd have beaten him with birch twigs too – "But Comrade Gramsci, this helps the circulation of blood..." – if he hadn't for once put his foot down and refused. This twice-weekly torment left him feeling and looking like a boiled fish, and mystified as to what benefit he was supposed to be deriving from it.

At other times he lay for hours on end attached to tangled webs of wires and probes. He was never entirely sure, and didn't always feel able to ask, which of these were administering things to him – intravenous "tonics", small electrical shocks, or less easily discernible "magnetic waves" – and which were monitoring the impulses and "signals" he gave off in response, let alone what the medical rationale of all this rigmarole might be. He also sometimes wondered, in these long forcibly idle hours of "treatment", whether it might not all be some monstrous positivist or behaviourist "scientific" experiment in which he had found himself an unwitting guinea pig. More than once he allowed himself the heretical thought that he had stumbled upon (and into) a horribly apt metaphor for this latest "constructive" phase of the Soviet revolution, with its stated aim of forcibly creating "new socialist man" out of the messy muddle of human history.

"They seem to think we are machines," he whispered to Evgenia on their third or fourth meeting, "in need of a bit of oil and tightening of a screw or two. Or musical instruments requiring retuning or restringing..."

He even overheard two senior doctors discussing the new

"revolutionary" medicine of grafts and transplants. A dead peasant had been brought back to life for several minutes with the surgical insertion of the heart of a dog, while donated glands and even nerves had been used to rehabilitate atrophied limbs and organs. Then there were the junior doctors' check-lists. Evgenia had told him all about her own latest diagnosis of "acquired invalidism". They tried to attach this label to him too, but with a rather different emphasis in the check-list of causes and symptoms.

"Do you have blue rings under your eyes?" asked the young man in spectacles who came to see him, barely old enough to shave, let alone probe the psyche of a man in his thirties. He peered closely into the face of the olive-skinned Sardinian, clearly unsure what colour the bags under his tired eyes should be.

"Do you suffer from an inability to do maths? Tumours and nosebleeds? Cold hands, hair loss and anaemia?"

"Not especially," Gramsci responded. "And doesn't everyone here have cold hands?"

"Too much intellectual work without sufficient breaks?"

"An occupational hazard among professional revolutionaries, I'm afraid..."

"Shaking and irritability, excitability, insomnia and troubled sleep, severe headaches, dizziness, ear and eye irritation, back and chest pain, heart palpitations and irregular heartbeat, stomach upset, frequent mood swings, memory loss and the inability to concentrate?"

"Well, all of them sometimes, especially the headaches..."

"Do you have suicidal thoughts?"

"No, never!"

"Are you a frequent masturbator? Once, twice or three times a week?"

"Is that any of your business, Comrade junior doctor?"

"Let's say once then. Do you suffer from anxiety about the

ramifications of masturbation? Self-reproach and self-chastisement?"

"So, is feeling guilty about masturbating worse than actually masturbating?"

The young doctor looked nonplussed, thanked Gramsci for his cooperation, and said "That will be all for now, comrade..."

Even sitting outside was considered part of his "therapeutic regime", swaddled in blankets and invalid clothing for strictly prescribed and recorded periods of time, taking in what his doctors clearly regarded as the magical properties of the Russian country air. They had even advised him on the correct way to breathe, in order to achieve "the maximal beneficial admixture of oxygen in the blood." He was supposed to inhale through his nose for five seconds and exhale from his mouth for three. He tried to follow their instructions, but invariably felt the early symptoms – light-headedness, irrational euphoria and auditory hallucination, dizziness and blurred vision, pounding heart and head – of hyperventilation, before forcing himself to breathe normally.

At least then he could return to what he himself thought he was here for, the real business of recovery. That is, catching up on his reading, note-taking and correspondence, all the interests and contacts he had put aside during the last few years of frenetic political activity, coordination and argument. He was also trying hard to learn Russian, with the aid of the excellent new dictionaries and grammars being compiled and produced by the State Publishing House. Words first, dozens at a time, deciphered from the Cyrillic alphabet, read out loud and memorised, digested like morsels of bread and regurgitated quite unconsciously on encountering their object: *spectacles, teacup, book, medicine*. Then gobbets of syntax, which could be trusted to fall into place around the meaning.

Increasingly he found himself slipping into the colloquial Russian of his surroundings. More than once he had occasion to remark, to the raised eyebrows of the attendants who had come to tuck in his blankets or drag him away to his latest "therapy, Comrade Gramsci", that this business of getting better was *chrezvychainiy tyazheliy trud*, seriously hard work. Was this direct translation from the Italian wrong, or were they simply taken aback by his use of their native language? The treatments certainly passed the time. It also meant that he was more or less constantly under supervision, "if not necessarily," as he put it to Evgenia with a wary glance during one of their precious Italian dinner table conversations, "surveillance..." It left very little space for any interest or pursuit which might be considered personal or private.

Sitting together, in the dining room or on the terrace, their attention would turn instead to other patients. Some would enter the sanatorium in apparently good health, then rapidly decline and withdraw from public view. Only the occupation by some newcomer of their customary place at the dinner table or in the treatment room would indicate their fate, which almost always seemed to be some long-term effect of the Spanish Flu epidemic unleashed on a vulnerable world in the last months of the war. Gramsci or Evgenia might enquire of their attendants, "Whatever happened to Comrade So-and-so?" to be told that Comrade So-and-so had "passed away" or – from one orderly who wore a cross on a necklace whose outline could be faintly discerned beneath his starched white overall – that he or she had "gone to a better place..."

"Oh yes," said Gramsci when he first heard this absurd religious euphemism for death. "And where might that be? New York? Paris? Shangri-La?"

But there were also other patients whose time at Serebranyi Bor took the opposite trajectory, towards rapid recovery and full health and vigour. These were almost always, Gramsci observed to Evgenia, hard-bitten proletarians or peasants, "whose robust nerves can stretch and vibrate to a higher tension without tiring", unlike the milky-pale intellectuals with hollow cheeks and darting eyes who would just fade away and die, the wraiths and phantoms Dostoyevsky had called "the injured and insulted." The workers and kulaks would come in sick and wasted, and after three to four months of sleep and half-decent nourishment, "better in any case than they are used to", emerge completely recovered and able to resume their normal life and responsibilities.

"They just don't seem to feel things the way we do..." Evgenia remarked one afternoon, as she and Gramsci watched two particularly hulking specimens – both at death's door just weeks ago – lug their bundles and backpacks of meagre possessions and provisions down the sanatorium track to the main road back to Moscow.

"Well, you could say that," said Gramsci, sitting beside her in his blankets and dressing gown. "I prefer to think they are more suited to these historical moments and *milieux*, when gigantic collective forces press down painfully on single individuals to obtain the maximum creative response from their will. These ordinary folk are utterly untouched by romantic fantasies of any kind, morally healthy and balanced... They never create insoluble problems and hence don't despair about not being able to resolve them. Nor do they see themselves as inept or lacking in willpower and personality. They don't spit on themselves, as we say in Italy..."

* * *

In the lingering heat of the Russian late summer, September 1922, Julia "Julka" Schucht came to Serebranyi Bor to visit her sister Evgenia. Julka was living with her mother and father and her sister Anna in Ivanovo Voznesensk. She had been working as a music teacher at the *Lycée* there until the year before, when she was assigned a job as a translator of documents for the NKVD, the Soviet Interior Ministry. This allowed her time off to play her part in agitation and propaganda in the factories.

"She's the busiest of all of us," Evgenia had told Gramsci, "and brings more money home than the rest of us put together..."

Their parents were able to come to Serebranyi Bor whenever they chose, usually fortnightly but sometimes weekly, and stay at one of the Moscow hotels commandeered by the party for its officials and leaders and luminaries. Julka could only visit Evgenia when she had the time for the round journey and the overnight stay in Moscow, which generally meant holiday periods or the occasional weekend. This was her first visit since Easter, and her first encounter with Evgenia's new friend and comrade Antonio Gramsci. She was sitting with her family around Evgenia's bed, catching up with everyone's news, when she became aware of a small figure standing at the door.

"Comrade!" Evgenia exclaimed. "Come and join us!"

The Schuchts turned to face him directly. Their mother and father had already been briefly and formally introduced on another recent visit. Apollon and mother Julia greeted him courteously and correctly, switching easily to Italian, and with the traditional formalities which even here and now, in the topsy-turvy of social upheaval, were deemed appropriate between generations.

"Good day, Signor Gramsci!"

"Good day, Herr Schucht, Frau Schucht..." said the funny little man with a slight hesitant bow, slowly stepping into the room. He had a heavy head, with a high broad brow and thin lips, on a square-shouldered, hump-backed body. Framed in the large hospital doorway, he stood barely five feet tall, the size of an older child.

"And this is my little sister Julia..." said Evgenia, extending her hand palm upwards to the younger woman sitting to her right. Gramsci seemed momentarily transfixed. Then with a flustered look on his face he nodded towards Evgenia's sister too, and extended a surprisingly fine, long-fingered hand towards her.

"Fraulein Schucht..."

"We call her Julka!" said Evgenia, over her sister's nod of acknowledgement and extended hand, "or Giulia in Italian of course, after the month she was born."

Gramsci, taking a seat on the opposite side of the bed to Julka and visibly relaxing, quipped, "Most of us get a name day... you get a whole month!"

The family laughed politely – not the first time, everyone understood, that Julka had been the subject of this mild joke about her name and month of birth – and drew him into their circle of conversation. They had been, not unnaturally, talking politics. The Schuchts were delighted (and not a little surprised) to hear that "Comrade Gramsci", as Evgenia now referred to him, would be attending the Fourth Congress of the Communist International as a delegate of the Communist Party of Italy. They admired the Comintern identity card which Evgenia insisted he pass around, reading aloud the words "Administration of the Affairs of the Council of People's Commissars" and "Moscow, 13th September 1922, The Kremlin". When it reached him, Apollon exclaimed approvingly "Delegate number 704!" What's more, the card made clear, "Comrade Gramsci" would be sitting on the Comintern's *Ispolcom* and its Presidium.

"Health permitting, of course," said Gramsci, "which is why I'm here..."

"Revolution requires considerable personal sacrifice," pronounced Apollon, his first substantial contribution. "Take our daughter here, for example," he said, his hand turned towards Evgenia in her bed, "or Comrade Ilyich himself..."

Gramsci, who knew from Evgenia of the Schucht family's acquaintance with Lenin, and of Apollon's personal friendship, asked, "And how is our great leader?"

"*Allora...*" replied Apollon. "He still suffers the after-effects of the assassination attempt four years ago. He finally had the bullet removed from his neck in April, but he suffers minor strokes. We are all concerned..."

"But we must not foster alarmism!" Evgenia exclaimed.

"No, indeed," said Apollon. "And he continues to work as hard as ever, even when confined to bed. He visited us in Ivanovo last month, to discuss improving energy supplies with the city soviet, and he told us all about his plans for wind turbines in remote rural villages."

"And I for one," said Gramsci, "cannot wait to hear him address our Congress!"

"Hear, hear!" said Apollon, and sat back in stately silence.

Gramsci too sat back in his chair, and let the women turn the conversation towards more immediate and local family matters. While he listened to the pleasant hum of their lilting voices, and noticed the sporadic inclusion of words or phrases or even entire sentences of German, French or Italian into their customary Russian, his gaze alternated between Evgenia and her sister Julka. Actually, it would be more accurate to say that it was torn, because while Evgenia occupied his direct line of vision, his attention was drawn – as it had been since he had first stopped and stood in the doorway – to Julka's breathtakingly beautiful face.

Julia "Julka" Schucht was tall and fair and slender, with shoulder-length auburn hair, and large sad eyes in a perfectly proportioned oval face, hinting at depths of loneliness which Gramsci found immediately appealing. She was the ideal blend of Jewish delicacy and refinement, from her mother presumably, and sculpted Teutonic angularity from her father, with high cheekbones beside a noble, slightly upturned nose. The combination gave her the finest features of Slavic beauty. By contrast, Gramsci found himself reflecting, Evgenia seemed to have inherited the coarser features of her forebears: high forehead rather than cheekbones, and a larger nose – which she was in the habit of momentarily covering with her hand – than she (or anyone else) would have liked.

Gramsci later remarked to Evgenia, when the family had left for Ivanovo and the two of them had slipped back into their easy confidence at the dinner table, that when he had first set eyes on Julka at her sister's bedside she looked to him like a "Byzantine Madonna". Evgenia responded, with a mildly sardonic tone which surprised him, that he would not be the first man to fall for her younger sister on first sight.

"Oh come on!" responded Gramsci, laughing and singing in his high reedy voice. "I only have eyes for you!"

He explained that it was an Italian popular song from before the war.

"Oh yes," she responded, laughing along, "but seriously..."

One of Julka's previous suitors had sought Evgenia's advice about his prospects, and remarked that her younger sister's was a face that always seemed to be asking questions of you, or posing a challenge, even if only, "How will you respond to my beauty?" Otherwise, and unlike everyone else who ever met her, Evgenia said, Julka seemed quite unconscious of her own iconic allure. If anything, the male attention and frequent devotion which her beauty inspired seemed to discomfort and mystify and, if it was too brazen or aggressive, irritate and anger her. She would freeze in their gaze, and determinedly avert her own eyes, which would fascinate them even more. Julka was even more beautiful and beguiling in profile than face-on, not least because it seemed to suggest that she was slipping away and into herself. Before they knew it, she would be informing the Schuchts that Herr Such-and-such or Monsieur So-and-so would no longer be visiting the family home. Some other handsome devil would soon take their place in pursuit of Julka's affections and mysterious charms, which were wholly invisible to her older sisters, to whom she would always be an annoyingly needy baby.

"Men are such fools," Evgenia said to Gramsci, apparently

oblivious to his own gender. "They're always drawn towards abstraction, some distant point on the horizon, in women as much as art and argument; a destination to aim for, a problem to solve, a prize to win, a quarry to capture..."

In her twenty six years, Julka had left a trail of male frustration behind her, pretty much unknowingly and apparently indifferently, with several sudden embarkations to foreign parts and at least one rumoured suicide. *Infuriating*, Evgenia thought, on the occasion of the family's next visit a couple of weeks later, as she watched Comrade Gramsci's gaze flit beyond her to her sister on the other side of the bed. Glancing sideways, Evgenia watched Julka embark upon her usual ice-maiden act, and Gramsci's glances become not far off a steady stare. Over succeeding visits, she watched Julka soften and Gramsci's initial polite reticence around her family crumble, until he was making a beeline for Julka, even drawing up a chair to sit right beside her, and engineering their own separate cocoon of conversation. She saw Antonio – "Call me Nino, my family do..." – adopt that familiar male air of eager intrigue in Julka's presence, just a small step away from captivation, *as they always do*.

Evgenia knew herself well enough by now to recognise that she would melt under such scrutiny. This had quite the opposite effect on men, who were repulsed by her all too evident adult neediness, not to mention the faint hints of odorous secretions her body would give off at such critical moments. Fully seven years older than Julka, now aged thirty three and still unattached, Evgenia always suspected (and feared) that she reminded men of their mothers, and that she was destined for the life of a maiden aunt. *No, they prefer the fragrant Julka. For all his personal disclosures and expressions of regard or even "love" for her, Evgenia, this Comrade Gramsci's no different.*

Well, that's not entirely true, Evgenia acidly observed from her bed, already beginning to turn away in embarrassment from her own initial warmth towards him, as she watched "Nino" and

Julka conduct the first skirmishes of serious flirtation. *He's a dwarf for a start, barely up to the shoulders of any normal adult, including all the Schucht sisters. And so slight, hardly more than fifty kilos...* Julka has already seen off several much taller and finer and better connected suitors, to her parents' considerable exasperation. *Then there's his hunchback, which he explains (rather too early in any opening conversation) with some unlikely story about being dropped as an infant by a nurse, when it's more probably the result of poverty and disease on this wretched faraway desert island he keeps going on about. Didn't rickets sometimes have that effect?*

And hadn't he pretty much admitted so himself, when he'd told her – again rather too soon – about him and his brothers and sisters struggling to help their beloved mamma to recover from their father's disastrous imprisonment? 'Don Ciccillo' Gramsci, the son of a Bourbon colonel, had chosen the wrong side in a parliamentary election in Sardinia. "Sardinian political parties are merely the personal followings of those able to provide the largest handouts," Antonio explained, "and my father just happened to fall out with the most powerful." Don Ciccillo had been convicted of some minor infringement in his administrative duties as Town Registrar, which elsewhere would have been completely disregarded or attracted a minor admonishment. He had received a five year prison sentence, later reduced to three and a half; his livelihood and reputation were destroyed. This had cast the Gramsci family from comfortable small town security into grinding rural poverty, blighted their childhoods and, in Antonio's case, severely exacerbated his ill health and disability.

He had plainly not been with any women before either, Evgenia suspected; at least not respectable, willing, non-charging ones. He was by turns shy and ungainly, then over-solicitous to the point of prying. This really ought to have turned Julka off completely, but to Evgenia's further inward fury, it seemed to have quite the opposite effect. Julka was plainly charmed and beguiled by his awkwardness, the sense of something missing in his masculine sense of himself, a great ocean of vulnerability under the superficial sharp wit, swarthy complexion and worldly affectations. The Italian delegate to the Communist International and newly appointed member of its Executive Committee, acquaintance of Bukharin and Zinoviev and Trotsky and protégé of Lenin himself, was also a lost crippled little boy a long way from home. For the first time ever, Evgenia acidly observed, something resembling a maternal instinct had been aroused in her beautiful younger sister.

Between the family visits to Serebranyi Bor, Gramsci still sought solace or diversion in Evgenia's company. They discussed politics as if their lives depended on it, which of course they did, though in ways in which they – with their still optimistic, urgent enthusiasm – might not yet appreciate. There was the forthcoming Comintern Congress, and daily accounts in *Pravda* and *Izvestia* of the preparations: "A new world to win!" as one of the Congress slogans put it. A widening range of delegates were making their way to Moscow from all over the world, in pursuit of the Bolshevik recognition that might propel them from obscure clandestinity or bourgeois absorption into the vanguard of history. Draft reports and resolutions were being circulated on the rapidly improving economic situation here in Russia, and distributed all over the world through *Inprecor*, the Comintern's news bulletin. Finally there was some sign of let-up in foreign support of the counter-revolutionary White brigands and mercenaries, even if only because the British and French and all the rest of them had troubles of their own to contend with at home. There was even talk of America, that other young society in dynamic upheaval, recognising the USSR. In contrast, Gramsci told Evgenia about the worsening situation in Italy. The Fascists were getting bolder and more violent by the day. Ever weaker Liberal governments cobbled together by Giolitti and his cabal came and went. A general strike called by a broad-based Labour Alliance, which included the communists alongside the reformist Socialists, collapsed in ignominy and recrimination. To make matters worse, the faction fighting in the young *PCd'I* was intensifying. The comrades were now arguing not just over the correct way forward but over what was to be learnt from the recent past.

"And rather more to the point," Gramsci said, "who is to blame for our failures and defeats..."

He was trying to stay above it all – Bordiga advocating a clean break from the reformists and maximalists of the residual Socialist Party, and Gramsci's old Turin comrade Angelo Tasca arguing for a United Front of all anti-Fascists based on the trades unions – but finding it increasingly difficult. The latest dispute was over whether the *PCd'I* should contest parliamentary elections, as Tasca advocated (with strong support from the Comintern), or stand aside from what Bordiga called the "bourgeois democratic charade."

"I can see merit and fault in both their arguments," said Gramsci, "but I don't mind telling you, Comrade Evgenia, the thought of returning to Italy in these circumstances fills me with dread. Then again, I can't stay here forever..."

Stuck in Russia, here at Serebranyi Bor, he was physically as well as politically isolated. Evgenia tried to offer comradely support. He discussed his official correspondence with her, and sought her advice on the cogency of his political arguments as well as the accuracy and appropriateness of his language. In July he wrote to Karl Radek, the Secretary of the Comintern, attacking the "maximalist rump" of the Italian Socialist Party under Giacinto Serrati and arguing against their admission (under serious consideration within *Ispolcom*) into the International.

"This lot betrayed the Turin proletariat just two years ago by refusing to organise a general strike, yet here they are hanging onto the coat-tails of world revolution!"

"Perhaps a little too combative," advised Evgenia, offering several more emollient phrases.

"Yes, you're right," said Antonio. "I'm sounding like Bordiga..."

In August he wrote to Zinoviev about developments in Italy, anticipating a Fascist *coup d'etat.*

"My goodness," she said. "Is that really what you foresee?"

"Indeed, with moral and material assistance from elements within the state and around the monarchy. The King himself is reported to hold daily conversations with Mussolini..."

In September he responded to a request from Trotsky for information about the Italian Futurists, for inclusion in Leon Davidovich's collection of articles *Literature and Revolution.* The Futurists had once been promising enough to prompt from Gramsci an article proclaiming "Marinetti the Revolutionary!" but now they were glorifying war and imperial expansion and sucking up to the Fascists. Even their art and poetry, once so modern and adventurous, was showing signs of conformity and contrivance. *It would be sad if it weren't so pathetic,* Gramsci wrote. They were like "a gang of naughty schoolboys who escaped from a Jesuit college, whooped it up in the woods, and were brought back indoors under the forest warden's stick."

"Oh that's very good!" said Evgenia, always glad to see "a bunch of Bohemians" put in their place.

They discussed the defeat of the small Soviet republic in Hungary, the only foothold the international proletarian revolution had yet established in any industrialized western country.

"Oh well," said Evgenia. "Let's hope it's only a temporary setback..."

They exchanged the latest news from their families. There was always more from the Schuchts than the Gramscis.

"I'm afraid I have rather neglected my familial duties," said Gramsci.

He confessed, to Evgenia's evident shock, that he had gone over ten years with only intermittent contact with his family back in Sardinia, and several of those years with hardly any letters at all. He had been home only twice in all those years. It was an almost conscious decision to cut himself off from where he had come from, he admitted, and begin again as if it had never happened.

"Revolutionaries tend to do that, as if we can remake ourselves as thoroughly and brutally as we are seeking to remake the world."

He was beginning to understand the folly and cruelty of it, especially when he felt the warmth and easy interaction of the Schucht family, and the fond pleasures of their shared memories, but Sardinia really did feel a long way away.

"Besides," he said in attempted mitigation, "there is always more going on in Ivanovo than back in dusty old Ghilarza! Now tell me about your mother's attempts at cloud berry jam, or Anna and Julka's latest violin recital..."

Antonio and Evgenia continued to share observations and quips about their respective "treatments", some of which they actually recommended to each other as unusually beneficial or simply pleasurable, like the course of full-body massage which a new, young and enthusiastic doctor from Turkey had introduced to the end of the *banya* treatment.

"They even use perfumed oils!" said Gramsci, delighting in both the story and Evgenia's startled look in response. "It makes me feel like a Muslim satrap being prepared for an evening in his harem!"

In quieter moments, or in notes he slipped under her door in the middle of the night, Gramsci regularly expressed his devotion to Evgenia and sometimes "love"; or at least the Italian phrase *ti voglio bene*, which she understood to mean "I love you". But he made no move to take the relationship forward, towards real emotional intimacy or any kind of physical consummation. He did not even offer a chaste kiss on the cheek, which Evgenia understood to be common among the slightest acquaintances under both Russian and Italian manners. And for all her encouragement of him to use her family pet-name of Zhenya, or *Genia* in Italian, he insisted on calling her "Evgenia" or more often simply "Comrade Schucht". Just what was this man up to? She knew him to be shy, and awkward in company, but surely they knew each other well enough by now to beyond that in their personal relations. She also knew from what he said that he was lonely and isolated, and deeply troubled by aspects of his past. Perhaps he simply sought her company for solace and distraction. *Most perplexing...*

* * *

In early October 1922, into his fifth month at Serebranyi Bor, the doctors pronounced Comrade Antonio Gramsci rested and well enough to resume limited political activities and official duties. He was still suffering from convulsions, but they were mild and brief enough for him to retain control of his movements by sitting quiet and still in a darkened room. From the sanatorium, he would be allowed out to attend preparatory meetings for the Communist International. He could even, so long as it did not take him too far away and demand too much of his precarious health and delicate constitution, contribute to public education and agitation on the purposes and importance of the forthcoming Congress.

His first excursion was as part of an official visit to the Soviet State Library in Moscow, where in the building of the State Publishing House GIZ he watched a beautiful new Russian language edition of Rudyard Kipling's *The Jungle Book* under preparation. Gramsci delighted especially in the simple blocky constructivist two-colour illustrations by El Lissitsky of Rikki-Tikki-Tavi and the boy Mowgli who was brought up by wolves. He watched closely – always fascinated by the skill and dexterity of advanced handicraft, and feeling his own relatively clumsy fingers and thumbs twitching involuntarily in sympathetic imitation – as the lithographic printers transferred the pictures to the stone. Afterwards he asked his translator to walk with him back to the tram stop, his first proper chance of Moscow sight-seeing. He had taken a liking to this young man, a student called Pasha who had grown up in the Austrian Tirol and moved here with his communist parents during the Revolution. After all the starchy middle-aged brusqueness of the official delegation, Gramsci relished a bit of younger company. Together they admired the city's old Italian and Byzantine architecture, above all its innumerable churches, most now commandeered for strictly, pointedly secular purposes like food storage or vehicle repair, or in some cases ramshackle residential accommodation.

They traversed semi-clandestine markets, wretched but colourful, taking up vast squares. In one of the markets, the Futurist painters had been given a free hand by Lunacharsky, the People's Commissar for Public Education and himself a well-regarded poet, and they had transformed the stalls into gigantic flowers. Palaces and gardens were decked out with banners and displays welcoming comrades to the Comintern Congress in dozens of languages, some of them unfamiliar even to the philologist Gramsci. Whole avenues of government buildings displayed gleaming new plaques at their heavily guarded entrances, declaring their new Soviet status and function. There seemed to be People's Commissions and Commissariats for every conceivable human activity and historical contingency. Gramsci imagined dozens of grandiose projects to transform the country, which he was already beginning to suspect – noting the Soviet propensity for bombast, but without daring to say so for fear of offending his hosts – would come to nothing.

As early evening darkness fell, the circular, still leafy boulevards filled up with a buzzing, amorous crowd, gaily and brightly dressed for a few hours' carefree carousing under the recently restored street lights. Red Army soldiers mingled with pretty perfumed girls released arm-in-arm from the government offices where they worked as typists and secretaries, and black marketeers barely bothering to disguise their activities and wares under the free-for-all of the New Economic Policy. On Tverskaya Street, as they approached the Hotel Lux, where Gramsci would return to stay when he finally left the sanatorium for good, the young translator pointed out the poets' cafés. Heavily made-up women and black leather-clad men leant on marble counters, sipping coffee and sucking on cigarettes, frowning and tight-lipped in concentration. Gramsci peered in at a handsome young man in a white silk smock with flowing golden-blond hair, incanting his poetry, whose violent images jostled each other as though in a fight.

"This is Sergei Yesenin," whispered Pasha alongside him. "He also chalks his poems on walls all over the city."

Further up the street, they stopped to examine the glass cases where the bourgeois newspapers had been displayed before the revolution. Some were still scarred by cracks and bullet holes from the civil war, but they were now being used to display huge collages and posters and strident artistic manifestos. Gramsci stopped at one, his eye caught by a stark agitprop poster against the encircling Great Powers, Lloyd George and Clemenceau and the global scourge of capitalism, this last symbolized by a pot-bellied character in a top hat smoking an enormous cigar. The simple, primary coloured illustrations were accompanied by sharp bursts of blank poetry exhorting greater revolutionary effort against the "capitalistic bloodsuckers".

"This is by Mayakovsky," said Pasha. "They say he is mad..."

The posters, with their bold colours and stark slogans and the official imprimatur of the *Glavpolitprosvet* (Chief Political Education Department), looked sane enough to Gramsci. But he had to remind himself that, to much of the watching world, the Soviet Revolution represented a kind of collective madness. And if madness consisted in irreconcilable opposites, they might just have a point. Beyond the brightly lit boulevards, with their jostling crowds and cafés and posters, Gramsci sensed a rather different Moscow, normally kept well away from foreign delegates and visitors like him. Down the alleyways and on the upper floors of tenement buildings you could see the real live city if you looked hard enough, and deployed your powers of imagination and sympathy.

You could just about make out shadowy figures scurrying and scuffling around in the dirt. They could be children or old people, abandoned to their fate by revolutionary upheaval, tipped out on their ears by a society which had turned itself upside down. This was a city of daily struggle to live, of suppressed shouts and haggling over meagre rations, of unannounced arrests and desperate pleas for mercy or release, of anxious women and ravaged men begging stony-faced bureaucrats through metal grilles for some small favour, all of it within an economy of moral barter and petty racketeering and shouted accusations and orders.

The comrades of the Comintern saw very little of it, shepherded from museums to model nurseries, from clinics to libraries and printing presses like the one Gramsci had just been cooing over, and sumptuously fed among almost universal misery. Its practical problems remained for most of them matters of abstract theory, presented in charts and columns in Research Bureaux documents and *Ispolcom* presentations. He would have liked to explore the real city with Pasha, but suspected this might embarrass the young translator, and just possibly place them both in real danger. They parted with a warm handshake at the tram stop.

* * *

His next engagement was to be a factory meeting in Ivanovo Voznesensk, which he had chosen from a list circulated among the Comintern delegates. It would require at least one overnight stay, so he made arrangements with Apollon and Julia Schucht, on one of their visits to Evgenia, to stay with them. He also asked – trying very hard to suppress any suspicion of ulterior motives, while deliberately underplaying his own facility in Russian – if he could engage their daughter Comrade Julka as his translator.

"Of course, Comrade Gramsci," said Apollon. "I'm sure Julka would be delighted."

Evgenia, who for some months had been assisting Gramsci towards fluency in Russian (certainly enough to address a factory meeting), looked on in uncharacteristic silence.

On the morning of the meeting at Ivanovo, Gramsci took unusual care over his appearance. He dragged a comb through his unruly hair and even through the small bush of bristle on his top lip. This was now, he noted to his own satisfied reflection in the mirror, almost worthy of the term "moustache". He put on his spare, clean set of clothes: the flannel shirt his older brother Gennaro had passed on to him before Antonio left Turin for Moscow, with his customarily curt "you'll need to keep yourself warm up there, little 'un"; the nearly new suit he had acquired for a few roubles from one of the sanatorium doctors who happened to be very nearly his small size; and the sturdy boots he had bought in Milan with most of his very first salary cheque back in the middle years of the world war, newly re-soled and heeled by the sanatorium cobbler. It was all topped off with a rather natty felt fedora he had bought from an old peasant woman at a Moscow flea market shortly after he arrived in early June. He even sprayed himself with a bottle of *eau de cologne* he had borrowed from the English chap – a bit of a dandy who, or so it was rumoured, was here to overcome opium addiction and some unnamed sexual perversion – in the room next door to his, at the back end of the sanatorium.

He had been offered a car to take him all the way to Ivanovo, but he insisted on travelling by train, not just because this was the people's mode of transport, but also because he much preferred travelling by train. He could stand up and walk around, smoke without bothering the driver, read and write without feeling sick, or simply gaze out of the window at the passing countryside and the intermittent human habitations. He did accept a ride from the sanatorium driver into Moscow. It was unseasonably warm for late September, a real Indian summer as the Americans called it, and he would have found the six kilometre walk a challenge after four months of mainly sitting and lying down. One of his doctors also warned that he might be bothered by *bezprisorniki*, street children.

At precisely 10.15, he stepped out of the car in front of the main railway station from which he would catch the train to Ivanovo Voznesensk. It would take four and a quarter hours, and deposit him there in the early afternoon, with plenty of time to meet up with Julka and travel to the factory for the meeting between day and evening shifts. Gramsci settled himself at a window seat in a carriage near the front of the train, but not right behind the engine, whose smoke and steam would obscure the view if he was too close. He put his valise between his feet on the floor, and sat as upright as this would allow so he could get a good look out of the window. As the carriage filled up, he scrutinised his fellow passengers, mostly men. It was a remarkably similar crowd to what you might find on the Turin-Rome express, a rather longer distance but a similar journey through age-old countryside and more recently burgeoning industrial cities and towns.

For all their differences in climate and vegetation, this was not the first time he had found himself likening his country of birth and usual residence to this one, this strange hurly-burly place of startling change and just as startling continuity. Everything in Russia seemed to be in constant flux but underneath remained essentially the same; *just like Italy, where* (he thought) *the gap between what one sees and what one does not see goes wider and deeper than in any of the other so-called civilised countries...The past is always present...* These countries, Russia and Italy, were very young and very old at the same time, paradoxically puerile *and* senile, like the Chinese philosopher Lao-Tzu, who legend had it was born with white hair after eighty years in his mother's womb.

Ivanovo lay to the north east of Moscow, beyond the city of Vladimir and amidst low-lying countryside most notable for its several substantial rivers. At this time of the year, they were in full flood and the surrounding land was veiled in patches of mist which the faltering early autumn sun was struggling to disperse. The winter cold was lurking just below the surface of the yellowing fields and muddy cart tracks, ready to pounce on the complacent or unwary. Gramsci had never been this far north before, so far away from Sardinia and Turin. He found himself unconsciously catching his breath when he thought about it, as if to guard against inhaling the chill. *A childish Italian habit,* he thought, *born of morbid mediaeval fears of "miasmas" and "fluxes", as if germs had never been discovered... Silly people,* he murmured at his countrymen and his own reflection in the window, largely ignorant of medical science and mired in superstition. *Cold does not cause infection – if anything it discourages it – but simply depresses the spirits and inhibits recovery.*

The surprisingly well-appointed train hurried along the occasionally juddering track through long stretches of open countryside, slowing only for towns and the sturdy iron bridges that carried it over the wide rivers. His fellow passengers were mostly NEP-men (for "New Economic Policy"), the new breed of businessmen authorised by Lenin to revive the market economy within the strict framework of the young state's socialist norms. The Bolsheviks had finally realised that Trotsky's "War Communism" could not go on forever, with the military discipline that was required to make people turn up for work, not to mention its starvation rations, requisitioning expeditions into the countryside, and widespread famine and typhoid. There was one story that was always deployed, in hushed tones, to illustrate the horror of those times, about enraged peasants slitting open a commissar's belly, packing it with grain and leaving him by the roadside as a lesson for all the others.

Fear of meeting a similar fate no doubt helped persuade the comrades of the wisdom of NEP: freedom of trade and production by craftsmen, concessions on attractive terms to foreign capital, in effect a partial restoration of capitalism. Leon Davidovitch and his supporters might rail against it, and call instead for "permanent revolution", but everyone else knew this was completely unrealistic, the final stand of a dwindling minority of old purists and ultra-leftists. After a few months of NEP, things had rapidly improved. Factories and workshops resumed production. Workers returned to their jobs, willingly and productively. Proper wages were restored, and people went back to spending them. Restaurants were open again, and pastries which were actually edible were on sale at a rouble apiece. The NEP-men had been tasked with getting stuff back into the shops, and earning themselves a tidy profit in the process. *And good for them,* thought Gramsci, surprising himself with his magnanimity towards this new breed of capitalist entrepreneurs, and looking around his train carriage at the NEP-men on this busy train to Ivanovo. *That's how they can afford their new suits and overcoats, shiny shoes and bowler hats...* Some carried leather cases brimming with catalogues and samples in their laps, clasped tightly in their arms, as if they didn't quite trust the briefly relenting Bolsheviks not to suddenly snatch it all back. *Not surprising really, considering the confusion among the Party rank-and-file over this ideological about-turn and the sudden re-emergence of the hated business class... What was it Lenin said just a couple of years ago about "saboteurs in the first and second class carriages"? That they should all be arrested and shot...*

Others, perhaps slightly higher up the business chain, carried only newspapers and magazines, which they read avidly and folded over page by page. They might have been high state officials, but for their workaday clothes and the hunger with which they scoured their papers for any item they might turn to their advantage. They reminded Gramsci of the way in which the workers of Turin had devoured the printed word during the red years of the factory councils and occupations; news and opinion which actually had some direct bearing on them and their daily lives. The market economy had that effect, brought global affairs to personal attention.

Amongst the Ivanovo-bound NEP-men, there were a number of scruffy but noticeably well-fed kulaks, wealthy peasants also benefiting from Lenin's relaxation of economic regulation, unencumbered now and presumably returning to the country from the capital having sold their surplus wares. Their clothing – rough woollen tunics, baggy trousers and thick *puttees* wrapped around the tops of their sturdy boots – was spattered with residues of their produce: fruit stains, husks of wheat, small bloody feathers. They held their bulky wallets, presumably stuffed with roubles, firm in their huge callused hands, and surveyed the carriage suspiciously from between prominent, sometimes bulbous noses. They didn't read anything, except their fellow passengers' faces. *Presumably they're illiterate...Let's hope their children won't be...*

As the train rattled along, Gramsci read his own book – one of Tolstoy's lesser works, in atypically dense Russian which he was forcing himself to decipher – and let himself nod off after every couple of pages, lulled into fitful sleep by the rocking of the carriage and the thought that there was still quite a long way to go. At Vladimir, roughly half way there after two hours, he unpacked the packet of bread and sausage which the sanatorium canteen had thoughtfully prepared for him. He bought a cup of hot tea from the steaming samovar wheeled along the corridor of the train by a starched uniformed and curly moustachioed waiter, another restoration from pre-revolutionary times. Feeling nicely replete, he let himself drift off again into pleasant half-sleep.

"Ivanovo Voznesensk!" shouted a voice from outside the window, muffled by the tight glass and the competing noises of bustle around, onto and off the train. "Ivanovo Voznesensk!"

Gramsci awoke with a start somewhere between the two announcements and, aware that the train did not hang about at station stops, gathered up his few belongings into his small valise. His book got all mixed up with the notes he had made for his speech and the small wrapped and beribboned gift he had brought for Comrade Julka in return for her translating services. *Oh never mind,* he thought, snapping the valise closed on its jumbled contents and pushing his way past boarding passengers to get to the carriage door, *I'll sort it all out later.*

The first thing he saw in front of the station buildings in the middle of the long platform, around a hundred metres away, was a big white banner proclaiming "The Workers' and Soldiers' Soviet of Ivanovo-Voznesensk welcomes Comrade Antonio Gramsci, EC member at the Fourth Congress of the Communist International!" in bold red letters. *My goodness, how embarrassing...* was his first thought, followed by a rather more measured *How nice!* and then *They've spelled my surname right!* Holding a heavy pole at one end of the banner he recognised Julka – how could he not? – and smiling widely walked briskly towards her. She was wearing a black silk dress he'd never seen before, and shoes with patent leather and silver buckles.

"Julka!" he exclaimed, reaching up towards her shoulders and head, and attempting to kiss her on the cheek.

"Er Comrade..." she responded in some awkwardness, encumbered as she was by the heavy banner pole. She was also aware that she stood at least eight inches taller than him, and that their fumbling embrace was being closely watched in some disbelief by her comrades from the Workers and Soldiers Soviet of Ivanovo Voznesensk. They had never heard Comrade Schucht,

NKVD translator, cultural worker and daughter of a revered old Bolshevik, addressed by her family pet-name, let alone embraced by a dark-skinned bushy-haired dwarf.

They boarded a tram car outside the station, and with lots of clattering bells and hooting whistles, trundled off towards the factory district. Gramsci looked out at the new concrete buildings going up around the old one-storey wooden dwellings. Beyond them he could see the mills and factories of this industrial settlement, belching filthy smoke from chimneys which were the highest constructions for many miles around. He quickly tired of the grim view, so reminiscent of the grimier districts of Turin, and stole sly glances at Comrade Schucht on the opposite bench.

He was aware of her comrades from the Soviet addressing her with smirks and titters as "Comrade *Julka*", and of her blushing discomfort in response. She caught his eye and raised her eyebrows in silent apology for their silliness. He smiled back and tried to indicate that it really didn't matter. There was a kind of protective fondness, he could see, in the rough factory workers' manner towards the young woman, not too far removed from his own growing affection for her. The banter among his Italian comrades was really far worse, especially on the Turin factory floor, and even that was nothing compared to the stream of organised sarcasm he usually had going on in his own head.

There were more of Julka's raised eyebrows – *just as perfectly beautiful as the rest of her face,* he noted – when the Ivanovo comrades started to make disparaging comments about "this giant of a man" whom "Comrade *Julka*" had been going on about all this time; "this high-up fellow" come amongst them to spread the word about international proletarian revolution. They obviously didn't realise that he could easily understand what they were saying, even in their heavily accented and idiomatic Russian. Until, that is, they saw him laughing along when the burliest and loudest comrade noted how far they had come in just five years of Soviet socialism. "Why, we are all a whole head taller than foreigners like this funny little *Italianetz*!" After that they quietened down until they reached the factory.

He was ushered into a large room at the back of the building. From the look of the racks of deep shelves around the walls it had been used for storage in Tsarist times, but it had since been converted into a canteen – the workers must be fed! – with long tables and benches in neat rows and an impromptu kitchen at one end. From the rafters hung banners exhorting ever harder work and proclaiming the imminent triumph of world socialism. The centrepiece was a painting of factory workers – men and women though, Julka apart, Gramsci had only so far seen men here – marching arm in arm holding spanners, hammers and picks in their enormous hands. Their joyous faces were raised to a glowing orange and yellow sky emblazoned with the words "Forward to the Fourth Congress of the Communist International!" *You can feel the enormous expectations in that picture...*

Huge cooking cauldrons on makeshift stoves emitted steam clouds and the savoury smells of the evening meal which would reward the day shift for their labours and prepare the night shift for theirs. One table had already been laid with a clean white tablecloth, glasses and bottles. Gramsci was greeted by an older man, dressed in a suit rather than the quilted jackets and overalls everyone else – again, Julka apart – seemed to be wearing. He introduced himself as "Comrade Manager", and showed his "honoured comrade guest" to a seat at the long white table. They were joined by Julka and what Gramsci was now thinking of as her entourage of awkward giggling workers.

At a sign from the manager, the bottles were opened and their clear contents poured into the waiting glasses, which were then distributed around the table. When Gramsci received his, and lifted it to his mouth, the smell of vodka hit his nostrils like a dose of the smelling salts he had been treated with after a particularly gruelling *banya* session. He took a sip and felt the smooth heat of the vodka – far more pleasant than scalding steam and a switch of birch twigs across your back and buttocks – slip down his throat and radiate across his chest. An involuntary "Mmm" rose from deep inside. Meanwhile his companions were emptying their glasses in single gulps and greedily refilling them from the rapidly emptying bottles. After their third or fourth they were called to order by the "Comrade Manager" with a curt demand for "some socialist discipline, comrades" and a pointed reminder that most of them still had a full night-shift to work.

"And now," he declared, "I call upon our esteemed comrade Granuski..."

Flustered – *is this the actual meeting?* – and still feeling the effects of the strong drink, not to mention yet another variation on his surname, Gramsci reached down for his valise and pulled out his bundle of notes. He had quite forgotten that he had put them back in disorder when he had got off the train, and as he lifted them from underneath his Tolstoy book, several sheets fell out on to the floor. In amongst them was his gift for Julka, which fell at her feet as she came to his aid.

"Oh dear!" he said, taking the mislaid sheets back from her in mounting panic, and disgusted with himself for having spoilt the surprise. "You might as well keep hold of that, I was going to give it to you later..."

Julka looked up at him in some amusement. *That glorious smile...*

"So comrades!" he exclaimed, standing upright and trying to look like he had some command of the situation. He had been advised by a Comintern secretary to keep his speech simple – "the Ivanovo Voznesensk Workers' and Soldiers' Soviet will be keen to know that they are not entirely alone in the world proletarian revolution, and that they should resist the blandishments of the objectively counter-revolutionary Trojan Horse of the Socialist Revolutionaries, but anything beyond that would be a waste of time and breath..." – so he was not planning to say too much or anticipating any great controversy. There was no sign of the SR oppositionists Julka had been tasked by the party with struggling against, which must be some measure of her success. He brought greetings from the Italian communists, and described how they had watched from afar and with boundless admiration as their Russian comrades undertook the first true and successful proletarian revolution in the history of the world.

The Italians were now trying hard, he said, in the rather different circumstances of bourgeois parliamentary democracy, to emulate their efforts and draw courage from their inspiration. They were seeking in their own way to instigate the dictatorship of the proletariat and usher in another workers' state to stand shoulder-to-shoulder with the glorious Russian Soviet Federative Socialist Republic. They were waiting eagerly for the Fourth Congress of the Communist International, and the proof it would provide of the growing hegemony of the working class and the unity of its political representatives under the guidance of the party of Marx, Engels, Lenin and Trotsky.

As he spoke, haltingly at first but with gathering momentum as he beheld the expectant upturned faces of his audience, Julka translated his words from Italian to Russian. He listened to his words changing shape and texture, as always fascinated by their transformation from one linguistic structure and cultural tradition into another, and keeping an ear out for unfamiliar Russian words he could add to his own growing lexicon. He watched her beautiful mouth enunciate clearly the words and phrases he had written and spoken. The returned gazes of the workers were all on her – even, in some cases, while he was speaking – as they digested the news from this strange faraway country they might have heard of but never been anywhere near. He might as well have been, he found himself thinking as he waited for Julka to finish translating his latest sentence, *a fuzzy wuzzy from darkest Africa*. Goodness, he'd been called that often enough by workers in Turin when he'd first arrived from the south.

His speech came to an abrupt halt when he turned to the next sheet and realised that it was the last, out of order from when he and Julka had gathered up his papers from the floor. He went from a close and detailed analysis of the balance of class forces in the Italian automotive industry – with some of the Ivanovo Workers' and Soldiers' Soviet comrades showing clear signs of fatigue, perhaps boredom, or the later soporific phases of intoxication – to a loud and ringing call for the workers of the world to unite and cast off the chains of capitalism and the dead weight of bourgeois hegemony!

At this the comrades sprang awake and, sensing that this was at last the end of it, came to their feet applauding and shouting their approval, while Julka struggled to make herself heard above the din with her final words of translation. The Comrade Manager, slurring his words and swaying slightly, proposed one last toast to "our esteemed Italian comrade Anton Grumpsky", and excused himself. He had to attend to some "urgent technical matter"; *and may well,* Gramsci thought, *need to call in at the lavatory on the way...* Draining their glasses, raising them and slamming them down in final gratitude, the workers also dispersed into the factory.

"That seemed to go alright," Gramsci said to Julka, when at last they found themselves sitting alone. "Do we go to your place now?"

"Oh no, comrade professor," she said, pretty much the first words she had spoken directly to him since his arrival. "We have to do the factory meeting now..."

"Oh my goodness!" This first gathering was just some kind of preliminary.

He made his speech in full and in the right order this time from a balcony overlooking the factory floor itself. The entire day and night shift workforce was gathered before him, gazing upwards or shuffling around. He spoke as loudly as his small reedy voice would allow, and Julka translated for him over the distant din of clattering machines and break-time chatter. This time he couldn't help but notice a small group of men and women circulating among the workers handing out leaflets, and trying unsuccessfully to engage them in conversation. Their leaflets were being crumpled up and tossed to the floor, and their advances rebuffed with scowls and loud shushing noises. This must be what was left of the famous, fearsome Socialist Revolutionaries of Ivanovo Voznesensk.

He also noticed small discrepancies between what he'd said and how Julka translated his speech. "United Front", a new formulation whose political vagueness made him feel uneasy, was substituted for the more properly Marxist "cross-class alliance under the dictatorship of the proletariat", for example. When afterwards he pointed them out, there was the first hint of discord between them – slight irritation on his part, mild humiliation on hers – but it was soon dispelled by her fulsome apology.

"Oh, Professor, I'm so sorry!"

"And I'm sorry for being so pedantic!" he responded.

Sheepishly she handed over an envelope.

"What's this, Comrade Julka?"

"A contract for my services today, Comrade Gramsci. I prepared it especially..."

He smiled at her careful formality – *perhaps a trace of her German ancestry?* – and promised that he would send her written confirmation of its receipt and of her highly satisfactory performance, "with some small hopefully constructive pointers for improvement", when he returned to Moscow.

* * *

After the factory meeting Antonio and Julka walked through the park and along the river back towards the town and the Schucht family home. For the first time they spoke freely and easily. They explored each other's personal backgrounds and characteristics, skirting carefully around what they really wanted to know about each other – above all, what each thought of the other – and both surreptitiously saving that for later. Instead they filled in the bare details of their lives. Julka spoke about her travels and sojourns with family. Much of it was familiar to Antonio from his conversations with Evgenia, but it was fascinating to get a slightly different perspective on it from another family member. The family wanderlust, for example, had been much more disruptive and burdensome for Julka, who after her peripatetic childhood spent almost all her adolescence settled in Rome and would clearly have preferred to stay there.

She told him about her training at the Santa Cecilia music school under the famous violinist Ettore Pinelli.

"I can't say I've ever heard of him..." said Gramsci, embarrassed by his cultural limitations. This was where she had first learnt to play the violin, and to express herself in ways that never came easily to her in words. As a young girl, she used to imagine she could transform the world with music. She clearly loved Rome, and relished the opportunity to practice the fluent Italian with which she recalled her time there. She asked him about Turin, and said how lovely it sounded.

"Well, I'm not so sure about that..." he said. "It's very industrial." As they walked along the riverside, Gramsci felt a pang of longing. Was it for his country, his native language, or his new companion? He put this faintly indecent, troubling thought to the back of his mind where it more properly belonged, perhaps to resurface when he had time alone to mull it over.

Julka had joined the Bolsheviks in September 1917. She was the first of her sisters to follow their father into the party of Lenin, she pointed out with a hint of competitive pride, before the October revolution. Her application had been processed and accepted unusually quickly because of her musical prowess and spreading reputation. Soon after, at New Year 1918, the first new year of the socialist state – *O quelli giorni innocenti*, "Oh, those innocent days!" – she had given a violin recital at the Alexeev School in Moscow for eight thousand people. She had played Wienawski's *Legende Opus 17*, one of her very favourite pieces, "not least," she said, "because when they first heard it in 1865, the composer's future wife's previously reluctant parents agreed to their marriage!"

She received, she said again with evident pride, a very warm review in *Izvestia* by the famous critic Alexander Serafimovich. Her playing, Serafimovich wrote, seemed to float above the clouds and over the mountains. It had reduced the audience to breathless silence, some to tears, followed by minutes of rapturous applause. Since then, she had performed regularly at party cultural events and private gatherings, usually in a duet with her sister Anna. Their rendition of Bach's violin concerto was especially renowned, though she feared Bach was going out of fashion. She had also composed her own musical settings of Russian poetry, of which her favourite was Lermontov. Her audiences were especially appreciative of her setting of *On the Death of the Poet*, about Pushkin's fatal duel: "He could not bear the burning shame," Julka recited from memory. "The petty calumnies, the stain, they sought to put upon his name... Alone he stood, and now is slain!"

"Delightful! Quite delightful!" Gramsci exclaimed.

Later that summer, as the war staggered to an end, Julka had caught Spanish flu. Unlike a number of her friends and comrades in Ivanovo, she had survived and recovered, but the illness had weakened her and left her prone to blackouts and fits, during which she stared blankly for minutes on end.

"Sometimes," she said with a shy smile and a slight blush, "my sisters say I look even more like a statue than I normally do!"

Gramsci felt another pang, this time of sympathetic concern.

"Do you know why it was called Spanish flu?" he asked.

"Actually, no..."

"Well, it's because of Spanish neutrality in the war. Everywhere else they suppressed the news of infections and deaths, because they didn't want to undermine public morale. Somewhere between fifty and a hundred million people died, out of the five hundred million infected, many times more than in the war itself. So all over the world, people were dying in complete ignorance and isolation. Except Spain, that is, where at least they knew what they were suffering from. Oh, and Japan, where the authorities took the simple but highly sensible and effective precaution of issuing everyone with breathing masks, so there were very few deaths. Interesting country, Japan... I once knew a worker in Turin who reduced every issue of global concern to what was going on in Japan. We used to tease him by asking 'And what are the Japanese planning to do about it?' The other strange thing about Spanish flu is that it spread during the summer and affected mostly young adults like yourself..."

"Goodness me," said Julka, and moved the conversation onto less morbid terrain. She told him about her work for the Soviet Interior Ministry, which was largely administrative but occasionally involved translating intercepted documents from abroad to counter-revolutionaries. Of course "for obvious reasons" she could not say much more than that. More effusively, she spoke about the students from the *Lycée* she was still teaching privately, the latest piece of music she was trying to get them to master, and the difficulties of obtaining new violin strings and good-quality horse-hair for their bows.

"Of course it's getting easier now. You can get pretty much anything under NEP, for a price!"

Antonio listened in rapt fascination as this shy young woman disclosed herself to him. For some reason he felt a strong impulse to give an entirely fictitious and fantastical account of himself – he was a trained and experience aviator, who one day could confidently expect to fly to the moon and plant the workers' red flag on its dusty surface; he was on a waiting list for a new and revolutionary surgical procedure, which would place his head on the body of an Olympic athlete (*that would show them!*); he had spent his childhood in a travelling circus troupe, with the stage-name *Angelo*, walking the high wire the entire length of the Italian peninsula – but he suppressed it. He reasoned that if he wanted to get to know Julka better, as he undoubtedly did, he'd do well to stick to the prosaic truth. They would have time enough together, he dared hope, to compose new and equally dramatic if rather less fantastical memories.

When they arrived at the Schucht family home, he was taken over by Apollon and mother Julia, engaged in formal discussion about the prospects for the Fourth Congress by the former and plied with heavy Prussian food by the latter, which meant he had to fight hard to talk coherently with the former. Apollon was a man who was used to being listened to, *as you might expect in a family of so many daughters*, Antonio thought, and not so good at listening to others, as he heard another carefully crafted and enunciated sentence of his own curtailed by Apollon's response. Julka melted into the background, into some other part of the family home beyond the range of the grown-ups. When they had eaten and the dinner plates had been cleared away by Julia Grigor'evna and the housemaid, Julka reappeared with her sister Anna. Had they not eaten? What was it with these Schucht sisters and food? He had never seen Evgenia eat a hearty meal at the sanatorium, or even clear her plate of the few morsels she had accepted. How did these people subsist? On fresh air?

It was now entirely dark outside. The candles flickered in the draught. There were no gas lamps out here in Ivanovo, the cause (Antonio recalled) of Lenin's recent visit. With the girls back in the family drawing room with their parents and what Apollon called their "esteemed guest" – causing Antonio to wonder momentarily if someone else had arrived – the atmosphere abruptly changed. The conversation turned flighty, hysterical almost, an exchange of quips rather than ideas, and left him floundering. The formal Italian gave way to colloquial Russian, which soon exhausted Gramsci's recently acquired facility and, at this late hour, mental energies. Apollon lapsed into an amused, indulgent, postprandial, paternal near-silence. Julka seemed to emerge from out of herself, giggling at some remark of her mother's, and competing with her sister to offer some sharp observation of an incident they had witnessed earlier that day before Gramsci had arrived. Something to do with a dispute over a tram ticket. He glimpsed her life without him, an independent young woman about her adopted town.

Apollon heaved himself to his feet and declared that he was retiring for the night, and called the housemaid to show Comrade Gramsci to his room, "after your busy day!" This was an airy chamber at the back of the house, with a large double-glazed window offering a view over an extensive garden in luxuriant early autumn bloom. Antonio slept unusually soundly – the quiet of the residential quarter of this provincial backwater came as a pleasant change from the bustle of Moscow, where even the sanatorium was never entirely silent at night – and the next morning he returned to Serebranyi Bor. Before he left he witnessed a curious incident in the Schucht household. Returning from a short walk around the town, he found the front door open and walked straight in to hear a furious outburst from Julka directed at no-one in particular; perhaps she wasn't so shy after all. *She certainly has a temper on her. Oh well, perhaps it's something to do with me being here.* When she had recovered her composure, Julka walked with him to the station, and waved him off as the train pulled away. When he was settled on the train, he thought back on their conversations, and reflected on how little he really knew of her. They had exchanged little more than pleasantries really, and she had always kept him at some distance, but it was clear to Gramsci that she would welcome further personal contact. She had even reached down to kiss his cheeks, Italian style, as he turned to board the train.

They began to correspond, still formally and tentatively, as autumn turned to winter and Gramsci and his doctors considered his discharge from the sanatorium. Julka called him "Professor" and largely confined her remarks to safe subjects like the weather – "Today I found the sun! It seemed to have gone missing..." – or politics – "Father says that Trotsky is over-reaching himself..." – in letters which (she later confessed) underwent as many as five careful drafts before she dared send them off. Evgenia confided in a slightly mischievous note that "Julka's purse is full of letters to you, begun and not finished." Meanwhile he continued to address her with the formal Italian "Lei" rather than the familiar "tu", and took care to maintain a rather impersonal business-like tone, signing off his letters with "a cordial handshake". It was as if they had to keep reminding themselves and each other that their relationship, if such it was, was for the moment entirely comradely.

And at least to begin with, Julka's only obvious reason to visit Serebranyi Bor was to see her sister in the company of other family members. Her exchanges with Gramsci, increasingly warm and exclusive as they were, had to be conducted in awkward asides and glances when they found themselves sitting near each other. If this was an early phase of courtship, it had to be made to look entirely accidental, not much more than common courtesy between casual acquaintances. Over time they made increasingly calculated, and obvious, attempts to engineer such proximity. Eventually Julka was clearly detaching herself from Evgenia's party of visitors and sitting with what her family and other interested observers were beginning to call "Julka's new friend" or simply, with a knowing nod, "the Italian". It wasn't quite intimacy, but it was clearly heading that way.

By this time it was Julka's turn to be intrigued, not least because after his initial torrent of attention to her and what she had to say, Gramsci had himself pulled back from the brink of open flirtation and romance. On occasions he was downright cool, and even more icily ironic than usual in his observations of other people or situations. He was working hard at his political duties, with several taxing trips to Petrograd for special sessions of the Comintern *Ispolcom,* and still not entirely recovered from the nervous exhaustion with which he had entered the sanatorium, manifested now in faint-inducing anaemia, bouts of amnesia and his perennial insomnia. But she detected another layer of reserve. Much later, in a letter to her, he would attribute this tendency to withdraw inside himself at moments of uncertainty to patterns formed in his own childhood and background – "I became used to hiding my feelings behind a mask of hardness, or an ironic smile..." – and ask for her forgiveness for subjecting her to that same hands-off treatment. "I suppose my only excuse is that I was trying to gauge your interest in me..." But for now, she could not help wondering if it was something she had said or done.

So she started making more of an effort with him, to pay attention to his funny little anecdotes or what he had been reading or had seen at the theatre, even to ask him – *my goodness,* thought the ever watchful Evgenia, *the ice maiden melts* – to elaborate or even strike out on an entirely new line of conversation. Over these intermediary days, which constituted the second phase of their fumbling courtship, Julka found herself drawn inside those grey-blue eyes looking for the earlier familiar hunger. And he was, she felt for just about the first time about any man she had ever met, a genuinely fascinating and engaging character. He had a range of experience and insight well beyond his age and his physical stature, or anything she had ever encountered in what she now saw as the surprisingly narrow *milieu* of cosmopolitan malcontents, dispossessed toffs and utopian dreamers she had grown up and lived amongst in her father's *émigré* circles. This man seemed to have grown from, and remained firmly rooted in, the real world, where people made and grew things and truly belonged to places and other people.

He was also of course, and despite his own deep personal reserve and coruscating rationality, vigorously and boldly Italian. Whenever she picked up her violin, Julka told Nino, the music itself seemed to bring back to her the warmth and the light of Italy, especially the Vivaldi pieces she loved to play for her own private pleasure. Teaching them to her own Russian students now, with their thick clumsy fingers and wide chins clamped to their cheap violins, she tried with her own much more refined instrument to convey some of that warmth, in the hope (usually vain) that it would enable them to relax into the beautiful sprightly music. Listening to her speaking now, Nino watched her come alive when she talked about her music. He told her he would love to hear her play. She blushed and said that one day he would.

All this time she was aware of the knowing glances between her relatives, and watched out for some sign that she and Nino were infringing the rules of the sanatorium or some unspoken social etiquette. But no one seemed to object to this new level of intimacy in what was quite clearly now a dalliance, if not a relationship. So clearly in fact that Nino accused her semi-seriously of standing him up when illness had prevented her from joining a family visit to Serebranyi Bor. Here was a man who, for all his physical frailties and deformities and his manifest romantic inexperience, was used to getting his own way. She caught a glimpse of what had enabled him to attain his present status in the *Partito Comunista d'Italia* and the Comintern, a seam of iron in his will. She would be sure to make definite arrangements in future, she wrote, and to let him know of any last-minute alterations; again, a sign of their growing attachment.

They took to walking out together around the grounds of the sanatorium, after first gaining approval from his doctors of this new development in his "treatment". And when it was time for her to leave, he accompanied her to the main gate and the road back into the city. They both felt, they later disclosed to each other when their intimacy was well and truly established, the wrench of separation and the delicious tingle of anticipation for their next meeting.

* * *

The situation in Italy was worsening by the day. Mussolini and his Fascist *squadristi* had set about "restoring order" to the cities and the countryside, with the active connivance of the King and the offices of state. These behind the scenes negotiations and manoeuvres had culminated in the grotesque pantomime of the "March on Rome", with thousands of Blackshirts converging on the capital mostly armed with sticks and whips and even, it was rumoured, toy rifles and revolvers carved from wood. The march took place two days *after* Mussolini had been invited by the King to form a government, with the participation of right-wing mavericks from the Popular Party and the Liberals. If this was any kind of revolution, as Mussolini kept bellowing, it was being imposed from above on a cowed nation and populace.

Gramsci spent his final days at Serebranyi Bor preparing an article on *The Origins of the Mussolini Cabinet* for the Communist International's bulletin, *La Correspondence Internationale*, popularly known and read around the world as *Inprecor*. He wanted to dig beneath the newspaper headlines and radio bulletins, and the absurd grandstanding of the Fascists themselves, and explain the class character and the political contingencies of the crisis. He began by explaining the historical weaknesses of the Italian bourgeoisie and their failure to achieve a properly modern, integrated national state in the face of the quasi-feudal alliance between the big landowners and the Vatican. In the resulting political vacuum, the liberal Giolitti had assembled an electoral coalition of city-dwellers and agricultural landowners. Through parliamentary manoeuvre and paternalistic concessions, all the old tricks of what was known as *trasformismo*, Giolitti had managed to organise a series of precarious government majorities behind his programme of industrialisation, free trade and social harmony. This fragile settlement had lasted around twenty years in one form or another, from one century into the next, but was finally blown away by the world war.

The popular opposition, clustered around the old Socialist Party, consisted mainly of share-cropping or smallholding peasants. This meant that post-war upheaval was largely a struggle over land ownership. But for all their mass peasant membership, the Socialists were incapable of concerted political action. Rather, these "Maximalists" engaged in noisy pronouncements in Parliament, in sticking up posters, and in songs and fanfares. They were all sound and fury, but no systematic organisation or mass education. Meanwhile the small Italian industrial working class went largely unorganised and unrepresented. Italian workers remained politically ineffectual when compared to the other developed countries of Western Europe, with their huge and highly effective trade union movements and Labour and Social Democratic Parties. Proletarian struggles like the Turin Factory Council movement were left isolated or even blamed on "irresponsible agents of the Moscow government", and suppressed by Socialist Party officials and trade union leaderships protecting their own positions. The European wave of post-war agitation and upheaval might have swept Italy along in its wake, with wildcat strikes and massive rumbustious demonstrations, but they achieved very little beyond local inconvenience and anxiety, and their participants soon grew confused and demoralised.

In March 1920, the industrialists, bankers and landowners began their counter-offensive, with feverish counter-revolutionary organisation and action, and the active assistance of the state. Demobilised army officers were allowed to keep four-fifths of their pay if they joined the *Fasci di Combattimento*, previously a small organisation of socialist, anarchist, syndicalist and republican eccentrics who had supported Italian participation in the war. These interventionists – previously "leaders without a following", as Gramsci dubbed them – were suddenly flooded with money and recruits. This provided the armed nucleus for Mussolini's campaign of terror. For all this ex-Socialist's "revolutionary" phrase-mongering and bombast, he was for the moment merely a willing tool of the most reactionary elements of the Italian bourgeoisie.

The article was published in *Inprecor* on 20th November 1922, and brought Gramsci many kind words and nods of praise around the Hotel Lux in Moscow, where he was now re-installed while he resumed his official duties at the Comintern. Comrades from all the European parties and beyond made a point of stopping Gramsci in the corridors and dining rooms and asking when the next instalment would appear. How did the Italian comrades propose to defeat the Fascist insurgency and new Mussolini government, this strange mutation of nationalism and socialism, reaction and revolution? It shouldn't be too difficult, should it? From the perspective of the international proletarian revolution and its Moscow powerhouse, this piece of reactionary buffoonery looked like a comic opera staged by a bunch of disillusioned ex-Socialists, almost consciously aping the propaganda methods, military manners and repressive apparatus of the Bolsheviks, but without the underpinning of an organised, self-confident proletariat. It was little more than a diversion from the main thrust of historical progress towards international socialism and then global communism, a Punch and Judy show to thrill and frighten the children. Surely it couldn't last, could it?

"Of course not!" Gramsci would respond, and make his own analogies between Mussolini and other grotesque figures in popular folklore besides Punchinello, trying to sound more confident than he felt.

As he offered further detail and explanation, he could feel his authority and stature grow among his comrades and Comintern functionaries and fellow delegates. He had reached that point, familiar from school and university, and later the struggles in the streets and factories of Turin and the formation of the *PCd'I*, where people ceased to notice what he looked or sounded like and concentrated instead on what he had to say. Gramsci was even approached by the Hungarian *Ispolcom* member Matyas Rakosi and – he told Julka on a walk around Serebranyi Bor – "...asked point-blank why I don't become leader of the Italian party in place of Bordiga. Amadeo's implacable sectarianism runs counter to the current Comintern line of seeking alliances with other workers' parties and even coalition governments. He will be expelled from the Comintern if he persists with his opposition to fusion with the Socialists and participation in parliamentary elections..."

"They want you to become party leader?" Julka asked, with a note of incredulity she immediately felt ashamed of and wished she could withdraw. Antonio passed over it, apparently oblivious.

"Well, Rakosi does. And he's a fool, without a single ounce of political intelligence in his big Hungarian head. But he wouldn't have approached me without some kind of authorisation from higher up... The problem is that it would split the Italian party in two, and as things stand Amadeo would take most of it with him. They love him back in Italy, in the piazzas and the factories, where he can always be relied upon for a barnstorming performance at a public meeting. With the Fascists on the rampage, and the Socialists looking for any sign of weakness amongst us, a split would be disastrous. I told Rakosi it's a much bigger political task than replacing Bordiga. In any case, in terms of general capacity for work, Amadeo is worth at least three of any of us..."

Julka looked down at Nino walking along beside her, and

recalled her Ivanovo comrades' jokes about "this giant of a man."

"I couldn't possibly replace him," he continued. "Most of the time I feel like I'm walking on hot coals, with Amadeo ranting away on one side about the need for purity and hardness, and people like Angelo Tasca on the other arguing for immediate and total fusion with the Socialists. Or else I'm wriggling like an eel to find some kind of compromise..."

He had eventually come up with one, he said, whereby the Socialist Party faction which fully accepted the twenty one founding principles of the Communist International – the so-called *Terzini,* Third Internationalists, gathered around Giacinto Serrati – should be merged into the new Communist Party. This was much better than trying to absorb the Socialist Party as a whole, large parts of which would never accept the tenets and practices of Bolshevism, or even much of Marxism. Even Bordiga, in private gloomier and more quarrelsome than ever, had felt obliged to accept this half-way house.

"Quite involuntarily, I have won myself the reputation of being infernally cunning," Antonio said to Julka, with a smile and a sideways glance.

Hotel Lux, Moscow 1923

The Hotel Lux was a squat four-storey building, at 36 Tverskaya Street in Moscow. Originally called the Hotel Frantsiy, it was commandeered by the Bolsheviks and used to house officials and delegates to the Communist International. Despite its name, it was by no means luxurious, even by Russian standards. Originally designed for no more than a hundred guests, during Congresses and other official events it struggled to accommodate many hundreds from all over the world. Some became more or less permanent residents of what they called their "golden cage", wholly reliant on their Russian hosts, as revolutions failed or conditions in their own countries made it impossible to return home, or they proved more politically useful here in Moscow. There always seemed to be lots of Germans staying at the Hotel Lux, even when their own political star was on the rise. They even set up their own Karl Liebknecht School, after the KPD leader assassinated alongside Rosa Luxemburg in 1919, to educate (in German) their children.

Guests were lodged according to their place in the Comintern hierarchy, and in most cases had to share rooms with several others. Heating was erratic. People clustered round primus stoves in their rooms, and small fires were a common hazard. Hot water was only available twice a week, and people had to shower in groups, as many as four at a time. There was much ribald humour about communal life under socialism, and how the poor privileged capitalists had to do these things all on their own. Children played in the corridors and meeting rooms, or in the street and alleyways outside. In the communal kitchens, pots of food were cooked right next to boiling pans of nappies. The place was infested with rats and cockroaches, and required the regular laying of poisons and traps in a half-hearted attempt at pest control.

During his longest stay at the Hotel Lux, for the final months of 1922 and into 1923, Antonio Gramsci shared a small room with his Italian comrade and near namesake Antonio Graziadei, with whom he had travelled to Russia from Italy back in May. Graziadei was an aristocrat, a fully-fledged Count, who had been a prominent member of the Socialist Party and joined the Communist Party when it split from the Socialists at the Livorno Congress in 1921. Tall and imposing, he wore a substantial moustache whose waxed ends he would twirl in moments of contemplation. Socially and politically, he and Gramsci could not have been more different.

Graziadei had a persistent and comprehensive distaste, common among Italians of his intellectual background, for all things Italian, which were almost automatically in his opinion inferior to those of other nationalities. He could go on for hours about how "shiftless, cowardly and socially inferior" Italian people were. Gramsci found this odd, and sometimes annoying; a direct counterpart to the fond, indulgent Italophilia of the Schuchts and most of the transnational bourgeoisie. It was a kind of anti-patriotism, derived (he thought) from distant and no longer respectable class hatreds. Graziadei had simply found in communism a new outlet for his aristocratic disdain. It always threatened to revert to a general contempt for all the lower orders, even when (as now with Graziadei) it had found a clear focus for its scorn in the reactionary politics and mean-minded morality of the Fascist-supporting petty bourgeoisie.

Graziadei had made an academic career, before his membership of the Communist Party, in political economy. He had held several university professorships, and there always seemed to be several others "in the offing", which he could defer indefinitely or graciously take up when the fancy took him. He was the new party's principal expert on land reform, and closely identified with the minority Right faction led by Angelo Tasca and its policies of "United Front" with the socialists and the contesting of elections. He was to advocate and represent these policies at the Fourth Congress of the Communist International.

Gramsci got on well enough with Graziadei, for all their political and social differences and the inevitable irritations of living in the same small room for several months. They had a shared love of the theatre, and spent many enjoyable nights together at the Meyerhold, the Bakhrushin and the Bolshoi, watching superb productions of new plays by Gorki or Sukhovo-Kobylin, or radical new settings of Lermontov or Hoffman, Aristophanes or Shakespeare. Some evenings they preferred to go "slumming it", as Graziadei put it to Gramsci with an inviting sneer, at the Variety Theatre or even the various circuses erected in tents on scrubland on the city's outskirts. They were especially fond of the magic acts at the Variety, which offered a delightful combination of guilty pleasure and innocent childlike wonder, all the more delightful for the free tickets Graziadei was able to procure through what he called his "connections".

They also found common cause in fond reminiscences of the Italian climate and cuisine (if not of Italy's people and popular culture) – lying in their hard beds late at night recalling city strolls or trips to the seaside, or reciting recipes and menus – and in revulsion at the grey freezing damp of the Moscow winter and the inadequate conditions of the Hotel Lux. Both hated, for example, the communal showers and bluntly refused to take part, not least because other nationalities – the Germans especially – seemed so heartily enthusiastic about them. Gramsci would go back to Serebranyi Bor once a week or so, partly to see Evgenia (and Julka if she happened to be visiting her sister) but also to make use of the private shower down the corridor from his old room. Graziadei also said he made "alternative arrangements" for bathing. Gramsci never learnt any more than that, and suspected that his high-born and always well-kempt and groomed room-mate might be using his considerable private income to purchase personal services from the thriving black economy of NEP-period Moscow.

* * *

Ever since he had been fully discharged from the sanatorium, Evgenia had turned oddly cool towards Antonio. It was as though the end of their time as fellow patients at Serebranyi Bor, with its pleasing cocoon of conspiracy and gossip and grievance, had drained the vitality from their relationship. Sometimes when he knocked on her door, eager to impart a snippet of news and some small gift from the outside world, she would barely look up from her book or newspaper, her embroidery or her own inner reflections. More than once her opening remark was a desultory "Oh, it's you..."

Now it was his turn to feel perplexed, and sad at the souring of a friendship he valued and enjoyed. It was all the more confusing because Evgenia herself was finally showing signs of full recovery, after almost four years at the sanatorium, and of the restored capacity to walk unaided. She still had to lean on walls and furniture every few metres but, as she herself remarked sardonically, this was a marked improvement on leaning on people. In a few weeks or months at most, she told Antonio wearily one afternoon in early December, her doctors had said she would be discharged back to the care of her family. There was even talk of her returning to work as personal assistant to Krupskaya. Gramsci had brought news of the Congress proceedings, and was keen to press on with his account. Evgenia would have lapped it all up before. But this previously fervent Bolshevik now seemed oddly uninterested, almost apathetic.

"And then Lenin interjected..."

"I had forgotten how tiring walking can be..."

"...that social democracy may well be the left wing of the bourgeoisie but at least it's left wing..."

"...and it's not as if there is anywhere interesting to walk to around here..."

"...and we need all the help we can get to break the capitalist encirclement, especially with no immediate realistic prospect of further revolutions in Western Europe..."

"...I've been here so long I know the view out of that window like the back of my hand..."

"...And Zinoviev said that from the historical point of view Fascism is a comedy. I wish I could find it funny, historically or otherwise. Hysterical perhaps..."

Then there was the smell. On each of his visits to Evgenia's room over the last couple of months it had been getting worse, a strong sulphurous odour that hung around the room. *Like a...* he thought when he first noticed it, *well, exactly what it is... a bad smell.* It was impossible to identify, and even more impossible to dispel, even by throwing open the window, which everyone rushed to do when first entering the room. Until, that is, Evgenia objected to the blast of icy air from the Moscow mid-winter outside.

"I'm ill!" she would squeal. "Do you want me to get worse?"

She didn't seem to notice the smell, even though it was undoubtedly emanating from her bed and quite possibly – her visitors really didn't relish the thought – from her own body.

Antonio ceased looking forward to his weekly encounters with Evgenia. In fact, if he himself was feeling tired or crotchety, which he often did after long days at the Congress, he would positively dread them. More than once he even considered foregoing his weekly shower at the sanatorium, at the risk of his own personal hygiene and body odour. It wasn't just Evgenia's frostiness; it was cold everywhere in this country, and heating always sporadic and inadequate. It took all his determination to remove his many layers of clothing, even indoors. In the lingering gloom of the endless Russian winter, not to mention the broader political climate of stasis and stagnation here and across the rest of Europe, his spirits were generally low.

He was still feeling the lingering effects of his own illness and nervous exhaustion: a lethargy that would afflict him for days on end, and blinding headaches if he pushed himself too hard. He was wary of anything that might threaten his fragile equilibrium, and this included Evgenia's irritability. Why did she suddenly seem so antipathetic, if not downright hostile and angry, towards him? He racked his brains for something he might have said or done to cause real offence. But beyond his general tendencies towards disputation, pomposity and pedantry – in reality nothing much worse than intellectual over-exuberance and male self-absorption – he couldn't identify anything. *Something else emanating from deep inside her?*

She had become really angry on his last visit when he had dared to criticize her embroidery. The swallows and other ornaments and even the monograms she sewed into handkerchiefs, he observed with a chuckle, always ended up looking more like lizards. She looked up in fury. But this was no worse than the gently scornful remarks she used to laugh at when they first met. They had even agreed early on that this affectionate ribbing, which Evgenia more than repaid with banter of her own about his funny ways or looks, was more effective "therapy" than any of the other batty treatments they were subjected to at Serebranyi Bor. In just a few months her ready laughter had turned into righteous indignation.

"How dare you criticize my handiwork? And what would you know about it anyway?" she exclaimed, before laying down her needle and frame and lapsing into a pursed-mouth sulk. He would take these darts of anger as his cue to leave, or take his shower.

More than once Antonio wondered whether there might be something deeper, more serious and permanent in Evgenia's "nervous debility" than the paralysis of the legs; a truly frightening thought. For all he knew she might have always been like this, and it had only just become apparent to him after six months of acquaintance. That was, in his experience, about how long people could maintain a front over their real personalities. Perhaps Evgenia always had been a rat-bag. Their early easy, open dealings with each other had been the aberration, in a lifetime of irritation and impatience with other people. Now he thought about it, her family did seem to treat her with kid gloves, a kind of wary formality and distance, as if they didn't want to get too close for fear of provoking another sudden outburst. Perhaps Evgenia would always eventually poison any relationship she embarked upon.

This might explain her lack of friends outside her immediate family circle and why, at the age of 34, she remained doggedly unmarried. Persistent moodiness had that kind of repellent effect. Perhaps it was only his naivety in personal relationships, especially with women, that had deferred his own disillusionment for this long, but he now began to realise just how dispiriting Evgenia's company could be. He would emerge from half an hour in her room feeling drained of all energy and joy. It was ridiculous to imagine that a psychological condition might somehow be infectious, in the manner of a contagious physical disease, but he was well aware that someone's permanent poker-faced gloom – what he came to think of as Evgenia's "barbed wire mask" – can drag another person down with them.

He had other examples from his life to call upon, at home with his mother and sisters during particularly "moody" spells, or with fellow students and activists in the long hard years of the war. Depression might not be a disease, but it could clearly be an all-pervasive illness, a real "miasma" as the first Florentine doctors might have called it. Only on the odd occasion, roughly monthly, when Julka happened to be there too did Antonio's own spirits lift when he looked into Evgenia's room and knocked lightly on the door.

"Good day, Comrade Julka!" would be his first words, to Evgenia's further evident annoyance.

As Antonio told a captivated Julka all about the Comintern's deliberations, with his own witty asides and cheeky pet-names for prominent party personalities, Evgenia would herself become newly attentive and inject fresh aggression into her embroidery. Only it wasn't the latest twists and turns in the debates about relations with the Socialists or the appropriate response to Fascism that she was attending to – or even the latest gossip about "the Pelican" or "the Crocodile" or "the Albatross" – but the growing warmth and affection between Comrade Gramsci and her flighty, previously frosty, little sister.

One Sunday afternoon in mid-December the family was assembled in Evgenia's room, with Antonio and Julka ensconced in their now customary huddle of lively murmured conversation. Evgenia herself was at the far end of the corridor outside, demonstrating to her father how far she could walk on her own. He had brought along a tape measure this time, and was recording in a small black notebook the length of each unaided walk between chairs, tables and handrails. The family could hear his shouts of encouragement – "Go on, Zhenya, just another couple of steps!" and "That's five metres, the longest yet!" – over her gasps and groans of effort and complaint.

"Oh for goodness sake! I'm going to get to the bottom of this!"

Mother Julia had stood up and spoken out, in uncharacteristically determined, forthright terms.

"She's not in here, so it can't be coming from her..."

The sulphurous smell was especially bad today. It was so cold and damp outside that nobody could bring themselves to open the window. The heating had been on full blast for several days, through the night as well as the day, which made the smell seem somehow cooked. Or brown.

Julia Grigor'evna was now examining the bedclothes and looking under the mattress. Nothing there... Then she threw open the wardrobe where Evgenia's "outside" clothes were hanging, mostly unworn for several years and looking increasingly bedraggled and unfashionable. Muttering to herself, Julia rifled through the pile of shoes, scarves and empty bags at the bottom. Again nothing there... Nothing either in any of the drawers of the chest where Evgenia's undergarments were stored.

"Well, stuffed more like..." her mother said, as she ran her hands through the jumble of stockings, chemises and bloomers.

She stood upright, apparently defeated. "Where can it be coming from?"

Finally, she spotted a suitcase under Evgenia's bed, bent down and pulled it out. She pressed the catch and threw it open, to reveal hundreds of eggs, some cracked and mouldy, and all of them various shades of yellow and brown.

"My goodness!" she exclaimed, as loudly as she could through a covered mouth and nose. "There must be at least six months of breakfasts!"

Antonio and Julka, the room's only other occupants and witnesses to Julia Grigor'evna's rummages, looked on in horror. Evgenia had reappeared at the door, holding tightly onto her father's arm for support. All eyes turned to her as her face crumpled, her secret revealed, tangible and odorous confirmation of her frequent declaration, "You can't force me to eat!" and of the lengths to which she would go to resist. Amid the various moans of disgust and incredulity, Antonio could be heard saying to Julka, "My Dad would have beaten me senseless for that..."

The ensuing silence was broken by a single shriek of laughter, a potent mix of hysteria and despair, from Julia Grigor'evna Schucht.

* * *

At Christmas 1922, the Schucht family gathered in Evgenia's room at Serebranyi Bor. She had been told that very morning that she would indeed be able to leave in the New Year. At the family's cheerful insistence she had walked the full length of the corridor unaided and without pause. For all her own ambivalence at the prospect of returning to the outside world, the Schuchts were pleased at her rehabilitation, and making plans for reintegrating her into the family circle. As Julia Grigor'evna put it: "It will be wonderful to feel complete again!" No one said so, but after all these years of visiting Evgenia they would not miss Serebranyi Bor or the five hundred kilometre round trip either.

When Evgenia was tucked up back in her bed, with a sigh of relaxation into its mound of soft pillows, the rest of the family – Apollon, Julia and Anna – went off to watch and listen to Julka give a long-promised concert for the other patients and the medical staff of the sanatorium. This would be her last chance to fulfil her obligation. Evgenia said she'd heard her sister play often enough, and preferred to stay in her room. As she was nodding off, she became aware of someone standing in the doorway; or rather, of someone standing in the doorway holding a Christmas tree in a bucket of earth. The tree was not especially big, but it was not much smaller than the person holding it. It was a man, Evgenia could see from the shoes poking out beneath.

"Antonio!" she exclaimed in surprise, when he moved the tree to one side so he could greet her and she could see his sheepishly smiling face through the foliage.

"I brought this..." he said unnecessarily, and with some difficulty set the tree down on her bedside table, grunting and gasping from the effort.

Closer up she could see that it was actually a pretty poor specimen. It looked like a branch of a much larger tree which presumably had been bought from a kulak and sub-divided by an enterprising NEP-man. Most of its spindly twigs were off to one side, where the weight of the needles had pulled them towards the ground. It did not look securely rooted in its bucket of earth, and presumably had just been shoved into it when cut from the larger tree. Sure enough, Antonio told her how he had managed to buy it at the tram stop on his way here, one of the very few of this year's crop of trees left in Moscow this close to Christmas.

"I left most of the needles at the tram stop. And don't ask how much it cost me..." he murmured.

He proceeded to pull out from his coat pocket a handful of wax tapers for decoration. Evgenia helped Antonio fix them to the lop-sided tree, twirling their paper ends round its spindly prickly branches, and trying not to dislodge too many of its few remaining dry needles in the process. As they worked, he shared some troubling personal news he had just received. This was the first chance he'd had to share it with anyone, and he sensed that Evgenia might be more interested in this than in the latest from the Comintern. For once, the Gramscis were as interesting as the Schuchts.

The news concerned Antonio's older brother Gennaro, whom the Gramsci family knew as Nannaro. He had been the first to leave Ghilarza for good in 1900, for national service in Turin then for work in the Sardinian capital, Cagliari. From there he sent home socialist pamphlets and periodicals, which his younger brother read avidly and used to form his own world-view. Antonio had stayed with Nannaro in Cagliari between 1910 and 1912 while he finished his schooling and prepared for university. They didn't get on, Antonio said. In the tiny damp room they shared in Cagliari, "...Nannaro was always in a foul temper, always fighting with me..." Money was extremely short, so that Antonio had to sell food and other provisions sent from home just to buy books. This earned him several severe scoldings from his mother. Nannaro took no notice of his brother's fragile health and welfare, which got so bad that he ate just once a day, "...and arrived in the third year of high school in a state of grave malnutrition."

"But it wasn't entirely unproductive. I learnt to avoid him, charm him, soften him, to manage him; skills I would later put to good political use. Nannaro was just a typical young migrant worker. With my own eyes I've seen how capable he is of being strong. It's only when he feels isolated that he loses his head and grows utterly discouraged."

Like many thousands of adventurous or desperate Sardinians, Nannaro migrated to the proletarian metropolis of Turin, with which the island had close historic ties. This was at around the same time as Antonio won his university scholarship there. This time, by unspoken agreement, they lived separately. Nannaro found work in printing. His socialist politics drew him into paid positions on the production side of several socialist newspapers and reviews. As he demonstrated his efficiency and responsibility, he would also be entrusted with their financial affairs. This eventually included *L'Ordine Nuovo*, the magazine Antonio had founded, and which played a key role in coordinating the Turin Factory Council movement of 1919/20. When the Communist Party was founded in 1921, and *L'Ordine Nuovo* became an official *PCd'I* publication, Antonio engaged his brother on the production, financial and circulation side.

In truth, Antonio told Evgenia, he and Nannaro were never that close. They were seven years apart, and had quite different interests, temperaments and outlooks, and separate circles of friends. Even when they were both living in Turin for almost ten years, Antonio said, they rarely saw each other outside work. He would struggle to describe how Nannaro spent his spare time, where he ate and socialised, or even where he was living at any one time. Like their father Francesco and their brother Carlo, Nannaro fancied himself as a businessman, though nothing ever seemed to come of his (or their) schemes and "propositions". Antonio wasn't too sure either where Nannaro stood on the burning issues of the day, whether he shared his little brother's positions on the party line and prospects for the future, or even if he had actually left the Socialist Party and joined the new

PCd'I. They rarely spoke, beyond sharing family news, or offering or requesting basic practical help they couldn't find elsewhere.

"Nannaro is a strange character. He was a sergeant-major in the 21st Sappers at Monterosso, Montenero and Caporetto. As a miner underground, with only a thin partition separating his tunnel from the Austrian one, he could hear the enemy trying to set off a mine to blow him to pieces, and he came back from the war even more cold and irascible than before. I just can't work him out any more, or what he makes of me. Sometimes he seems excessively proud of me, as if he wants to borrow my prestige and show off to his friends. At other times he seems to resent my achievements and wants to put me in my place. He can be terribly cutting, especially about my physique..."

"So what's happened to him?" Evgenia asked, with a touch of impatience.

"Well," said Antonio, placing the final taper on the tree and sitting back in his bedside chair with a heavy sigh. "This is the thing. He was beaten up and seriously wounded by the Fascists in Turin last week. He lost a finger and a lot of blood. I don't know much more than that, but I gather there were knives and clubs involved, even a bayonet or two. He fought back, as I would expect of him. But that only made matters worse, not least because he was on his own and there were five or six of them. He'll recover, but he's obviously very shaken up. Eighteen other comrades were murdered in the city on the same day, including workers I know from the car factories. The Fascists have shut down *L'Ordine Nuovo* and charged the staff with subversion and possession of arms and explosives, which is preposterous. They wouldn't know a stick of dynamite from a firework, or one end of a rifle from the other. It's caused uproar in Italy. Nannaro wants to leave the country, which is why he contacted me. But what really seems to be bothering him is why the Fascists beat him up. They thought he was me..."

"How come?"

Antonio let out another deep sigh. "It turns out that he has been drawing my salary from the party account all these months I've been here at the sanatorium and in Moscow. He presented himself as usual at the Banco Commerciale in Turin, and the cashier pointed him out to a bunch of thugs waiting at the door... I'm not especially bothered about the money, but he thinks I am. I think he also blames me for the beating, which I can understand. I'm more bothered about something else he wrote me..."

At that point, Julka returned from her concert with her parents and Anna, and brought Antonio and Evgenia's conversation to an abrupt halt. They were excited about the concert, which had ended with several encores and a standing ovation. Julka had even had to play her favourite Vivaldi piece twice, at the Sanatorium Director's insistence.

"Well, I'm glad you're back!" said Antonio, indicating the spindly, decorated, tilting Christmas tree. "We've been waiting for you so we can start the celebrations!"

He leapt to his feet and began lighting the candles with a swift round of an expertly held and deployed match, breaking off only to light his latest Macedonian cigarette. As the family clapped in delight and sang a rousing *O Tannenbaum* – with Antonio showing off to Julka by singing some of the words from the English Labour Party anthem *The Red Flag*, in somewhat arcane and barely understood English – Evgenia lay looking on sourly, wondering quite who Comrade Gramsci had brought the tree and lit the candles for, and what he had been going to tell her about. *Oh well, I'll tease it out of him later*. She insisted on blowing all the candles out, before the bare little tree caught fire and set her room ablaze, "Then I never will get out of this place!" Julka lapsed into sullen silence, just as she had when Evgenia – eight years older, and always in Julka's memory a fully grown woman – had scolded her as a child. Antonio sat quietly too, observing the change in atmosphere as the Schuchts steered the conversation onto more formal family affairs and the rapid, faintly troubling improvement of the economic situation they observed around them in Moscow and at home in Ivanovo.

"Suddenly there is music coming out of the taverns..." observed Julia Grigor'evna.

"...And children selling flowers on the streets..." said Anna.

"There are still plenty of beggars," said Apollon, "but they're no longer dying of hunger as you step over them."

This might not feel like a resumption of revolutionary momentum, or even historical progress, they all agreed, but at least it was some kind of relief, a lightening of the mood.

* * *

At this point, six months after his first acquaintance with this fascinating and often bewildering family, Antonio was as unsure of his own desires and intentions as they were. Julka was beautiful, so beautiful that he would find himself looking at her face and realise that he had not taken a breath for what seemed like minutes on end. In turn she was genuinely interested in him and what he had to say, not just about politics, but his own obscure background and personal history; even if in telling her about it, he tended to slip unknowingly into the manner and language of the "professor" she still occasionally, and slightly tongue in cheek, addressed him as.

So long as he controlled what he derided in himself as a tendency towards "bloodless erudition" – with reels of statistics and grand historical sweeps – he could certainly tell a story. She lapped up all he told her about Sardinia, this extraordinary place so different and so far away, which he pointed out was actually much more typical of the rest of the world than any of the large cosmopolitan cities she had lived in or visited. It sounded to her like the desert island of Robinson Crusoe – for both of them a favourite book in childhood, in a famous Italian translation –

though she hesitated to say so for fear of offending Antonio's evident pride in where he came from.

Sardinia, he told her, consisted mostly of untilled pasture land or bare rock. There were hardly any streets or roads or other means of communication with the interior. It was a parched landscape where people scratched a bare subsistence from the dust. Or, in the metal mines on the south west coast, from deep under the ground in conditions little changed since Roman times, working long hours on their hands and knees with picks and shovels for a pittance. Industrial injuries and illnesses were so common people expected to die of them, and were surprised if they didn't. Union organisation and action was put down ruthlessly. Protests were routinely dispersed by the army. The authorities acted like an occupying colonial administration, and kept the people in a state of grinding poverty and ignorance. In his own home village of Ghilarza, only two hundred out of two thousand inhabitants could read or write.

This included his mother, unusually for a woman. She served as a kind of village scribe for her friends and neighbours, writing down their pleas for official clemency or favour, and their communications with emigrant relatives. The tasks which brought her both the most satisfaction or anguish, depending on their contents, were other women's love letters to their husbands, away in the army, the industrial cities of the mainland or – closest to home and most painful of all, for her as well as them – in prison. Her writing brought her favours and gifts in kind, but no money. For that she made and mended clothes. She had sustained the family of seven children through their father's imprisonment by working long hours with needles and threads and fabrics in her busy hands. She had also taught all her own children to read and write, and passed on to them her own love of books and learning and folk tales. This extraordinary woman, who had never spent a night away from home or travelled further by train than forty kilometres, was able to quote entire passages of Boccaccio and Dante, and could and did entertain her children for hours on end with Sardinian folk tales and rhymes. Even now, Antonio could recite those passages from the *Inferno* which had become his own personal favourites; and this in turn prompted long and impassioned discussions with Julka over their meaning.

That apart, Antonio confessed to Julka, his own childhood was "a sewer of bitterness", especially after his father's imprisonment. With so many brothers and sisters and so little money, and the sense of shame brought upon them by their father's disgrace, it could hardly be otherwise. From the age of ten, Antonio said he had been made to feel like an intruder in his own family. Because of their misfortune and poverty, he had to start work when he was only eleven: "Ten hours a day, including Sunday mornings, in the local Land Registry office. The work consisted of moving huge files that weighed more than I did. At night under my blanket I wept from the pains wracking my whole body." Nannaro was his immediate boss at the Land Registry, and at that time the only other wage-earner in the family. He had bullied him as only an older brother can, carelessly and offhandedly.

"I reminded him of it a couple of years ago, and he couldn't remember a thing!"

Julka listened to him closely, sometimes straining to catch unfamiliar words in Italian, or in the Sardinian dialect which she had to ask him to translate.

"I'm sorry!" he'd say. "Sometimes I imagine I'm still back there!"

At other times his thin reedy voice would trail away, as though he was reluctant to overburden her with the full misery and occasional horror of his story, and she would have to ask him to speak up or repeat what he had said. Or he would grow uneasy at the increasingly sentimental or self-pitying turn of the conversation and clumsily deflect the focus back onto her.

Despite himself, he would then adopt the inquisitorial tone and manner of the professional journalist he had been for much of the last ten years. She would try to answer his questions about her own childhood and young adulthood fully and honestly, straining against her own barriers of reserve and shyness and self-effacement.

Though her family had always been comfortably off and well provided for, even during the years of famine and typhoid, because of Apollon's private income and his political status, she had not had an easy childhood. As the youngest of five lively highly-strung sisters she had always had to fight for attention. Most of the time she concluded that it wasn't worth it, so had learnt to be entirely emotionally self-reliant; perhaps dangerously so, because this induced a self-containment that was frequently taken as aloofness or even arrogance.

As Evgenia had previously observed, Julka's beauty was something of a burden which had brought unwelcome attention from men throughout her life. There were hints of inappropriate advances from older male friends of the family, including a current serving member of the Soviet Politburo, whom Gramsci thought he could identify from current gossip around the Comintern and a hilarious, graphically explicit *graffito* in the men's lavatory in the Kremlin. Protecting Julka would cause the family considerable embarrassment and potentially political disfavour. This had given her a sense of never quite fitting in, rather like he had described, or at least of not being a convenient or even welcome presence, and sometimes even a handicap. *Was this mutual sense of exclusion,* Antonio wondered then and many times afterwards, *a healthy basis for an intimate relationship?*

But then Nino and Julka would exchange glances and smiles, as if to say that now they had met each other everything would be alright, that together they could face both the past and the future in what he routinely called "this vast and terrible world" with hope and confidence. He would tell her some funny story from his boyhood about his antics with animals or a neighbour, or what he and his brothers would get up to behind their mother's back, and she would talk about family holidays at the Italian seaside, or something a colleague or student at the *Lycée* had said which made everyone laugh. And after all, nothing was ever entirely bad or hopeless. She had her beauty and musical talent and teaching skill, he would say, while she pointed out his learning and intellect and political authority. After mutually difficult, disrupted childhoods, things had not turned out too badly for them as adults.

So they proceeded, in what was (if they but knew it) to be the most carefree period of their relationship, in their own separate bubble of conversation in Evgenia's room or on walks along the corridors and, weather permitting, around the grounds of the sanatorium. He made her laugh by lying on the ground and sweeping his arms and legs around to create a stunted snow angel, then proceeding to smoke a cigarette in a manner of *faux* relaxation, one leg over the other, blowing smoke into the slate-gray sky and causing bemusement among several passing estate workers. Julka made sympathetic remarks or even gasps at the hardships Nino had endured at almost every stage of his life. He teased from her lesser disclosures of her own: how her love of music was offset by her frustrations at the limitations of her talent and her disappointment that she could not make a decent living from it; the dull routine of her job with the Interior Ministry, especially the drudgery of translating other people's frequently clumsy and garbled communications; most profoundly and repeatedly, her longing for Rome and the warmth of her youth. Antonio regarded these revelations as all the more precious because of her natural reticence. She told him more than once that she had never spoken to anyone like this before. For several days afterwards he glowed with a sense of privilege.

On his part, he told her what he had been working on, some

article or document, or about meetings he had attended at the Comintern, and the continuing difficulties over fusion with the Italian Socialists. The joint committee that had been established at the Congress in November was threatening to fall apart, with Bordiga refusing to have anything to do with it and everyone else struggling to attend meetings either in Italy, where they risked arrest, or abroad, from where they might not be allowed back into Italy. Gramsci said he "was the only one who showed up for the last meeting!" He told Julka as much as he felt able to disclose of what were often confidential discussions, that is, and without testing her patience with too much organisational detail.

He talked more broadly and expansively of the future and how he imagined it. It would never be easy, at least in the short to medium term, and would always involve struggle or even "going into battle." After all they were engaged in a war, albeit the class war. It promised better outcomes than the usual bloody militaristic adventures of the great imperial powers, but there would still be casualties and sacrifices. He hoped nonetheless that he and his comrades, "including yourself, Comrade Julka, and your lovely sisters", would still find the time and the opportunity to make homes and families of their own, as well as helping the working masses and their families make better lives out of the wreckage.

Alone again afterwards, on his way back from Serebranyi Bor to the Hotel Lux, or lying awake in bed late at night while his room-mate snuffled and snored nearby, Antonio would try to sort out the way he felt and what he should do about it. He would start by calculating his chances of getting anywhere with Julka, totting up the fors and againsts in just the same way he would weigh up an inner-party debate or the prospects for the latest revolutionary upheaval somewhere in Europe. It was a matter of assessing his own subjective will and the objective circumstances, and their relative weight, and calmly and rationally reaching some realistic view of his prospects. Surely she was too beautiful for him, this tall upright artistic young woman who stood and walked a full head above him. On the other hand, he could not deny his feelings of longing and desire, and a special kind of giddiness which welled up inside whenever she was near or he thought of her. He finally understood what people meant when they talked about "butterflies in the stomach", a phrase which had previously mystified him. Was this at long last the stirrings of true and full romantic love?

Antonio felt real affection for the shorter plainer Evgenia, and a lingering bond from their months together at the sanatorium. They were near-contemporaries in age and experience, and had so much in common in temperament and outlook, most obviously a harsh and sometimes exacting realism that veered towards an abiding and thorough-going pessimism. They could be open and honest with each other, and refreshingly frank in ways that sometimes caused raised eyebrows among onlookers. There had been occasions at the sanatorium when they had played together with the innocence of children. For example, he took her for rides around the grounds in a Sardinian-style cart or buggy he had bashed together out of some old pram wheels and planks of wood, provoking yelps of delight and mock-alarm from her when he let the cart go down a slight incline then brought it to a sudden halt at the bottom. He felt that he knew Evgenia, and that she knew him, whereas when he thought about Julka, she remained a pretty much total mystery. No matter what she said about herself, no matter how effusively and sincerely she spoke, there was always something just beyond reach.

Most confusing of all, he couldn't decide whether Julka consciously withheld these parts of herself, or had no idea of her own what they were. And really, from all that she had said to him during their long exploratory conversations around the sanatorium, he had no clear idea what she thought of him. She had shown sympathy and concern, and on occasions a kind of comforting pity, but beyond that it was all a bit of a blank. Could she reciprocate his feelings for her, which he was beginning to think of as love? Did she even like him, or just happen to find herself in his occasional company? These ellipses and quandaries could, in moments of quiet anxiety alone in his bed, seem positively dangerous. In particular there was something truly alarming about a beautiful woman who did not understand, accept or even realise her own beauty, like a wild animal or an unexploded bomb. This continued to prompt in him a wary formality. He could not imagine, he reflected more than once to himself, taking *her* for a ride in his Sardinian cart.

* * *

One of Gramsci's final notes to Evgenia Schucht at Serebranyi Bor, early in 1923, told her: "We'll soon have you jumping over streams!" At the very end of the letter, before his customary "tender embrace" , he reassured her: "You mean so much to me."

"Oh yes..." she said to herself as she read it.

She was sitting alone in her room on the bedside chair he usually sat in when he came to see her. Her embroidery and the book she was reading had been set aside on the bed where she had until very recently been permanently confined.

"...I mean so much to you that you hardly ever come to see me anymore."

He made his final visit a couple of weeks later, at the end of March, with the snow and ice receding in the gardens and fields beyond Evgenia's window, and an open suitcase on her chest of drawers. It was the same suitcase where she had stored the cracked and mouldy eggs, now cleaned out and fumigated. She was preparing to leave Serebranyi Bor at long last, and had already packed the clothes she didn't need for her remaining days here, along with the nightdresses and bed-jackets she wouldn't need in what she referred to, with a shiver and audible trepidation, as "life on the outside." The garments were weighted down with books she had already read but wanted to keep. Among them Gramsci noticed several volumes he had lent her. He made a mental note to ask for them back at a more opportune moment.

She was sitting opposite him stony-faced in her chair, attacking her embroidery. He decided to stick to the safe terrain of Comintern politics, which was now consuming much of his time and energies.

"They're calling meetings repeatedly, at the most unlikely hours..."

Ispolcom was seriously concerned about the worsening situation in Italy. Perhaps it wasn't just a comic opera after all. Much of the *PCd'I* leadership had been arrested, including Bordiga on 3rd February.

"A warrant for my own arrest was issued in January. Strange, being a wanted man..."

It meant that, for the time being, he would not be able to return to Italy. Those comrades who remained free were busy squabbling amongst themselves. There had been no hard news sent to Moscow for many weeks about what exactly was happening.

"Just one letter," said Gramsci, "and we're not at all sure of its authorship or its authenticity. It simply said that everything was destroyed, that there was no point trying to put it all back together again, and that the author of the letter was the only person we should think of contacting. Most peculiar, and highly suspicious... *Ispolcom* keeps asking me what we should do, and all I can think of is reconstituting the party from outside. Oh well..."

"And have you heard anything from your brother?" asked Evgenia.

"Which brother?"

"The one who was beaten up."

"Mario?"

"I don't think that was his name..."

"Oh, you mean my older brother Nannaro! The funny thing is – well it's not at all funny really – my younger brother Mario's with the Fascists, silly boy, and he was beaten up by communists at about the same time..."

"You were going to tell me something else about Nannaro..."

"Oh yes, I remember..."

Whatever it was, Gramsci did not seem quite so keen to recall. He visibly stiffened in his chair, and took a deep breath.

"Well, there are some aspects of this I've never shared with anyone..."

Evgenia leant forward, put her hand on his arm, and said softly, "You should know by now that you can trust me, *Comrade Nino*."

After a further brief pause, Antonio steeled himself and gathered his thoughts.

"Years ago, back in Turin, I had a woman friend called Pia Carena."

The mention of her name caused him to blanch. *Almost a wince*, Evgenia thought. *A woman friend, eh?*

"Pia's brother Attilio helped to distribute our cultural review *L'Ordine Nuovo*, and took part in the discussions we organised in the cafés and the streets. Pia was a professional stenographer, who specialised in taking shorthand notes of meetings and drafts of articles. Her brother got her involved in producing the paper, and very useful her shorthand was too, though like all of us she had to turn her hand to other things as well. *L'Ordine Nuovo* became more than a cultural review, more like the official organ of the Factory Council movement. And I have to admit that Pia became more than a friend. In fact she was the first woman..."

He struggled for the appropriate term.

"... I ever became close to. But we were so busy we never spent that much time alone together. My God, I used to work through the night, pretty much every night. I don't know where we found the time to do anything else. I think Pia felt a lot more deeply about the affair than I did. She also spent quite a long time away from the paper in the summer of 1920, and when she came back she had changed. She was older, quieter, paler and noticeably thinner. She said she had been visiting relatives in the Alto Adige region of northern Italy, up near the Austrian border. I suspected, though I never found out for sure, that she had had a child. I presume she had given it away..."

My goodness, thought Evgenia, Papa Nino. *You're not quite as innocent as I thought...*

"I can't say I'm too proud of the episode and my own small part in it," said Gramsci, "but to be honest I thought very little more about it. As I said, we were very busy... Anyway, it turns out that Nannaro has been carrying on with Pia in Turin, and that she has lent him the money to settle in Paris. He has even implied that I might settle the debt. Needless to say, it makes me feel highly uncomfortable."

"I can well imagine," said Evgenia.

An uneasy silence settled on the room.

"I think I'll take my shower now," said Antonio.

"I suppose I should too," said Evgenia. "They've been rationing the hot water recently..."

"Ah! Not as severely as the Hotel Lux, I hope!"

"No, not quite. Just every other day."

Antonio picked up his wash-bag from the floor, with his towel and soap, and headed for the door. The shower he normally used, down the corridor from his old room at the other end of the building, was occupied, so he made his way back towards Evgenia's room looking for an empty one. In the first he came to, the water tap just wouldn't turn. Either it had stuck fast with limescale, or been turned off deliberately, perhaps another economy measure. He ended up in the shower directly down the corridor from Evgenia's.

He stripped off his clothes, hung them from a couple of pegs on the door, and stepped under the hot running water. "Aah," he said in joyous relief, "nothing as simply pleasurable as a strong hot shower..." He soaped himself down and let the hot water rinse away the dirt and stale sweat of the previous week. As he did so, he reached for his penis to relieve the sexual tension that had built up over those seven long days, just as he had been doing since he first learned to masturbate twenty years ago in his lonely bed in Santulussurgiu, where he was lodging while he attended secondary school. As he was reaching orgasm, and too late to prevent the involuntary spasms of ejaculation, he heard the door to the shower cubicle open behind him. He turned sharply, his right hand still on his spurting penis, to see Evgenia standing there in her dressing gown holding her towel and wash-bag tightly across her breasts.

"Comrade Gramsci!" she exclaimed, her gaze fixed upon his engorged penis, which like the engorged penises of all small men, looked disproportionately, alarmingly huge.

For reasons he could not easily account for – Consoling her? Enticing her? Assaulting her? – he reached out towards her with his free left hand.

"Take your filthy hands off me!" she screamed. She turned and fled back to her room.

O mio dio! thought Gramsci, over and over again, as he hurriedly rinsed, dried and dressed himself, and fled back to the Hotel Lux.

* * *

In the middle months of 1923 Antonio Gramsci set about consciously and doggedly courting Julia "Julka" Schucht. He had just turned 32, no longer a young man. This was, he had convinced himself, the love of his life, most probably the one chance he would get at serious romantic attachment. He meant to capture Julka's heart in turn, and planned and pursued a campaign of seduction. He bought her flowers and sweets and small knick-knacks he picked up at roadside stalls. He sent her parents gifts – cigarettes for Julia Grigor'evna, books of poetry and short stories for Apollon Alexandrovich – with a clear signal of his intentions towards their youngest daughter. Julka responded; not eagerly – this would not have suited her natural reticence – but willingly. His advances were not rebuffed, even if – as he concluded in his late night calculations – he could not say they were being fully reciprocated. *It's more like,* he decided before drifting off into his customarily fitful sleep, *she's going along with it...*He made the arduous journey to Ivanovo Voznesensk a couple more times but during the Mayday holiday and with her parents' blessing she came to see him in Moscow. They walked around Red Square and ate at the canteen in the Kremlin reserved for Comintern functionaries. They talked mostly in Russian because Antonio felt it would help him improve, and also not draw unwelcome attention to themselves. Though he didn't feel able to say so, he also enjoyed hearing Julka talking freely in what had become her first language, with the slight lisp which softened the harsh Russian consonants and the mumbled descant with which every Russian sentence seemed to conclude. He wondered too whether he might just get closer to this enigmatic young woman in Russian than in Italian.

Not that she took the conversational lead; she left that mostly to him. He told her about the latest debates concerning the *PCd'I* organisation in Italy, which were taking up much of his time and attention. As he had advocated, the party leadership was being reconstituted with comrades who had not yet been arrested, including his old friends from Turin and the early days of their cultural review *L'Ordine Nuovo*, Palmiro Togliatti and Angelo Tasca. But even this was not a straightforward matter, because their political perspectives had seriously diverged since Turin. Togliatti was supporting Bordiga's electoral abstentionism and purist sectarianism, while Tasca was advocating the opposite line of standing in elections and alliance with trade unions and what remained of the Socialist Party.

Gramsci told Julka in rather less detail about his own efforts to protect an old Torinese anarchist friend who had ended up in the brutal care of the GPU, the Soviet secret police. He spoke more circumspectly than usual, aware that he was talking about what were ultimately his *confidante's* employers, the NKVD or Interior Ministry, albeit a branch a long way removed from her translation department with its slightly fusty, almost academic atmosphere. There was little Gramsci could do to get the old fellow off the charges of subversion, which he cheerfully admitted: "Yes, I've spent my whole life as a subversive and it's too late to stop now, no matter what name you give your shiny new state!" But Gramsci might just manage, he told Julka, to get the sentence commuted from summary execution to expulsion from the country, "…a forged passport from the OMS (*Otdiel Mezhdunarodnykh Sviazy,* International Relations Section of the Comintern) office and a one-way ticket to Milan, instead of a bullet in the head." Julka, similarly circumspectly, promised to let him know if she heard anything about the case.

She told him less guardedly the latest news about her family. Evgenia was having some difficulty adjusting to what she still referred to as "life on the outside." She had refused to take up the post with Krupskaya or to look for other work, despite her previous substantial school teaching experience and extensive qualifications, and spent much of the day in her room with her popular novels and her embroidery, "or even, as far as anyone can tell, simply asleep. She even suggested the other day she'd be better off back at Serebranyi Bor. She says she misses the peace and quiet..." Here she gave Antonio a sly glance, with just a hint of a smile, which he took as an invitation to join her in a little unspoken mockery at her older sister. They both knew that for at least the last six months of her stay at the sanatorium, Evgenia had constantly complained how isolated and bored she felt.

Anna Schucht had moved with her husband Theodore Zabel

into lodgings of their own, which gave the family more space. "But also, as you might imagine, makes the house feel a little empty. I really miss her, especially with Zhenya behaving so strangely, and I miss our duets..." With Anna gone, she had no one to practise with, which made it much less enjoyable. She told him about the new music she was struggling to learn and teach, "...difficult pieces by the new Soviet composers... I can see what they are trying to achieve, but in my hands it just sounds like screeches and squeaks!"

"I can't imagine that," Antonio said. "The fault must be all theirs!"

For her next visit Julka agreed to come for the weekend and to stay overnight with Antonio at the Hotel Lux. Graziadei had returned to Italy in the winter, and been replaced by Egidio Gennari, a respected organiser and much less of a character, though with a similar taste for female company. Antonio had made arrangements for his room-mate, repaying several similar favours, to make himself scarce and stay elsewhere for the night. He met Julka at the train station and they spent the afternoon and evening in tentative conversation about trifles and the exchange of surreptitious glances, both aware – deliciously and anxiously at the same time – of what lay ahead. Antonio had spent the morning cleaning and tidying his small room, and packing Gennari's few personal things away in the wardrobe. He decorated it with candles, for a rather softer source of light than the bare electric bulb, and flowers he had picked himself from the less publicly exposed beds in the Neskuchny Palace gardens. Julka gasped with delight when he opened the door and hurried to light the candles from his Macedonian cigarette. She entered the room and closed the door behind her. When the moment came, they were both awkward and quiet. Antonio undressed to his undershirt, and paused to watch Julka fumble with her pins and fastenings and stays. Was he supposed to help her? Take charge of the situation? Or would that seem overbearing, just too *experienced*? On previous occasions, with Pia, they had just got on with it, between other personal and political functions. Or, with prostitutes, he had felt able to rely on what he coyly thought of as their "professionalism". This included the time in Turin when, short of money, he had to call upon his friends to pay his bill before the brothel keeper would let him out. For several years afterwards, they took every opportunity to remind him of it.

When Julka was down to her own undergarments, she sat down on the bed and beckoned him towards her. He hesitated for a moment, overcome at the sight of her face and loosened hair in the soft candlelight, and his amazement that something he had longed for over so many months had finally, actually come to pass. She felt beneath his undershirt and drew him towards her mouth, looking up at him to check his response and communicate her own desire. He felt for her breasts and between her legs, and she offered herself to his touch. Finally she lay back and drew him inside, and they lost themselves in their union. Thought dissolved into feeling, feeling into sensation, and sensation into fulfilment. Or at least that's how he recounted the experience to himself afterwards, marvelling at the wordless ease of it all, before scoffing at his own inability to describe the miraculous absurdity of sex.

After that they spent as many nights and (work permitting) afternoons together as they could, stealing time from the revolution which they both knew (when they thought about it) they were owed. He wrote to her: "I'm not sure yet if I can come on Sunday. They are chasing me hard for a report on our trade union strategy, but I will try to tear myself away. I must, I absolutely must have you go on loving me." Another time a telegram came from Italy, warning him that a further warrant had been issued for his arrest and advising him not to return home. The messengers went with it to the Lux early in the morning. He was not there, and none of the other Italians had any idea where he might be; he had left no word. They went the rounds of Moscow by car, but could find no trace of him. Now deeply worried by his disappearance, fearing kidnap or worse, they called in the secret police to help. When Gramsci finally turned up at the Lux late the next afternoon, having spent the night with Julka at Ivanovo, he was greeted (as he put it in a letter to her sent that day) "like someone who had returned from the dead."

In a later letter, he asked her, "Did you come to Moscow on 5th August as you told me you would? I waited three days for you. I didn't dare leave the room for fear of missing you like that other time... You didn't come to Moscow, did you? You would certainly have come to see me, at least for a few moments... Will you come soon? When can I see you again? Write to me. Everything you say to me does me good and makes me feel stronger." There was in this note a tone of urgency, a neediness bordering on desperation, with an unmistakeable undertow of rebuke. It gave Julka some pause for thought, before she wrote back that political work and violin practice for a forthcoming recital had kept her in Ivanovo. She apologised for not letting him know earlier, but this cancelled visit had only been a vague arrangement, made in haste over her shoulder as she was boarding her departing train from Moscow and before she realised the scale of her workload. If she had thought about it further, she might have seen in his admonishment a premonition of the tone of much of their later correspondence, only slightly softened by the outcry of romantic yearning.

Very much later, in very different circumstances, he would write to her: "I've been going over it all again in my mind, over all the memories of our life together, from that first day I saw you at Serebranyi Bor and didn't dare go into the room because I felt so timid (yes, you made me feel timid, and today I smile as I remember it), until the day you went away on foot and I went with you as far as the main road through the forest, and stood motionless there for so long watching you grow smaller and smaller down that road, carrying a bundle across your shoulders on your way back to the vast and terrible world outside. Then those few blissful months in Moscow, when we finally gave in to ourselves and each other."

The experience of falling in love for this first (and only) time had a profound effect on Antonio Gramsci, and would haunt him for the rest of his life. He had never felt like this before in any of his dealings with other human beings. As he wrote to Julka, she had given him "the greatest, most beautiful, most powerful reason in the world to go on living." The physical sensations – the churning stomach when he saw or thought of her, the heavy heart, the welling eyes, the feeling of total, unquestionable rightness about the act of sex – were entirely novel and almost overpowering. The sense of psychic connection to another person was palpable but inexplicable, especially within the terms of the philosophy of historical materialism he tried to apply to every other facet of his life. This was so much more than "social relations", the rather prosaic Marxist conception of human interaction. He felt a wide-eyed joy he had not known since his early childhood, before his father's imprisonment and his family's disgrace, running around the hills near Ghilarza with playmates or communing with his latest tame bird or furry animal. He discerned in his own *weltanschaung* a sense of the future which almost amounted to reasoned optimism, a temperamental luxury he had never previously dared to allow himself.

But over all of this there was a shadow: a sense of personal vulnerability, projected onto Julka in a fit of protective altruism, so that he worried for her too. Falling in love was a dangerous business for everyone involved. He was not only exposing himself to the risk of being hurt, but exposing another person he cared for deeply to his own tendency – all too manifest in his everyday dealings with comrades – to coldness, callousness and even cruelty. The witty remark, rewarded by a hearty round of laughter, could so easily topple over into barbed insult, sharp intakes of breath and uncomfortable silences, and for those on the receiving end wounded pride and hurt feelings. This was what Gramsci's Revolutionary Liberal friend from Turin, Piero Gobetti, had called his "tone of irony turning in no time to a blow-pipe of lethal sarcasm", in an early profile for the Italian press.

Gramsci found the simple everyday uncertainties of love very difficult to cope with. Did this other person feel the same, and to the same extent? How could they possibly know, or communicate something so ethereal? After a life of study and action, he was bewildered by the chaos of his own feelings. He often likened himself, especially during still frequent bouts of illness and exhaustion, to a "bear with a sore head", retreating with a scowl and a growl into its hole in the mountain. Well, this old bear had been well and truly enticed out of its cave and into the bright open sunlight of the plains. What would it do now? It bothered him deeply that he had not the faintest idea. Yet he knew that the cave bear would find it very hard to go back up the hill and into the darkness. Now that he had found love, he simply had to go through with it, as much (when he thought about it, and fighting its inherent ridiculousness) for political as personal reasons. He wrote to Julka:

> *"How many times have I wondered if it is really possible to forge links with a mass of people when one has never had strong feelings for anyone, not even for one's own parents? Is it possible to love a collective mass when one has not been deeply loved oneself by individual human creatures? Hasn't this had some effect on my life as a militant? Has it not tended to make me sterile and reduce my quality as a revolutionary by making everything a matter of pure intellect, of mere mathematical calculation?*
>
> *I've thought a lot about this, and it has come to my mind again these last few days because I was thinking of you, and of how you came into my life and gave me love, gave me what I had always lacked. It was this lack that made me cross-grained and spiteful. One*

cannot divide oneself into fragments and make only one part function. Life is a whole, and each activity is strengthened by all the others. Love fortifies the whole of one's existence. It creates a new equilibrium, and intensifies all other feelings and sensations."

Is love a luxury or a necessity? A distraction from or concentration of all that is noble and worthy in human existence? In the bleak lonely years ahead Antonio would return many times to this simple basic quandary. But for now he knew that he could not live without his Julka and the prospect of a life together with her, however hazardous and unrealistic that might prove. He would be a fool to turn his back on love and the chance it offered of lasting happiness, and return like that grumpy old bear to his cave.

* * *

On the 21st September 1923, the reconstituted *PCd'I* executive, surprised by the police in a worker's house on the outskirts of Milan, was arrested *en bloc*. They were accused of conspiracy against the state, and though they were eventually acquitted on the basis of inconsistencies in the still-fledgling Fascist legal apparatus, would spend three months in prison. This would further disrupt the small party's fragile networks and communications. The old leadership around Bordiga was also on trial during this period, though they too would be acquitted on 26th October. The acquittals were all achieved on judicial technicalities, and were not received with any great triumphalism. Everyone knew that these were just opening salvos in what was beginning to look like a remorseless and very one-sided civil war. The Fascists would drag their opponents back to court as soon as they had brought the law sufficiently in line to make their vague charges of subversion stick.

The *Ispolcom* decided that Gramsci should move to Vienna, as near to Italy as he could safely go without risking his own arrest under the warrants issued earlier in the year. From there he would coordinate the party's faltering domestic operations and attempt to rebuild its shattered infrastructure. He would leave Moscow as soon as the necessary transit arrangements were made. Train tickets and a passport were procured by the OMS office, along with a residence permit which his old comrade Angelica Balabanova undertook to organise in Vienna.

Antonio and Julka were married on 23rd September, in a simple ceremony at the Moscow Registry Office witnessed by Egidio Gennari and Evgenia Schucht. It was, in the manner of the brisk new morality of the proletarian state, hardly a "ceremony" at all, simply a formal public recognition of their private relationship, with no obligation to each other or anyone else beyond what they chose to offer freely. They paid over a small fee at the cashier's kiosk at the entrance to the building. The certificate they received in return from the smiling registrar might look impressive, with its stamps and state letterhead and flourishes of signature, but really it carried no more weight than any of the other paper documents dished out by the offices of the new dispensation in an attempt to convince the world that the revolution was permanent.

It was, Antonio remarked sardonically over a simple wedding feast in the Kremlin canteen, just like rural Sardinian tradition, where "couples separate quite amicably if the marriage is a failure, free to pair up with another man or woman from the same village. Before the war at least, trial unions were common. The couple got married only after the birth of a child, and if they couldn't reproduce, both parties were free once more to go off with somebody else, with the full blessing of the church. Sensible arrangement for such a backward culture, don't you think?"

Most of the party laughed, except Evgenia, while Julka looked on silently, with a hint of confusion in her almond eyes. But for Antonio at least, getting married was curiously comforting. It felt like he had finally passed over into full satisfactory adulthood, that he was the recipient as well as guarantor of certain basic obligations towards another human being. As such, his marriage was some kind of bulwark against his essential loneliness. He also felt like he was repaying some distant obligation to his family, who as town-dwellers were not quite so attached to Sardinian country tradition as the free-loving and hard-headed peasants might be. He remembered them, especially his mother, being scandalised by Nannaro's refusal to marry the mother of his child, Edmea. Antonio never got round to asking Julka exactly how she felt about being married to him. Again, she just seemed to go along with it.

In a similar vein, she came to live with him at the Hotel Lux. "As would be expected of a married woman," she said, in consenting to Antonio's proposal. He did at least detect something of his own sense of achievement and pride in the way she described herself as "a married woman", with a very definite lift in her voice and her bearing. She kept her job, but was allowed to reduce her hours and responsibilities in the light of her new status. They moved to a new room reserved for married couples, and set about establishing the daily routines of an established relationship. They would rise in the lifting darkness at 7am. She would prepare breakfast while he collected the newspapers and any mail from the hotel reception. When he left for work at the Comintern, she would tidy and clean the room, then herself leave for work. When he came home, often late into the evening after a day of meetings and report writing, he would find her reading or darning by candlelight, or simply sitting in her chair and welcoming him home with her beautiful smile. They prepared a meal in one of the wretched communal kitchens, and caught up with each other's news and feelings as they ate. If they felt like it, they made love before they went to sleep.

During this period the big political topic was the final defeat of the German revolutionary movement. With it went the prospect of some kind of link between German industry and Russian agriculture that would break the isolation of the Soviet economy and drive a stake through the faltering heart of the capitalist system. Nino freely shared with Julka – far more openly than he would have dared at the Comintern – his own scorn for the way the catastrophe had been allowed to unfold. The Comintern and the *Kommunistische Partei Deutschlands* had set the insurrection for 25th October, the sixth anniversary of the Bolshevik takeover of Petrograd ("actually it wasn't; the idiots neglected the two-week difference between the Russian and western calendars"), as if you can make an appointment with history.

It turned out to be a complete fiasco, called off at the last minute because they knew they didn't have enough arms and men to defeat the army and topple the Social Democratic government of the Weimar Republic. Except in Hamburg, that is, which failed to receive the order to abort the revolution in time. Three hundred poorly armed communists took over the city centre, but were easily defeated by the army and the *Freikorps* when they realised they were on their own. Elsewhere in Germany there was just a vague sense of atypical disorder and indiscipline, which was as much to do with economic collapse and hyper-inflation as any serious prospect of revolution. People scoffed in the Comintern corridors and canteens about how German workers would form an orderly queue to take power, and insist that any breakages be paid for. A story circulated about the looting of a shoe shop in a working class district of Berlin, where people had emerged empty-handed if they couldn't find anything in their own size.

"Can you imagine that here?" Antonio asked Julka incredulously. "Or anywhere except Germany?"

Shortly before he left for Vienna, the couple conceived their first child. From Vienna, on 7th June the following year, he wrote to his mother in Sardinia: "My companion shares my ideas completely; she isn't Italian, but she lived for a long time in Italy and studied in Rome. She's called Julia (Julka by her own family) and she has a degree from the music *lycée* of Santa Cecilia. She is courageous and has a strong character. You will all like and appreciate her when you get to know her. Next summer or autumn I hope to come with her to Sardinia for a few days, and introduce you all to her and the baby we are expecting."

Vienna, 1923/4

Antonio Gramsci left Moscow at the end of November 1923. He had been in Russia for a year and a half, played a small but significant part in the affairs of the Communist International and a rather larger one in the *Partito Comunista d'Italia,* grown a moustache then shaved it off when he decided it made him look just too Russian, met and married his wife, lived with her for nearly two months in relative comfort and privacy at the Hotel Lux, conceived their first child, learnt to read and converse and write rudimentarily in Russian, and grew in personality and confidence more than during any comparable period of his life. Professionally and politically, he felt more settled and fulfilled than ever before. But if he resented being parted from his wife and her puzzling family, and from the other emotional and personal attachments he had formed in Russia, he did not let it show. It was commonly understood and accepted that such personal sacrifice was necessary, for the greater cause of proletarian revolution and international socialism.

After a complicated five-day rail journey, multiple changes of trains with either a few frantic seconds or many idle hours to spare, and several fraught border crossings, Gramsci arrived in the Austrian capital Vienna on 3rd December. The city was recovering from its own post-war privations, under the stern control of the Austrian Social Democratic Party, much more stridently than NEP-era Moscow. Everywhere he looked Gramsci could see solid blocks of workers' flats being built by the Viennese Social Democrats for their million proletarian supporters. These pioneers of municipal socialism, with its complex moral economy of favour and obligation, could mobilise instant demonstrations of fifty thousand solid citizens, dressed in sportswear and surreptitiously armed, to deter opposition and force through some new welfare measure. They even produced a comic newspaper, *Lachen*

Links ("Left-wing Laughs"), full of party-approved jokes for the masses. Teams of council workers toured the city in shiny new vans removing abandoned refuse, stray dogs and neglected children. Here, it seemed, history was still plainly progressing, albeit more languidly and complacently than elsewhere. There was a gaiety in the cafés and streets that seemed quite spontaneous, unforced.

Gramsci stayed a few days with Josef Frei, the General Secretary of the Austrian Communist Party, then took up longer-term residence in a scruffy suburb, in an unheated barely furnished room sublet by an unfriendly Catholic *hausfrau*. She was forever complaining that her communist husband was making her keep a Godless foreigner under her roof, and that surely the *polizei* were on their way right now to arrest them all. After a lifetime of sheets and blankets, it was Antonio's first encounter with a duvet, "which *(he wrote to Julka)* keeps slipping off in every direction, so that I'm always waking up with either a foot or a shoulder frozen stiff."

His only immediate colleague in Vienna was his secretary Mario Codevilla, a dim tubercular Italian whose conversation consisted solely of small talk. Codevilla was constantly clearing his throat and tapping his fingernails one after the other on any available hard surface. They spent much of their time together composing letters to Moscow or Rome: "So many letters! I'm writing at least half a dozen a day. I've never written so many letters in my life as in these last few days!" Gramsci wrote in another letter to Julka. He also wrote articles for *Inprecor* on the situation in Italy. "They suggested I use a pseudonym," he told Julka, "though I'm not at all sure why. At least I got to choose my own mangled version of my name, which no one else has yet come up with. I'm now called, for *Correspondence Internationale* purposes, G. Masci! Not too far off the Italian words for manly, *maschio*, and scoundrel, *mascalzone*! I'm sure you sometimes think of me in those terms..."

The small circle of émigrés and subversives Angelica Balabanova introduced him to offered little by way of open honest social contact. They all seemed to be running away from something, and always on the lookout for whomever or whatever might be following them. In some cases, marked out by a rather less haunted look, they were following someone else. This alone, Gramsci feared, revealed much about the present state of the international revolutionary movement: *are we becoming just a gang of fugitives and spies?* Conversations were conducted in whispers and codes, with one eye over your shoulder and another over your partner's. Introductions were always draped in suspicion, and arrangements to meet again necessarily provisional because "you never know..." People went to extraordinarily elaborate lengths to devise signals – a folded or unfolded newspaper, a tug on a right or left earlobe – to indicate that they were or were not being followed or watched.

To Gramsci it all seemed faintly preposterous. It wasn't so much a requirement of the current political conditions of stolid if brittle parliamentary democracy across most of Western Europe, as a leftover from the tangled undergrowth of pre-revolutionary conspiracy and repression. All these subterfuges really had no place in the brave new world of socialist reconstruction and developing proletarian hegemony. He understood the need for care and trust, but there were also heavy doses of preening self-importance and nostalgia for simpler times and polarities in all the furtive nudging and winking and whispering and signalling. These class warriors were much more comfortable, it seemed, in permanent discomfort.

People would somehow appear as if out of thin air, in cafés or apartments or meetings, and then just as mysteriously disappear, never to be seen again. Everyone else would then spend weeks and months trying to figure out whether they were police spies or secret agents – and if so which branch or agency they had been working for, one of a bewildering array of acronyms and abbreviations – when in most cases they almost certainly weren't. They were probably just dissolutes or dilettantes, or displaced bohemians, or congenital conspirators and lifelong intriguers, people who spent their days attaching themselves to one vaguely interesting cause after another in the absence of anything better to do.

Much of the conspiracy and intrigue in Vienna emanated from the ancient intractable enmities of the Balkans, all those broken countries of craggy mountains and fertile valleys to the sun-seared south, for which the Austrian capital had been an imperial centre and now provided a point of access to the sympathies, attentions and resources of Western Europe. Gramsci would seek explanations in the cafés and meeting rooms of just what the latest feud, assassination or bomb-plot was actually about, only to find his head spinning within minutes from the torrent of accusations of betrayal, corruption and genocide by one ethnic or political group against another. They were basically a set of tribes, dignified by grand ideals and organisational networks, each with their own growing band of heroic martyrs and alleged traitors, busily filling up their calendars with macabre anniversaries and holy days. Their customs and codes were interesting in their own right, from a strictly anthropological perspective, but of no great historical or political importance.

The atmosphere in émigré Vienna was further poisoned by news of the constant factional turmoil back in Russia, where it really did count for something, and was getting worse with Lenin's illness and decline. Gramsci's sponsor Angelica Balabanova herself was under a cloud, having fallen out with Lenin and Zinoviev and been expelled from the Comintern, which she had briefly served as its first Secretary in 1919. That's how she'd ended up in Vienna, unwelcome either in Moscow or in Italy where she had spent most of her earlier life. Even here she seemed incapable of settling anywhere. She was constantly moving from one small furnished room to another with her only personal possessions: a spirit-stove for tea, a small pan for omelettes, three cups for her guests, and several huge and ferocious portraits of the famous old Italian maximalist Socialists she had learnt her politics from in the last decades of the nineteenth century. Sitting there sipping weak tea and picking at a bland, unseasoned omelette, Gramsci always felt they were scowling down at him.

The only other person Gramsci got close to in Vienna was the ex-anarchist, sort-of-Trotskyist, Victor Serge. He took great care to refer to Serge in his conversations and correspondence only as "a/the Frenchman", because Serge was already under suspicion of "oppositionism" among the Comintern majority. He was an extraordinary character, an almost exact contemporary of Gramsci's, and seemed to have already packed several whole lifetimes into his thirty three years. He had been, successively, the child of displaced Russian intellectuals, a juvenile delinquent in Brussels, an anarchist convict in Paris, a trades union militant in Barcelona, and an active participant in the first, harshest but purest years of the Soviet Revolution. Because of his skills and experience he was made a senior official in the Comintern, working directly for its President Zinoviev (whom he quickly came to loathe), despite never being a member of the Bolshevik Party.

Most recently Serge had been dispatched to support the various failing revolutionary causes around Western Europe, in Berlin then Prague and finally here in Vienna. He had only accepted the posting because it got him out of Moscow. He was thoroughly disillusioned, horrified by the descent of the Soviet state bureaucracy and security apparatus into what he was already calling "unaccountable and coldly vicious totalitarianism." He had spent most of the last two or three years, he told Gramsci, trying to save hundreds of friends and comrades from arrest, imprisonment or execution by the thugs and heresy-hunters of what he still called the *Cheka*, the old Tsarist secret police, many of whom had simply switched sides after the Revolution. Indeed, some of the names of these turncoats and their unfortunate victims were familiar to Gramsci from Julka's whispered evening accounts of her day's work. Serge said he understood and accepted the need to eliminate the enemies of the revolution. The problem was that the Bolsheviks had lost any clear sense of who were their enemies, and by corollary their friends. They now had all the hallmarks of an exclusive, contemptuous elite.

Serge retained a profound sympathy, respect and admiration for their leaders – Lenin and Trotsky in particular – but saw clearly the historical contradictions overwhelming their best intentions, and bringing out their autocratic tendencies at the expense of their democratic ones: "Lenin endowed an immense movement of faltering masses with a political consciousness that was supremely clear and resolute, but even the greatest of individuals can only achieve so much against the tides of history and the dead weight of social backwardness and inertia."

"Vladimir Ilyich," Serge confided to Gramsci, "has spent much of the last few years railing privately against the counter-productive brutalities of the secret police, the crass stupidity of much of the state bureaucracy, and the rank careerism of most of the party's recent recruits. But," he continued in little more than a whisper, "it's now plain that much of this degeneration was inherent in the Bolshevik model of organisation that Lenin above anyone – proud of what he has destroyed, not so proud of what he has created – has brought about.

"Lenin, hundreds of times, has stressed that the dictatorship of the proletariat is a truly ruthless dictatorship and at the same time the broadest possible workers' democracy. He believes and wants it to be so. He goes to give an account of himself before the factories; he asks for merciless criticism from the workers. At the same time he argues that socialism is quite compatible with personal autocracy, oblivious to the corrosive contradiction within that formula. Think of it in terms of one of those proletarian revolutionaries, spouting power to the workers in the factory then going home to beat his wife, a democrat in the workplace and a dictator at home.

"It's bound to unravel eventually... just look at Lenin's own personal record. He has old friends and comrades jailed or dismissed because they confront him with embarrassing objections. He welcomes Makhno's peasant anarchists into the Red Army, which tips the balance in the civil war, then proceeds to outlaw anarchism and expropriate the peasants. He promises religious freedom, but keeps saying that religion is the opium of the people. Even while proclaiming the restored economic liberties of NEP, he continues to deprive his critics of their political and personal freedom..."The revolution remained the only hope for mankind – under the leadership of "our sick Party; sick, but what else on earth is there?" – and for the uncountable millions ground into dust by capitalist profiteering and imperialist warmongering. But it was exacting a very heavy price for historical progress, not least in the honesty and integrity of its leaders. "If you keep trying to face all ways, you just end up spinning around in circles and getting dizzy..." It took incredible fortitude and intelligence, which only one or two truly possess, to keep your eye on the main prize in the distant future. Once Lenin, already "a shadow of his former self", had gone, the party unity only he could maintain would shatter.

When the great man finally died in mid-January 1924, Gramsci and Serge discussed the quarter of a million workers who were enrolled at one stroke into the Russian Communist Party on the day after his death. How much were these proletarians worth, they wondered, if they had to wait for the death of Vladimir Ilyich before coming to the Party? Further, Serge said, these were uneducated, inexperienced, completely uncultivated people, ignorant of the ways of the world, of Marxist philosophy and Leninist political practice. Their "communism" was just another religion to replace the Orthodoxy of the Tsarist autocracy, or worse, a simple career move. Their dull dead weight would swing the balance of power inside the party firmly towards the bureaucrats and careerists and opportunists in the leadership.

Serge and Gramsci's misgivings were deepened by the farce over the embalming and interment of Lenin's corpse: "An outrage to any self-respecting historical materialist, surely including Lenin himself," as Serge put it. It was only done to placate the backward masses who had travelled in their millions to Moscow to view the body of this new saint in its coffin in the Kremlin, and kept on coming even after the end of the official state period of mourning. Lenin himself had apparently left no clear instructions. Allowing this absurd sanctification to happen, and not specifying a simple burial in the family plot, was "the final oversight of an ailing and overstretched leader."

Gramsci was often troubled by Serge's revelations and insights, which served to undermine his own previous convictions and hasten his disillusionment, while at the same time delineating and reinforcing some of the doubts he had begun to feel in Moscow. If he could, he would steer their late-night conversations onto safer, more enjoyable terrain, in discussion of literature or art. Serge was already writing and publishing stories, and beginning work on the series of novels which would make his name and reputation. Gramsci loved his detailed characterisations of famous or not so famous revolutionaries, and would ask Serge to repeat particular favourites: "Tell me about Bukharin again... or Emma Goldman... or Bill Hayward..." In turn, Serge admired Gramsci's caricatures of leading Italian Fascists – with flailing arm movements and great windy flights of pompous rhetoric, and telling personal details like a limp wrist or a lisp or a stutter – whom Antonio had known when they were maximalist Socialist Party firebrands before and during the war.

Victor Serge later described Gramsci himself as "...an industrious and exotic exile, late to bed and late to rise... His head was heavy, his brow high and broad, his lips thin; the whole was carried on a puny, square-shouldered, weak-chested, humpbacked body. There was grace in the movement of his fine, long-fingered hands. Gramsci fitted awkwardly into the humdrum of day-to-day existence, losing his way at night in familiar streets, taking the wrong train, indifferent to the comfort of his lodgings and the quality of his meals."

In fact Gramsci moved lodgings as soon as he practically could, but not before receiving a harsh lesson in Austrian anti-Semitism and (from Serge) some judicious advice on how to deal with it. A comrade from the Soviet embassy who had heard Gramsci was moving asked him to reserve the room for his wife. The pinch-faced landlady agreed, but wanted to know if the new tenant was Jewish: "I don't let to Jews." The Soviet diplomat's wife was in fact a Ukrainian Jewess. Antonio asked Victor Serge what to do. There was only one solution: "To tell the old woman you couldn't decently ask the new tenant if she was Jewish, but that you know she's a secretary in one of the embassies." Serge explained that the Austrian petite bourgeoisie might hate Jews, but they worship the Diplomatic Corps far more. Sure enough, the landlady replied, "...of course she can have the room. I know you can't go asking Embassy people if they're Jews or not."

Antonio really didn't take to Vienna, which (he wrote to Julka) "...seems very sad and depressing compared to Moscow. There are no sleighs jingling cheerfully along the white streets, only the dreary rattle of street cars ploughing through slush." He spent most of his spare time alone, reading or composing long love-letters to his wife. He felt their separation keenly, and a deep sense of loss after their two short months of living together in Moscow. He begged her to come and join him, even though it would mean giving up "...the interesting, active life going on around you. I am too much alone... it's like living in mid-air. I think constantly and with infinite longing of the times we spent together, so close and giving endlessly of ourselves. I can almost feel your cheek against mine, and my hand caressing your head, telling you how much I love you even while my lips are silent." In those of his dreams which were not about her, he now saw *himself* floating ten centimetres off the ground, amongst solid, frumpy Viennese crowds securely rooted in earthbound reality.

In late February 1924 Julka informed him in her latest letter from Russia, unceremoniously and almost in passing, that she was twelve weeks pregnant. He responded that he was "...overcome with desire to hold you in my arms and feel for myself the new life uniting our two lives even closer than before." But the subsequent letters he received from Moscow, where Julka was back living with her parents and Evgenia in an apartment near the Hotel Lux on Tverskaya Street, were not encouraging. The middle months of Julka's pregnancy were difficult, and on several occasions she feared she had lost the baby. Weeks went by without any communication, until a terse note from Apollon or Evgenia informed Antonio that Julka had been unwell in some unspecified way, and implied (in a foretaste of later correspondence between the older Schuchts and Gramsci) that his written bombardment wasn't helping. He could feel Julka – the beautiful, fragile, brittle young woman only he had come close to reaching – drifting further away from him again.

When Julka was well enough to write to him herself, her letters took on a curiously dissociated tone, as though she was mechanically recording some formula she had picked up elsewhere. They were dull and dutiful, with very little detail or intimate disclosure or sincere endearment, always indicative of low spirits and growing distance. She also took to signing off as Julia, something she had never done in their previous correspondence. More than once, Antonio suspected that her letters were being dictated to her by someone else. In general, her explanation for not joining him in Vienna was that she could not leave her family. But again there was no specific explanation, beyond some vague sense of daughterly duty. The clear implication was that they could be trusted to look after her properly and, he reckoned, that he couldn't. He might have understood better if she had argued that her pregnancy would make the long arduous journey from northern to southern Europe even more difficult than it would be otherwise, but she didn't. She made no reference whatsoever to the fact that she was carrying his child.

He picked up on her depression, and began to argue that living with him would lift it: "I think I could find lots of ingenious ways to cheer you up and make you smile again. I'd make you clocks of cork, papier-mâché fiddles, and wax lizards with two tails; my full repertoire of Sardinian folklore. I'd tell you stories of my wild and woolly childhood, so different from your own, each tale more fantastic than the last!" He had hoped that her pregnancy "...would lend you strength, and help you overcome the crisis which I've long felt was latent inside you, and all bound up with your past, your childhood and your whole intellectual development... During that brief period when we were utterly happy, I did think very definitely that our happiness would be completed if you were to have a child, but after you told me you were expecting you have said no more about it."

* * *

Vienna in 1923/4, long after its *fin-de-siècle* heyday as the epicentre of modern European civilisation, sat comfortably in its middle-aged social democracy but with a very definite sense of trouble brewing in the surrounding hills and countryside. It had been the capital of an empire of fifteen nationalities. As it crumbled and dissolved in the ruthless contest of European imperialisms and the internecine squabbles of the Habsburgs,

Vienna enjoyed its final heyday, as a bubbling melting pot for all their cultural elites. In the last days of the nineteenth century and first of the twentieth, all the experiments and innovations that would come to define modernity and modernism had emerged here. But by the 1920s, the Vienna of Klimt and Schoenberg, Mahler and Freud, Hoffman and Schiele had been shattered and scattered.

It may not have made a particularly congenial place of residence for Gramsci, but it offered a perfect vantage-point from which to observe the ebbing of the proletarian revolutionary tide, if not (at least for Gramsci) to do much about it. The news from Russia was vague but always disturbing, especially when filtered through the jaundiced accounts of willing or not so willing exiles like Serge and Balabanova. Lenin had been paralysed in 1922, struck dumb in 1923, and died soon after on 21st January 1924. The other leading Bolsheviks – Trotsky, Stalin, Zinoviev, Radek, Kamenev, Bukharin et al – were fighting bitter, outwardly incomprehensible and endlessly shifting factional struggles over his legacy and who should succeed him.

From a distance, Gramsci found it all as bewildering and dismaying as his dealings with the Schucht family, and confessed to feeling "misled by my ignorance." He wrote an editorial obituary for Lenin in the relaunched and refashioned *L'Ordine Nuovo,* headed *Capo* ("Chief"). It was followed a fortnight later by an editorial headed *Contro il Pessimismo,* arguing against the mood he himself was beginning to feel overwhelmed by, and pleading for calmer and more congenial dealings amongst the Soviet comrades. There was a venom in it all he just could not begin to comprehend, and which friends like Serge could not begin to explain in anything other than metaphysical or even mystical terms.

It all came down, apparently, to thoroughly un-Marxist intangibles like the "Russian soul" or the necessary blood-letting of revolutionary upheaval. They all seemed to find their historical reference-points in the French Revolution, with its Jacobin terrors and Thermidor purges. They had endless discussions about who might be the Russian Robespierre or Danton or Bonaparte, as if history was a piece of theatre that was simply re-staged every hundred years or so, with the same plot and cast of characters updated for a new century. Gramsci would find himself struck atypically dumb in frustration at the lack of historical specificity in these discussions. Whatever was going on, it threatened to consume them all in biblical-scale catastrophe. If the Bolsheviks were set on destroying each other, why did their capitalist enemies abroad or even at home need to bother? They simply had to bide their time while the revolution tore itself apart.

The quite separate factional battle inside the tiny, shattered Italian Communist Party continued to rage, a blurred miniature compared to the angular iron monument of Soviet Bolshevism. The majority group in the Italian leadership, loyal to the imprisoned Bordiga, were still refusing fusion with the Socialists, "accepting the International line formally, while working on the old lines behind the scenes", as a secret factional memorandum put it. In this poisonous atmosphere each wing of the party was intercepting and publishing letters and documents which exposed their opponents' subterfuges and deviations. Bordiga proposed from prison that the *PCd'I* should split from the Communist International altogether. When the round-robin reached Gramsci, he refused to sign it, as much because of its sectarian tone as its inevitably destructive consequences. At the same time he kept his distance from Tasca and the other right wingers. His principled stance didn't do much good, but simply served to illustrate and deepen his political and personal marginality inside the *PCd'I*.

Bordiga remained the party's dominant personality, "stubborn and inflexible to the point of absurdity" as Gramsci put it in a letter to Alfonso Leonetti, at that point his only close comrade inside the leadership. All Gramsci's inquiries and surveys indicated that Bordiga retained overwhelming support in what remained of the party inside Italy. A large majority of local and regional officials and activists was still attracted and swayed by Amadeo's incendiary rhetoric and calls for immediate insurrection, even though anyone with any sense could see this would mean the final and total destruction of the party. Meanwhile the right of the party were ever more determined to engineer fusion with the Socialists on any terms, and active collaboration with any other anti-fascists to restore constitutional norms to Italian government.

All Gramsci could propose in order to resolve the conflict was "a clear, frank argument which goes right to the bottom of things." It sounded inadequate as he wrote it, and pathetic when he received his own copy of the memorandum. He resisted Leonetti's suggestion to reconvene the old *L'Ordine Nuovo* group from Turin as the core of a new leadership, because "it would only look like a clique reassembled around my own person for bureaucratic reasons... It would all end in personal feuds over the right of inheritance to a legacy of mere memories and words."

More to the point, he could not be sure that he and Togliatti and Tasca could ever work together again, given their political divergences since Turin. Instead he worked hard to bring the party round to the Comintern view, mainly by correspondence, urging a "united front from below of mass revolutionary action radiating out from the workplace." This was, he argued, the only strategy which promised to stop Fascism in its tracks and revive any prospect of proletarian revolution. What's more, it had the support and authority of the Communist International and of the successors to Lenin, the recently deceased father of the great and glorious October Revolution. He might have added, but thought better of it, "whoever those successors turn out to be..."

Gradually the other party leaders were won over, or at least pacified. A new leadership group was reconstituted around

Gramsci, who agreed "to put all I can into this group. I won't be able to do all that I'd like to do, because I still go through periods of atrocious feebleness which make me fear a relapse into the kind of stupid coma I have suffered from in recent years." The party press was revived inside Italy, taking full advantage of the relatively liberal atmosphere the Fascists had sustained since coming to government in an attempt to prove their respectability and keep the bankers and industrialists on their side. On 12th February 1924 the first edition of the new *PCd'I* newspaper *L'Unita* was published in Italy, and by June circulation had risen to 50,000. A fortnightly *L'Ordine Nuovo*, a rather more conventional political review than in the heyday of the Turin Factory Councils, had appeared in March, soon selling 5000.

These were real measures of revival, especially when possession of communist publications could be used as evidence in criminal proceedings or excuse for a Fascist beating. The struggle between reaction and revolution was still in the balance: "We might still get history back on track," Gramsci wrote in *L'Ordine Nuovo*. On 6th April the *PCd'I* won 270,000 votes in a general election. A "Proletarian Unity" list of nineteen Comintern-supporting MPs (thirteen communists, five *terzini* and one independent) was elected to the Italian parliament, including (in his absence) Gramsci representing a constituency in the Veneto region. They would be massively outnumbered by the "national list" led by Mussolini and the Fascists, who had won a parliamentary vote to change the electoral law so that the largest single bloc would gain two-thirds of the seats. This gave the national list 374 out of 535 seats, and provided a constitutional veneer to the Fascist dictatorship, but Gramsci's parliamentary seat gave him immunity from arrest if he returned to Italy.

There was the added incentive, he told Victor Serge, of escaping the worsening atmosphere of the International and the feuding inside the Russian Party. In his final weeks in Vienna, Gramsci sought out Serge's sympathetic and always congenial company, and shared stories and strolls around the city, evenings at plays or readings and more obviously political events. They attended meetings of Social Democratic activists: middle-aged men, sinking into mental inertia and physical atrophy, and cultivating their paunches with beer and pies while they listened to and failed to be roused by fiery speeches. Serge told Gramsci about a Communist Party newsletter he had read, complaining about unfair treatment of working class families by social workers employed by the city council. One family had their welfare support reduced because they had "gained property" in the form of a bag of apples. He had seen for himself the forced removal of children from his apartment block to a diagnostic centre which "resembled a police raid." Serge and Gramsci together witnessed a march past the Town Hall with 30,000 bicycles garlanded with flowers, and stood speechless before bursting into uncontrollable laughter. At night they watched quite different groups of people, in uniforms and berets, marching in step in small groups to the outlying hills for weapons training: Officers' Associations and ex-servicemen, carrying banners decorated with crosses and swastikas. One evening, with patches of snow still on the ground, they were walking through the city semi-consciously in step with the ever-present *um-pa-pa, um-pa-pa* of Strauss waltzes from the cafés, when an explosion rang out beneath the arcades of the Opera House. A despairing unemployed man had blown himself up with a stick of dynamite which, Serge calculated, would have cost him a whole week's dole. The beneficence of municipal socialism, it seemed, could only extend so far. If NEP-era Russia was demonstrating the impossibility of socialism in one country, "Red" Vienna demonstrated its impossibility in one city.

Throughout this period, Antonio continued to correspond with the Schuchts, in the face of ever more explicit discouragement from Evgenia. To Julka he wrote on 15th March: "Will I ever be able to stick my tongue out at you again? We're serious persons now and mustn't set a bad example to the children... The truth is that I love you, I think of you continually, and every now and then feel you close, very close in my arms. Strange things happen to me. When I'd read your last letter I began to feel sure you must have arrived in Vienna, and that I would bump into you in the street... Darling Julka, you are the whole of life to me, for I had never felt what life was until I loved you... I believe that when we live together again we shall be invincible, we shall find a way of defeating even Fascism. We want a free and beautiful world for our child, and we shall fight for this as we have never fought before, with a cleverness we have never had before, with a tenacity and energy that will overcome every obstacle in our path."

He received no direct reply from his wife to this or any other of his subsequent letters from Vienna. But Evgenia wrote to him to say that his letters to Julka were confusing her, with their expressions of endless devotion and what Evgenia called "…your rather embarrassing and lustful propositions." These were, he should understand, "deeply unsettling to a woman in her condition." Not long ago, she reminded him, he had even been flirting with her, Evgenia. Did he not remember telling her "*ti voglio bene*" and singing "*I only have eyes for you*" in her room at Serebranyi Bor? And of course, as only she and he knew, he had made other personal displays of himself towards her during their time together at the sanatorium.

"Quite honestly, Comrade Gramsci," she concluded, "we never quite know what to make of your outbursts..."

He wrote back (in his final letter addressed directly to Evgenia) that he was sorry to have caused confusion in the Schucht family, for whom he felt such great respect and admiration. He felt particular gratitude to her, Evgenia, for having made his stay in Russia so delightful, but perhaps it was time to clear the air. He truly loved Julka, and he needed her and the whole family to understand and accept this. She was now, after all, his wife. That relationship superseded all others. Evgenia herself had witnessed their marriage in September the previous year, and soon their child would be born as further proof of their deep bond.

He was sorry that Evgenia had ever felt misled about his intentions towards her. He felt genuine affection for her, as a person and sister-in-law and fellow communist. Furthermore he hoped that they could remain friends throughout whatever trials life still had to throw at them all. She had assisted his recovery as surely as any of the doctors at Serebranyi Bor, with their mysterious "treatments" that had given him and her such cause for mutual merriment and grievance. He treasured the frankness and honesty of their exchanges over that whole six month period of rest and recovery, and regretted any discomfort or embarrassment he might have inadvertently caused her towards the end of it. Now, in that same frank and honest spirit, he felt compelled to tell her that he had never felt the slightest physical or romantic attraction towards her.

Rome, 1924

Antonio Gramsci returned to Italy on 12th May 1924, nearly two whole years after leaving. Everyone he met had horror stories to tell from the time he had been away. Comrades had been murdered or savagely beaten, with that peculiarly methodical technique – force-feeding large quantities of castor oil, and kicking or beating with cudgels on the kidneys – the Fascists had taken as their own. Offices, meeting rooms and printing presses had been smashed to pieces or burnt down, including most of the places Gramsci had worked in during the war and the "red years" afterwards. People had been forced out of their homes and families, or targeted simply because – like his own brother Gennaro – they were associated with known communists, socialists or even Liberals. All you needed was a record or even suspicion of opposition to the Fascists, and you were fair game for the *squadristi*.

"This isn't just a restoration of the pre-war reactionary status quo," said Alfonso Leonetti, over a welcoming-back dinner at his poky little flat in the Roman workers' district of Trastevere. "It's like a return to the bloody dark ages!"

The worst thing was that the entire machinery of the modern state, above all the police, had been absorbed into this apparatus of terror. The *carabinieri* could be relied upon to stand idly by while the Blackshirts went about their business, or even to join in if they felt like it. There was no point complaining afterwards; collaboration went all the way up to the highest courts, with only small isolated murmurs of misgiving.

"The best you can hope for," said Leonetti, "is a shrug of the shoulders and the name of a lawyer who just might offer you more than sympathy..."All the legal, constitutional and moral safeguards of liberal democracy and the bourgeois order, which the comrades of the Socialist and Communist Parties had been so scathing towards during their own ascendancy, but also exploited so assiduously to advance their own cause and protect their own standing and institutions, had simply been cast aside by Mussolini and his sidekicks. Every conversation Gramsci had back in Rome – always conducted in furtive whispers and sideways glances – seemed to end on this note of rueful irony. What they would give for a few legal niceties now! Sadly shaking heads had replaced fond embraces and claps on the upper arm or back, or (Gramsci recalled with a twinge of embarrassment) ostentatiously raised clenched fists, as the favoured gesture of greeting and farewell between comrades. Even physical contact might give you away or be used as evidence of subversive activity against the New Order, so people now seemed to shrink from touch in this most tactile of cultures. *My goodness,* Gramsci thought when he first noticed a comrade flinch before his outstretched hand, *the Italians are turning English...*

His first formal duty as *PCd'I* General Secretary was a clandestine party conference near Lake Como a few days after his return. He travelled there from Rome via Milan in lovely late spring weather, with two comrades whom he had to pretend to ignore the whole journey. They made sure to leave the train at Como from separate carriages, and only meet up outside the station when they were sure they were not being followed. They could then safely join the crowd of holiday-makers and day-trippers, including several other comrades with whom they exchanged wary nods, making their way to the resort. As previously instructed, they found their directions to the conference – a simple account of which roads to take – on a card pinned to the notice-board of a large hotel, lost to anyone except those in the know amongst advertisements for tourist excursions and holiday services.

"Comrades," Gramsci began, when everyone was sure that most of those who were expected had in fact arrived, "I'm not going to give a great long speech, because I'm more interested in what you've got to say. After all, you know the situation here first-hand, while I've been away for two years..."

They were sitting or in some cases standing in a lovely little valley, white with narcissi flowers. The meeting place had been carefully chosen because it could only be seen from the surrounding ridge. There were around sixty of them, central committee members and regional leaders, with a couple of local rank and file comrades keeping watch from the hill above. Looking round at their upturned faces, some familiar but mostly not, all of them bemused and anxious and strained, Gramsci wondered who and what they were actually representing. Current estimates of national party membership were just a few thousand, and only a handful of those – not many more than those sat here in this sunlit field – were in any real sense active. What could they possibly do about the political catastrophe engulfing them and the country, this carnival of reaction? Could they even be relied upon to follow the strategic direction of himself and the newly reconstituted Comintern-endorsed leadership?

The answers to these key questions emerged during the day's debates and votes on the three motions put to the conference. The first was proposed by the new leadership around Gramsci, still known as the "communist education" group after the study circles the original *L'Ordine Nuovo* had organised for the Turin Factory Councils. It was supported by four central committee members and three regional secretaries; seven votes in all. The second, from the right wing minority calling for a broad anti-Fascist alliance and the restoration of constitutional democracy, won four votes from the central committee and six from the regional secretaries; ten votes in all. The third, communicated from Bordiga in prison by his solitary remaining acolyte on the central committee, called for immediate armed insurrection and transition to proletarian revolution. It won support from that one CC member and no fewer than thirty nine local leaders; forty in all. A small forest of clenched fists pumped the air, accompanied by a roar of triumph.

Gramsci had listened to the debates in mounting concern. It was like the last five years had never happened, and these bellowing extremists had somehow been transported through time directly from the hungry, embattled streets of Turin and Milan and the tumultuous final conferences of the old Socialist Party, with the bright glow of the young Soviet Revolution on the distant horizon. They were still confident of imminent victory, and bathing in its warm seductive allure. They thought they could simply vote an insurrection into being. Nothing had been learned from the failure of the Factory Council movement, the defeat of the factory occupations by the industrial employers, the big landowners' brutal resistance to peasant land seizures and rural reform, the sectarian squabbles of all the various sects and coteries descended from the Socialist Party, and finally the inexorable rise to mass support and state power of the Fascists.

He could see the fatigue, disappointment and suffering in their features – dull eyes in lined foreheads, thinning hair and slack mouths, the blank face of defeat – but all he could hear in their voices was high-pitched sloganeering and barely digested formulas echoing around the pretty sunlit valley from Bordiga's prison cell. Old Amadeo – stuck there for the foreseeable future – was entitled to a few comforting delusions, but these few still free communist militants could ill afford to share them.

During the lunch break, they retired to a large local hostelry on the southern shore of Lake Como. They pretended to be employees of a Milanese firm on a works outing, singing Fascist songs between cours*e*s*e* – the anthem *Giovinezza* providing a rousing finale over the tiramisu*e* – and making florid bombastic speeches in honour of *Il Duce*. Gramsci deployed his full range of impersonations of the Fascist lackeys he had once known as maximalist Socialists, trying hard to avoid the cruder caricatures which he knew would have the comrades in suspicion-arousing stitches. For all their enforced straight faces and subdued posturing, they enjoyed themselves enormously. It was as if five years of pent-up fury and dismay were suddenly being released; catharsis through play-acting. It would help to lift morale for the battles ahead, he concluded, far more than all the hours of windy speeches and arm-waving posturing he had just had to sit through in the valley of the narcissi.

* * *

Gramsci took a room on Via Vesalio in Rome in a house occupied by a German family, the Passarges. They didn't know he was a communist MP, and he went to some lengths to avoid them finding out. As he wrote to Julka: "I try to look like an ultra-serious professor. They hold me in some awe and go to the most exasperating lengths to leave me in peace." Sometimes, during the long warm evenings and summer nights, he would hear them creeping along the corridor outside his room, while he read without absorbing much, scribbled some note or reference, or slept fitfully thinking of his wife and longing for some intimate human contact. Sometimes the Passarges youngest child, a rather plain four year old girl, would creep into his room, offer her cheek to be kissed and ask him to play. It was a welcome break from the long hours of reading and writing.

In fact it felt to him, after his two busy years in Moscow and Vienna, his demanding job and his brief taste of married life at the Hotel Lux, that he was living more like a student again. He noted with a mixture of amusement and dismay, and the evidence of his own nose, the sharp decline in his personal hygiene. The intervals between stripping his bed for inclusion in the Passarge family laundry got longer and longer, until Frau Passarge began dropping heavy hints. He was no longer grooming and dressing himself for another person. His hours became even more irregular, and sometimes he would realise with a start that he had read or written or simply day-dreamed right through the night and that the sun was coming up on the eastern horizon.

It would have already been light for several hours in Russia, he reckoned, especially in the northern cities with their white nights. If he had been thinking of Julka, he would wonder what she was doing in the warm mid-morning sunshine of Soviet Moscow, with its post-NEP bustle and urgency of reconstruction. Would she be at work or giving a violin lesson? Or would she – heavier every day – have allowed herself the morning off to go shopping for baby clothes? Whatever it was, it would certainly be much more interesting and purposeful than anything he might be up to in sleepy, lazy, ancient, reactionary Rome. Here, the sun was taken as a signal to slow down rather than rise up.

Even in Vienna, with its sobriety and respectability and steady unspectacular reform, and on roughly the same longitude and time-zone as Rome, there would be more going on than here. Its one million proletarians would be up and off to work in what they thought of as *their* factories and workshops, warehouses and building sites; *their* cranes swinging into action across the city; *their* scaffolds resounding and bouncing from the heavy tread of strong work-boots; *their* lathes and saws pressing and grinding raw metal and wood into tools and joints and fastenings, building new lives. In retrospect there was something fundamentally serious and grown-up about the Russian and Austrian capitals. By contrast Italy just seemed silly and childish, especially with the Fascists parading around like toy soldiers.

Friends and comrades, including many of the old *L'Ordine Nuovo* crowd who now felt safer in Rome than in Turin, occasionally visited him at Via Vesalio and talked politics late into the night. He got to know the Sardinian nationalist, MP Emilio Lussu, and relished the chance to talk in their shared dialect about developments on the island. As he grew concerned about disturbing or alarming the Passarges, and increasingly embarrassed at the chaotic state of his room, he would arrange to meet people at a restaurant near Termini station. Afterwards, they would stroll around the city talking or, if they felt like being entertained, go to the cinema and catch the latest *Americano* comedy or melodrama. While the cultural life of the Italian capital had markedly declined under the dead hand of Fascist censoriousness, which made Gramsci fondly recall the mad poetic turmoil of Moscow, there were at least plenty of "movies" to see. Gramsci had a particular penchant for Buster Keaton. Comrades would nudge his arm and point to Charlie Chaplin, to whom Gramsci bore a passing resemblance, especially in the photos taken of him in Moscow with his moustache.

L'Ordine Nuovo groups began to meet around the city to discuss the latest issue of the *PCd'I* fortnightly review and provide cover for more obviously political activity and organisation. Members were very young, in their teens and early twenties, and hungry for information and guidance. Gramsci sensed that they were beginning to look through and beyond the crude simplicities he'd encountered at Como, and attended as many and as often as he could, introducing discussions and always trying to prompt responses and other contributions. He exercised his authority as an MP and experienced militant judiciously, so as not to overawe these very much younger and less experienced comrades. They had been children before and during the war, and knew very little of the "old" Italy before Fascism, that unruly society of sharp political discord and ideological tumult, with widespread class warfare struggling for expression and resolution within a formally liberal-democratic legal and constitutional order.

"A cracker in a matchbox... " he observed ruefully, "all gone now..."

He tried to encourage fresh thinking about how to revive the fortunes of the workers' movement in these radically altered, reduced circumstances. It was very difficult. All these young comrades seemed capable of suggesting was more of the same. More copies of the fortnightly *L'Ordine Nuovo,* and of the *PCd'I* daily paper *L'Unita* and the new weekly *Lo Stato Operaio,* sold to more workers at more factory gates and in more workers' districts of more industrial cities. More outings to the countryside, to spread the word to more peasants. More members of the party, more discussion groups like this one, more public and street corner meetings. *More of everything,* Gramsci thought to himself, always careful not to demoralise these bright, enthusiastic youngsters, *which got us into this position in the first place...* Shouting ever more loudly to be heard above the hubbub, rather than educating people, truly changing them and their minds.

He didn't spend much time in Parliament. Against the Fascists and their "national list" allies' massive rigged majority, there wasn't a great deal of point voting or even speaking. He and his comrades were happy to leave all that to the windy old buffoons of the Liberal Party and the various strands of reformist Socialism who held out some hope for some kind of constitutional resistance and restoration. Nor did they feel any obligation to their notional constituents in the far flung corners of the Italian peninsula; at least no more than any other MPs, who might deign to return at election times, dispensing smiles and waves and (in most cases) *lire* in return for votes. Most of the communists preferred to devote their limited time and energies, and their parliamentary salaries and privileges, to propaganda and organisation, rather than what Gramsci routinely derided as "the squalor of parliamentary life." Then came the Matteotti affair, which briefly rocked Mussolini and his friends back on their heels.

Giacomo Matteotti was a moderate Socialist MP with an independent streak and a pragmatic approach which had made him a long-time natural opponent of both the flamboyant Mussolini and what he called the "communist secession" from the Socialist Party. He had compiled a mass of hard evidence of electoral fraud and financial misconduct by the Fascists in the recent general election, and presented it to parliament in a blistering speech on 30th May 1924. He accused Mussolini of being ready to use force if the Fascists had failed to win at the polls. A great clamour of "Yes! Yes!" arose from the Fascist benches. As he sat down, he remarked to fellow Socialist MPs: "Now you can prepare my funeral oration..." A furious Mussolini made it clear in his response that he wanted Matteotti punished for his insolence.

A few days later Matteotti was beaten and stabbed to death by a gang of *squadristi*. They were led by a certain Amerigo Dumini, who was on the payroll of Mussolini's press secretary Cesare Rossi. They dumped the body in a wood fifteen miles outside Rome, where it lay undiscovered for a further two months. The new "national list" government was badly shaken by Matteotti's disappearance, as its non-Fascist components took fright at the public expressions of outrage at his assumed murder on Mussolini's orders. The communist daily *L'Unita* ran a full-page headline: "Down with this Government of Assassins!" At the opposite end of the political spectrum, the industrialists of the great northern cities actively contemplated a restoration of the old Liberal order they had less than two years previously helped Mussolini to overthrow. They were known to be holding preliminary discussions with the old Prime Minister Giolitti.

Over succeeding weeks and months, as Gramsci wrote to Julka:

> *"Fascism was isolated in the country, to the point where its leaders panicked and its hangers-on deserted in droves. We worked feverishly, taking decisions, issuing orders, trying to give aim and direction to this flood of popular feeling... Our paper has trebled its circulation, and in many places our comrades have assumed the leadership of the mass movement and attempted to disarm the*

Fascists, while our slogans were acclaimed and repeated in motions passed at factory meetings."

The murder of Matteotti also united all the anti-Fascist parties and groups in Parliament, who agreed to withdraw in protest. They would meet separately, and call themselves "The Aventine Secession" after the Plebs of ancient Rome who once withdrew from the Senate to the Aventine hill outside the city. There they went about their usual business of long-winded debate and empty resolutions, with the small band of communists and *terzini* socialists deriding their "narrow parliamentarism" and trying to get them to "do something".

* * *

One hot day in June 1924, Gramsci was returning to his lodgings on the Via Vesalio when he saw a familiar figure on the other side of the road. It was his comrade and ally from Turin, Alfonso Leonetti, in the company (Gramsci could see from behind) of an attractive woman. They were arm in arm, walking closely together. *Who's old Alfonso got himself attached to?* He hurried across the road towards them. As usual, two other men on either side of the road stopped in their tracks to see what he was doing.

"Alfonso!" called Gramsci, not too loudly, when he had got to within a few yards of his old friend.

Alfonso turned around to see who was calling him, in the process detaching himself from his companion, who also turned towards Gramsci. It was Pia Carena, his old – *well, what should he call her? Flame? Friend? Acquaintance?* – from Turin. They greeted each other awkwardly – "Hello Pia", "Hello Nino" – while Alfonso, clearly apprised of their former relationship, looked on.

"What are you doing here?" was all Antonio could think of to say to her.

"Well," she responded diffidently, her eyes downcast, "I've

been living here quite a while. Ever since Nannaro left Turin for Paris, in fact. I decided it wasn't safe to be in Turin, or much fun with so few of our old comrades still there."

Gramsci turned towards Alfonso, to gauge his view of this uncomfortable encounter, but also for some assistance in dealing with it. Alfonso was normally pretty helpful; *on my side* was how Antonio generally thought of him, especially in the recent disputes inside the *PCd'I*. On this occasion Alfonso was unusually deadpan, hard to read... *I wonder how much he knows...*

"You know," Alfonso said, "I've got to be somewhere. You two have clearly got some catching up to do." Turning to Pia, he said, "I'll see you back at the flat..."

Antonio and Pia stood for some moments in awkward silence. He had not seen her for several years. She had aged, settled into herself, lost her youthful edge and carefree fizz. But then, he reminded himself, so had he. *It's called growing up...* And these last few years had knocked the fizz out of lots of people.

"There's a café just round the corner," he said at last, "where we can talk without too much interference or concern for who might be listening. Shall we?"

Pia nodded her assent, and they turned towards the corner. Antonio's "tail" followed from a distance. He and Pia didn't speak until they had settled at a table with their cups of coffee and glasses of water.

"So how are you doing? Are you managing to get by?" Antonio asked.

"I still do short-hand," replied Pia, "and I've got some part-time work in the Museum of Antiquities. Alfonso's very kind..."

"I heard about you and Nannaro..." said Gramsci.

"How is he?" Pia replied. "He was in a pretty bad way when he left..."

"I don't know. I haven't heard from him since he left Turin. I assume he's got himself settled in Paris. He usually manages to land on his feet. Did he ever pay you back what you lent him?"

"No, but I didn't expect..."

"How much was it?" asked Gramsci, reaching inside his jacket for his wallet.

"Oh, that's not necessary," said Pia firmly. "I managed to sell some jewellery I didn't need..."

"Including that locket I gave you?"

"Oh Nino, that went a long time ago..."

Just like me, he thought. He reached across the table to lay his hand on top of hers.

"You know, I don't know whether I should say sorry..."

"There's nothing to say sorry for. We were both young, we had no idea what we were doing."

"We still are young..." said Gramsci, surprised by how unconvincing he sounded.

"Do you think so?" said Pia. She clearly didn't.

They drank their coffee, like perfect strangers who just happen to find themselves sitting opposite each other in a café.

"Would you like to come up to my room?" Antonio said suddenly, surprising himself this time with the urgency of his desire. It had been, by his reckoning, over half a year since he had felt the touch of a woman; and that after several months when he and Julka had made love almost every day. Pia was still a highly attractive woman. Perhaps not young any more, but could it be that her experience since they had last been together had made her more desirable than ever?

"Nino, I don't think that would be a good idea. I'm with Alfonso now..."

"Yes, I saw..." Now there was jealousy in his voice, and an undercurrent of resentment at exclusion from a site of human warmth and intimacy. *That old feeling of being left out... Stupid to imagine it didn't follow me around like that fellow in the hat and overcoat over there.*

They parted on friendly enough terms, at the corner outside the café, with kisses on the cheek and promises to keep in touch, though they both knew they wouldn't. There was too much pain from unhealed wounds. Gramsci nodded towards the two policemen waiting to resume their dogged pursuit, and smiled ruefully. As he kissed Pia once more, this time more lingeringly and with some pressure, he murmured, "They claim they're protecting me! I suppose I should feel flattered that they think me important enough to follow..."

Pia murmured back, as she returned the kiss with some suppressed passion of her own, "Nino, you will always have people looking out for you..."

* * *

Personal letters from Moscow were still few and far between. When Julka did write, her letters were brief and cursory, with that same mix of forced cheerfulness and banality – "the weather here has been glorious!" – that had aroused his suspicions in Vienna. He tried to break through the formalities with his letters to her, which were full of fond reminiscences, bold declarations of love and pleas for her to join him: "How I would love to go for a stroll with you so that we could see the beauty of Rome together... I shut myself up in my room. I seem to have become a cave bear once more! I think of you, and the sweetness of loving you, and of knowing that you are very close as well as very far away. Darling Julka, even far away the thought of you helps me to be stronger. But my life can never become normal again as long as we're separated; loving you has become too much part of my personality for me ever to feel normal again without your presence."

On 18th August 1924, while Mussolini's government tottered in the wake of the Matteotti crisis, Antonio wrote to Julka about the *PCd'I's* desperate attempts to exploit the public mood of disgust: "The meetings I go to are very satisfying in one way, because of the goodwill and enthusiasm of so many comrades, but in another way they make me pessimistic because of the general lack of preparation... we are still so few, and so badly organised." What he did not know was that his wife had given birth eight days previously, because there had been no word from Moscow. He knew the baby was due between 8th and 15th August. As the days passed he grew more anxious, and wrote hopefully to Julka: "Perhaps as I am writing now the child is already born and lies there beside you, where you can caress him after having suffered to bring him into the world."

Finally, after a two week trip to Milan and Turin on party business, he arrived back in Rome on 3rd September to find two letters from Julka waiting for him, dated 11th and 18th August. The baby had been born on 10th August, weighing a very healthy three and a half kilos. He had, she wrote, "a lot of brown hair, and a well-formed head with a high forehead and very blue eyes." She observed in her second letter, atypically poetically, that "he looks as if he has been a long time in the sunlight already, like a ripe fruit still attached to its tree." Julka had called him Lev, for "Lion", which Gramsci in immediate and joyous reply thought a little ridiculous for "a tiny baby without a single tooth in his head! But really I don't care what he's called; all that matters is that he is a living child, our son, and that we shall love each other more every new day because we see ourselves in him, only stronger and happier... Please tell me every phase of his development. Personally I am convinced that the day a child puts his foot in his mouth is of prime importance. Don't fail to inform me the moment this act is accomplished, symbolising as it does official possession of the outermost limits of the national territory."

In fact Gramsci insisted, not long after, that the child's name be changed to Delio, after a beloved cousin who had died very young. As the weeks passed, other aspects of their distant liaison also proved troublesome. He found some of her descriptions of the baby somewhat odd – "He sticks his tongue out at me to make me angry"; *surely that's the suckling instinct...* – while she steadfastly refused to accept his practical assistance, which she mocked as "pretensions". He sent her some money via an old friend exiled in Moscow, Vincenzo Bianco. It wasn't a huge amount – a small part of his now substantial earnings from journalism and parliament, "not much more than a packet of cigarettes or a cup of coffee", which he would only otherwise have given to the party press – but he hoped it would make some improvement in Julka and the baby's material conditions. She sent it straight back through Bianco, with a short note saying she could cope perfectly well on her own.

This was their first substantive disagreement, and it introduced a new and sour note to their correspondence. "I think of all the time we've spent away from each other, of all those aspects of your life I have been absent from," he wrote. "There is so little I can do for you and the child, and I would like to do something. It would make me so happy to feel that I was important in your life, and could help you over some difficulty. I would then feel that a new bond had been created between us, something to give us at least the illusion of being close to one another." The grinding poverty of his own childhood had made him appreciate the value of even the smallest gifts, "which create bonds, feelings of solidarity and affection nothing can destroy."

She wrote back – *are these her own words?* – that these feelings of personal and family solidarity seemed to her "bourgeois", especially when expressed through material objects and money. His gift was an offence to the communist principles by which they were supposed to live and raise their child. All the help she and the baby needed was available from the Soviet state. "There are Soviet laws which entrust the care of children to society as well as to the parents," she reminded him, "and didn't Engels himself decry the so-called sanctity of the bourgeois family?" She described approvingly the Soviet maternity ward where she had lain for the statutory prescribed week while recovering from giving birth: "The children are all brought along in a big trolley before being distributed to their mothers to be fed."

He replied, measuring his words carefully but perhaps not carefully enough, that, "This scene seemed so real to me that I was tempted to provoke you by suggesting that maybe they give a different infant to the mother each time, given that Soviet discipline is so imperfect, and scarcely likely to reign among the nurses in a children's hospital." He brought the exchange to some kind of conclusion with: "It's a great pity I have not been able to share the anxieties and joys of this time with you. This will always be a great gap in my life." Again he had the unnerving feeling that he had been corresponding not just with Julka, and that her replies were being shaped or even dictated by someone else.

That was not all. Those feelings and opinions that were undeniably hers were in many ways just as troubling. For the first time since they met, he began to dwell on the differences between the two of them, in temperament, in attitude, in outlook on life, without ever really being able to say definitively what they were. He would calculate, late at night or in the gentle Roman dawn, just how much time they had spent together – roughly six months as a courting couple, nine weeks and three days as husband and wife – and ponder just how little it was. What chance had their relationship really had to develop, to blossom, to deepen into a complete partnership?

He had known all along that as long as he loved her, Julka's full character would always remain tantalisingly out of reach. That was a major part of her romantic appeal, her entirely unself-conscious and uncontrived mystery. But now he asked himself, *just how much does she actually know me?* Or rather absorb or even listen to what he told her about himself, face-to-face or by letter? In her busy daily life, with a small helpless baby to care for and a responsible job to return to as soon as she could, so far away and in such different circumstances, how much time did she spend thinking about him, Nino?

Finally, while out walking (almost) deserted streets in a vain attempt to shake off his early morning torpor, he stumbled upon what now seemed the most crucial difference of all. He had sought self-knowledge throughout his life, until by force of habit it had become a constant internal dialogue and systematic process of adjustment. Wasn't that the basic point of each person's life, to open up their personality, as it responded and retuned itself to events and circumstances and other people; the dialectical interplay between thought and action, theory and practice, the properly Marxist or even "communist" approach to an individual, personal life? Julia "Julka" Schucht, it occurred to him, was not like that at all. Through fear or choice or arrogance, he knew not which, she spent her whole life avoiding self-awareness, pushing it away as if it were a contagion or a trap or both. The very last thing she wanted was to be understood, to be opened up, to be laid bare, for fear of what she or anyone else might find. What had seemed mysteriously alluring to him was in fact dangerous to her, an uncharted reef of jagged rocks beneath the tranquil surface of the sea. And her refusal to get to know herself, to confront her own personality and compose some kind of guide or map to her inner life, was in turn dangerous to the people around her. Above all to him, Antonio Gramsci, who had felt such joy and fulfilment at being finally able to open up to her, another person, after so many years of keeping himself to himself, at being fully understood at last by someone else. He began to wonder whether she really cared for him at all. Their love began to feel more and more like a hopeless folly. Through these first months of separation, he felt his longing for her curdle into an acute sense of loss. Several times he even thought he saw her, on a passing tram or at the far end of a dark street.

Not for the first (or last) time, Gramsci threw himself into political work as a way to overcome his personal frustrations and disappointments. He tried to convince himself and his party that things were looking up. In a report to the Central Committee he wrote: "The Matteotti crime was the definitive proof that the Fascist party will never become a normal governing party, and that Mussolini is capable only of striking picturesque poses, not of being a real statesman or dictator. He is no national figure, no Cromwell or Bolivar or Garibaldi. He will go down in history as a quaint phenomenon of our provincial rustic folklore. Fascism is being propped up by its allies in industry and agriculture, but only as much as the rope holds up a man who has just been hanged."

In fact Mussolini soon recovered his composure, and the Fascist "revolution" its forward momentum. He conducted a purge of his more "extremist" aides, including those most clearly implicated in Matteotti's murder, and a reshuffle of his ministers to appease his allies and public opinion. Meanwhile the Italian economy had begun to benefit from the upturn all across Europe. The big industrial firms were increasing investment and production and exports, and new small companies opening up, all of them encouraged by the harassment of the trades unions, the raising of prices and the reduction of workers' wages.

The drastic cuts in secondary school and university places which Mussolini's Education Minister Giovanni Gentile had introduced in 1923 began to bring down under-employment and, perhaps paradoxically, disaffection amongst young people. Fewer new graduates meant more and better opportunities for the older graduates who had struggled to find suitable work. It was a kind of middle class protectionism, reversing decades of educational expansion, which Gramsci observed to his comrades, "brought to a grinding halt the upward social mobility through education of tens of thousands of poor, talented young people like so many of us." Along with measures to discourage internal migration from the countryside, and vacuous talk of the "rural soul of Italy" and the emergence of something called "super-country", which flattered the peasant masses while doing nothing concrete to alleviate their poverty and ignorance, it represented a serious step backward in the country's economic development and social progress.

In September Gramsci heard from Turin that his one of his oldest and closest friends, the Revolutionary Liberal Piero Gobetti, had been viciously beaten up, and the family home where he lived with his parents burnt down. On 12th September a Fascist deputy Armando Casalini was shot and killed in a Rome tramcar by a deranged young man, Giovanni Corvi. For the Fascists this made up for Matteotti, and full-scale repression resumed and intensified. Mussolini felt confident enough to dismiss the "vociferous nagging" of the Aventine parties. In a speech to Parliament, still occupied solely by his own adoring supporters, he threatened, "On the day they actually try to do something, on that day we shall make hay of them, and use it as litter for our camps!" Between 3rd and 5th October, in front of horrified foreign tourists in Florence, the *squadristi* went on a rampage against the local opposition, leaving several dead and many injured.

* * *

Gramsci spent much of the autumn of 1924 rushing around Italy rallying the comrades and assessing their capabilities for practical action against Fascism and for the revolution. He was still able to travel freely but constantly aware that he was being followed and on occasions pointed out. His stature and his deformity made him even more conspicuous than his politics and occupation would have done. As he said more than once to anxious comrades arranging to meet him, trying to put them at their ease with a touch of self-deprecating humour, "You can't miss me, you just have to look down!" Police surveillance became increasingly blatant. After Casalini's death it got very much worse, as the Fascists recovered their morale and motivation.

They had a martyr of their own, and could pose as victims as well as victors. Gramsci felt less and less like he was being "protected", and more and more like he was being watched. Apart from anything else, it made getting about much more expensive, because taking taxis rather than trams was the only way to shake off his "tail".

In late October he returned to Sardinia, by boat across a strangely still sea from Genova. He spent much of the journey on the open deck, looking out over flat water, mulling over the worsening situation on the mainland and wondering what he would find on the island. In fact he was shocked at how little it had changed, as the boat docked at the port of Cagliari and he disembarked and sought out his lodgings. Once he was reacclimatised to the town's dusty provincialism, he was shocked at himself for expecting any different. His memories and associations of the island capital, where he had lodged with Nannaro while preparing for university, were not especially fond. He was to attend the regional Party Congress to be held clandestinely in a field between the Cagliari salt-pans and the village of Quartu. He spent the night on a camp bed in a lawyer's office in Cagliari, listening to the Fascist militia carousing in the street outside while they gathered for the second anniversary celebrations of the March on Rome. The next morning, a Sunday, he was collected by a young factory worker, Antonio Bruno. It was still dark outside, with a notable autumn chill and patches of mist on the lower-lying fields in and around the quiet city.

"Comrade Gramsci?" said Bruno, shaking the famous deputy awake. He was covered only with a blanket, and still dressed in the clothes he had travelled in: the shirt Nannaro had given him in Turin to take to Moscow, now worn and faded and dirty, and a cheap suit with stains on it. No tie or hat or overcoat. Bruno found it hard to equate this scruffy little cripple, unshaven and with a great shock of uncombed hair, with the colossus he had been led to expect.

"Yes, yes, yes!" said Gramsci, springing awake, folding the blanket and setting it neatly on the camp bed. "Let me just splash my face..."

He poured water from a jug into a bowl, drank a glassful and washed his face and hands with the rest.

"So my friend!" he said in Sardinian dialect, drying himself on a cloth. "Let's be off before the Fascists have slept off their bloody hangovers!"

Bruno led the way on foot, a circuitous route around the town in near darkness. For all his ambivalence of the previous evening, Gramsci seemed delighted to be back in Sardinia, walking with a fellow Sardinian and talking Sardinian.

"This is the first time I've been back in four years," he told Bruno, "and before that I'd hardly been back in seven, not since before the war..."

As they walked, he pointed out buildings in the city – "There's Santu Palmeriu! I see they've still not finished the tower..." – and features of the landscape, its flora and fauna. "I used to walk up that hill with my friends when I was a student at the *lycée* here. Look! There's a lizard! Or could it be a *scurzone?"*

They reached the meeting place at around seven o'clock, just as the sun came up over the surrounding vineyards. Delegates arrived singly or in small groups, until everyone who was expected had arrived. The *PCd'I* had never been big in Sardinia, where progressive opinion was normally channelled towards Sardist separatism, the basis of Gramsci's own politics until he moved to Turin and joined the Socialists. But he was shocked by how few comrades there were here now: just twenty, representing an active membership barely twice that, in a population of several hundred thousand.

Admittedly, the island's most adventurous young people, including Gramsci himself and a number he had grown up with, had left for a better life on the mainland or in America, as they always had. There had never been much to detain them here, by way of education or employment, social and financial prospects. Sardinia tended to get what the rest of Italy didn't want, including its school teachers, who he remembered would sometimes show up at village elementary schools like his own and promptly disappear when they saw where they'd ended up. But with the economic upturn, whose benefits were being felt even here in Sardinia, the exodus had eased slightly. He would have expected the Party's vigorous and well-publicised efforts against the Fascists during the summer to have brought in many more new recruits. It had elsewhere, though he had his doubts about the quality of the influx.

Gramsci sat in the shade of a large tree and addressed the comrades assembled around him. He spoke about Bordiga – "Comrade Amadeo's imprisonment has unfortunately taken him out of the struggle and out of touch with the true state of the nation and world affairs" – and about the need to reorganise the party for conditions of repression and clandestinity, mainly through a network of "cells" which would not give each other away, and could if necessary be directed from outside the country. "Fascism will one day topple under the weight of its own contradictions, and having destroyed its bourgeois rivals leave the nation leaderless. We need to be in a position to step into the breach." For now, the party's strategic priority had to be persuading the peasants "and here in Sardinia the shepherds and fishermen" to side with the workers across Italy, "who remain stubbornly resistant to Mussolini and his goons!"His speech was applauded politely in the early morning sunshine. The comrades were not exactly roused, but they were not disinterested either. In discussion, only one delegate spoke up for Bordiga, in a hectoring harangue that seemed to Gramsci to have been modelled on old Amadeo's personal rhetorical style. Perhaps this ranting, arm-waving, head-jerking fellow had attended one of the Bordighist summer schools in Naples, where it was rumoured comrades were instructed in how to stand and gesticulate, even when to use one arm or both, as well as the stock phrases to repeat while giving a speech. To everyone's great relief, the one remaining Bordighist in Sardinia had to leave early to catch the two o'clock (and last) train to the south west mining town of Iglesias.

They enjoyed a simple lunch of pasta, bread and cheese, apples and wine, and continued calm and constructive discussion into the evening. To the delegates' surprise, the great Communist politician from the mainland seemed as interested in their stories about Sardinian life and folklore as the prospects for international proletarian revolution. There had been an upsurge of labour militancy in the Sulcis-Iglesiente mining basin, with even the new Fascist union organisers threatening a strike against the French mine-owners and managers. Gramsci wanted a full account, and an assessment of the chances of broadening the dispute beyond wages and hours onto matters of industrial management and social welfare, which he said were just as important to workers and their families, and crucial to the prospects of proletarian hegemony. But he seemed just as interested in the acts performing in Cagliari's musical theatres, and which particular songs and jokes were proving especially popular.

The next day Gramsci took the same two o'clock train up the west coast to his home village of Ghilarza. This was the first time he had visited his family there since 1920, when he had returned briefly for the sombre occasion of his older sister Emma's funeral after she succumbed to that year's cholera epidemic. He was met by a group of old friends at the railway station in nearby Abbasanta. "Peppino! Enrico! Gaetano!" said Gramsci, stepping sprightly down from the train, winking and nodding his head discreetly to his left, and leaving the carriage door slightly open. Two other men had got off the train and stood on the platform, trying hard to look inconspicuous and disinterested.

"Yes, the journey was fine," Gramsci said in answer to his

friends' polite opening enquiries, then stepped smartly back into the carriage when the station-master blew his whistle. The two policemen also scrambled back onto the train. As the train pulled away, and his friends pretended to wave him off, Gramsci jumped back down onto the platform and slammed the carriage door behind him. The train sped off, with Gramsci's "tail" safely on board, down the single line towards Sassari and the other grim mining towns beyond. It felt like a small victory, with which to start the walk home.

As Gramsci and his friends approached Ghilarza, he observed how little had changed here too: the lava-stone houses with plumes of smoke fluttering like pale blue ribbons from their squat chimneys, the orange groves rising from their backyards into the surrounding hills, stamping donkeys tethered to their posts for the night, raising their heads from their mealy-bags to investigate passers-by; the smell of dung and baking bread. Villagers nodded their greetings at their low doorways or in the narrow street. Behind him, Gramsci could hear them talking about "Don Ciccillo and Peppina Marcias' boy, the famous MP", and sensed his three escorts walking slightly more proudly erect beside him. The only surprise was a bicycle coming clattering down the street, ridden by a young peasant boy with a great pile of sheepskins on the back.

"My goodness," he remarked. "That's the first one of those I've ever seen here!"

He told his friends about bicycles on the mainland, and the march-past of 30,000 flower-bedecked bicycles he had witnessed with Victor Serge in Vienna. Surveying their blank faces he realised he might as well have been talking about the dark side of the moon, here in rural Sardinia where there was as yet no sign of radio or too many other symbols of modernity. *In fact,* he reflected during several subsequent conversations, *this place is closer in spirit to America than Italy, because they receive more direct, reliable, uncensored news from émigré relatives in New York and*

Chicago than from anyone on the mainland. Stories about mobsters and hoodlums or the latest Hollywood sensation meant more to these people than what Mussolini's government or the coterie of career politicians who made up most of the opposition were up to.

He barely had chance to greet his mother before a procession of village worthies came to pay their respects to the visiting dignitary. Even the local Fascists came by, revelling in the success of a fellow Sardinian, even if he was a communist: "The Sardinians are doing well, eh? Good for Sardinia!" A group of labourers from the local Mutual Aid Society asked him all about Russia and the Communist Party. He told them about the October Revolution, and the ongoing struggle to create a society which was equal and fair. The Soviets were creating an economy where workers and peasants were justly rewarded for their labours, and everyone could be sure of enough to eat and a decent place to live. This was a revolution against misery and poverty. The labourers looked puzzled, until one of them piped up: "But Signor Gramsci, why leave Sardinia, which is so poor, then join up with another load of poor people over there?"

Finally he was left alone with his mother and what remained in the *casa Gramsci* of his family. Throughout the visitations from the local worthies she had muttered in the corner or clattered around the kitchen, deeply resentful that after all these years other people still had first call on her son's time and attention. Now she sat him down at the table and they exchanged family news. How was Don Ciccillo? The same as always; he would be back soon from the village hall where he'd gone to play draughts and dominoes with his cronies because he couldn't stand waiting around for his son to arrive. The Gramscis never were very good at waiting for things. Had Nino had any word of her eldest son Nannaro? No, not since he'd moved to Paris after what Gramsci called his "altercation" with the Fascists, sparing his mother the distressing detail. Talking of Fascists, how was Mario getting on?

Less involved with politics, thankfully, said Signora Peppina, and more bothered about his new business and young family.

"His wife's a funny one, she doesn't seem to want to have much to do with us. A bit hoity-toity, if you ask me, nose to the heavens. But what about your news, Nino? I want to hear all about your wife and your child. Of all of you I thought you'd be the last, or would never get round to it."

"Is that why you put me forward for the priesthood when I was eleven?"

"Well, it was never a serious possibility, I doubted they'd have you, especially after what happened to your father. And you always asked too many questions. So many questions..."

"Yes, and their refusal to offer plausible answers is what turned me away..."

He did not pursue this line of argument, for fear of offending his mother's religious sensibilities. Instead, she delighted in his account of his marriage and Julka's maternity, and made him promise to send her regular photographs and news of every significant development in the child's life. She was pleased they'd called him Delio after Nino's cousin on her side, and said how pleased his uncle was too. Several times she remarked upon Nino's new-found serenity and maturity, patting his hand and arm on the table between them. It clearly brought her much relief after years of worry over what would become of him, her brightest but most vulnerable child. He paused to reflect on the inter-generational transmission of anxiety: *just as her worries ease, mine begin...* A couple of times she reached across the table to stroke his cheek. *I can't ever remember her doing that when I was a child...*

Don Ciccillo returned and embraced his son, clapping him on the back while taking care to avoid his hump. As always they struggled to find things to say. Ciccillo asked about his brother, Nino's Uncle Cesare, who was a civil servant at the Ministry of Finance in Rome; had he been to visit him? No, replied Nino, more sharply than he would have liked, not since Cesare had found out about his politics and refused to answer the door to him some years before. "He knows I'm in Rome, and he can find me at the Parliament building. If he hasn't done so by now, he must have his own good reasons which I have no wish to discuss or put to the test." Don Ciccillo looked wounded, and withdrew into his shell.

Nino's older sister Grazietta, four years his senior and a determined spinster, the quietest and most dutiful of the Gramsci girls, returned from the market and busied herself in the kitchen. Finally, his youngest brother Carlo came home from the shoe shop he ran in town, and sat himself down at the table. The shop was doing well enough to support him and, he said proudly with a glance at their parents, contribute to the upkeep of the family and the household. With opening pleasantries out of the way, the family sat down to a hearty dinner of roast game, shellfish and Sardinian sweetmeats. Grazietta and her mother must have been preparing and cooking for days.

"Well," said Carlo with a wink to his brother, both of them gnawing on rabbit bones. "It's not every day we host an MP!"Afterwards Antonio played with his four year old niece Edmea, Nannaro's child, who had been left with her grandmother to raise. She was a quiet, reflective child, who had barely said a word since he arrived, just observed this funny looking and talking stranger from her place by the hearth. As they played, and Edmea was quickly absorbed in the joy of the game, he could not help thinking of his own small child so far away. Later he wrote to Julka about their game:

> *"She'd been scared by the sight of some big boiled crabs, so I made up a whole story for her about 530 wicked crabs under the command of General Chewbroth, with his brilliant General Staff Fieldmistress Bloodsucker, Fieldmarshall Cockroach, Captain Bluebeard etc., who were foiled by a little band of good crabs Fidget, Thudbang,*

Whitebeard, Blackbeard etc. The wicked ones pinched her on the legs with my hands, while the good ones came scuttling to her defence on garlanded tricycles, armed with brooms and skewers. The whole house echoed to the whirr of the tricycles, the thump of brooms, and conversations between the scampering crabs. The little girl believed it all absolutely, and took the story so seriously she thought up new episodes and twists to it herself. It was all very much more entertaining than receiving the village dignitaries!"

Gramsci stayed in Ghilarza for ten days, from 27th October to 6th November 1924. After their opening salvo of news, he and his mother struggled to establish meaningful contact. He had never been quite so aware of the gulf between their daily lives and outlooks. It occurred to him that as he had grown up she had grown down, or never really expanded her horizons beyond her immediate family and the life of the village, while his had broadened to take in the whole wide world. He was aware for the first time of her intellectual limitations, whereas previously he had always marvelled at how much she had read and remembered. Even in her case, book learning was no substitute for lived experience, of which at half her age he had ten times the amount.

All they really had in common were distant memories, and he was none too sure how accurate they were. He had left Ghilarza as a very young man, in his mind much earlier, while she had stayed where she felt she belonged. Somehow they had missed each other along the way, and failed to establish a proper independent adult relationship. Perhaps, he reflected sadly, parents and children never did get to know each other as adults, however old they grew. Observing Grazietta and Carlo, his only siblings left in the family home, he could not help but see them as still dependent children, and give thanks that he had managed to get away. At least he had not turned out *un mammino*, a mummy's boy, like so many Italian men did. If only he could re-establish contact with these people, his mother especially, on a fresh basis...

It was too late now. Perhaps they had never been that close, and he was romanticizing his childhood, as he was inclined to. There was so much business that would have to remain unfinished. He and his mother had barely seen each other in almost twenty eventful years, either side of the biggest and most catastrophic war the world had ever seen. Many of those years had passed without any form of communication between them. He appreciated the sacrifices she had made for her family, and the true heroism required to hold it together during Don Ciccillo's disgrace. Against all the odds she had enabled her children (Emma sadly apart) to grow up and realise their potential. For most of them, and especially him, Nino, that meant leaving her behind. All her best efforts were bound to result in loss. For her part, she was clearly proud of her successful son, but had no meaningful way of expressing it, or any clear sense of what his success amounted to. Apart, that is, from all the local worthies coming to pay homage as soon as he appeared over the hill.

He was also well aware that his memories of her and his childhood were deeply unreliable, shrouded in impressions that came from sources other than his own mind or true feelings at the time. The proof of this was that he could never arrive at a settled judgement of his life and place in the family. Was it, as he led friends and comrades to believe, a carefree existence roaming the village streets and surrounding countryside, tracking animals and building ships out of sticks; or as he had told Julka, "a sewer of bitterness" in which he was made to feel he never belonged or was fully loved? Perhaps it was all of these things, foremost at different times or operating at different levels at the same time. As for his father, he had always been a remote stranger, scowling in the corner if he was actually there at all. Their shared, all too accurate and reliable memory of his imprisonment and its effects upon the family hung over them all like a dark cloud, always there but never spoken about. It was the one hard reliable fact in their store of family lore.

On Gramsci's final morning in Ghilarza, his mother gave him a traditional Sardinian baby's bonnet to give to Julka for their child. Edmea, who had grown quite attached to her Uncle Nino, scampered at his feet and hung on to his coat, making funny noises and faces to attract what remained of his attention. The family assembled awkwardly, embraced and said their farewells. They parted at the foot of the hill where the boundary of the village met the surrounding orange groves. Antonio set off alone for the station at Abbasanta and the long journey back to the mainland, with a final wave before a bend in the road took him from their view. He would never return to Ghilarza or Sardinia, and his parents would never see him again.

On 3rd January 1925, Mussolini announced that he would no longer be accountable as Prime Minister to Parliament, which he regarded as nothing more than "a bivouac for my Blackshirts." What he called the "fascistization" of Italy would now gather pace, with suppression of all political debate and organisation. The press and the opposition parties would be subject to state control, and local government would be replaced with appointed officials. From his balcony overlooking the Piazza Venezia, *Il Duce* told thousands of delirious supporters, "I consider the nation in a permanent state of war." With all constitutional, legal and political obstacles removed, he set about creating the military-industrial system which would sustain Italy's war on itself and in time on anyone else who stood in the way of his plans and dreams.

The short-lived Aventine opposition collapsed in a shower of windy rhetoric, futile protest and party machinations. In November 1924, the 19 Communist and *terzini* MPs had withdrawn, frustrated by their failure to get the other parties to actually do anything, and returned to confront the Fascists in the official Parliament at Montecitorio. The other opposition parties continued to press Mussolini to "respect legal norms". He responded with a wave of repression, closing down politically suspect clubs and societies, dissolving opposition parties and movements by decree, ransacking the houses of opponents, arresting their occupants and taking over their newspapers. This time Mussolini did not even bother to blame rogue elements amongst his subordinates, but accepted "full political, moral and historical responsibility for every single thing that has happened... If Fascism is a criminal conspiracy, then I am the chief conspirator!"

* * *

"Good evening, Signorina Schucht. At last we meet!"

Tatiana Schucht, the Schucht sister who had been missing the longest and furthest away, presumed by the family to have been left behind in Rome, had finally been located. Since Gramsci had arrived here in May 1924, and bearing in mind promises he had made in Moscow, he had been keeping an eye out for her, or at least for someone matching her description. In truth he had not been looking too hard or closely, because he had plenty else to bother himself with. And the description he had been given of her was oddly vague: smaller than her sisters, a lot like Julka, a bit like Evgenia, not much like Anna, most like the deceased Nadina whom he had also never met. In fact, he now realised with some discomfort, the pale distant figure he had imagined in his delirium of self-pity was Julka was almost certainly Tatiana, whose journey between home and work intersected his own.

Further, though he barely dared admit it to himself let alone to Julka or any of the other Schuchts, he was disturbed by the thought of what he might find and what he might get himself involved in. From what they said about Tatiana, or Tanya for short, this second oldest of the sisters was just as troubled and complicated as the rest of them, with her own spells of "nervous exhaustion" and prolonged hospital treatment. She was also, at almost forty and as far as anyone knew, unattached and unmarried. This was in itself a warning sign. For Antonio, Julka and Evgenia were quite enough to be going on with.

It wasn't him who tracked Tanya down, and set up this first meeting on 2nd February 1925. That was an old family friend, Leonilde Perilli, Nilde for short, who traced Tatiana to the Crandon Institute in the Via Savoia, where she was working as a science teacher. Tanya had been out of touch since 1917, when Apollon finally left Rome to rejoin his wife and other daughters in Russia in time for the October Revolution. For reasons which were never made clear, at least to Gramsci, Tanya had stayed behind. He had subsequently surmised that it was to pursue a medical career of some sort, following her nurse training before and during the war, but no one seemed to know what shape this had taken. From what scraps he heard of Tanya's life in the intervening years, it seemed to have petered out altogether, and been replaced by school teaching and other scraps of temporary work.

He was getting used to unspoken complications in his dealings with the Schuchts, and this new sister seemed to bring a whole new set of her own. Nilde told the family, and Gramsci when they asked her to relay the news, that Tanya had behaved very strangely when she had made contact. She was plainly depressed and downcast, and could only imagine that someone in the family had died, so refused to write to them herself or believe Nilde's reassurances that they simply wanted to know that she, Tanya, was alright.

"Yes," said Gramsci to Tanya now, over a coffee near the Spanish Steps. "I can assure you everyone's fine. Julka and I married in Moscow, fifteen months ago, and our first child Delio was born in August."

"Oh I'm so relieved! I was convinced someone had died..."

Gramsci had seen photographs of Tanya as a very much younger woman. Of all the sisters, she did indeed most closely resemble Julka and, he had thought, rivalled her younger sister's beauty. She was still very recognisably a Schucht, and identifiable from her small size among the gaggle of sisters he had seen in a photo from twenty years ago. *Hardly any taller,* Gramsci noted with some satisfaction, *than myself...* But she had aged much more quickly than the others. She had evidently not thrived in solitude, and whatever she had been through in Rome was etched in her pale lined face and superficially brittle manner. Her dress was far from elegant, functionally sufficient, almost scruffy, with patches and rows of stitching on her coat and skirt. Her Slavic features were somehow less clearly defined than either Julka's or Evgenia's, supplicant rather than defiant, cowed rather than haughty. Perhaps the light and warmth of Italy had somehow faded her, like a photograph left on a windowsill. *One of life's librarians,* was Gramsci's rather uncharitable but telling first impression, *devoting their lives to keeping other people's thoughts in order, inside or outside their heads.*

He warmed to her during their first evening together, as their conversation roamed far more freely than it ever did with her sisters, over politics, their impressions of Rome and their lives here, her work and his. Perhaps there was more to her than met the eye. There must be something about her that had enabled her to strike out on her own and live independently for nearly ten years. They went to eat at a restaurant, and he noticed that she ate as little as the other Schucht sisters, but otherwise appeared to be in good physical health. He had been given to understand that Tanya did not share the family's loyal and thorough-going Bolshevism, but like much else he'd been told about her this was not entirely true. As he wrote to Julka the next day, "politically she's much closer to us than I had been led to believe... The only things she takes exception to are the denial of free speech to the Russian opposition and the imprisonment of some of their leaders. I was very happy to meet her because she is very like you."

They met again several times over coming weeks, over *trattoria* meals – hearty in his case, sparing in hers – in the centre of Rome. He enjoyed her company as much as the food. She reminded him of Julka, but without the secrets and obstacles he always seemed to be confronted with within five minutes of conversation with his wife. "She's like you in so many of her features and movements," he wrote to Julka. "The music of her voice is like the echo of your own. She would be pleased to know I wrote 'echo', because she objected to my comparing her voice to yours, which she says is very beautiful."

For her part, Tanya was charmed and amused by Gramsci, and (despite her worries about what it might entail) glad of this unexpected chance to re-establish contact with her family. "She wanted to buy some shoes for you," he continued in his letter of 7th February to Julka, "with the most terrifying heels. I resisted strenuously, insisting that you would certainly never wear such horrors, and pointing out that she would never wear them either. She wants to buy little shoes for the child too. What a terrible woman, with her mania for shoeing the whole world!"

* * *

Gramsci had told Tanya that he would soon be travelling to Moscow, and she had decided that he could take her gifts of fine Italian shoes with him. There was to be a meeting of the full Executive Committee of the Comintern on 21st March 1925, and he was to lead the Italian delegation. It would be the first time he had been to Moscow, and seen Julka, since November 1923, nearly a year and a half ago. He would at last meet his son Delio, "a real living child, rather than a faint impression on photographic paper", as he wrote to Julka. This time he travelled openly and legally as an MP, which still counted for something, with an ordinary passport, which took weeks to arrange but finally came through at the end of February. His "tail" was obvious but discreet and unobstructive.

He arrived in Moscow in early March, with the first hints of spring: traces of blue in the unrelenting pale grey of the midday sky; the steady drip of melt water onto the pavement from the huge iron downpipes on the more prominent public buildings; the occasional warning crack of overhanging icicles and the rushing roar of loosened snowdrifts on pitched roofs; the emergence from the dirty receding snow of snowdrops and bluebells on patches of communal ground that had once been tended gardens; the emergence of those other kinds of "snowdrops", homeless old people and abandoned children who had died of disease and hunger over the winter, been buried and preserved in the snow and ice where they fell, and now lay or sat blue-faced and stinking till the city authorities' cleansing squads got round to clearing them away and dumping them in some huge hole in the ground on the city's marshy outskirts.

The human detritus of the Revolution, Gramsci thought but dare not say aloud, for fear of offending the Comintern officials who had met the Italian delegation at the railway station and showed them to the limousine that would whisk them away to the Hotel Lux, a shiny new product of the ZIL vehicle factory that had recently resumed production after a seven year hiatus. But not before they were surrounded by a gang of *bezprisorniki,* who clearly thought that Gramsci was some rich kid they could bully or beguile into throwing them some scraps of food or something they could trade for vodka or glue. When they saw the adult face under his fedora and noticed the hump on his little frame, they fled in shrieking terror, convinced he was some kind of golem or folk-devil. They were helped on their way by the shouts and kicks of the security officers among the escort, not to mention their hands reaching towards ominous bulges inside their heavy overcoats. *Even a leather overcoat amongst them,* observed Gramsci, *I thought they'd gone out of fashion with the Trotskyites...*

The Italians left their meagre luggage at the Lux, and were

immediately taken on a round of official receptions and public meetings. There was an air of formality and officialdom about proceedings that had not been present when Gramsci was last here. He tried to convince himself, not wholly successfully, that this was a sign of the increasing confidence, security and authority of the new workers' state. Similarly with the endless tables of statistics and charts and graphs, demonstrating "scientifically" that fully fledged communism was within reach by the year 1935, in ten rigorously planned, realistically timetabled and rationally organised years. The great Lenin's legacy would soon be brought to fruition, capitalism exposed and overcome as the necessary but now redundant phase in human history it truly was. Socialism would be put in its place, if necessary in this one country but eventually, when every other laggard country caught up with the helter-skelter pace of change in the motherland of proletarian revolution, across the whole world.

And all in ten years... thought Gramsci, the snowdrops and *bezprisorniki* still fresh in his mind. He found himself thinking similarly sardonic, not to say heretical, thoughts when he surveyed the banquet all the foreign delegations were assembled at that evening in the Kremlin. *Subjected to, more like*; unused as most (but not all) of them were to such extravagant fare. *We haven't seen much of this on the Via Vesalio, or on Tverskaya Street either...* There were whole roast animals turning on spits, fresh fruit and vegetables he had never seen north of the Alps, and as many different types of caviare as there were species of fish in the sea: "That is where this stuff comes from, isn't it?" he asked an Italian comrade, as they spooned it onto their plates from a silver salver held out towards them by a stiff unsmiling waiter hovering at their shoulder. Again that troubling, necessarily unspoken question: *is this progress or reaction?*

After the banquet he had to attend a late night meeting at the Lux of the Italian delegation, who struggled to stay awake after their long journey and a meal of such unaccustomed plenitude.

It was reconvened early the next morning to ratify the statement on Fascism which Gramsci would present to the *Ispolcom* later that afternoon. "Three o'clock sharp, Comrade Gramsci!" he had been told by the powdered, starched female secretary assigned to the delegation, who came knocking at his door at 8am. Finally, approaching lunchtime, with the statement agreed by the still drowsy Italians, he managed to hurry down Tverskaya Street to the recently restored apartment block where the Schuchts were now living.

He had sent word, so they were prepared and waiting for him. Julka stood at the door, holding baby Delio, with Evgenia standing in the corridor just behind. Apollon and mother Julia Grigor'evna hovered uncertainly further back into the apartment. No sign of the maid, who must have been left behind in Ivanovo Voznesensk. At Evgenia's prompting, Julka held the child towards Antonio and instructed, "A kiss for Papa!" From Julka's stiff formality, Gramsci could tell that the move had been rehearsed. But confronted with their real guest, the preparations counted for nothing. Delio was plainly terrified by the sight of this dark-skinned, stunted stranger, whoever his mother said it was, and recoiled from the touch of his bristly cheek, whining miserably and holding his hand to his mouth.

"Excuse him!" said Evgenia, pushing past Julka and taking hold of the mewling child. "He's not well..."

The child, it turned out, had whooping cough. Every breath, in and out, gave off a high-pitched wheeze, interspersed every few breaths with a harsh cough which shook his whole body and flushed his face and induced yet more miserable whining. His crying face was barely recognisable from the grainy posed photos Gramsci had received every few months.

"We're taking him to see the doctor this afternoon," said Evgenia. "Perhaps you'd like to come?"

"Well, I have to be back at work in an hour or two..." *Still no direct word or look from Julka. What is going on here?*

In the hour or so he spent with the Schuchts, he could not work it out. Julka and Evgenia continued to fuss over the child, while Apollon engaged him in awkward conversation about the Comintern and the political situation here in Russia. Antonio just about had time to convey news of Tanya, her love and best wishes and sincere hope that she might see some of them in Rome.

"She expects us to come to Rome?" said Evgenia sharply.

"Well, I have to say I too was rather expecting Julka and the boy..."

"But how would we travel? We can't just drop everything here! Julka was planning on going back to work full-time."

Still no direct word from Julka, who sat with the baby held tightly to her breast. *Are you supposed to hold them so tightly? Like some kind of shield...*

"Of course they should go to Rome!" interjected Apollon, asserting his authority. "A woman should wherever possible be with her husband, and a child should be with his father."

Evgenia, deeply upset by her father's edict, stormed out of the room.

"Don't worry about her," said Apollon to Gramsci. "She'll come round eventually. Of course she'll have to come too..."

So that was settled. As soon as the necessary arrangements could be made, Julka and Delio – and Evgenia – would come to Rome.

Official business continued to keep Antonio busy during his time in Moscow, and he had very little time to spare for the Schuchts. He managed to snatch a few spare hours on the occasional afternoon and, as the child recovered from his whooping cough, would take Delio in his pram down Tverskaya Street to a pretty little garden reserved for Comintern officials and delegates. There he would play the proud father, as comrades peered into the pram at the tightly swaddled child and cooed over him. The other Italians always remarked approvingly on Delio's olive skin and bush of thick black hair, and how closely he resembled his Italian papa. The child slept on, or looked impassively back. Or screamed in distress and pain, which was Antonio's signal to return to the apartment.

When Delio had been given a clean bill of health, Antonio suggested to the Schuchts that they should give their doctor – an especially attentive and competent female paediatrician – a gift to say thank you for helping the child make such a speedy and full recovery. They agreed, and together Antonio and Julka chose a reproduction of Correggio's *Danae* in one of the art shops that had come back to life near the Kremlin. This was about the only time they got to spend alone, pushing the pram around the centre of the city like normal, proud young parents, and fussing over the child propped up inside it. Julka even cast a few shy smiles in Antonio's direction.

When they got back to the Schucht family apartment, where Evgenia was waiting anxiously at the door and immediately took hold of Delio, they wrote their best wishes on a small card attached to the brown paper wrapping. At the bottom, Antonio and Julka signed their names. Evgenia, who had been witnessing the scene from over their shoulders, then deposited Delio on Julka's lap, signed her own name beneath Julka's, and alongside wrote "the mothers". Gramsci chose not to say anything about this most peculiar behaviour, and the strange web of relationships it implied. But later, as he was preparing to leave with the picture tucked under his arm to deliver to the clinic, and wondering whether he could "accidentally on purpose" dispose of the small card along the way, he overheard Apollon scolding the child back in the living room: "Auntie Zhenya is not your mother! Delio has only one mother, only one mother, only one!"

* * *

Gramsci was back in Rome on 28th April. He saw Tanya the following evening, conveyed the news and best wishes from

Moscow, and shared his concerns about Julka's almost total silence and Evgenia's odd behaviour. To his immense relief, Tanya also found it all very strange, *though* – he thought to himself – *she doesn't seem at all surprised...* She had received a letter from her mother, who said that they had found Antonio "moody" and "apathetic" while he was in Moscow ("I was exhausted!"), that she (Julia Grigor'evna) had been disappointed because he had not brought her chestnuts from Italy ("But I told her they weren't in season!"), that Evgenia objected to his heavy smoking ("I smoked no more than usual!"), and that more than once Julka had been reduced to tears by things he had said or done. Gramsci had no idea what this last was all about – Julka had been largely impassive in his presence, apart from murmurs of pleasure over the reproduction they had bought for Delio's doctor – and he was left utterly perplexed.

He threw himself back into his political work. There seemed to be so much to do, so little time, and so few people to do it. He slept little and poorly, startled awake by something he had to do the following day, then lying awake worrying he would be too exhausted to do it. His headaches, which had almost disappeared in Moscow, returned with a vengeance: a constant dull throb, with regular peaks of pain that would lay him low for useless hours on end. At best they were a kind of ticking in his head, corresponding to the beating of his heart. At moments of uncertainty or acute stress they would speed up, so that it seemed that time itself was running out on him and his few scattered comrades. There were always articles to write for the party press; so many articles, whose quality and coherence he fought like a tiger to maintain. In reality a daily paper, a weekly magazine and a fortnightly review were far too much for a small struggling party like his, but they couldn't close them down for fear of looking weak, losing influence and capacity, or disappointing their still substantial national readerships. Sometimes he ended up writing, anonymously or under some other ridiculous pseudonym ("Raimondo Rocchi" was his proudest creation), almost entire editions on his own.

He was acutely aware of the low political consciousness amongst those few comrades who remained in circulation and active, and even amongst those older cadres in exile or in hiding, whose substantial experience was no compensation for their lack of information and engagement with the contemporary, constantly changing political scene back here in Italy. If anything it was proving a handicap, because these senior comrades were still thinking and arguing in terms of the situation when they had left or gone underground. The party's MPs weren't much use either. They were of variable quality and commitment, and some even bridled at the ten per cent levy the party had agreed they should pay from their salaries towards its costs. One or two refused to pay altogether, threatening to inform the press about "improper use of parliamentary funds." Political organisation and influence was limited or non-existent back in their constituencies, so they couldn't be pressured there either.

Somehow or other, the quality of party organisation, activity and consciousness had to be raised. So Gramsci devised what he called a "Party School", a kind of communist university, based on correspondence courses in history, philosophy and culture, as well as matters of political theory and organisation. Two batches of study material were mailed out in the spring and summer of 1925, both with long introductory essays written by Gramsci and extracts from other Marxist writers edited and translated by him, until it became clear that they were being used by the Fascists – often tipped off by sympathetic *postini* – to identify their communist opponents.

On 16th May Gramsci finally made his maiden speech to Parliament. The Fascists were proposing a new law to restrict public servants' involvement in "associations, clubs and institutes." Its stated target was the Freemasons, but the Communists feared it was also designed to bring their own activities under even tighter state control. Fascism would in the meantime reach an accommodation with Freemasonry, which was too weak to resist but too strong to destroy. Parliament was unusually attentive as Gramsci spoke quietly and steadily, with none of the flights of windy rhetoric they were used to. Even Mussolini was pictured in the newspapers leaning forward with his hand to his ear.

"Fascism simply seeks to supplant Freemasonry as the main source of patronage for official and civil service jobs," Gramsci began. "The so-called Fascist revolution is nothing but the replacement of one set of favoured administrative personnel by another."

"Then why are so many bankers and industrialists against our revolution?" asked Mussolini.

"There are plenty behind you, and the rest will come over eventually, in order to safeguard their wealth and their jobs," replied Gramsci. "They'll join the Fascists as well as the Freemasons!"

Mussolini sat sneering, chin jutting out and arms folded, as his loyal deputies howled their disapproval.

Gramsci continued. "But this is just a sideshow. The real question is why, although the Communist Party has not been declared an illegal organisation, our comrades are arrested every time they are found together in groups of three or more?"

"Just like in Russia!" shouted Mussolini. "In Russia you're very good at rounding people up. Quite right too! At least here we let people out again. We only pull them in so we can get to know them..."

His cronies bayed their amusement.

"You're doing what they used to do in the South before the war," Gramsci said through the hubbub, "when they hired thugs to arrest anyone who voted for the opposition... so they could get to know them."

From across the chamber a voice shouted, "You know nothing

about the South!"

"I am a Southerner," Gramsci responded, then turned back to Mussolini.

"The truth is you know that in order to exercise power you have to place yourself at the head of the class which controls the state. Here is the grain of truth in your muddled, reactionary perversion of Marxist teaching. You could not be leader of the proletariat, so you became a bourgeois dictator. We know your face, we know that trick of rolling your eyes round in their sockets, that mechanical ferocity that was once meant to make the bourgeoisie shit themselves with fear, and that's now turned against the workers. But you can't maintain the pretence forever. The workers in the north and the peasants in the south already realise that the state steals from both alike to reward the bourgeoisie. *Your* bourgeoisie! One day those workers and peasants will unite to consign you and them to the dustbin of history. You may conquer the state, you may change the statute book, you may try to ban opposition, but you cannot prevail over objective historical conditions. Let me say here and now: the revolutionary forces of this nation will survive, and your dark dream will never be turned into reality."

As he finished, the Chamber erupted in massed shouts of fury, and just a few of acclamation. Over the following days, a story circulated that Mussolini saw Gramsci immediately after the debate, drinking a coffee in the parliamentary bar, and approached to congratulate him on his speech. Gramsci, according to this story, just carried on sipping his coffee and ignored *Il Duce's* outstretched hand. When the story got back to Gramsci himself, he scoffed and dismissed it, and wondered to himself why it was that Italians had to turn everything into opera, or worse into melodrama? And why did everything have to be black or white, with no shades of grey in between, and every individual a hero or villain, when most people spent their lives wading around the mess in between? In this case, how likely was it that this proud violent man, with his "rolling eyes" and often stated contempt for the niceties of parliamentary debate, would have risked being doubly mocked by the leader of his keenest adversaries? Or, Gramsci reflected upon his own reputed role in the exchange as compared to his actual feelings at the time, that the awkward débutante MP of a minor and embattled party, winding down over a coffee and well aware of the utter futility of his rhetorical defiance, would have spurned the hand of the most powerful man in modern Italy?

He wrote to Julka soon afterwards:

> *"The Fascists accorded my parliamentary début an unusually favourable reception, heckling rather than just howling me down, so from a revolutionary point of view I started off badly... I am so tired, and have to be very careful in my everyday movements. I'm oppressed by solitude more than anything, partly because of the illegal operation of the Party, which forces us to operate individually and independently. I try to escape this political desert by seeing as much as I can of Tatiana, who reminds me so much of you. But there's no real way of making up for your absence. Everything I see in the world around me reminds me of you and Delio, and so makes me more acutely aware of my unhappiness. I can't even bear to look at babies and small children, who I've always been so fond of, because they just remind me of what I'm missing. But it will pass, because I know that you are coming to Italy. We will recover our energies, and our personalities will grow together as we watch Delio grow up."*

For all the oddities of their last encounter in Moscow, he remained hopeful that they could rekindle the spark of their early days together, re-establish their loving contact and find a new shared focus in their parental responsibility; especially here in Italy, away from the deadening influence of (most of) Julka's family, the chill and the dark of Moscow, and the spreading stench of polemical dispute and factional intrigue emanating from the Comintern and the Russian party. If he could just find the old Julka, the Julka of their huddled conversations at Serebranyi Bor, their walk along the river at Ivanovo Voznesensk, and of their precious few weeks of married domesticity at the Hotel Lux...

* * *

At around this time Gramsci bumped into Victor Serge, who was passing through Rome on some obscure political mission to do with the Balkans. He said he couldn't talk about it, and Gramsci replied cheerfully that he didn't really want to know. Serge brought more deeply disturbing news from Russia. There was what he called "an epidemic of suicides." He had undertaken research in the city hospitals and clinics, and written an article about it for the party press, which was turned down because of its "defeatism". In Leningrad alone, he said, "there are ten to fifteen suicides a day, mostly among the under-thirties." He knew a number of them personally, including most recently the poet Sergei Yesenin.

"I saw him performing in Moscow in 1922!" said Gramsci, with a sudden pang of loss, and fond recollection of a joyous evening in the bustling city with his young interpreter. It might have been a mere couple of years ago, but it felt like a thousand.

"Well, I saw him laid out dead on his bed," said Serge, "like a young soldier dying alone after some bitter defeat. They'd found him hanging with a suitcase-strap around his neck, and his forehead bruised from banging against a heating pipe in his death throes. I saw his last lines, which he'd written in blood because he had no pencil or ink: 'There is nothing new about dying in this life, but there is surely nothing new about living either.'"

It had been clear for some years that Yesenin and his fellow poets and artists of the Great Awakening had lost faith in the Revolution. Serge recalled the last time he had seen the great poet perform, describing himself as "a stranger in my own land... I am not a new man, I have one foot in the past, and yet I wish, I the stumbler, I the cripple, to join the cohorts of steel once more." There, if he was permitted, he would bear witness while "The sickle cuts the heavy stalks, as one cuts the throats of swans..."

"My God," gasped Gramsci, impressed as much by Serge's capacity to quote verbatim from other people's poetry as by the poetry itself, and impelled to a poetic image of his own: "So if that's what the sickle cut, what did the hammer strike?"

"A whole generation of revolutionaries, my friend," said Serge. "And there is much worse to come. We are watching a rebellion of poets turn into a rampage of butchers... I was in the bar of the Hotel Europa a while ago, trying and failing to get drunk and wipe it all out of my mind, when Mayakovsky came and joined us. All right then? I asked him. 'Yes,' he replied, 'but one day I'll blow my brains out. Everybody's a bastard!' And old Vladi's making a good living with official poetry..."

It wasn't just poets and intellectuals suffering from the stifling of revolutionary hope. There was mass unemployment far worse than anything from the Tzar's time, with 150,000 in Leningrad alone. "At least they get a dole of 25 roubles a month on average, which is just about enough to live on, and progress of sorts from the days when they'd have starved to death. But that didn't stop them rioting and burning down the Labour Exchange. Not that you'd find anything about that in *Pravda*...There are beggars and prostitutes everywhere, and an estimated seven million *bezprisorniki*.."

"Yes, I saw them in Moscow..."

"And only enough orphanage places for a few thousand at a time, and they're the lucky ones! They're more likely to be rounded up and sent to prison or labour camp, where they'll be among the first to drop dead from disease or injury because they're so unhealthy and malnourished. We had an outbreak of gang rapes recently, and the rapists' defence was what did it matter if there were four, five or six of them involved? The girls didn't belong to anyone, and besides they would still have got pregnant or diseased if it had been only one..."

An epidemic of rabies was sweeping the country, with mad dogs in the cities and rabid wolves in the countryside. There was widespread racketeering and corruption under NEP: "Twisters start up a fake co-operative. They bribe officials for credits, raw materials and orders. They become the universal middle men between socialized industry and the consumer, and double the price of everything. I tell you comrade, it's a disaster!"

"Indeed," replied Gramsci, growing concerned that his friend might be going just a bit too far, especially when Serge began to equate Russia and Italy, Mussolini and Stalin, "who lords it over the party like some evil puppet-master!" *Just where might Serge be headed? And who might he take with him?* And why did he keep going on about the *Cheka*, when the Special Commissions had been turned into the GPU in 1922, and regularised as a normal secret police within the NKVD, the Interior Ministry? The Interior Ministry his own wife, Julka, had been working for since 1920...

When Serge talked about a wave of what he called "totalitarianism" sweeping across Europe, this was surely too simplistic, and failed to take into account local and national conditions, and the different patterns of economic development and political hegemony in each country and region. Wasn't there a real risk, in this sweeping unhistorical generalization, of the very "totalitarianism" Serge was decrying, in outlook upon if not necessarily ways of running the world? He reminded himself that his friend "the Frenchman" was a close if somewhat critical friend of Trotsky. He sought safer ground by enquiring after Serge's wife and family. That was no better, because Victor's wife Liuba had cracked under the pressure and been certified insane. Gramsci thought it better not to share his concerns about his own wife and her family, not least because they seemed so vague and minor by comparison. Furthermore, he had never told Serge that his own wife worked in the same government department as the cursed "Chekists". He and Serge parted on terms which were not quite so friendly or open as they had been before. They would never see each other again.

* * *

Julka, Delio and Evgenia Schucht arrived in Rome in late October 1925. Antonio found out about their impending arrival quite by accident, at a reception at the Soviet embassy, when a secretary happened to mention that she was looking forward to working with his wife, "Comrade Julia, er... we have been told she's called Schacht; is that right?"

"Well, yes..." he replied, somewhat flustered. "Nearly. It's actually Schucht, with a –u."

"Oh, I'm sorry!"

"Don't worry, it's an unusual surname and a common mistake. It probably was Schacht in the original German, and it changed when her family settled in Russia, and the name was Russified. At least that's what her father told me. I have similar problems with my surname, which was originally Albanian. I get all kinds of spellings and pronunciations..."

"So that must be why your wife did not adopt it?"

"Well, perhaps it was a factor..."

Somehow it had never occurred to anyone, himself included, that Julka would or should take his surname. It wasn't as if it was any kind of asset, and in these days of female emancipation it wasn't unheard of for wives to retain their own name, especially amongst the intelligentsia. He began to wonder about the child. He remembered all too well the fuss over his first name – Lev or Leo? Finally Delio; he now wished they'd called the child

Leonardo – but what surname had he been given? As for the job, well, apparently Apollon had used his party connections to fix something up. The diplomat for whom Julka would be working explained that it was in effect a transfer within the NKVD, though of course the Soviet Interior Ministry was not supposed to be active in a foreign country, especially an unfriendly one, so they would all have to be discreet.

This was the first Gramsci had heard of any of it, the actual date of their arrival or Julka's job, but he didn't want to make too much of it. Instead he tried to exult in the fact that they were definitely coming. And when he thought about it, it showed commendable foresight of Julka to arrange worthwhile employment before she arrived. If her father was able to ease the process with his political connections, so much the better.

"I don't know what to think of this, since I've heard nothing from you about it," he wrote to Julka the next day. "I told Tatiana about the rumour as soon as I heard, and she was so affected by it she couldn't sleep! She does have a tendency to get over-excited, rather like a small puppy! But I am even more excited, if that's possible, at the prospect of you and Delio finally coming to be with me. At last we can start to live like a proper family."

As the date approached, and his excitement and apprehension mounted in equal measure, Antonio received further unsettling news from Tanya. There had apparently been considerable discussion amongst the Schucht family about their living arrangements in Rome. It had been decided, at Evgenia's insistence, that they would all live together. Tanya was told to find somewhere suitable, and that she should move in with her sisters. This despite the fact that she had lived in her own rooms in Rome for over eight years now, and for the last five years had been comfortably settled in the house of the principal of the school where she taught science.

To Antonio's considerable surprise, she told him about her forced move as though there was no possibility of her refusing.

She said she had already found a furnished apartment on the Via Trapani, with two sizeable bedrooms and – luxury of luxuries, especially compared to what the Schuchts had become used to in Russia – its own separate bathroom.

"Well, that suits me," said Antonio, "because the Passarges are moving too."

Tanya looked downcast. He wasn't sure why, and offered a cheering thought.

"And it will be so nice to live with all of you!"

"But Antonio, that's not going to happen..." she said meekly.

Evgenia had further insisted that he, Julka's husband and Delio's father, was not to live with them. She said she had been advised that his presence would constitute a "security risk". If his relationship with them were known, the Italian authorities might revoke their visas.

"But Tanya," he protested. "The police already know that Julka's my wife, because I told them when I was asked to sponsor the visa applications! Who told Evgenia such nonsense?"

Tanya looked back chastened, but apart from a slight shake of the head did not respond. Perhaps she knew no more about any of it than what she had told him already. He decided not to pursue the matter for now, because it was clearly making her deeply uncomfortable. She had enough to contend with, not least the prospect of living with her sisters after all these years of independence. She herself was clearly apprehensive at the prospect. He suspected that Evgenia was making it all up about the "security risk" and their visas, for her own peculiar purposes, but he couldn't query it without challenging her authority in the family. He couldn't risk another crisis, especially now, when they might still decide not to come.

He realised that he couldn't force himself upon them either, so he moved with the Passarges to a house on the Via Morgagni. Just days after he had moved with them, the police ransacked his room. The four-hour search was overseen by Commissioner

Belloni, the deputy head of the Roman police. Belloni was pleasant enough, and engaged Gramsci in long conversation about the legitimacy of Italian claims to Corsica and even parts of the French mainland like Nice and Savoy. But the Passarges finally discovered that their lodger was not a "Professor" after all. There was no question of him moving out, at least for the time being, they said when the police had finally left empty-handed, but they were noticeably less quiet and respectful around him and his room. He decided to spend as little time there as possible.

Evgenia, Julka and Delio arrived at Termini Station, with several heavy chests and suitcases. They also brought a large pram for the child, though – Gramsci noted with delight – he was eager to take his own first faltering steps. When he met them from the train, with Evgenia holding Delio tightly by the hand as they stepped down from the carriage onto the platform, he encouraged the child to "run to Papa!" But the child looked terrified and clung to his aunt, hiding his face in her skirts. *Oh well, he must be tired from the journey, and alarmed by the noise and bustle of the station...* Instead Antonio embraced Julka, "My darling Julka!" She also looked tired and drawn. *Hardly surprising...*A comrade with a small motorised van had offered to transport them and their baggage to the Via Trapani. Once they were safely indoors with their belongings, it was made clear that Antonio's presence was no longer required, though Tanya made a point of saying that he would be welcome as soon as they had settled in.

"Perhaps," she said, turning tentatively towards the stony-faced Evgenia for approval, or rather the absence of disapproval, "tomorrow evening?"

Antonio settled into a pattern over the next few weeks of visiting for dinner in the evening, when he had finished his political duties and Julka had returned from her job at the embassy, and staying there for the rest of the evening. He would have liked to help put Delio to bed, but Evgenia had taken on this and – as he had noticed within seconds of their arrival – almost every other aspect of the child's care. He also couldn't help noticing that Julka seemed to have very little to do with the child, who at nearly a year and a half was fully weaned.

In fact she seemed to have little interest in very much at all. He understood that it was best not to broach her work, so that closed down one substantial line of conversation. He tried to consult her about his own work, or propose joint projects like translations between Russian and Italian, but the best he could hope for was dutiful compliance. After the first few sentences of an article or a communiqué, she would complain about its complexity or a growing headache, and didn't he understand that she was tired after a busy day doing just this kind of thing at work? Once or twice her general air of listless apathy gave way to the morbid outbursts of repressed passion she had always been prone to. One morning, alone in the flat, Antonio and Julka were discussing the circumstances of her oldest sister Nadina's death seven years before. The family had finally received notification of when and where she was buried. Julka insisted that it should be kept from Evgenia, even though Antonio knew from his time with her at Serebranyi Bor that she knew all along that Nadina had died. Julka argued with him to the point of bitter tears. He let the matter rest. At this stage, this and her other strange behaviours were picturesque traits, aesthetically interesting, not the symptoms of sickness.

The whole family – Tanya aside – were plainly not interested in the Italian political situation in which he was otherwise totally, daily immersed. It seemed that the petty squabbles and difficulties of his tiny and ineffectual *Partito Comunista d'Italia* really were nothing compared to the titanic battles going on inside the Russian Party and the wider efforts to construct the new socialist society of the Soviet Union, with which the Schuchts kept in close and interested contact. Julka relayed news from the embassy much more enthusiastically than anything she might say to him. The Schuchts spoke Russian between themselves at home, with its barked and mumbled pronunciations; even in the presence of Tatiana, whose Russian was even more rudimentary than Antonio's. The words which Delio was beginning to form and utter were all unmistakably Russian; the child stared blankly back at his "Papa" when Antonio tried to teach him the equivalent Italian.

If he could coax any clear opinions out of Julka at all, they were generally negative. She was plainly disappointed in Rome, and found it dull and dowdy compared to the gay sunlit city of her youth or even the NEP-era bustle of Moscow. Antonio argued that Rome was never at its best in the winter, when the fogs drifted in from the sea and the ancient stone absorbed and gave off a damp chill, but yes, the economic privations of capitalist adjustment and the political repression of Fascism were having a very definite effect on the atmosphere and range of civic life. Was this what she meant? By then she had lost interest in the conversation. Another time he offered to acquire a camera for her, so she could at least record "outings we might take on fine days", but she seemed uninterested in either the camera or the outings.

She had also given up on her music, saying she no longer found it "useful" to herself or "society", especially now that her livelihood did not depend on it. He said he found this sad, because she had played so beautifully and derived such obvious pleasure and fulfilment from it. She said that he, like all non-musicians, did not appreciate the amount of work, discomfort and occasional pain that music required. She was glad to leave it behind, the aching muscles and tendons and occasionally bleeding fingertips. Instead she had taken up embroidery, following Evgenia's lead, and (Antonio couldn't help noticing) showing a similar lack of talent at it. They also bullied Tanya into joining them, which she did half-heartedly, so that when he called round in the evening he would often find them sitting around their sewing box, fumbling and stabbing at their squares of material stretched tight in their wooden frames. As before, all of their efforts tended to look like lizards, though this time he took care not to say so.

Julka frequently complained that she was tired from her job, that she wasn't used to the work it involved, mainly administrative with very little translation called for because everybody at the embassy spoke Italian and Russian, or to working full-time. She seemed to spend most of her days filing. He tried to show sympathy and support, and suggested that she might try to reduce her hours. This, she said, was out of the question because there was so much to do. She did not want to let down her employers or show anything less than total commitment to their common cause. It might look like dull routine to him, but she was still making a contribution to the proletarian revolution and the building of socialism.

Just once, when he too was feeling especially run-down from work, he allowed himself to respond that if it was "so bloody important" she shouldn't complain about how tired it made her, but this induced more angry tears and a painful hours-long sulk. In fact, Antonio concluded, she was even more withdrawn and impassive towards him than she had been the last time in Moscow. She refused requests to go out with him in the evening but, he noted sourly, was always eager to go out with her sisters or her old friend Nilde Perilli to shows at the Argentina or Adriano concert halls.

What might he have done to offend or alienate her? And what might he do to win her back round, at least to the state of amused interest she had displayed towards him before he left Moscow for Vienna? Passion or even sustained interest might be too much to ask from his wife, but surely he had a right to some level of warmth and intimacy. He sought out Tanya's advice, one late afternoon when he met her coming home from work, and suggested they go for coffee "like the old days". Tanya told him that Julka's Russian doctors had investigated the possible causes of her fragile health before she left Moscow, over and above the general nervous debility that seemed to run in the family. The latest hypothesis was that she might have a form of epilepsy, yet another long-term reaction to her infection in 1918 with Spanish flu.

"This would explain her blank spells, when she goes all glassy-eyed and distant," said Tanya, "and her general air of not being quite all there."

What an odd way to put it, Gramsci thought, *almost poetic*. But thinking over the couple of weeks since Julka, Delio and Evgenia had arrived, the awkward atmospheres and his failure to make proper contact with any of them, Julka in particular, he knew exactly what Tanya meant. As for what he might do about it, all Tanya could suggest was small gifts.

"Julka always did like to receive things from male admirers... But honestly I'm not sure. Antonio, you have to remember that she's even more of a stranger to me than you. I haven't seen her for over eight years, we've all changed a lot in that time, and I don't understand her illness or behaviour either. You at least have been close to her for some of that time. She is your wife. Perhaps you could consider what worked before..."

He thought back over the time he had spent with Julka at Serebranyi Bor and Ivanovo Voznesensk, and then in Tverskaya Street in Moscow, at the Hotel Lux or the Schuchts' apartment. But he found it hard to remember any particular incident or moment when his awkward courtship had achieved clear results. Instead, he just remembered the initial sparks of mutual interest, months of warily circling around each other, and then the huge relief and satisfaction when they both realised they felt similarly towards each other and were free and able to embark on a proper intimate relationship.

It was, looking back, a long seamless process which required little conscious effort beyond listening to their own and each other's hearts. That was the beauty of it, for him at least his first and only experience of a truly loving, unconditional and open-ended relationship with another human being. The very fact that he *didn't* have to think about it was what had made it so special. It seemed so long ago, just two years but in emotional time (*if there is such a thing,* he thought) so much longer. So much had changed since then, including Julka and himself, and not all for the better. In so many ways they now seemed like totally different people. He would just have to start all over again but, following Tanya's advice, be much more calculating and strategic this time.

So he began to take Julka gifts whenever he went to the Schuchts – flowers, sweets, small glass baubles or wooden carvings that he picked up at street markets or in department stores – until one day Evgenia commented pointedly on how much "these unnecessary fripperies" were costing. Wouldn't the money be better spent on the upkeep of the child and the household? Besides, Antonio soon realised that Julka never seemed too impressed by the gifts from her latest "male admirer" anyway. She would unwrap them, examine them cursorily and lay them aside, then look at him blankly as if to say, "What else have you got to offer?" Even the sweets sat there mouldering and unconsumed, in this household of women who seemed to have the diets and appetites of small birds. On several occasions Delio, rummaging and rampaging around the flat, was found with sticky hands and a mouthful of sugar or chocolate, and forced by Evgenia to spit or even vomit them out. Julka's appetite for flattery and seduction and "male admiration" seemed to have waned as thoroughly as for everything else in life.

"Mamma Zhenya" was in firm charge of the family. She did the housework and cooking, neither of them particularly well, and looked after Delio while his Mamma Julka and auntie Tanya went to work. She refused to allow Antonio to smoke in the apartment, which left him – by now a sixty a day man – even twitchier than he would have been in her presence. She called his favourite Macedonian brand, "foul-smelling Turkish donkey manure"; he muttered in response, "Why don't you call it Turkish donkey *shit*? Everyone else does..." She even objected to the smell on his clothes, and insisted that he leave his jacket and coat on the landing, "and stay well away from me!" Antonio needed no further encouragement.

Aspects of her care of Delio disturbed Antonio profoundly. The child was allowed to run riot around the apartment, with no structure or purpose to his time, and no restraints on what he might do or delve into. The mouldy sweets were the least of it. Gramsci regularly had to remove sharp or fragile objects from the child's tight grasp before he broke them or hurt himself or someone else, to the child's howling chagrin, which could only be soothed by "Mamma Zhenya". When Antonio presented Julka with his latest gift, a 400 lire wristwatch he'd bought from a German watchmaker on the recommendation of Signor Passarge, Delio grabbed it and threw it on the ground. When they realised it was broken, the child was allowed to keep it, until even Evgenia realised that he was ingesting its smallest pieces. Gramsci recognised in all this the precepts of Rousseau, whom Apollon Schucht was known to admire and espouse, in the upbringing of this "noble savage". In fact, when old Apollon came to stay in the spring of 1926, he took one look at the situation – in the household, the city and "my poor dear Italy" – and promptly returned to Russia.

Without sentimentalising or harking back to some traditional ideal of family life, this arrangement – with Evgenia setting herself up as "the mother", and Julka and Tanya under her, all three of them self-styled neurotics – just felt all wrong. Antonio would read alarming reports in the paper about the mistreatment or even murder of children, and find himself imagining morbid scenarios of what might happen here. One particular report stayed with him for days, about a woman in Genova who had poisoned herself and her five year old nephew, leaving a note saying that she had had to take the child to paradise with her because she could not do without him even there.

But the worst thing for Antonio was that Evgenia seemed determined to stand between him and Delio, and to poison whatever relationship they might be able to cultivate in already trying circumstances. To begin with, the child had called Antonio *dyadya*, Russian for uncle. He had clearly been coached by Evgenia, and this went on for several days until an outraged Tanya plucked up the courage to object. Evgenia would never let Antonio hold Delio for longer than a few seconds, complaining variously that he was "restricting", "upsetting" or "coddling" him; or that he was going to drop him, adding casually and cruelly that "you of all people should know what that can lead to..." Antonio refrained from relaying the latest medical advice he had received – that his hump and his stunted growth were the result of poverty and disease, most probably rickets, rather than the family myth of him being dropped by a maid – and handed the child back.

Then there were the sleeping arrangements. Evgenia had placed Delio's cot right next to her own bed, on the opposite side of the large bedroom to Julka's. Evgenia claimed her sister would need all the undisturbed sleep she could get after working all day at the embassy. More often than not Delio ended up sharing Evgenia's bed, because at the slightest murmur she would scoop him out of his cot and in with her. Tanya told Antonio that Nilde Perilli had heard from several of her acquaintances around town that Evgenia was passing the child off as her own. Out on walks with him in the pram, or holding him in shops and cafés, she would talk about "my baby", and even about aspects of his birth and infancy which could only have been experienced by Julka. Matters came to a head when Evgenia discovered Gramsci in Julka's bed one morning.

"What are you doing here?" she shrieked, clutching the child tightly and setting him off on another crying bout with her high-pitched tone. The two of them – Evgenia and Delio – looked furiously down on Antonio, two faces locked together in anger, while Julka simply murmured in sleepy protest and burrowed deeper under the covers. After that, Evgenia insisted on Julka moving into the smaller bedroom on her own, swapping with Tanya, in case Comrade Gramsci "forgets himself" again. It wasn't just the risk of the police coming round and finding him there; what if the child should witness his parents "poking about"? Did they not understand the psychological damage that could do to a small child?

All this time, Antonio pressed for some kind of response from Julka, both to his own feelings and needs and to what was going on around them, in what he was beginning to call openly "this peculiar ideological atmosphere." But he just could not seem to break through her fog of reserve. When it became obvious that the gifts were having no effect, he decided that as a matter of routine they should have sex when he visited. They were after all husband and wife, and wasn't this what husbands and wives did? Perhaps this would break through the miasma of confusion and apathy, and bring them truly back together again. So after dinner, he would quietly take Julka by the hand and lead her to her room, ignoring Evgenia's cold stares and tut-tutting in Russian to the child. But even this seemed to make little impact on Julka, who would mechanically undress and go through the motions. *Really,* he would think as he looked down on her, *she's just going along with it again...*

A further unfortunate incident brought what he called their "second honeymoon" to an abrupt end. He arrived at the Schucht apartment early one evening, and as he hung up his coat on the landing, saw Julka sitting alone at her embroidery. *Thank goodness,* he thought, *it looks like we have the place to ourselves*. He decided to surprise his wife, who obviously had not heard him come in, into some unusually animated response, perhaps even an unprompted embrace. He crept up behind her, nuzzled into her neck and put his arms around her and his hands on her breasts, only to find that it was Tanya sitting there. Startled, she shrieked and stabbed herself with her needle.

"Tanya!" he said as they both stood upright. "I'm so sorry!"

His sister-in-law had a look of utter horror on her face – *so much like Julka's used to be, or rather how I imagined as we grew old together* – as she looked past him towards the doorway. He turned to see what she was looking at. There stood Julka and hovering behind her, Evgenia holding Delio, still in their coats and presumably just returned from a walk moments after his own entry, glowering over what had just transpired. They all silently went about their business. The incident was never mentioned again – not even when Antonio mistook Tanya for Julka a further time and called out to her up the stairs of the apartment building – though at least for him it hung in the air like a bad odour. It considerably dampened his ardour, which truth be told was never that fiery in the first place.

In January 1926, he proposed that he and Julka should formally register their marriage with the Italian authorities, in a small ceremony at the Registrar's office in the civic buildings near the Piazza Navona. He hoped, without saying so, that this might reawaken in her some sense of her wifely duties, of the obligations they had publicly made to each other. But there were also further considerations over the Schuchts' legal status here in Italy, not quite as stark (*or as ridiculously self-serving...)* as the ones Evgenia had raised before, but serious nonetheless.

This time, he said, he had heard from a fellow MP who had contacts in the Justice Ministry that the Fascists were reviewing the residence status of foreigners, with a view to tightening up visa requirements and favouring those with some kind of hereditary connection to Italy. This did not include the "Slavic race" where the Schuchts – for all their other cultural and national affinities – would be formally placed under the newly devised framework of ethnic categorisation. In the light of this nonsense, said Gramsci, it would do no harm for him and Julka to have their relationship formally recognised in Italy. It would also clarify the status of Delio "...and any other children we might have..."

"Will there be any?" Evgenia exclaimed at this point, followed shortly by, "And where does this leave me?"

"Well, I'm not sure," responded Antonio, "I'll have to make enquiries..."

But of course he didn't. Tanya's position was straightforward enough; she had after all resided in Italy for all her adult life. But for reasons he could not easily explain, he preferred to leave Evgenia's position – she had been born in Siberia, and was much more clearly Russian in her speech and manners – indeterminate. This time, Tanya witnessed the marriage registration, and Evgenia only found out about it over dinner on the evening after the ceremony. She received the news in her customary stony silence.

Soon after this, Julka informed him that she was indeed pregnant again, and that all being well the baby would be due in August, at around the time of Delio's second birthday. Antonio was initially delighted, but soon realised that early pregnancy added another set of complications to the brittle domestic atmosphere of the Schucht residence. Julka seemed to withdraw even further into her shell, with lots of time in the luxurious bathroom and interludes of solitary weeping face down on her bed. A raised hand, held palm outwards towards him, made it clear that he was not welcome to join her there. Evgenia became even bossier in her solicitousness, keeping an even tighter hold on Delio and even keener eye on any approach Antonio might make towards him or his wife. She already seemed to be claiming this new child as her own.

The best times were actually when Julka and both her sisters had gone out for the evening, and Antonio was left alone to look after his son. He was supposed to put him to bed at seven o'clock sharp, but invariably he kept him up beyond that, playing or telling stories or play-acting like he had with his niece Edmea in Ghilarza. They sat at the family piano, now little played and out of tune for lack of use and attention, and plonked away on the keys. To Gramsci's astonishment, the little boy began making animal noises to accompany the notes, "from the bear's baritone right up to the high notes of the chickens at the other end!" as he reported excitedly to the Schuchts on their return. They didn't seem quite so impressed: "It's late and we're tired," said Evgenia. "I hope you didn't over-excite him or we'll never get him to sleep!"

Or they would work on drawings with Delio's crayons and big rolls of printing paper Antonio had requisitioned "on behalf of the People's Republic of Gramscis" from the party press. Delio's pictures were mostly random scrawls of colour which would occasionally and haphazardly assume some recognisable shape, which his father never failed to point out and praise. For the most part, however, Delio was more interested in the complicated patterns and cartoon-like caricatures Antonio was making with his crayons on his side of the roll. He would look up to find the child staring intently as his efforts took shape, clearly fascinated by the process of pictorial representation – summoning up an image out of nothing, *literally exercising one's imagination* – but quickly look back down at his own drawing when he realised that his father had noticed his interest.

Certain games never ceased to amuse Delio, no matter how many times they were repeated. Almost as soon as Antonio arrived for the evening, the child would urge him to take the wall clock down from the wall – "*Chasy! Chasy!*" in Russian – and move the hands into all their possible positions. To begin with, Gramsci thought the child was learning to tell the time, but when questioned Delio showed no sign of understanding what the time, or time as a concept, might be. He reasoned that it was more likely that Delio, aged barely two, was fascinated by the removal of an everyday household object from its usual place, where it sat untouched, its conveyance to another place entirely, and its transformation into a plaything, something you could actually alter with your hands. The process was far more interesting than the object.

Gramsci bought Delio a small wooden train for Christmas, with passengers that slotted into their seats in the open carriages and a track which could be reconfigured into lots of different shapes; itself an educative activity which Delio could be engaged in, passing his father rounded or straight interlocking pieces on request or even making suggestions of his own. But the child quickly grew frustrated at his inability to manipulate the small parts and figures, and threw one of the carriages at the wall, where it broke in half. *A noble savage indeed,* thought Gramsci, imagining the treatment he would have received if he had behaved like that as a child – *not that we could have afforded something like this* – and bridling against the Schucht family's "Rousseau-ian" prohibition on punishment. Delio was more impressed and fascinated by the fact that his father, after some mild admonishment of the child's destructiveness, managed to repair the carriage with a few judicious drops of glue.

"See, good as new!" he said triumphantly.

The child mechanically repeated the Italian phrase – "Good-as-new, good-as-new..." – as though the magical, adhesive properties of the glue resided in the words themselves.

The Schuchts had brought a stack of children's books with them from Moscow, beautiful examples of the kind Gramsci had seen being printed at the State Library two years before. He looked for, and was disappointed not to find, the translation of Kipling's *Jungle Book* he had watched in production, and resolved to order it for Delio. *For the most part,* Gramsci thought, *the text of these new books do not match up to the stark modernity of the illustrations. A definite shift from the verbal to the visual in Soviet cultural practice* ... The best stories were actually adapted folk tales, which had the satisfying narrative arcs and archetypal character-types of classical literature. Delio seemed to prefer the new, searingly Soviet books, mainly for the constructivist block-style illustrations, which he would point at and touch, as if he was trying to pick them off the page; *surely a sign,* Gramsci thought, *of the illustrator's success and skill.*

Delio's favourite book, which he would never tire of hearing and looking at, was *The Children's International* by Yuri Gralitsa. Though he could have very little grasp of the meaning of the words, which were nothing special anyway, it had especially delightful illustrations of heroic Young Pioneers striding purposefully into the countryside to help with the harvest, and then back into the grateful city with sheaves of golden wheat. *That's one way to depict requisitioning,* thought Gramsci to himself, *and at least we're spared the disembowelled commissar...* When they got to the passages where the Young Pioneers went marching around, Delio would pretend to stride purposefully himself, even while sitting down, thrusting his arms and shoulders forward one after the other and joining in the chant of "Left! Right! Left! Right!" *Young children find nothing quite so captivating as older children,* Gramsci decided, *a glimpse of their own future perhaps...*

One evening he and Delio were halfway through the book when Julka, returned early and alone from her evening out because she wasn't feeling well, appeared at the door to the bedroom. He gestured to her to come and join them on the bed, and she sat on Delio's other side while Antonio finished the book. For just a few moments, Gramsci realised, this would look from the outside like a serene picture of a normal happy family. It would even make a nice children's book illustration: *Mamma and Papa and little boy, settling down lovingly and peacefully for the night.* He tried to hang on to that thought, and the image that went with it. He remarked to Julka in Russian when he came to the last page that it was "...beautifully illustrated and told, and without a doubt ideologically correct", then switched to Italian to say, "But darling Julka, is it any match for *Robinson Crusoe*?"

He thought he saw a flicker of a smile on his wife's beautiful face, and tried to burn this new image even deeper into his memory.

* * *

There were several bungled assassination attempts on Mussolini in the year between late 1925 and late 1926: in November by a former Socialist MP called Tito Zaniboni, in April by a deranged sixty two year old Englishwoman called Violet Gibson, and in October by a fifteen year old boy in Bologna called Anteo Zamboni. With each failed attempt, the Fascist crackdown grew more severe, and the myth of Mussolini's superhuman invulnerability ever more inflated, when the only wound he ever suffered was a slightly bloody nose. "What doesn't kill you makes you stronger!" he declared to the adoring crowds in the Piazza Venezia.

When he spotted this paraphrase of Nietzsche in the *Corriera della Sera* report, this elicited a wry guffaw from Gramsci, who considered the attacks on *Il Duce* utterly counter-productive and "quite mad." As far as he knew, they were the work of isolated individuals, incompetently executed, and nothing to do with the *PCd'I* or any of the other anti-Fascist parties. If anything, he suspected, they were put up to it by dark forces within the state and the Fascist combat apparatus.

Meanwhile Gramsci's efforts to reshape and redirect the *Partito Comunista D'Italia* were beginning to bear some fruit. At its third National Congress, held necessarily over the French border in Lyons, he and his supporters won 91 per cent of the votes for the Executive Committee. They won the same overwhelming majority for the main resolution, "The Lyons Theses", which

Gramsci had put up for debate. Bordiga's faction got 9 per cent and was reduced to an extremist rump. At subsequent EC meetings, Gramsci's positions on the rebuilding of the labour movement and alliances with the peasants and elements of the middle class were also endorsed and put into action.

He was under no illusions over what had caused this apparently spectacular about-turn in the party's politics, in the fifteen months since the disastrous Bordighist jamboree in Como. Above all there was encouraging news from Russia. The *PCd'I* could now bathe in the glow from the worldwide prestige of the first workers' state, which by the mid-1920s was apparently established as a going concern after years of civil war, terror, privation and famine, and rapidly developing under the state-directed capitalism of the New Economic Policy. The USSR was even receiving limited international recognition from the previously hostile western powers, most notably that other "young country" and beacon of modernity: the USA.

This served to obscure the increasingly vicious in-fighting amongst the Bolshevik leadership that followed Lenin's death, apparent only to insiders and contained by the rigours of inner-party discipline. But there were other, more local reasons for this new mood of unity and loyalty in the battered ranks of the *PCd'I*. As Tasca and Graziadei and other right wingers repeatedly pointed out during debate, for polemical purposes of their own, the small vanquished party was almost totally reliant financially and organisationally on the Comintern from which the inveterate splitter Bordiga wished to disaffiliate. If he had prevailed, the embattled party would almost immediately have ceased to exist. Under constant harassment in Italy itself, it kept going on Soviet money and glory.

But behind the façade of Soviet triumphalism, the internal political situation was getting worse in Russia as well as in Italy, with the conflict inside the Soviet Communist Party crystallising into permanent factional struggle between the majority around

Stalin and Bukharin and the opposition minority around Trotsky, Zinoviev and Kamenev. It now threatened to break out of the corridors and meeting rooms of the Kremlin and the Smolny, and infect the wider party and the worldwide movement. The substantive issue was the pace of industrialisation and the collectivisation of agriculture in Russia, which Trotsky, et al., wished to hurry on, as against the continued operation of the NEP free market, which Stalin and Bukharin advocated.

But what concerned Gramsci most was the poisonous atmosphere within the party and the risks to Communist unity. There was a great deal of personal rivalry and animosity, and jostling for the undisputed position of leadership vacated on Lenin's death two bitter years before. The whole shouting match, and the vicious personal denunciations of which it largely consisted, had very little principled political basis. The different sides could amend or even overturn their positions in a moment if it conferred some factional advantage.

In October Gramsci was asked to write on behalf of the *PCd'I* Executive to the central committee of the CPSU about the growing crisis. He wrote that: "You are degrading and may even annul completely the leading position the CPSU acquired under Lenin's leadership. It seems that your absorption with Russian questions is making you lose sight of their international implications..." The Italian party had no desire to tell the Russians what to do, or which course to take in their own internal affairs, but they should always act in a spirit of comradeship and communist unity: "We would like to ensure that the majority of the CPSU central committee does not go too far, abuse its victory and take excessive measures against the minority." All of them had played a leading part in the world's first proletarian revolution, notably Trotsky, for whom Gramsci expressed special sympathy and respect.

Palmiro Togliatti, Gramsci's comrade and friend from Sardinia and Turin, was the *PCd'I* representative in Moscow at the time.

He had abandoned Bordiga some time before and supported Gramsci's position inside the party. They had collaborated closely on the "Lyons Theses" for the *PCd'I's* most recent Congress. But when he received Gramsci's letter to pass on to the CPSU, he considered it ill-advised and withheld it. Far better, Togliatti wrote back to Gramsci, to support the correct (and by implication, winning) position of the majority around Stalin and Bukharin, than dwell on the split itself and its consequences, which might be taken as veiled support for the opposition. And though he didn't spell it out, Togliatti clearly didn't share Gramsci's "sympathy and respect" for Trotsky.

Gramsci sent an angry note by return, rejecting Togliatti's arguments and insisting that he submit the original letter to the Russians. Togliatti continued to suppress it. In Moscow, the Stalin-Bukharin majority pressed home their advantage. Trotsky and Kamenev were expelled from the CPSU executive, while Zinoviev was removed from the Presidency of the Comintern. The objections of the Italians or anyone else were brushed aside, in a climate of stifling conformity. There was to be no further direct contact between Gramsci and Togliatti.

At around the same time, Gramsci received a private letter from his other old friend and comrade from Turin, Angelo Tasca, who was now living in exile in France. Tasca was still involved in the *PCd'I*, albeit as figurehead of its small right-wing minority faction, and representing the party abroad and in Moscow, but with growing misgivings. He described his present "state of resigned discontent" and aired his deep-seated suspicion that he was "unsuited for life as a communist militant." He said his uppermost concern was his wife and child, their welfare and future prospects, and the health of his relationship with them. He was desperate to avoid becoming the husband and father his own father had become, distant and cold and frequently cruel. "You may remember from your own encounters with him..." *Yes indeed*, thought Gramsci, recalling a tall fierce patriarch trapped in mourning for the young wife he had lost at Angelo's sister's birth.

For Gramsci, reflecting privately on his altercation with Togliatti and this dispiriting communication from Tasca, and reports of many other good comrades' disillusionment and despair, it felt like everything was falling apart. But he resisted suggestions that he himself should go into exile, expressed repeatedly and more forcefully by the rest of the party leadership as the general situation in Italy darkened, because "leaders should remain in place until it becomes quite impossible." More than once he made sardonic use of the hoary old nostrum about captains being the last to leave a shipwreck; he would come to regret deeply what he would later call this "perversity of desire" and "heroic vanity", and wish he had got out when he could. He and his fellow communists had not yet fully grasped the severity of the Fascist terror and clampdown, its radical historical distinctiveness, and the political catastrophe about to befall them and their country. Beguiled perhaps by their small local inner-party successes, they lost sight of the gathering storm around them.

Throughout this turbulent period, Gramsci continued to see as much of the Schuchts and his son as he possibly could. One evening, when Evgenia had gone out, he helped Julka to bathe Delio, and delighted in her exclamation "We really do have a handsome son!" But they had not settled in Rome, and were becoming increasingly anxious about the political situation and whether it was safe for them to stay there. Evgenia was making it plain that she wanted to go back to Russia. While Julka continued to work at the Soviet Embassy through the middle months of her pregnancy, she did not dare disagree. *Going along with it again...* Evgenia even suggested that the family's departure would make life easier for Antonio, because he would not have to worry about their safety and would be free to pursue his political duties wherever they took him. At some point, she said, he might even have to go into exile like other *PCd'I* leaders. He could even come to Russia "and live near us." Her final and decisive argument was that Julka would be better off giving birth in the special maternity clinic for party and state officials in Moscow, and that her baby would also be better looked after there. Gramsci, well aware of the deterioration in Italian health services under the Fascists, found it hard to object.

The problem remained of exactly how they would travel, and get across the border without the appropriate documentation, which would be very difficult if not impossible to acquire. They needed a ruse. So in late July, Evgenia, Tatiana, Julka and Delio travelled as holiday makers to Trafoi, a resort near Bolzano in the Alto Adige region of north eastern Italy. Julka crossed the border alone on 7th August, reached Moscow three days later, and gave birth on 30th August to another boy, Giuliano. Meanwhile Antonio had joined the others at Bolzano, and enjoyed a couple of relatively carefree weeks with Delio. He wrote to Julka: "We played a lot. I made some little toys for him, and we lit fires out in the fields. There weren't any lizards so I couldn't show him how to catch them."

Without Julka there, Evgenia also seemed much more relaxed and unobstructive. There was just one moment of unpleasantness, when he tried to teach the boy a ribald Sardinian song, *Lassa sa figu Puzone* ("Leave the fig alone, bird"), and Evgenia realised the double-entendre. "The things you try to put in that poor child's head!" she said, scooping him up and away.

Evgenia left with Delio for Moscow in early September 1926. Antonio would never see them or his wife Julka in person again, or meet his second son Giuliano at all. At the end of October he travelled to Genova for a secret meeting with a representative of the Comintern, Jules Humbert Droz, who was to explain the controversy in the Russian party to the *PCd'I* Executive and try to allay their concerns and fears. Gramsci was eager to attend, to receive a clear first-hand account of what was going on in Russia, and to clarify the *PCd'I's* position in return. But on the way there, he was intercepted by the Milan police and advised by an Inspector to return to Rome. There had been yet another attempt on Mussolini's life, and the police could not "guarantee your safety, Signor Gramsci." Antonio had a definite sense, which he tried hard to dismiss as the product of his own gnawing fear, of the net closing in.

On 5th November the government cancelled all passports and ordered border guards to fire on any illegal fugitives. All anti-Fascist publications were suppressed, and parties and organisations dissolved. Opposition MPs were expelled from Parliament, on the spurious grounds that they had absented themselves during the Aventine period (doubly spurious for the Communists because they had returned long before the others). On 8th November 1926, the police began to round up Communist and other opposition MPs and activists.

After an afternoon and evening of frantic messages to make his escape to Switzerland according to a pre-arranged plan, which Gramsci persisted in ignoring, he was arrested at 10.30pm at the Passarges' house on the Via Morgagni. He had been under close round-the-clock surveillance for several days, so more than likely would have been followed and captured wherever he'd gone. The MPs' parliamentary immunity and other legal safeguards, which they had thought right up to the last moment would protect them, were wholly disregarded. The "exceptional measures" were to be applied retroactively, to a time when the Communist Party was still legal and represented in Parliament; a juridical nonsense which summed up the bold and sweeping "totalitarianism" of this next phase of Fascism.

The communists were to be put before special tribunals created by decree for disposing of all opposition to the Fascist regime, superseding all established legal and juridical procedures, and staffed by members of the Fascist militia and army officers. These tribunals were empowered to impose summary terms of *confino* or "internal exile" for up to five years at a time.

Their conditions would be more relaxed than ordinary prison sentences – with subsistence allowances, provision for private accommodation and even for detainees' families to join them – but crucially would remove them from political life, disperse them to the remotest parts of the country, and prevent them escaping abroad. Mussolini was pictured on his balcony overlooking the crowds in the Piazza Venezia, smiling widely and rubbing his hands.

Part Two: Experiences of Prison Life

"I don't want to talk about my thoughts about all of you and the children; this part you must imagine." Antonio Gramsci, letter to his sister-in-law Tatiana Schucht, 23rd May 1927

"Our years of darkness were his years of stubborn resistance." Victor Serge

"You know, writing has to replace conversation for me, and I have the impression I'm actually speaking to you as I write!" Antonio Gramsci, letter to Tatiana Schucht, 19th March 1927

"Half-winged, half-imprisoned: this is man!" Paul Klee, Pedagogical Sketchbook 1925

"Tonight I committed suicide. Of course I only dreamed it, but with such clarity of detail that on waking I looked at my wrists to see the stigmata. Why did I want to die? No special reason: weariness. I had that morning a long talk with the secretary of the party that left me feeling sick." Angelo Tasca, diary entry 13th February 1929, on being expelled from the Partito Comunista d'Italia he had helped to found.

"Gramsci's language was as remote as possible from the usual baroque rhetoric, the prolix emotionally emphatic style of the official Italian literature of the day. The writing was meticulous, dry, tight,

often twisted in on itself and obscure, but always stubbornly clamped to the argument at hand, indeed relentlessly turned to ideas and objects, with no space left for sentimentality, self-pity or the like." Lynn Lawner

"I totally lack atmosphere. So I must work in a solitude so total that I can't describe it and you can't conceive it. It oppresses me never to be able to consult anyone, to hear a living voice, discuss an idea or a text. Only my old prisoner's habits allow me to work like this. And so I continue... but don't think for a minute that I have made my peace with this." Victor Serge, letters to Marcel Martinet, 1930

"The most common type of appeal from urban citizens to the Soviet state was for help in tracing an absent husband and collecting family support payments." Sheila Fitzpatrick, Everyday Stalinism

1926 -1928: Rome, Ustica, Milan, Rome

The conditions of the political prisoner – lodgings and sustenance, privacy and personal hygiene, correspondence and visiting rights, writing and reading materials – are in almost every respect superior to those of the ordinary or "common" criminal. The authorities thereby acknowledge that within the normal legal framework of civil society the political prisoner has done nothing wrong, and that he is detained only for their own narrow purposes.

For his part, there can be no question of guilt or remorse in the traditional legal/penal sense; only regret at not having taken the necessary steps to evade capture. In their treatment of him, the authorities reveal their relative brutality or sympathy, malice or dispassion, consistency or arbitrariness, sensitivity or indifference to public opinion; and they express the starkest judgement of the humanity (or lack of it) of the regime.

After his arrest on the evening of 8th November 1926, under the "exceptional measures" introduced four days before, Antonio Gramsci was taken to the Regina Coeli prison in Rome. For the sixteen days he spent there, he was kept in absolute solitary confinement and subject to the most stringent prison discipline. His guards knew exactly who he was, and would mutter under their breath or refer to him amongst each other as "you/the bloody commie bastard" and other such epithets. They were plainly under orders to shock him into a full realisation of his dire predicament.

Gramsci drew some quiet satisfaction from the fact that he was still regarded as important and dangerous enough to warrant such treatment. This was an arena of battle. He was an active combatant in the political front-line of the class war. He had simply been unlucky, and lost this latest engagement. His cause was just and strong. He should remember at all times, and remind everyone else, that he had done nothing wrong. Apart from opposing the government, that is, which in normal circumstances and in most parts of the civilised world was not considered a crime.

He and his party had not taken up arms or committed any kind of organised violence, apart from isolated and largely ineffectual token gestures at self-defence. Personal attacks on Mussolini and other individual fascists had been carried out by other people, always alone and sometimes deranged. They were disowned by the communists, and condemned as utterly counterproductive. This was despite the sore provocations of the last few years and the urgings of their own hotheads, who would continue to urge "insurrection" from the safety of exile or provincial obscurity but did not constitute any actual threat.

For the moment, the priority was simple survival. The communists would endure, and maintain a presence inside and outside the country. For all their misgivings and regrets, above all over their failure to anticipate and pre-empt what was coming, they would prevail sooner or later, and regain their liberty and legal rights. "I will not give in," Gramsci found himself repeating, day after day of his solitary confinement, to keep up his resolve. At this stage, the conviction of his innocence fuelled his stiff sense of grievance and his calm determination to resist. For his first three days at Regina Coeli, Gramsci was kept in a filthy cell crawling with bugs, with nothing to read and only basic prison rations to eat. When he was finally and officially put "on payment", a simple kind of credit that was deducted from the political prisoners' subsistence allowance of ten lire per day paid by the government, he was able to buy food and supplies, "victuals" in prison terminology, from the prison canteen. He was then transferred to a cleaner, fumigated cell, with fresh sheets on the bed, and simply but adequately furnished with "barrack accessories". It also had an electric light that, to his considerable frustration and annoyance, he couldn't switch off in the night, forcing him to try to sleep with his hands over his eyes.

The hour's morning exercise was spent alone in a circular courtyard divided into segments by very high walls, supervised by sneering guards on top. "Once, just for a bit of variety," he wrote to Tanya, "I was kept out there for half an hour in the pouring rain." The cells were regularly inspected for signs of attempted escape, with guards bustling about checking the window bars and the door hinges. This included a nightly inspection at 3am, which made it hard to get back to sleep. For nearly three weeks, these gruff strangers were the only people Gramsci saw. All he had for entertainment or simple distraction were scraps of conversation through the walls or from opposite cells, swiftly suppressed if the guards overheard. At this stage he was utterly unaware of how long this would go on, but half-suspected that he was in some kind of holding pen while the authorities decided what to do. He took to describing the experience to himself as "my holiday in hell", which seemed to provide some sardonic comfort.

On 19th November Gramsci was informed that he had been condemned to the maximum sentence of five years' *confino*, internal exile under the supervision of the police. There was no further explanation or detail, or possibility of appeal, but he overheard one of the guards say that he would be going to the Italian colony of Somaliland. This would involve a voyage of almost two months in chains, crossing the equator, which he very much doubted he'd survive. In fact he was informed on the 24th that he would serve his sentence on an Italian island, at that stage unspecified. On the 25th he travelled by train to Naples, in the company of four comrades, linked by chains and manacles. Their *carabinieri* escort were much more respectful and correct than the prison guards, and allowed free conversation and the sharing of food and cigarettes.

This was Gramsci's first proper human contact since his arrest, and he made the most of the opportunity to catch up with the news and simply remind himself what the company of other people felt like. The group spent two nights in Naples, then on the evening of the 27th went by boat to Palermo in Sicily. There they stayed in relative comfort, in a house overlooking Monte Pellegrino, while other groups of political prisoners gathered for embarkation to their final destinations. Gramsci discovered that he and most of the others, including his old comrade and more recent adversary Amadeo Bordiga, were bound for the island of Ustica, north of Sicily and many miles from anywhere.

Because of rough seas, the voyage to Ustica had to be attempted four times. This was a real torment. "Just imagine," he wrote to Tanya, "reveille at 4 in the morning, the formalities of handing over money and various valuables and other objects to be deposited; then, handcuffs on, a prison van to the harbour, the climb down to the boat which takes us to the ship, then clambering up the ship's ladder to get on deck, then down another ladder to the third-class compartment. All this in handcuffs, and chained to three others. At 7 o'clock the steamer leaves and sails for an hour towards Ustica, pitching and rolling like a dolphin, then turns back because the captain considers it too risky. Then we go through it all again in reverse, back to our cells but by then it's gone mid-day and too late for lunch, so we don't eat till 5 o'clock, having had nothing all day. This whole caper four times, till we finally arrive at Ustica."

Once on Ustica, on 7th December, life settled down and improved considerably. For now, the political internees were pretty much left to their own devices, as if having rounded them up and shipped them to this remote island the Fascists weren't sure what to do with them next. More than once, walking the hills or sitting in the weak winter sunshine, Gramsci remarked sardonically to a comrade, "I could get used to this..." He gained weight and, for him, slept well. His headaches eased. It began to feel like a proper holiday. To Tanya he wrote, "Ustica is much prettier than it looks in the picture postcards I will send you. It's a small village of the Saracen type, picturesque and colourful. I feel perfectly well and that my stay here is ridding me of all my old aches. I really needed to take a long rest." He asked her to convey his good news to Julka: "I wouldn't want her worrying unduly." In a photograph taken of him and his comrades on Ustica, which was sent abroad and circulated around the party leadership in exile, Gramsci looked happy and relaxed.

At most there were around thirty communists in *confino* on Ustica. The six most prominent – including Gramsci, Bordiga, Virginio Borioni and Enrico Tulli, who was soon joined by his wife – had a house to themselves, with three bedrooms, a kitchen, a wash room and a terrace overlooking the beach. From there they could gaze out at the sea by day and up at the sky at night, and marvel at the changing colours and moods of the water or the countless stars and brilliant moon. The weather on this isolated island was mild, but it rained frequently, which created double or even triple rainbows of the most extraordinary size and vividness. They bought their food and provisions with their pooled ten lire a day allowances, and prepared their own meals communally. Gramsci wrote to Julka on 15th January, "It's my turn today to act as waiter and kitchen-porter. I don't know yet whether I'll have to peel the potatoes, clean the lentils or wash the salad. My débute is awaited with much curiosity; for some reason they don't think I'm up to it! Several comrades have offered to take my place, but I'm insisting on doing my bit!"

The "politicos", as they were referred to by themselves and everyone else, were subject to a loosely enforced night-time curfew. But they were otherwise free to roam the island, an area of around eight square kilometres of mostly scrub and bare rock. Of its permanent population of roughly sixteen hundred, around a thousand were islanders of Sicilian extraction, identified in the old demotic Italian of these parts as *Christiani*. Fully six hundred were ordinary criminals from all over the country, *confini* to others and *soldati* (soldiers) to themselves. Both criminals and islanders were decent and hospitable towards the *politicos*. It was as though the new ideological dispensation of the mainland had not yet reached this far out, or had tarried at least some way behind its exiled opponents, hovering over the sea like one of those peculiar flying machines its more artistic advocates were always going on about. *Perhaps Fascism would never wholly arrive here,* Gramsci reflected, *like electricity or motor vehicles.* Ustica had been left behind by the modern world, and by any of its inhabitants that had the means and the gumption to leave. Those that remained, permanently or temporarily, were united in suspicion and contempt for the bosses and big shots of "the mainland", *by which they are as likely to mean Sicily as Italy!*

Gramsci was fascinated by the ordinary criminals or *soldati*, their habits and pastimes, regional identities and moral codes, and sought out their company whenever it was permitted and safe. That usually meant catching them on their own, well away from the prison guards who watched over them loosely, or the fellow convicts who kept a much closer watch. There was no paid work for most of them, he discovered, so they relied on the ordinary criminals' *mazzetta* (state handout) of just four lire a day. Most of this was spent on wine, so drunkenness and alcoholism were common. "They would sell the shirts off their backs for a drink," he wrote to Tanya, "and many appear to have sold their shoes and jackets too." They borrowed more from moneylenders among their fellow prisoners, at a weekly interest of thirty per cent, so ended up paying over almost all their *mazzetta* every week, with just a single lira retained for basic subsistence of pasta and herbs. It was not unusual to see these particular wretches supplementing their minestrone with grass from the fields. The interest was collected in full and on time by the money-lenders, surrounded by hulking lackeys "…who would disembowel their great grandfathers for a drink; so, the indebted convicts are consigned to a downward spiral of obligation and decrepitude."

As well as a much smaller allowance, the common criminals were subject to much harsher treatment from the police and prison warders, with frequent beatings and solitary confinement. They had to observe a stricter curfew than the politicos, from 5 in the evening till 7 in the morning, locked up for the night in large dormitories, where they played cards for what remained of their pathetic *mazzetta*. There were four distinct subgroups. The Northerners were mostly burglars, pickpockets or petty thieves and fraudsters. The Romans were tightly organised and loyal to each other, even those amongst them who acted as informers. The Southerners were divided into two distinct, mutually hostile sub-groups: the Neapolitans and the Sicilians.

Gramsci listened intently as a convict from Palermo gave him this ethnographic survey on a stroll along the Ustica beach one mild mid-December afternoon. Of particular significance to this fellow were the different groups' attitudes towards knife-crime, which was his speciality. The Northerners had no time or use for it, he said; the Romans and Neapolitans could look after themselves in a knife fight if they had to; but the Sicilians had elevated the use of the knife and the drawing of blood into a highly ritualised code of honour. "This fellow," he wrote to Tanya, "was very proud of having inflicted a wound on the boss who was mistreating him. It had been measured as ten centimetres deep, and ten centimetres it was, not a millimetre more or less. This was his masterpiece, and it filled him with intense pride..."

There was also a kind of intermediate group, known as "the Bedouins", from the Italian colonies in north and east Africa. It was never entirely clear what their "crimes" amounted to, traditional property theft and personal violence, or acts of rebellion against the colonial authorities. It all seemed to amount to the same thing, a kind of indiscriminate subaltern resistance, very like the old "brigandage" of Sardinia. They didn't seem to differentiate amongst themselves either, Gramsci observed, between *politicos* and *soldati*. The condition of "outlaws" in the colonies, as in much of southern Italy, indiscriminately covered a multitude of sins.

One particular Bedouin by the name of Haussiet took a fancy to him, would join him for coffee and tell stories from the desert in exchange for tales of Sardinian mountainsides and Russian winters. Their store of anecdotes for the moment exhausted, they would fall into an easy silence. For hours on end the Bedouin would sit and watch Gramsci reading and writing. He especially enjoyed looking at Gramsci's family photos, and complained that his wife was so stupid that she would never think of sending him photos of their son. Gramsci wondered whether this wouldn't offend one of the precepts of Islam, but the Bedouin said it was alright because Kemal Ataturk, the founder of modern Turkey, said so.

Of the indigenous islanders or *Christiani*, what caught Gramsci's attention most was their attitude towards animals. On the one hand their donkeys, their only means of freight or transport, were large and extremely tame. He took this as "a tribute to the kindliness of the inhabitants", in stark contrast with his own village of Ghilarza, where "the donkeys are half-savage and don't allow anyone near except their own master." On the other hand, on Ustica he witnessed "the arrest of a pig which was found feeding illegally in the village street and was led off to prison like a common thief... The way of arresting the pig was most amusing too. They got hold of it by its hind legs and pushed it forward like a wheelbarrow, with the beast screaming like a fiend!"

When he tried to buy ten packets of Macedonia cigarettes with a fifty lire note, the village tobacconist was dumb-founded and struggled with the change, because she was only used to selling cigarettes to convicts one at a time. "So she had to perform the difficult feat of multiplying the individual price by ten times twenty!" The prison authorities quizzed him about a letter from a friend offering to send him a radio, and "for security reasons" refused to sanction it. A few days later the government-appointed *Podesta* of Ustica himself came to tell Gramsci that the municipality would purchase the radio set for him, because he had been to Palermo several times and seen for himself that it wasn't possible to send outward messages with an ordinary wireless.

Gramsci was surprised by how well he got on with his old comrade and more recent adversary, Bordiga. Their common present plight appeared to supersede their several previous years of bitter animosity and dispute. What had seemed like bombast and self-importance in old Amadeo became in these straitened circumstances kindly affection, good humour and quiet efficiency. Bordiga remarked on Antonio's distinctive step first thing in the morning, that it was "the step of a man who has not yet drunk his first cup of coffee", sluggish but somehow impatient at the same time. Gramsci was much taken with this character sketch, and relayed it to Tanya. He further noted Amadeo's obsession, "characteristically Neapolitan", with food – in stark contrast to his own general indifference – and the iron conviction that you could tell from anyone's manner or speech whether their most recent meal was a good one.

In the evening, they played cards with their house mates, the first time Antonio had ever played. Amadeo assured him that he had it in him to become quite a dab hand, "if not a proper card sharp!" They argued amicably about the order and shelving of their rapidly growing library of books and newspapers. Antonio wanted to do it by subject and date, while Amadeo went by size and shape, with the result that Antonio complained he could "never find anything in this dreadful symmetrical mess!"

Together they organised a school for the other politicos, modelled on the communist "correspondence courses" Gramsci had organised back in 1925 (and the old "intransigent" Bordiga had scoffed at). There were three basic levels, depending on students' previous education, consisting of grammar, mathematics and basic science. The students had high intelligence and practical understanding but for the most part little formal education, so they "lapped it up like eager children." On top of that there were extra courses in history and geography, French (elementary and intermediate) and German for those who were capable of them. They used textbooks ordered by Gramsci from Sperling and Kupfers, a bookshop in Milan, on an unlimited credit account opened by one of his old friends from Turin, Piero Sraffa, now an Economics Professor at Cambridge University in England.

The courses were open to officials and inhabitants of the island, who also sought and received help in the upkeep of the place. The tower clock, which had not worked for six months, was repaired by a communist watchmaker from Bologna. Electricians undertook to install lighting, and builders planned a landing platform for the ferryboat so it wouldn't have to take its chances against the rocks. From there, they would be able to watch out for its four times weekly arrival (Mondays, Wednesdays, Fridays and Saturdays), with its precious cargo of mail. Its frequent non-arrival due to bad weather was the cause of crushing disappointment and, Gramsci wrote to Sraffa, "a certain melancholy settling on every face."

The ferryboat and the post it delivered were of course Antonio's only connection to the vast and terrible world he had recently been plucked from, his fragile link back to his birth family and the new family he had just begun with the Schuchts. At this stage both Julka and Tanya were writing regularly, but with quite different tones and subjects. Antonio's responses were similarly differentiated, easy and flowing with Tanya, wary and formal with Julka, whom he increasingly tended to address, refer to and think of as "Julia". To some extent this was governed by Tanya's continued residence in Italy, far away but at least in the same country, and her own admission of a growing sense of distance from her family. This contrasted with Julia's re-immersion in her old life in Moscow, not to mention her preoccupation with her two small children, *however much of that she is allowed by her older sister...* Julia regularly excused the rather cursory, scribbled nature of her forwarded notes by reference to the "fuss and racket" the children were making. But it also reflected Antonio's growing attachment to his sister-in-law and parallel estrangement from his wife.

His own early prison letters to Julia, or "Julka" if he was feeling well-disposed or making a special effort to reach her, consisted of homilies and pep-talks ("we two are still young enough to see our children growing up, all of us together") and fond reminiscences of their limited time together – the later months of 1923 and the spring of 1925 in Moscow, the first six months of 1926 in Rome – and of the much more limited periods within them which could be considered truly good times, a few scattered days and weeks which he could list and recall in fine detail. He soon ran out of things to write to her, and had to apologise via Tanya for the infrequency and "childish hesitancy" of his letters. It was partly, he reasoned, from the dull dispiriting realisation that they would pass through at least three pairs of hands and eyes before they reached hers, what his fellow politicos referred to as "real passion killers." Over the years this would evolve into what he called "a prison style of writing", guarded and stiff, full of hints and allusions he could only hope their recipient would understand or decode.

First there was the prison governor, to whom every item of correspondence with the outside world had to be submitted and, if anything caught his eye, explained. This caused a particularly absurd if amusing incident when Julia wrote to Antonio about Delio's developing sense of direction. She described the child lying in bed in a north-south position, declaring that in the direction of his head lived people who used dogs to pull their sledges across the ice. To the left was China and to the right Austria. His legs pointed to the Crimea and so on. The governor interrogated Gramsci for over an hour, without letting him read the letter, about the secret messages it contained: "What's this about Austria? Who are these people whose dogs pull them along?" Gramsci tried to explain, still without reading what Julia had written, until he finally exclaimed, "Aren't you married? Surely you understand how a mother might write to her distant husband about their child!" The *Direttore*, married but childless, handed over the letter without another word.

Then there was Tanya, who would enclose his letters to Moscow with her own, because he was not allowed to write direct from prison to the Soviet Union. It would be only natural if she glanced at them. Finally, he was sure, his letters would be scrutinised by the Foreign Relations Department of the GPU, with any political or otherwise sensitive information referred on to the Comintern and the *PCd'I's* "External Centre" based in Paris, plus any other agency which took it upon themselves to snoop for who knows what nefarious purposes. But beyond all this, there was the censor in his own head, wondering what and how much Julia/Julka could take, and how she would react to any particular item. More broadly, it is hard to write freely to someone you cannot feel sure will actually be interested in you and what you have to say, as by now he generally couldn't with Julia, this beautiful stranger who had seen him at his most open and vulnerable but had given so little of herself away.

When he did write, he tried to reassure her that he was physically fine and in good spirits. He was aware of reports of his poor health or even impending death circulating abroad as part of the campaign of protest against his detention. These politically motivated fabrications annoyed him intensely. As he wrote to Julia: "The truth is bad enough; why can't they just stick to that? In fact I'm probably in better health than ever!" His only illness, aside from his usual headaches and nervous debility, was a slight cold which he got over in a couple of days. Other comrades were having a much harder time of it, he told her: "Molinelli fainted three times in one night and suffered convulsions lasting as long as twenty minutes. My room-mate Pietro Ventura has wild nightmares that make him howl and jump about in his bed." He pleaded with his wife for more detailed letters, especially about the children, their development and illnesses, and for any photographs of them she could send. On the other hand, he advised her not to write anything which might cause the letter to be held up even further during its complicated transit: "We must stick to trivialities!"

His letters to Tanya were much franker and fuller, with detailed references to recently shared books and fulsome gratitude for gifts and supplies: "When I saw your writing on the first bottle of coffee I received, I felt like a little boy again." He even discussed the difficulties of personal writing under censorship, in particular, "...a sort of modesty; I don't care to write about certain feelings, and if I try to tone them down, I feel like I'm acting like a church elder!" She sent him much-needed warm winter clothes, a woollen jacket and socks. This prompted more profuse thanks, as well as mild rebuke that she should stick to what was allowed and not send things like chocolate and gingerbread that would simply be confiscated "and end up being passed around the police station!"

He began to outline to her his plans for captivity: "1. To keep healthy. 2. To study German and Russian systematically. 3. To study economics and history." He requested books he felt he would need, as well as personal equipment: "a safety-razor with extra blades, nail-scissors and a small file. I also need a bottle of aspirin in case the strong winds here give me toothache." He did not spare her the details of his various torments, from his recurrent ailments to his awful journeys between prisons. He complained if she went longer than a week between writing, "...because it's only from you that I receive regular letters. When there's no letter from you for such a long time I feel so isolated, as if my link to the outside world is broken altogether." In subsequent letters he would apologise for complaining, and beg for her indulgence and understanding. This felt like a real, ongoing relationship, with a present and a future, rather than (as with Julia) something that belonged firmly in the past and now largely consisted of reminiscences and formalities.

After just six weeks and two days of tolerable and recuperative *confino* on Ustica, Gramsci was suddenly transferred back to the mainland for trial by the Special Tribunal for the Defence of the State. This had been set up to deal with the most prominent detained communists. His first five year sentence of *confino* would be superseded by a much more formal and no doubt lengthy period of imprisonment, after a "show trial" which would have all the trappings of the judicial process but none of the inherent uncertainties of its outcome. The Fascists had apparently made their minds up what to do with their opponents. His journey to Milan took nineteen days, as a common prisoner with other convicts, part of it "tied to a criminal with epilepsy on a chain a hand long" (he later wrote to Tania and Julia). It exacted a toll on his health and his spirits from which he would never fully recover. *So much for a holiday...* He was now back in purgatory. It was as if he was being punished for having had such a good and restful and interesting time on Ustica. Its physical and emotional benefits were abruptly thrown into reverse. The authorities – probably all the way up to Mussolini, who notoriously took a close interest in such matters – had decided that the anti-Fascist opposition should be broken as individual human beings as well as collective political threat.

The *PCd'I* leaders in exile were at the advanced stages of an escape plan whose details were known only to Bordiga. The most prominent communists, Gramsci foremost amongst them, were to be collected from Ustica beach on a moonless night by a sympathetic fisherman, and transferred to a steamer which would take them first to French Corsica for registration as political refugees, then on to freedom in exile in Marseilles and Paris. In fact, given the exiled leadership's distance from Italy, and their limited resources and experience at this kind of thing, it was always pie in the sky. They even misread the lunar calendar. Gramsci was removed by the prison authorities from Ustica on 20th January 1927, under a bright half-moon on the rough sea passage to Palermo, just a few days before the escape plan was to be implemented.

* * *

> *"Imagine a huge worm creeping from Palermo to Milan, continuously reconstituting itself, leaving one ring in each prison and picking up new ones, shaking right and left before it settles into its next stage. At each stop, the worm deposits its cargo of prisoners for two to eight days in pigsties called transits, amidst the accumulated filth and poverty of generations. You arrive exhausted, dirty, unshaven, your wrists raw from long hours in chains, your sunken eyes stinging from sleeplessness and the strain of concentration. You throw yourself onto an ancient straw mattress, wrap your face and hands in soiled towels to keep off the bedbugs, and cover yourself with thin blankets for meagre protection against the cold. When you leave you feel dirtier and more tired than ever, and arrive at the next transit with wrists livid from the cold irons and the weight of the chains, and aching arms from carrying your own baggage..."*

So wrote Gramsci in his first letter from Milan to "My dear ones" Tanya and Julia. It was never received, but retained by the prison authorities because of its exposure of prison conditions and used as evidence in his trial. For most of the tortuous journey he thought he was going to Rome, and managed to send Tanya a telegram in the hope she might come to visit him there. But in fact he was sent to Milan, in a prison transport in the company of ordinary rather than political prisoners. This is why it took nineteen days, because people were joining and leaving the convoy at every stop. Along the way, he passed through Palermo, Naples, Caianello, Isernia, Sulmona, Castellamare Adriatico, Ancona and Bologna. He stayed overnight in the prisons there, except for two nights in the *carabinieri* holding cells at Caianello and Castellamare, which he described as "the two ugliest nights of my whole life", surrounded by scowling feuding convicts and baited by the provincial police as a "big shot red". Peering through the filthy windows of metal railroad cars which still bore the linings of frozen snow they had stood in overnight, and shivering uncontrollably in his thin shirt and threadbare overcoat, he recognized the names of stations from his own travels or in one case – Ravisindoli in the Abruzzo region – from Julia's accounts of Schucht family holidays when she was a child.

He was also able to describe the trip retrospectively as "an endless film" and "a fantastic novel", because of its generally nightmarish quality and the extraordinary characters he met.

> *"At Ancona, for example, a kindly old man who seemed of humble peasant origin asked me for some soup I'd left. I gave it to him gladly, impressed by the serenity in his eyes and the modesty of his manner, only to learn immediately afterwards that this repellent beast had raped his own daughter... During the exercise period in Naples, where I witnessed an initiation ceremony for the camorra, I met a man called Arturo who told me he was forty six years old and had already spent twenty two of them in prison. He was an expert shoemaker, and could cite Nietzsche. Tranquil and smiling, he had skin like yellow parchment or cured leather. I saw him again in Ancona, but he was a different man: hard angular face, sharp icy eyes, chest puffed out, a tense spring ready to snap. He reminded me of Farinata in Dante's Inferno, 'in contempt of Hell.'*
>
> *In Palermo I met a formidable anarchist from Turin, who refused*

to disclose anything to the authorities about himself apart from his nickname, L'unico: 'I'm the only one, that's it...' In Bologna prison I was approached by someone calling himself Dante Romani, who also said he was an anarchist, an engine-driver by trade who had been arrested after the riots in Ancona in 1920. He had just finished his sentence and was on his way back home, but he seemed strangely well-informed for someone who had spent years in prison.

One evening at (I think) Sulmona the other convicts organised a knife-fighting contest, strictly organised with spoons for weapons scraped against the walls, so that hits showed up on clothes as white chalk marks. They fought in regional teams – Sicilians, Calabrians, Neapolitans and Apulians – but not the Sicilians against the Calabrians, because they hate each other so much it would inevitably turn serious! The Apulians are the best knife-fighters of all, and the two finalists were both Apulians, a 65 year old and a young man, of amazing skill and agility, who fought for half an hour with no clear winner."

Gramsci finally arrived at Milan prison on 7th February 1927. Though he maintained his correspondence with Tanya and his Sardinian relatives, mainly his mother, he was limited to just two letters out per week, which had to be completed within four and a half hours on a Monday afternoon. For his first six months he did not receive a single visit, primarily because Tanya, the only person within reasonable travelling distance, was in hospital for much of this time. She had finally succumbed to the Schucht sisters' propensity for neurasthenia. In Tanya's case it was complicated by suspected appendicitis. She also suffered an acute bout of phlebitis, painful inflammation of the veins in the legs, but this had recurred throughout her adult life and was fairly easily treated with tight bandages and Aspirin.

Tanya's nervous exhaustion was more troubling for Antonio, firstly because she assured him that this was the first time she'd gone down with it, but secondly because he already understood how dependent he was becoming on her, his only close, attentive and reliable relative in mainland Italy. He could really do without her going the way of Evgenia and Julia. *Maybe,* he thought, reflecting all the while on the rather strange way that Tanya had taken him on as a kind of cause or project, with what he began to describe as her "animal protection psychology", and considerably rearranged her life around him, *she caught it from me... After all, I don't seem to have done her sisters too much good.*

* * *

Resistance can take many forms. It can be active or passive, violent or inert, useless or effective. It can demonstrate the strength or weakness of the resister, his aimlessness or his sense of purpose, his capacity for applying his always limited personal and material resources or for squandering them. As such the act of resistance represents the only kind of free expression remaining to the political prisoner. After all, the situation of an incarcerated man is historically tied to slavery in the classical period.

Perhaps the most difficult form of resistance is against his fellow prisoners, because it is at once so foolish and so necessary. There is no trace of solidarity in prison. Everyone mistrusts everyone else and tries to take advantage. Everyone is on their guard and lying in wait. Small groups seem united by common interests into something like friendship, but these connections are easily broken by the distrust that eats away at all relationships in prison. Acts of resistance against the authorities must be carefully chosen and conducted, because the political prisoner can easily wear himself out pursuing useless causes. He will end up banging his head against the wall, making no impression on the wall but plenty on his head. For much of the time, given the imbalance of forces between prisoner and gaoler, it's better just to go along with

the prison regime, however petty or spiteful.

On the other hand, the hardest thing of all for the political prisoner to resist is the desire to surrender. This comes from deep inside himself, and from his sincere and clear-eyed understanding of the weakness and loneliness inherent in his situation. This is what we mean by the "breaking of the spirit", the real but rarely stated official objective of imprisonment. This is the triumph of the authorities, and the final disaster of the political prisoner. And therein lies the dialectic of dignified captivity. Every moment is a finely calibrated interplay of resistance and submission.

He sat on the edge of his bed, looking up to the barred window of his cell. It was no ordinary window, but a kind of gash in the shape of an upturned crescent. The bars gave it the look of a "wolf's mouth" or *bocca di lupo,* its name in prison slang. It was high up in the wall, too high to see any more through it than a patch of sky. A band of sunlight appeared at two o'clock in the afternoon, reached about 25 centimetres across, and worked its way around a mid-point on the wall – well above his head – till it fell away in the early evening. He calculated from this trajectory that his current cell must be facing south-west-west. He compared this ration of sunlight to his previous cell, where the sun shone between ten and two o'clock, and at its highest created a band at least 60 centimetres wide at around chest-level. He had been able to stand for at least an hour every day with the warm sun full on his face, whereas now he could only reach it on tip-toe, stretching his fingertips towards the precious heat.

He felt a sudden sharp pang of inconsolable loss. It was all he could do to stop himself from crying. *What for? My freedom? My family? My party? And why? From rage or sorrow? In protest or release? And all for a shaft of sunlight on a high stone wall!* These things matter when you are confined in a single space, alone all day and all night, for as far into the future as you can see. *At least it's April,* he consoled himself, and the sunlight would get higher and stronger through the coming months, hence lower around his cell and just possibly on his wide raised forehead. *Unless they move me again...*

The prison of San Vittore in Milan consisted of eight radiuses extending from a central hub, like the spokes in a bicycle wheel, with cells on either side of broad high corridors. From where they sat at the hub, the guards could see what was happening on every radius and get there quickly if they needed to. It was, Gramsci had read in a well-thumbed convict memoir from the prison library, the typical design for the modern prison, invented by the French for the more humane, "scientific" containment of opponents of the Revolution; at least, those not consigned to the guillotine. Combined with more recent thinking in criminology, which had established through methodical observation and measurement that crime was more prevalent among certain "types", who therefore could not be held personally responsible for their crimes, it created the prison atmosphere and ethos of a holding pen. It was a warehouse rather than a rubbish dump, Gramsci reckoned, and that was progress of sorts, *even if it means that we Southerners, with our "natural" propensity for wrong-doing, are even more likely to end up here...* If there were "types", he wrote to Tanya, these arose from the negative effects of confinement on certain personalities and social backgrounds, so "The calmest are the peasants; then the factory workers, then the craftsmen, and finally the would-be intellectuals, who are prone to sudden bursts of infantile madness." There were fifty cells in each radius, which made for a prison population of at least four hundred, perhaps a couple of hundred more if you took into account the ordinary criminals who were trusted to each other's company and expected to share cells. On the way to his daily two hours of solitary exercise, strictly forbidden to converse or (as the Prison Regulations put it) "in any way fraternise" with those other prisoners, he had calculated that he was now in the twenty second cell of the second radius, having been moved (for no obvious reason he could see or that anyone was prepared to tell him) from the thirteenth cell of the first radius. *These details matter... or do they?*

He slept on a camp bed up against a side wall, with two thin mattresses, one woollen, and fresh linen once a fortnight. There was also a small table, a bedside cupboard, a basin and an enamel iron jug and – *wonder of wonders!* – a mirror in which he could shave. He had purchased a small cooking stove and a few aluminium utensils from the stall brought in once a week from a local department store. It really wasn't much worse – *a consoling thought...* – than most of the places he had lived, and considerably better than some. *Well, apart from the fact that I can't leave...* He had not slept well in the several weeks since his arrival, *but where and when have I ever slept well?*

He habitually rose at 6.30, half an hour before the guards roused everyone else with their shouts and a clanging bell. This felt like a small triumph of the human will over prison routine. He made himself his first cup of coffee of the day, *always remembering Bordiga and his remark about my early morning step...*, tidied and cleaned out his cell and his toilet, washed his face and hands at the basin, and combed through his unruly hair at the mirror, checking carefully for signs of illness or age and most days relieved not to find any. At 7.30 he was brought half a litre of hot milk, which he drank straight away with a few mouthfuls of bread. At 8.00 he was escorted to one of the exercise yards, where he strolled around reading and smoking for two hours. Most recently he had been reading *The Gentle Peasant Girl* by Pushkin, and learning roughly twenty lines of the original mellifluous Russian a day. The rest of the morning he perused the five daily newspapers and several weekly political papers and cultural reviews he bought and had delivered and, for light reading, the constantly replenished stack of popular novels from the prison library.

Lunch arrived irregularly, at some time between 12 and 3, soup or pasta with a bit of bread and cheese and a quarter litre of wine. Over lunch and afterwards he continued reading. A similar dinner, augmented by meat or a couple of eggs, would be delivered to his cell between 6 and 7. With the state of his teeth, he wrote to Tanya, he could not eat any vegetables, though he could nibble at dates and biscuits. To allay her concerns, he assured her that he drank only three coffees and smoked no more than fifteen cigarettes a day. At 7.30pm, the guards commanded silence with their bell. He would go to bed and read until between 11 and midnight. If he felt like it, he would make himself a cup of camomile tea at around 9 o'clock, and ruminate on another day of organised pointlessness. All this was paid for from his prison allowance of ten lire a day, and brought in from the outside by the grocers and newsagents who did good business from the prison. *Not a bad life, so long as you can forget that it's a kind of slow death...*

His present cell was, he estimated, about three metres by five, and four metres high, the dimensions of a student's bed-sitting room. It was situated right above the prison workshop, so the throbbing of the machines went on all day and into the evening if there was a job to finish. *Or so I imagine,* he thought, imposing on this small discrepancy in the daily timetable of prison life an assumed organisational purpose. Even a distant echo of the ideologies of Fordism and Taylorism, which had brought new levels of mechanical and human efficiency to industry. He further imagined a roster on the workshop wall, with the names of outside clients, allotted tasks and responsible prisoners, deadlines and tick-boxes for the completion of every stage of the production process. *Sometimes,* he noted, *the rhythm of the machines exactly matches the thuds of my migraine...*Or rather, he consigned this and other observations to memory, because he had no means of writing them down. In the same spirit of petty restriction that pervaded all the Prison Regulations – *that nit-picking masterpiece of mass organisation comparable only to the Catholic Catechism in its historical force...* – and limited his interactions with other prisoners to a mere glance and a nod in the corridor or staircase, he was not allowed any writing materials outside the strictly timed hours allowed every Monday afternoon for family correspondence. It took him all that time to transcribe the two letters per week he was allowed to send, with a scratchy quill pen on sheets of cheap coarse paper that had to be surrendered when the time was up, *like the university exams I was sitting fifteen years ago...*

To make the most of those precious hours of frantic scribbling, he spent much of the rest of his week composing in his head what he wanted to say. Inevitably these mental drafts and the responses he might anticipate would elide, in the long lonely hours of semi-darkness in his cell, into imagined conversation with his friends and family on the outside. Their physical forms, or rather what his anxious memory could conjure up of their faces and hands and keep desperate hold of, would emerge from the commingled miasma of the shadows of his cell and the mists of his past, and respond with mouths and minds of their own to his observations and queries. *Hello Mamma, how are your aching hands?... Hello Teresina, have you married your postmaster yet?... Hello Carlo, how's that business proposition coming along? Is there scope for a shoe shop in Ghilarza?...*When he felt at his most forsaken, he remembered that he had not seen any of his family or friends since the night of his arrest. They were mostly of course a long way from Milan, safely beyond the reach of his official persecutors, but their distance from him seemed to grow with every passing day. Their increasingly infrequent letters became more formulaic and uninformative, dutiful and dull. This was, it seemed to him, the cruellest aspect of his incarceration, all the more cruel for not being directly attributable to his gaolers. He fought hard against the thought, but didn't always succeed, *these people are supposed to love me...* He longed for their real physical presence, their faces and hands, minds and mouths, with an ache and a yearning he had not felt since early childhood. In the meantime, his imagination would have to make do.

> *"Dear Mamma, yes I'm managing to keep warm in this cold weather. One of the first things I bought when I arrived here in Milan was a nice big thick jumper! How are things in Ghilarza? Has the village street been paved yet, like the mayor was promising when I was last there with you? I would so much rather hear about these things than your concerns over my plight... I have a hunch – I don't really know why – that I won't be in prison longer than three years, even if I'm sentenced to twenty. In the meantime I shall get by like I always have. The last ten years of struggle have hardened me more than you might imagine. I could have been killed a dozen times, and between 1921 and 1926 I was actually prepared to die, yet I am still alive. What's more, I was truly happy for a while. I have two fine children who are being brought up as I would want them to be, and who will grow up into two strong healthy men..."*

> *"Dear Teresina* (his youngest and favourite sister), *I'm very worried by the state mother seems to be in. I cannot seem to persuade her that I am alright... there's a whole area of feeling, a whole way of thinking that stretches like an abyss between us. Please try to persuade her, using whatever arguments you think will work, that I am fine. While for me this is one episode in a political struggle being fought not only in Italy but all over the world, for her it is a terrible personal tragedy whose causes and effects she doesn't understand. Tell her that being in prison for political reasons no longer provokes disgust as it did with father... I remain hopeful but I have to be realistic. I think my sentence will be fourteen to seventeen years, but it could be heavier, precisely because there is no evidence against me. Without evidence, what crime might I not have committed?"*

> *"Dearest Tanya, it's been a month and ten days since I heard from you and I don't understand why. Your last letter was full of worries; above all, that your worries about me were making you ill. I can assure you I'm fine. I have always attended to my physical health, and taken great care to avoid excessive strain or indulgence. I really don't need you to worry on my behalf. It only adds to my worries! I imagine you serious and frowning, with never even a fleeting smile. I wish I could make you feel calm and well. What do I have to do? Threaten you? I could stop writing to you, then you'd learn how it feels to go for weeks on end without any word..."*

> *"Julka, my darling! Does Delio ever think about me? Please send me a photograph of Giuliano..."*

Only that last one was only ever thought, rephrased in endless variations and never sent, because in the absence of anything from her for many months, he had stopped writing directly to his wife. *If she wants to know anything she can find out from Tanya...*

In the summer heat of 1927 Gramsci composed and sent a letter to Giuseppe Berti, a comrade in the *PCd'I* leadership in exile, in which he wrote:

> *"I am undergoing a period of great moral stress because of certain family matters. My nerves are on edge and I'm very touchy. I can't succeed in concentrating on any subject, I have lost all sense of your circumstances, and I have no idea what sort of changes have been going on in the exile community."*

Word began to circulate among the communist exiles that Antonio "refuses to put pen to paper" because of "an exaggerated sense of caution" and some kind of family-related "moral crisis" which, apart from anything else, was leaving him seriously short of money. He was finding it ever harder to buy in provisions from outside, and for whole weeks was having to rely on the meagre prison fare, which was making his digestive problems worse. With Tanya in hospital and out of circulation, arrangements were made to transfer funds via his family in Sardinia.

There was a further round of rumours about Gramsci's health, typically exaggerated as they gathered political force, and culminating in yet another rash of stories in the émigré and foreign press about his imminent death. His old Turin friend and comrade (and now husband of Pia Carena) Alfonso Leonetti claimed in the Comintern bulletin to have heard "an anguished cry from Milan jail: Gramsci is dying of hunger!" The party leaders considered another escape plan but, after receiving coded messages from the *PCd'I* prisoners in Milan, it was quickly dismissed as "completely infeasible."

* * *

The prisoner regards visits from friends or family with deeply conflicting emotions. On the one hand they represent a precious link with the outside world and whatever part of his life has been and will be spent there. On the other they totally disrupt the patterns and rhythms of his present life on the inside. He longs for the physical presence of a loved one, and he relishes the sense of real lives being led elsewhere that is conjured up by their reports of other loved ones. But he feels the stab of loneliness brought on by the realisation that he is no longer a real living element in those lives. Then there is the abrupt shift from the muffled sounds of his cell to the racket of the crowd, with its dominant note of metallic female shrieks.

The first visit Gramsci received since his arrest in November (*over eight months now...)* was from his brother Mario, in late August 1927. It was a strange encounter, all the stranger for being the least expected or desired by either Antonio or his younger brother. Mario had been an official with the local Fascists in Varese, in the Lombardy region of northern Italy. But he had decided that it was bad for his business to be too openly involved and had withdrawn from active politics. Nonetheless he was able to use his contacts to persuade the prison authorities to approve a new medicine for the worsening indigestion Antonio had been writing home to his mother about. Antonio wrote to thank Mario for his intercession, giving him more detail about his various, mostly stable medical conditions.

Mario's wife Anna, commonly referred to in the Gramsci family as "that silly woman", had heard the stories about Antonio's supposed illness and looming death. Now armed with his letter to Mario, and with all the dreadful sounding Latin medical terms and complicated chemical compounds required to deal with them, she wrote in wild lamentation to her mother-in-law. Signora Gramsci was predictably distraught, and Antonio had to write to reassure his mother that he was in fact quite alright. All of this upset, made worse by delayed and muddled correspondence the length and breadth of the country, rumbled on for weeks on end. The various parties – Antonio, Mario and Anna, above all Signora Gramsci and the others back in Ghilarza – suffered agonies of confusion and worry while they waited for further letters, or for their own to reach their destinations. Each round of letters only seemed to make matters worse.

Antonio finally asked Mario to come to visit him at the prison in Milan, in the hope that this would clear things up and calm everyone down. In fact it had quite the opposite effect. For the fifteen minutes of the visit, Mario was deeply disturbed by the prison environment, "…jumping out of his skin at the slightest noise or commotion..." Gramsci wrote to his mother. Mario was also obviously embarrassed by the incarceration and the dishevelled appearance of his brother, whom he had not seen in many years. Not since 1921, in fact, when they had had a similarly uncomfortable encounter, involving discussion of their passionately held, diametrically opposed political views.

Oddly, Mario had visited Tanya in hospital before travelling on to the prison, and invited her to come for a recuperative holiday with him and his wife in Lombardy. He blurted out the import of their conversation to Antonio.

"Well, thank you for visiting her, and being so kind," responded Antonio, trying to put his brother at ease, all the while wondering why he should have to, and how they had managed to get themselves so tangled up in gossip and misunderstanding.

"She could use a holiday after all these months in hospital, and I know the Lombardy lakes are lovely... And how's your dear wife Anna?"

"She's fine, she's fine..."

"You know, I've only ever met her once, and she was heavily pregnant. Actually she was in the first stages of labour! Not the best circumstances to make the acquaintance of a lady..."

Antonio was trying hard to demonstrate his own vigorously good health and humour, smiling and laughing more than naturally, and struggling to suppress his annoyance at the muddle these silly people had managed to create, not to mention what he knew of his brother's politics. He told Mario a funny story from his early months in Milan, which he thought he would appreciate.

"A guard asked me if it was true I could have been a government Minister if only I'd agreed to change sides. I said a Minister would have been a bit much, but I could have been an Under-Secretary at the Post Office or the Public Works Department, because that's the kind of job governments gave Sardinian MPs!"

Leaning towards his brother, and glancing towards the guard to make sure he couldn't be overheard, Antonio said in a near-whisper, "He thought I was serious, and asked me why then I hadn't switched sides?"

Tipping back in his chair, and tapping his forefinger on his temple, Antonio concluded "He clearly thought I was mad..."

There was indeed the flicker of a smile on Mario's face. Antonio saw something of the lively, enquiring and funny little boy he had known back in Ghilarza, always doing skits and impressions of teachers and uncles and village elders. Mario had always seemed to be at the centre of a huddle of other small boys, telling some outlandish story or demonstrating some new trick. But he still didn't wholly relax. Antonio asked after his business, which likewise was doing "…fine, fine..." Not least, Mario implied, because of the custom his political connections had attracted.

"Yes, I'm sure that must be quite an asset..."

Antonio actually had no idea what Mario's "business" involved, and felt no inclination to ask. He simply assumed, watching Mario shifting around in his seat here before him, that it involved buying stuff from one group of people as cheaply as he could, then selling it to another group of people for however much more he could squeeze out of them. *Isn't that what small business usually involves? What more was there to know?*

After quarter of an hour, Mario got up to leave, still edgy and embarrassed, and making friendly overtures to the prison guards who looked on impassively. For a moment, Antonio thought he glimpsed the rest of Mario's present life and social milieu, the well-connected provincial Fascist businessman, *a big man around Varese*. He shook his brother's hand, bade him farewell and – "As you can see, I'm fine..." – hoped that was the end of the matter. "We need to do all we can to prevent undue alarm to Mother. She's had more than enough worry for one lifetime. All this must be bringing back to her what we went through when Father was in prison..."

But after the prison visit, Mario wrote a further alarming letter to his brother Carlo in Ghilarza, who set about organising a trip to Milan for himself and his mother to see their dying brother and son before it was too late. Antonio then had to write to both Carlo and his mother separately – using up an entire week's ration of precious correspondence – to reassure them that really and truly he was fine, and that on no account should they come and see him now, especially his mother, "a woman of seventy who's hardly been outside her village and never made a rail journey longer than forty kilometres."

To the clearly panicking Carlo he wrote curtly that "your present mood isn't worthy of a grown man" and, drawing on his own experiences of hardship as a student and an activist, outlined the philosophy of self-sufficient perseverance that had got him through all these years of penury and oppression, and would enable him to survive prison: "When all is lost or seems to be, you have to go back to work, starting from scratch with a cheerful attitude. I believe that you always have to depend on yourself and your own energies, without expecting anything from anyone, in order to avoid being disappointed. You must set out to do only what you know how to do and are capable of doing, seeking your own individual way. Anything else is romantic daydreaming."

It did not occur to him at the time that this stark homily, and the bitter wisdom it contained, might cause further concern to his relatives. Antonio wrote an account of the whole mess to Tanya, regretting whatever he himself had done to create it and resolving in conclusion that "I don't believe I can count on Mario or his precious 'connections' any more." He would just have to make do with the medicines and supplies he could get hold of in prison and that she might be able to procure for him outside and have sent in. He had no further direct contact with Mario, to everyone's evident satisfaction.

* * *

The prisoner looks forward to visits for days beforehand, planning what he will say but increasingly anxious that he

will say the wrong thing. But then he spends days afterwards wondering what was implied or truly meant by some small incidental remark from his visitor, or whether he could have expressed himself more accurately or effectively. Sometimes these visits leave behind a residue of bitterness far greater than the brief happiness of seeing your loved ones. It takes the prisoner a gigantic effort of will to convince himself that he wouldn't be better off without visits altogether.

"Tanya!"

"Antonio!"

She made to embrace him across the scratched, discoloured wooden table in the cavernous prison visiting room, which was much noisier and dirtier than the side room where Antonio had received his brother.

"No physical contact allowed!" barked the guard by the door. Antonio shrugged apologetically. *No such problem with Mario...*

Tatiana Schucht had arrived over half an hour earlier, anxious not to miss a minute of her officially prescribed and strictly supervised hour of visiting time with Prisoner number 7047, Gramsci A. "Very nearly the same number as my Comintern pass which so impressed your family seven years ago!" he had pointed out in an earlier letter. He had had to describe her to the prison authorities as his sister, to get around Regulation no. 84 subsection (ix) on "Special Measures" *confini,* which limited access to immediate family members unless "by prior notice and application to and permission from the Ministry of Justice". Rumour had it that this permission took many months to come through the prison bureaucracy. Other than birth family, only wives were exempt from this arduous procedure, but even they had to show their Italian marriage certificates at the prison gates. *My goodness,* he'd realised as he read that, *they'd let me see Julia but not Tanya. Not that I can imagine Julia ever coming here...*

This subterfuge of passing Tanya off as his sister might cause problems later on, *but who knows where any of us might be then...?* Tanya had only come out of hospital a few days before, in early September 1927. She had been there for nearly six months, ever since Antonio had arrived in Milan. Her suspected appendicitis had cleared up, if that's what it actually was, but she also had a particularly acute case of nervous exhaustion further complicated by what her doctors had only ever vaguely called "constitutional weakness." They seemed to mean that she was small, pale and thin, despite her repeated insistence that she was the most outgoing and independent, emotionally mature and physically robust of all the Schucht sisters. Hadn't she proven that in her ten years living alone in Rome, mercifully far away from them and what she called "all their melodramas and unnecessary complications"?

"Of course you have!" said Antonio, when she told him about her doctors' continuing concerns for her health. He wasn't really listening to these opening pleasantries, but bathing in the luxury of her face and voice, *so like Julka's*, even if their personalities were so different. He responded with an account of his own health and state of mind, still paying more attention to the facial expressions she made in response – *such an animated face, like a funny little mouse!* – than to what she said.

"You know, I feel less nervous tension now than I have for years," he assured her. "I was feeling overwhelmed by these strange bouts of dull rage, but I haven't had one for weeks... perhaps I'm becoming acclimatised to life in prison! I guard against it, but I realise it's inevitable, necessary even...The course of bioplastene injections is clearly helping. "

He was hungry for news from the outside.

"How are things in Rome? How is that lemon plant I left behind? Has someone thought to water it? And how are the Passarges? I know Signora Clara was feeling unwell, and my arrest must have come as a great shock to her and her husband. My first letter from prison was to her, asking for some of my books, but I never received them. Knowing how reliable she is, I suspect she never got the letter. Do pass on my best wishes..."

She answered his questions as thoroughly and discreetly as she felt able. In fact Signora Passarge had died in the summer, but Tanya had been reassured by a bereaved Signor Passarge that it was not directly caused by Gramsci's arrest, "...unpleasant though that had been..."

"My goodness..." was all Antonio could think of by way of response. *Another link with the outside world severed...*

Tanya had taken his lemon tree into her own care, and it was doing well on her windowsill. She would bring him a lemon on her next visit. For now she had brought him some fresh milk and cheese.

"Oh you are so kind! But you must bother less about me, and take more care of yourself! You're only just out of hospital..."

"Yes, I know, but I'm anxious to throw myself back into life," Tanya responded. "In fact I have an idea I want to run past you: how would you feel if I moved to Milan so I could see you more often?"

"Well, that would be wonderful..."

"That's settled then. I've already found a job at the Soviet trade delegation, and they tell me I can rent a room from one of their officials. Now, how are you occupying yourself, Antonio?"

He began to outline for her his latest thoughts on a programme of study, something to stave off "intellectual degradation" and provide "a centre for my inner life." He had in fact been thinking about this for much of the summer, and was anxious to get on with it, badgering the prison authorities for permission to write in his cell, outside the prescribed hours for correspondence, and to order the books he would need, some of them dangerously close to the proscription on "political agitation." He believed it would help him to survive his imprisonment, however long that might turn out to be, and have the added benefit of helping to make sense of the failure and defeat of the revolutionary struggle, at least here in Italy. Otherwise he just didn't know what he would do with himself.

"In here, the term 'killing time' takes on added meaning, and I might as well devote it to something that will help the cause, even if the cause doesn't seem to want the help I have to offer. Honestly, these silly campaigns in my name! Sometimes I think I'd be more use to them dead than alive..."

By taking on grand historical and cultural themes, he would hope to rise above the everyday turmoil of political life, not to mention the dull squalor of prison routine, and create something *fur ewig*. This, he explained to Tanya, was Goethe's term for research and writing that had no immediate practical application, and in that sense was "disinterested". But for precisely that reason, it would enable him to shed light on the epochal historical changes that had swept across Italy and the rest of the world in the last few centuries.

"My goodness!" said Tanya. "That sounds ambitious!"

"Indeed! And that's precisely the point. It's only ambition that keeps you going in this place. I'm doing plenty of reading, anything I can lay my hands on in the prison library and order in from outside. All I need now is some means of making notes and recording my observations, perhaps even working it all up into articles or even a book..."

For now, the themes he wanted to explore were: "Firstly the formation of intellectual castes and their role in the creation of national cultures. Then something on comparative linguistics, which was my degree subject before I dropped out of university. Thirdly, a study of the plays of Pirandello, which I reviewed for the socialist press during the war years when no one else was taking him seriously. And finally, a study of popular taste in literature, with a view to identifying just what appeals to those masses of people who devour the serialised stories in the periodicals. So what do you think of all that? You know how much I respect your opinion..."

Before she could answer – and he could see that she was a little thrown and, glancing at the prison guard and the clock, conscious that their time was nearly up – he said more familiarly, "And talking of popular literature, Tanya, who's buying adventure stories for you now that I'm not around to do it?"

She blushed at this mildly flirtatious turn in his questioning, and shyly assured him, "There is no one..."

The prison guard, looking hard at the large loudly ticking clock on the wall, came to her rescue and shouted, "Time!"

* * *

"The available company in prison is divided into two strata: common people or professional criminals, with whom conversation can be interesting for two or three weeks, until one exhausts the supply of the picturesque and the typical that is inherent in their condition; and the self-styled intellectuals, referred to in vulgar Italian as "mezzo-calzette" or half-stockings, accused of debt and fraud etc. This last lot don't even have the colourful stories of the ordinary criminals. I've had some of them as neighbours in nearby cells, and was struck by how they become demoralized in childish and primitive ways. They weep exactly like children, with great loud sobs, invoking Mamma. They're always asking for something, in order to be able to see the guard, exchange a few words, and so feel connected with life, proving they still have rights.

I am of course subject to the same material conditions and psychological processes, so I accrue my own stores of self-pity and colourful anecdote. Let me tell you about the peasant from Salerno who killed his father-in-law and thereby inherited his property – "I've killed and I've inherited" was his refrain – and about the Calabrian gangster, sixteen years old, to whom I gave a pair of shoes and a vest and who solemnly promised in return that he would never steal my chickens; and the shoemaker from Messina who recited for me all the adventures of Sinbad the Sailor in a Sicilian version, which he had heard from his grandfathers and refused to believe (I did not insist) was from A Thousand and One Nights... And we all of us, at some point in our own endless nights, cry for Mamma."

Through 1927 and into 1928 the legal and investigative proceedings against Gramsci and the other communist leaders in prison churned on relentlessly. The problem for the Fascist lawyers, as Gramsci had indicated in his letter to his sister Teresina, was finding credible concrete evidence against him. The regime had not yet cast such considerations completely aside. Police reports on Gramsci consisted of routine observations of his daily life as a communist MP, or vague generalities about him being "subversive", "a trouble-maker" or "a threat to public order." One report from the Rome *carabinieri* stated that he had been "found in possession of arms and explosives in November 1922", when he'd already been in Moscow for six months and would remain abroad for another year and a half.

So the authorities set about gathering "evidence" through other means. There was a sudden easing of the conditions under which Gramsci was kept at Milan prison, especially his contact with other prisoners. He had to give up his right to those of his periodicals that were classified as "political", in case he used them to incite insurrection, but he was bored with what now seemed to pass for everyday political life on the outside, and it seemed a small price to pay for some very welcome company. He and his fellow politicos were even allowed to organise an exhibition of photographs of their children. He wrote in a note to Julia, included in a letter to Tanya, that "Delio was greatly admired", and hoped that "this might make you smile; it's only with great difficulty that I can imagine you smiling."

At this point, "Dante Romani" reappeared, permitted to approach "Signor Gramsci" and even to spend whole afternoons in his cell. At first Gramsci was glad to see him, and set aside the doubts he had felt on their previous encounter in Bologna. When he said, "I thought you were being released..." Romani replied breezily, "Oh, I got into trouble again!" Gramsci decided he should just enjoy the company. He wrote to Tanya: "He's an alert and lively young man from a village near Monza, awaiting trial on a charge of theft and damages to a brothel! He says he was part of a self-appointed vice-squad of vigilantes, raiding the place for cocaine. Most picaresque and highly entertaining!"

They talked freely about their lives and families; Romani had "a charming and pretty little girl called Maria Luisa. In accordance with Sardinian custom we have decided that Delio should marry Maria Luisa as soon as the two have reached the age of matrimony!" But then Romani started offering to convey messages, letters and "orders" to the outside. The *PCd'I* was, he said, in a bad way, and needed Gramsci's leadership to put things right. This crude police trick only confirmed Gramsci's previous suspicion that "Dante Romani", or whatever was his real name, was an agent provocateur.

When a new warrant against Gramsci was issued in May 1927, accusing him of "provoking civil war and destroying life and property", it was clear from the supporting documents he saw that there was still very little hard evidence against him. In October, another prisoner introduced himself as "Corrado Melani" to Gramsci in the exercise yard. He said he was the lover of the sister-in-law of the secretary of the Milan Fascist federation, Mario Giampaoli. "He's persecuting me because I know certain things about him," said Melani. "For example, the attempt on Mussolini's life in Bologna was a set-up organised by Giampaoli. One of his sidekicks shot in the air, and Giampaoli jumped on the so-called assassin Anteo Zamboni and slit his throat. I've got documents proving Giampaoli's involvement with brothels and gambling, and that a number of Fascist MPs are homosexuals..."

If any of this got out, Melani confided to Gramsci, the Fascists would surely fall, which was why Giampaoli was out to get him. Melani offered to sell his documents to the *PCd'I*. Gramsci politely but firmly turned him down, and saw no more of "Corrado Melani". He wrote a strongly worded complaint to the Ministry of Justice about police attempts to entrap him. His conditions were tightened up again, with the limitations on contact with other prisoners re-imposed and stricter than ever surveillance by the guards.

His "worst problem" now, he wrote to his sister Teresina, was the "boredom of enforced leisure." He spent one whole month whittling away at a stick until it bore some resemblance to a letter-opener, which he conveyed to Julia via Tanya with great pride in his craftsmanship. He became quite adept at constructing papier-mâché balls from old copies of the *Gazzetta dello Sport,* with the vague intention of sending them to his sons to remind them of him. With the onset of winter, the trajectory of the sun – when it deigned to appear at all from behind dull cloudy Northern Italian skies – sank lower and lower, until Gramsci's daily ration was just a few minutes of pale light on a patch of ceiling just in front of the barred window. For company he was forced back onto the insects and birds that periodically joined him in his cell. The former offered limited possibilities: "I still haven't found a spider to train," he wrote to Tanya. "There aren't any mice and the remaining zoology is not very attractive." The local bird life was more cooperative. He was especially fond of the sparrows that flew in through the *bocca di lupo,* and he even managed to tame a couple of them by clipping their wings.

> *"The first sparrow was very proud and extremely lively. What I liked in him was his resistance to handling, beating his wings and pecking my hand fiercely. Then all of a sudden he decided I could be trusted. Before, he'd keep well away from me. If I offered him a dead fly in a matchbox, he never took it until I moved away. Then one morning he came right up to me, and started pecking my shoes for*

food. After that we were the best of friends. I think he ate some kind of toxin, because one evening he couldn't fly. He hid under my table and cried out like a child all night, and died the next day. The one I have now is very servile and unassuming, and quite nauseating in his domesticity. He likes to be fed, although he can eat perfectly well by himself. He hops onto my shoes and nestles in the turn-ups of my trousers. If I hadn't clipped his wings, I think he'd fly up and sit on my knee; I can tell from the way he stands up tall, quivers and then hops onto my shoe. I think he will die too, because he insists on eating burned match heads, and the phosphorus can't be good for him, quite apart from the fact that I feed him a constant diet of soggy bread and little else. At the moment he's quite healthy but sluggish, runs about very little but sticks close to me. In fact I've already kicked him by accident several times. I've ordered some lettuce with my food; not that I'm inclined to eat it, but it might do the sparrow some good..."

In late 1927 Gramsci – well aware of the edginess in his mood – received what he immediately regarded as "a strange letter" from Ruggiero Grieco, writing from Moscow on behalf of the exiled *PCd'I* leadership. At a time when the communist political prisoners were preparing a legal defence which rested on disavowal of their status as party leaders, Grieco referred to "the great responsibility assigned to you... as communist leaders." At one of the preparatory hearings, Gramsci was asked about this apparent contradiction by an examining magistrate, who observed: "Signor Gramsci, you have friends who seem to want you to stay in prison quite a while..."

The letter was probably little more than a routine rallying cry to all the communist prisoners, a rather clumsy attempt at comradely morale-raising, thoughtless rather than malicious. Gramsci conceded to Tanya that "perhaps prison life has made me more suspicious than common precaution requires." But the memory of the "strange letter" would remain with him for the rest of his life, and come to represent his own growing sense of isolation and the insensitivity towards him of those "on the outside" who were supposed to care for him. A second letter from Grieco, sent some months later from Moscow with news of the latest situation inside the Russian Communist Party, had a quite different secondary purpose. Grieco meant to reassure the Russian authorities, who he knew would intercept it, of the Italian party's whole-hearted support for the new Stalin-Bukharin majority's crackdown on the Russian opposition. Gramsci recognised another cack-handed political gesture, meant to quell the lingering suspicions amongst the Russians about him and his letter to them in October 1926. But even here he saw something "irresponsibly foolish" that could be used against him at his trial.

* * *

Tanya's next visit to Antonio in San Vittore was rather less amicable. In the meantime she had written to him, saying that he "seemed different" without specifying how. With so much time to brood between visits, he had agonized over what she might have meant, and wrote back saying he wasn't "aware of the differences you mention, though living here changes people so slowly they may not notice at all. I accept that I may have grown colder and adopted an outer insensitivity..." He apologised for causing her any upset, but added in mitigation "people always torment those they love most." He then went on to chide her for sending him books he hadn't asked for – "When I need something, I'll ask for it" – and for letting weeks go by without writing: "Any irregularity immediately takes on some sinister meaning..." He concluded on what he thought was a more positive note: "For a long time I had planned to offer you some flowers grown here in my cell (what prison romanticism!), but the plants dried up and I was unable to keep alive the five or six little flowers that budded..."

In her next letter, Tanya inferred that these closing remarks were some kind of comment on their relationship, at which point Gramsci threw up his arms in the air and decided not to write again until he saw her. *The perils of correspondence!* When she came next, in late September 1927, he was suffering from severe toothache which no amount of Aspirin seemed to touch, and contemplating another brutal bloody extraction by the huge monosyllabic guard who bore the laughable title of Prison Dentist. Gramsci had already lost five teeth to this butcher in the eight months he'd been here. The slightest complaint and it was, "That'll have to come out too!" On top of the teeth he'd lost in his years of freedom, it was beginning to feel like his mouth didn't have many left. So he was not in the best of moods for Tanya. Neither, it seemed, was she. Every fresh topic seemed to provoke further irritation.

First of all it was the flowers story, to which he responded, "You really mustn't read too much into these things. I was just trying to end my letter on a cheerful note!"

"Well that wasn't the way it came across..."

"Just go by what I say, for goodness' sake, and not what you think I mean! It's the same with all these books and gifts of food. How many times do I have to tell you? When I want something I'll ask for it..."

"But I'm only trying to please you!"

"But they just get confiscated! Really Tanya, you mustn't spend all your time thinking about what I want. I promise that if I have any real needs, I won't hesitate to let you know..."

He tried to divert the conversation onto more congenial topics. She had written to him some months ago that she was thinking of resuming her medical studies, with an eye to becoming a qualified doctor.

"Have you been going to the lectures at the *Policlinico*?" he asked her now.

"No!" she exclaimed, "I haven't had time, what with my job and visiting you and seeing my own doctors..."

And so it went on, into discussion of Julia's continuing refusal to accept Antonio's gifts or money – "I can't account for my sister's peculiarities!" – and Tanya's offer to procure a new suit for Antonio to wear at his trial.

"I have an old suit set aside!" he exclaimed. "And when I'm sentenced I'll be given a regular prisoner's outfit to wear! Why should I be an exception? And what will it look like if I'm dressed up like a dandy? No doubt with one of your precious bloody flowers in the buttonhole..."

Even when Antonio, doing all he could to lighten the mood and disregard his toothache, started demonstrating some of the new "callisthenic" exercises he had been doing alone in his cell, it left Tanya cold. She just looked on blankly, as he sat there flexing his arm muscles and pulling his face into an odd grimace which he said maintained the flexibility and tone of his skin.

"You just look pale and tired to me..." she muttered eventually.

"Well yes," he responded. "I am in prison..." *And you're not exactly a picture of health yourself...*

In the New Year, into 1928, Tatiana Schucht fell ill again with her nervous debility and "constitutional weakness," which this time took the form of bronchial pneumonia. For several months she was confined to hospital and unable to visit Antonio in prison. She had to give up her job at the Soviet trade delegation in Milan. He could not help reflecting that the demands and pressures he had put on her, not to mention the mutual irritations he had tried to pass off in a letter as "…normal between brother and sister, such as we are now my dear," had contributed to her relapse.

In the meantime he started, to his immense surprise, to receive letters from Julia again. The first was written on 26th December 1927, amended on 24th January and (to Antonio's puzzlement) finally arrived at the end of February 1928. Julia apologised for not writing when she was ill or "distressed", and hoped that he would forgive her. The rest of the letter consisted of news of Delio and Giuliano, now aged three and a half and eighteen months respectively. Delio was drawing ever more "graphically organised" pictures, and showing an interest in the construction toys now appearing in the Moscow shop windows. Giuliano had taken his first steps and begun to call people by their names and compose simple sentences. He was especially attentive to his big brother, and tried to copy everything Delio did and said. The news brought Gramsci equal parts delight and dismay. He was so proud of his family's development, but desperately sad that it did not include him.

He wrote straight back to Julia, via Tanya in hospital, trying hard to stay positive and not communicate his own mixed feelings at her news, while remaining truthful and sincere in what was his first direct contact for over a year. He told her how he was finally adapting to prison life, overcoming the "crises of resistance" of his first year in captivity, mainly by slowing down and allowing himself to succumb to:

> ***"…the routine, the privations and necessities, the enormous number of minute events that occur day after day, month after month, year after year, with the same mechanical rhythm of sand in an hourglass. Every molecule of me was tenaciously opposed to absorbing these external pressures, but my resistance was always overcome, despite all my best efforts to shake them off. I have now arrived at the serene decision not to struggle any longer but instead to seek to control the process, with the aid of a little irony.***
>
> ***I'll never become a complete philistine though, since I'm ready at any moment to toss off the brute second skin (half donkey, half sheep) that prison grows over your skin. There is one thing I'll never be able to do, however: give my own skin the smoky colour it once had! I fear that Delio, despite your***

> ***contribution, must be much smokier by now than I ever was. You don't believe me? This winter I went three months without seeing any more than a few remote reflections of the sun. The light that filters into my cell is somewhere between that of a cellar and that of an aquarium. It makes me feel like one of those monstrous fish that live at the bottom of the very deep sea, so pale that you can see through them!"***

In early April 1928, he received via Tanya a lock of Giuliano's hair – a lovely ash blond colour, the same as his own as a baby – and the latest report on the child's developing speech. He was now able to say clearly "Mamma Julka" and "Mamma Zhenya". In reply to Tanya, Antonio noted Delio's upcoming fourth birthday and asked her to purchase and send a Meccano set on his behalf, accompanied by a set of deliberations over whether these mass-produced construction sets were better than the much more primitive materials available to himself as a child, "which demanded so much more of your own imagination and creativity... I could even construct an entire naval fleet out of sticks and stones and horse-bone glue!"

At the end of that month, he wrote to his mother, enclosing "for safekeeping" the single photograph he had of Delio, taken nearly two years earlier in June 1926, and which he had displayed in the prisoners' exhibition in November 1927. He said he was eager to hear her impressions:

> *"...particularly whether he looks like us when we were children. You'll see how handsome your grandson is and be really proud of him. I want you to leave the prison stamps on the back. The photograph should remain just as it is, with the signs of its passage through the prison system where I've been held for so long. Far from feeling ashamed of my imprisonment, I consider it an extreme honour. This will certainly be the child's feeling too, when he is of an age to understand these things."*

* * *

There is a theatrical aspect to all forms of politics, which can from the outside make it look operatic or melodramatic, and more than faintly ridiculous. This theatricality is accentuated in a dictatorship, because in the absence of democratic debate this is how popular support is garnered and organised. The political prisoner has to play his individual minor part in the drama, and seize this opportunity to make whatever political impact he can.

It may look from the outside like play-acting, but this is a deadly serious business. Make no mistake, the political prisoner is playing for his life in all its aspects (even if a sentence of death is unlikely): its continuation, its purpose and significance, its intrinsic value as a process of experience and reflection, and above all the chance it offers to make life better for other people.

Antonio Gramsci was taken for trial in Rome on 11th May 1928, one of thirty two leading Communists, of whom eight exiles were to be tried *in absentia*. From 12th May he was held again in Regina Coeli prison, this time sharing a cell with his close comrades Umberto Terracini and Mauro Scoccimaro, who were due to be tried alongside him. It was becoming clear to him as well as others around him that his health was rapidly deteriorating, not least because he was now denied the special diet prescribed by the prison authorities in Milan, who had been anxious to stop the stories circulating internationally about his ill-treatment and impending demise.

"Here in Rome the situation is almost the opposite," he wrote to his mother. "I have no idea how to gain permission to obtain food – naturally at my own expense – that I can digest. There is no possibility of seeing the director. We're limited to one request a week, and for one thing only. If this is turned down, you have to wait a further week to make another one, so it's quite useless to make requests." All the same he was still trying to reassure his mother and others that his current state of physical and moral health was good, and that he felt "serene and satisfied in myself... Yes, life is difficult, and sometimes sons – for the sake of their own honour and dignity – have to make their mothers suffer."

The trial began on 28th May. It was meticulously planned and designed, with strong elements of theatrical production, and borrowing freely from church-style liturgy, language and ritual. Security was provided by dozens of Fascist militiamen with black helmets, daggers and rifles with fixed bayonets. Posing in cordons as "guards of honour" for the judges, they could have passed as sacristans in a cathedral, guns instead of crosses held aloft as at some perverted black mass. The proceedings were conducted according to an entirely new, specially devised "court-martial" protocol, with a general as President of the Tribunal and a jury of five colonels from the Fascist militia.

Gramsci and the others were accused of "conspiracy, instigation to civil war, justifying criminal acts and fomenting class hatred." They were further accused of being "directly and primarily responsible for the illegal and criminal activities of the Communist organisation as sponsored by the organs and general policy of the party itself." Defence lawyers continually asked for more specific charges, supported by new and concrete evidence, but none was forthcoming. The prisoners, they concluded, were being tried for their politics rather than any crime they might have committed.

Gramsci was represented by a lawyer from Milan, Giovanni Ariis. His brother Carlo was there, along with other prisoners' relatives, and the Rome correspondents of the *Manchester Guardian*, *Le Petit Parisien* and the Soviet News Agency *Tass*. Gramsci was the first to be questioned, on 30th May, and acknowledged that he was a communist MP and journalist. But he denied engaging in any kind of clandestine activities, not least because (he told the court) "for years now six police agents have followed me about everywhere. Supposedly to protect my person, a close watch was kept on me. This now becomes my best possible defence. How could I have done the terrible things I'm accused of when I was under constant surveillance?"

When the President of the Tribunal asked Gramsci what was meant in his writings by "talk of war and the seizure of power by the proletariat," Gramsci replied, "All dictatorships end sooner or later by being overthrown in war. Given their intrinsically coercive character, it's the only way it can be done. When that happens, it seems clear to me that the proletariat should replace the ruling class, assume the reins of power, and try to build the nation back up again."

In summing up the case against him, on 2nd June, the Prosecutor Michele Isgro declared, "We must prevent this brain from functioning for twenty years!" In fact, on 4th June, Gramsci received a sentence of twenty years, four months and five days. His fellow detainees received similar sentences. An appeal was immediately presented on behalf of all of them, and almost as immediately rejected. At first Gramsci was supposed to be sent to the prison at Portolongone, on the island of Elba ninety kilometres south of Livorno. But with his health still worsening, his sister Teresina wrote to Mussolini requesting a "careful medical examination" and transfer to "a prison hospital where he can receive the proper food and care his weak constitution requires, and endure his punishment more humanely."

A medical report of 6th July declared that Gramsci had recently lost twelve teeth and was suffering from "gingivitis with abscess formation (gum disease), caused by uraemic disturbance (kidney dysfunction) and accompanied by nervous exhaustion." It was decided to send him to the prison at Turi di Bari, a penitentiary reserved for sick prisoners, in the south eastern "heel" of Italy. Mussolini declared in the press that this demonstrated the "humane face" of his regime, and contrasted

Gramsci's treatment with "the expulsions, imprisonments and summary executions dealt out to some of his old comrades in Moscow."

1928/1933: Turi di Bari

The biggest challenge to the political prisoner is finding a structure and a purpose for all his otherwise empty time. It's different for the ordinary prisoner, the seasoned or even apprentice convict, for whom "doing time" is an occupational hazard. He is usually sustained and disciplined by some criminal sub-culture, which spans the gulf between "inside" and "outside". There is no such comfort or contact for the political prisoner, who is necessarily cut off from political society, as surely as a drowning man is deprived of air.

His most pressing obligation, to himself and the cause which has landed him there, is to do something worthwhile from within the inescapable, almost tangible mood of gloom and isolation in which he has been forcibly immersed. To accomplish this he has to claw his way to the surface, take a deep breath in and a good look around. He must then force a deep breath out, and turn his miserable existence to productive and purposeful use. Preferably that great determined exhalation will be in the face of his most taciturn guard, and will be gratifyingly foetid from the combined ill effects of the meagre prison diet and almost universally rotting teeth.

Antonio Gramsci's journey from Rome to Turi di Bari prison was, he wrote to Tanya some days after his arrival, "another taste of hell". He had been granted a medical certificate, meant to alleviate his travelling conditions, but somehow at the moment of his departure it had disappeared. It lasted twelve days, in an ordinary prison transport, manacled and shackled in transit, lurching southwards between holding cells in filthy provincial gaols, the "huge worm" heading back in the opposite direction from that which had borne him from Ustica to Milan. Gramsci had attributed his illness in Rome to "liver trouble" on top of his usual ailments, but on departure it flared up and got very much worse. At Caserta, about a third of the way to Turi, a brusque local doctor diagnosed herpes zoster, which Gramsci remarked sardonically to Tanya, "…is one of the few complaints I've not yet suffered..." This fellow refused to give him the gauze he needed to bandage his sores because "at the front soldiers went as long as six days without having their wounds bandaged", then demanded in lieu of payment half the big bag of cherries Tanya had sent him in Rome: "I couldn't eat a single one of them, so at least they were put to some use."

Whatever ailed him, it soon got very much worse: "At Benevento I went through two absolutely horrible days and nights; I twisted around like a reptile. No matter where I put myself, sitting down, standing up or lying down, I just couldn't get any relief."

A more sympathetic prison doctor diagnosed Erysipelas or "St. Anthony's fire", a bacterial infection of the skin which causes rashes, soreness and boils all over the body. But he couldn't offer any treatment: "It just has to take its course, Signor Gramsci." He didn't ask for payment either, but Gramsci gave him the rest of the cherries, in gratitude for a more plausible diagnosis. Between Benevento and Foggia the pain receded, and the rashes and boils started to fade and dry up. Gramsci stayed at Foggia for five days, and by the third felt somewhat better. The pain was just about bearable when lying down, and he managed to sleep a few hours each night. He finally arrived at Turi di Bari on 19th July, still suffering from skin inflammation, struggling to eat and digest, breathing with great difficulty and unable to walk more than a few steps at a time without leaning on someone. Every movement required careful forward planning and long minutes of heavy-breathing recovery. Altogether, he calculated, he had barely slept for twenty days and nights. There was some consolation, in the form of a letter from Tanya waiting for him, and another from his brother Carlo enclosing a very welcome 250 lire note.

The special prison at Turi was a traditional, squat, castle-type building with four floors or "landings", built from local stone and surrounded by a kind of moat whose high walls deterred escape and contained the exercise yards. The windows of the cells were heavily barred but mercifully large, with shutters against the winter cold and the early morning sun. Unlike the prisons in Rome and Milan, they let in plenty of air and light. There would be no fretful calculations of how many minutes and hours of sunlight Gramsci could expect, or how much of his cell it might reach and warm. To begin with, he was held in a kind of quarantine or assessment area, prior to being assigned to a permanent section of the prison. This was a communal dormitory with five others, strangers from all over Italy, anxious and wary of each other as only imprisoned strangers can be. Gramsci struggled to sleep, like (he surmised from their noises and movements) his cell-mates. Occasionally he would catch an open eye staring at him in the half-light, and wonder if it was conveying menace or kindly curiosity. After a couple of weeks he was transferred to another cell with four others, all political prisoners, but with a variety of bronchial and lung complaints. He managed to sleep a little better, and it was a great relief to be able to share news and opinions with other politicos, even if they belonged to different factions, organisations and movements. It was apparent to him that their perspectives were starting to seriously diverge, even amongst the communists. There were strange accounts about what was going on in Russia, with the factional struggles reaching some kind of climax and wild talk of expulsions and arrests and even executions. But nobody really knew what they were talking about, so their discussions were mainly speculation from which Gramsci largely abstained. Apart from the odd sardonic remark or – when he knew from personal knowledge that some new rumour could not possibly be true – a factual correction, he kept his own counsel.

But as he listened to their chorus of wheezes, snorts and great rolling boils of coughing, which were especially bad when they were lying down at night, he fretted about what illnesses he might catch on top of everything else. As soon as he was able, Gramsci asked to see the Prison Governor, Giuseppe Parmegiani, a pinch-faced career bureaucrat who was known by prisoners and guards alike as *il gran' formaggio*, "the big cheese". Parmegiani told him bluntly that he had received strict instructions "from above" that "the Honourable Deputy Gramsci" was to be treated no differently from any other prisoner. The huge portrait of Mussolini over his shoulder, in full oratorical arm-waving, eye-rolling mode, chin jutting out like the lump-end of a hammer, seemed to nod in confirmation.

"The authorities have already demonstrated their compassion," said Parmegiani, "by not sending you to a normal prison hell-hole but here to the *Casa Penale Speciale* at Turi, with our specialist experience, expertise and facilities in dealing with prisoners in ill health."

Gramsci had struggled to see any of this. It looked to him like any ordinary prison, apart from the preponderance of frail and elderly prisoners and the added risks of communal contagion.

"Let me remind you," he replied as civilly as he could manage, "that I was arrested while still a parliamentary deputy and theoretically protected by my office. Indeed I still am, at least until the next general election, whenever *Il Duce* deigns to allow one, no doubt in suitably rigged and gerrymandered form. You should be treating me like a Cardinal, rather than worse than a humble parish clerk..."

The Governor simply reiterated that the normal rules would apply, including – and here he picked up the two letters Gramsci had already written to Tanya and his mother – "one letter per fortnight." He said that Gramsci was to indicate which of the two he wanted sent now, and which could wait another two weeks. The Governor further pointed out his own underlining of Gramsci's written instruction to Tanya "never to send me anything unless I have asked you for it," and concluded, "I am pleased to see, Signor Gramsci – sorry, *Honourable Deputy* Gramsci – that you are already adapting to the exigencies of life here at Turi di Bari..."

Gramsci got even shorter shrift from the local doctor, Dr. Cisternino, who was responsible for providing the prison's rudimentary medical service and refused to see him for several days. When he finally did, conducting a cursory examination and simply reading out what the doctor in Benevento had written, he observed that Gramsci appeared "to be on the mend... Of course, as a good Fascist I would like nothing better than to see you dead." Gramsci heard later that when Cisternino was called out by the townspeople at night, he would look down from his window and fix the fee – "Is it a 5,000 lire or a 10,000 lire visit?" – before deigning to descend.

In mid-August 1928, Gramsci did at least manage to get a cell on his own, on medical grounds. He wrote to Tanya that "the Special Tribunal sentenced me to imprisonment but they did not specify that this should be aggravated by tuberculosis..." But to his great dismay the new cell was located right next to the guardroom, with noisy comings and goings all day and all night. He never again slept a whole night through at Turi. Sleep disturbance and deprivation became his principal torment and bugbear.

* * *

Prison tears: a study of prison tears would make a fine start to a study of the anthropology of incarceration, as much for the effects of weeping on other prisoners as for its causes in the weeping one. Those others sense whether the tears are

"mechanical", a kind of reflex reaction to the state of imprisonment, much like the jerk of an immobilised limb or the blink of an eye before a jabbing finger. These mechanical tears indicate some amorphous and unnamed sorrow, which is in most cases a simple cry of loneliness and longing for the intimate company and the tender touch of another trusted human being. It provokes a general response of indifference from the other prisoners; they have been there too, will go there again, and know that it will pass soon enough. Then there are the truly "anguished" tears, which derive from a stark realisation of what the prisoner has lost and what awaits him, of the people he has known and loved and may never see again. This awareness of a life slipping away is a perversion of the normal temporal processes of memory and anticipation. Both past and future are being erased. It's the annulment or appropriation of time, implicit in the notion of penal policy, and everyone involved understands its obscenity. The cries of anguish are shared around the whole prison, like a rumour or a hymn or an airborne contagion, and reflected back in communal rage and indignation. The air boils and bubbles like soup in a cauldron. At those moments the stark reality of prison is laid bare for all to see: the state-sanctioned theft of life under the moralistic guise of retribution, or worse (and even more moralistic, in the sense that it appeases troubled consciences among the moralisers), rehabilitation. Mechanical tears are treated as mere noise, like the clanging of doors or the shouted instructions of the guards, just another part of the prison routine. But the tears of anguish are a notable incident in the prison day and (more often) night, an abrupt break in routine, to be remembered and commented on for weeks or even months afterwards, forever associated with the name and appearance of the anguished one. They are quieter and more prolonged, draining the crying prisoner dry, and often carrying over into convulsions of

tearless sobbing which no one hears but everyone senses and some silently share. These paroxysms of loss and despair charge the prison atmosphere with the buzz and flash of static electricity. You could start a fire with this grief.

There is a noticeably different reaction again when someone screams "I want to die!" It is as though this third, final cry of despair has offended some essential rule of prison life and more broadly of human existence: that no matter how many miseries or types of torment we confront, or how much is taken from us without our consent, life must and will go on. There will be something after this, even if we have no idea what or where or even when it might be. There is life after prison, if not after death. There has to be, for humanity's sake there has to be. In these circumstances, self-willed death is seen as a kind of betrayal or even treason, a broken link in the chain of suffering and sporadically joyful humanity we are all shackled and manacled to. That is why suicide is traditionally regarded in Christianity and other faiths, at least those which consider suffering an essential element within human existence, as a mortal sin. It is both a betrayal of, and escape from, the rest of suffering humanity. Finally, the tears of the younger prisoners form a fourth, quite separate category. They cast a dull empty silence over the whole prison which is almost a noise in its own right. The idea of death presents itself for the first time. The young prisoner becomes old all of a sudden. The rest of us are reminded of our own first prison tears, and in that moment take a sharp lurch towards our own old age and death. We think of our mothers, where we all came from, the source of the only wholly unconditional love we have ever received (however fleetingly that might have been; in some cases only at birth). It's as though our mothers are assembled at the prison gates, waiting for the authorities to relent and grant these infantile pleas for succour; imagine a prison full of mothers suckling their adult

sons. Most of the time, older and younger prisoners regard each other with deep mutual contempt, but when a younger prisoner breaks down, it arouses an instinct in the older ones that can only be described as maternal. If they are within physical reach, this is the only time an arm will be raised in solace and comfort, not in threat or anger.

From the very start of his imprisonment proper, Gramsci knew that the first weeks and months would be the hardest. Apart from the uncertainty and disruption of the quarantine and assessment period, it was also a matter of getting used to this horrible new place, which largely came down to convincing yourself – denying all the evidence of your senses and intellect – that it was not quite so horrible as it seemed. He had never been adept at self-delusion, and now he lived, he wrote to Julia, "…in continuous fear of being overrun by the prison routine, this monstrous machine that crushes and levels everything."

From his own observations of the other prisoners, he could see that those who had been there for more than a year or so were acclimatised, resigned to their fate, but, "When I observe men who have been in prison for five, eight or ten years and observe how their minds have become warped, I shudder to think what will become of me. At least some of them must have been convinced at the start that they would never give in. Instead, without being aware of it, so slow and molecular is the process, they find themselves utterly changed today; and this change in them prevents them from realizing exactly what has happened. Of course I intend to resist but, you know, I'm not able to laugh at myself as I used to, and this is a worrying sign."He was, he knew, already adjusting, but he was only a short way into the process. The more recent arrivals like him still had a kind of nervy, street-level alertness, as though awaiting some sudden announcement that their incarceration had been an administrative blunder or a case of mistaken identity. They could return to the little lives that had got them into trouble and, as they put it when they bantered amongst each other, hope for "better luck next time!" Almost every day he overheard one of them explaining to a long-term inmate or a prison guard or official that he hadn't actually done the crime he had been convicted of, or that his part in it had been wildly overstated or misunderstood. To listen to them, you would think that every young criminal was "just the lookout" or "the fall-guy for the other bastards." These assertions would elicit knowing, sardonic responses – "Of course you didn't do it son..." – which the "new 'un" would almost always misinterpret as endorsement. He even heard one young prisoner ask a smiling old lag if he could write a character reference for his forthcoming appeal. *It would be quite comical really,* Gramsci observed, *if it wasn't also very sad...*

You could also measure the prisoners' levels and stages of adaptation to prison by the colour in their cheeks. The newer ones still blushed red and pink in anger or delight, while the "old 'uns" had a permanent pallor in shades of yellow and grey, and rarely showed much emotion of any kind. It was almost like a colour chart, such as Gramsci had seen in the printers' offices and workshops he had frequented as a journalist. Underlying this was a kind of common sense that seeped out of the prison walls and into the consciousness of every prisoner, and infused every glance or word of exchange they were allowed between each other. Its central tenet was that the primary obligation of the prisoner was submission, and that all – even the most vociferously "innocent" or violently intransigent – would eventually submit, and turn yellow and grey.

The passing of time was a constant, obsessive mathematical activity. For each prisoner the key figure was how much of his sentence he still had to serve, but he was known to other prisoners by how long he had been in here, and how well he had reconciled himself to his fate. This obsession with the passing of time had some surprising results, not least a kind of mutual assistance. Simple daily survival, counting down another day towards release from these definitively confined circumstances, required some level of consideration for each other's feelings. All those sentences, from eighteen months to thirty years, added up into a collective sentence of many millennia, slowly chipped away at with every passing day together. *This*, Gramsci thought, *was the nearest prison ever came to any level of rehabilitation, quite inadvertently, in that of necessity these generally insensitive thugs have to pay more attention to other prisoners than they ever did on the outside.* "How are you doing?" was the implicit sense of any glance or word, not just the first exchange in any encounter; meaning, "Can we, you and I together, manage another day in here?" This also, it seemed to him, provided the material basis or common currency for the curious moral economies among the different criminal or regional groups, all those slogans and formulas repeated in awe and reverence and carved into the walls of cells or their own skin, which served to formalise and codify the basic requirement for cooperation.

Then there was the intergenerational, almost tender kind of solidarity, which Gramsci began to notice extended beyond the phenomenon of "prison tears". The longer established prisoners showed a kind of pity towards the newer ones, the *pulcini* or "little chickens" as they were commonly called, undercut with some menace and cool-eyed appraisal of any vulnerability that might be thereby exposed and exploited. If the *pulcini* received this pity in good grace, without bridling against the inevitable overtones of condescension, while taking care not to dissolve into grovelling servitude, their prison lives were quickly and markedly improved. They were received into some kind of inner sanctum. Helpful advice, favours and protection, even food and other comforts would come their way. They became *soldati* in their own right, feared and respected, looked up to and licensed to look down on others.

In contrast the grovellers were tolerated but found that their patronage was soon withdrawn, while they themselves became a service traded around the prison. The cockiest little chickens had it the hardest, their proud gestures of defiance treated with withering scorn: "You can act the big shot on the outside sonny, with your runty mates and your giggling girlfriends, and your tales of *braggadocio* and derring-do, but in here you're just another piece of shit like the rest of us..." If their resistance went on for any amount of time, it was beaten out of them with feet and fists or improvised weapons in dark corners coldly watched over by the prison guards. It was in everyone's interests that these cheeky little sods should have the stuffing knocked out of them, before they caused any serious trouble that everyone else would have to pay for in a tightening of prison rules and conditions or in the extension of sentences.

Eventually they too adapted, learnt their place in the pecking order, and adopted the appropriate acquiescence and respect. If they didn't, they just kept getting beaten up, right up to semi-permanent maiming and senselessness, and in at least one case Gramsci learnt of through whispers in the exercise yard, officially hushed up "accidental" death at the hands of their fellow inmates. Again, it was part of prison folklore that the cockiest and most recalcitrant *pulcini* had no one looking out for them on the outside, which is why they threw their weight around in here and refused to give in. They had nothing to lose, and nothing to offer apart from trouble. They were fair game; no one would miss the little bastards anyway.

Sooner or later, Gramsci understood, he himself would have to submit to the prison mentality, despite his disgust at its effects on other prisoners. Aware from them what was coming, he wanted to get on with it, but it couldn't be rushed. He just had to wait for his nervous system to absorb the dull shock, and in the meantime suffer the jolts and pangs of adjustment. Of course, knowing that it would be hard did not make it any easier to bear. Quite the opposite in fact, because he had the wit and the nous and the self-awareness to see what was happening and to simultaneously resist and will it to go faster, which of course it wouldn't. In fact he had precious little control of any kind over the process of abandoning himself and his former life. It was a further kind of delusion, especially acute among intellectuals, to imagine that he had. That delusion would, just like every other aspect of his previous personality, have to be abandoned. He had to bide or rather 'do' his time, just like everyone else.

Little more than six months into his sentence, he wrote to Tanya:

"They say that the sea beyond thirty metres deep is always still. Well, I have sunk to a depth of at least twenty metres, a level that only moves when storms of a certain size, well above normal, are unleashed. I am sinking deeper and deeper, and I can clearly foresee the moment when by imperceptible degrees I will reach the level of absolute stillness, where even the greatest storms no longer make themselves felt and it will no longer be possible to see the motions of the upper layers. And worse, it seems to me that I have already fallen into the trance-like state of the drowning man, typical of old convicts, who no longer reason by making realistic connections but by intuitions of a magical or spiritualistic form."

* * *

The longer sentence from the Special Tribunal, the twenty-odd years that now formally superseded the initial five years of *confino*, had a kind of weighty finality about it. It was Mussolini's last word to his fellow *Avanti!* journalist and old Socialist Party comrade. Insofar as any kind of future was conceivable in the new order of Fascist Italy, rapidly beginning to feel like a permanent fixture, this really did feel like a life sentence. Finally, at Turi di Bari, with the journeys between other prisons and the brief stops inside them looking more like a strange interlude, and now settled in a cell of his own, Gramsci realised that he was not going anywhere else any time soon.

There was a kind of peace in this gloomy realisation. The fight was over. The war he had described so proudly to his mother just a few months ago had been irretrievably lost. The proletarian revolution and the making of socialism was an inglorious failure, at least here in Italy but quite possibly all across Europe too. All that remained was to figure out the reasons for its defeat, and hope for "better luck next time." To pretend otherwise was delusion, little better than the *pulcini* pleading their wretched innocence of their pathetic little swindles and assaults. The Honourable Antonio Gramsci, one-time delegate to the Executive Committee of the Communist International, with its abruptly modern acronym of *Ispolcom*, more recently Secretary of the *Partito Comunista d'Italia* and Deputy for the Veneto region in the lower house of the Italian Parliament, was now Gramsci A., Prisoner 7047 at the Turi di Bari State Penitentiary for Sick Prisoners. The stern critic and would-be leader of the Italian state was now amongst its most powerless captives, in body if never wholly in spirit.

As if to underline this transformation, the guards at Turi were very different from the edgy thugs he had encountered in Rome and Milan and all the other prisons along the way. They were calmer, and in some cases kinder, because they understood that this was the best way for them as well as their charges to get through their working day, and all the working days that made up their careers and sentences. That doesn't mean they made life easy for the prisoners, or for Gramsci in particular, but in most cases their cruelty was inadvertent, insensitive rather than wilfully malicious. The noise from the guardroom next to his cell was more or less constant, day and night, as the guards came and went, talked and joked amongst themselves, spoke on the telephone, or handed over to the next shift. *This was*, Gramsci reminded himself, *their workplace*. It required the same kind of procedural tasks, menial chores, practical collaboration and orderly communication as any other job. And they were also after all Italian, with their operatic sense of performance and ingrained fear of boredom, solitude and silence. But understanding all this didn't make it any easier to bear.

It was especially disturbing in the night. The guards who volunteered for the night shift had obviously been doing it for some time, and adjusted to the topsy-turvy routine of working in the hours of darkness and sleeping through the day. It seemed to attract a particular character type, duller and deeper inside themselves than the day shifts. They were fundamentally at odds with the calibrations of normal human existence, the natural impulse to get up with the sun and down with the darkness. The night guards had the same prison pallor and emotional numbness as the older, long-term prisoners, and without their uniforms might easily have passed for them. It was rumoured that some of them actually had been prisoners, but couldn't bear to leave when they'd served their sentences.

Perhaps their nocturnal existence had inured them to the feelings and needs of normal people, Gramsci reflected as he listened to them gabbling and cursing away through the night, barking orders at subordinates or trusties, rattling keys and clanging doors, ostentatiously farting or belching, or moving furniture and equipment around the prison, as well as conducting regular checks of the prisoners through the slatted grilles in their cell doors. One particular dumb brute would open and close the grilles with his cudgel, which would rattle the bars as he drew it across, creating a staccato noise like machine gunfire or a train going over points. When Gramsci asked politely if he could just use his hand instead, the guard responded incredulously, "You don't expect me to touch it, do you?"

He would try to sleep or at least doze through it all, but would more often lie awake, listening out for the next disturbance or for any scraps of information or revelation that might be interesting or useful. Strangely, the harder it was to hear, the more he listened out. Other prisoners he grumbled to were nothing like as bothered by it. It was for them just background noise, the distant rumble of humanity, which more than one claimed to find comforting. Gramsci decided that part of the problem was that he was just too interested in what other people had to say, and he tried very hard to convince himself that it really wasn't that interesting. The problem was that for at least part of the time it really was, for cultural or historical as well as practical reasons, and you had to stay awake to pick these nuggets out. Either that or, deeper down at the level of barely rational consciousness, he suspected they might be talking about him or something that might affect him, just as when he was a child he had lain awake listening to his parents talking in the next room.

Prison at night is a very different place to prison in the day. The dreams and nightmares of several hundred lonely suffering agitated men – signalled by odd shouts and sighs, as well as occasional tears – coalesce into a peculiar atmosphere, almost gaseous and tangible, and peopled by phantoms both devilish and angelic. It is even further removed from normal society than during the day, because each inmate is truly and (so it seems to them) forever alone. He cannot forget himself in the company or the bodies of others, or in the stream of incident and chatter which every human gathering creates. He is forced inside himself as well as his cell, a secondary and much more punitive kind of incarceration, especially for those who lack the personal resources to cope with such enforced introspection. There he meets adversaries and ill-wishers entirely of his own making, with no excuses to be found in anyone else's supposed culpability. Prison nights are when the prisoner truly serves his sentence, Gramsci decided. That is how it should be fixed and handed down, 7,425 nights (in his case) instead of twenty years, four months and five days. Stays in a hotel are counted in nights, so why not prison?

Like all prisoners with a shred of intelligence and curiosity, Gramsci watched out for accounts of prison life in the books, papers and periodicals he ordered or that came his way. It wasn't just so that he could compare them to his own experiences, or that these other convicts' accounts validated and illuminated his own, as they usually did, but that they also offered a moment of precious abstraction or objectivity, the purer air of a higher altitude. They lent the prison experience an air of novelistic memoir, and even on occasions historical significance. At least while he was reading them, they allowed some precious release from his own thoughts, or even – if they were substantial, evocative and accurate enough – temporary escape from the prison he himself was currently confined to. His own miserable existence became part of the historical tradition of incarceration.

The first such account to catch his eye was by Jacques Riviere, a French essayist and editor who had spent some years as a German prisoner of war. Immediately after a search of his cell, during which his matches, some prohibited food, writing paper and a book on Goethe were confiscated, Riviere wrote:

> *"I think about all that they have stolen from me: I am humiliated, ashamed, naked. I long for my release but I'm no longer sure I can make it till then. This slow misery takes more out of me than any single ordeal. I feel it pressing down on me from all sides, entering my cell, entering me, robbing me of whatever I have left and leaving me discarded in a corner like a piece of trash. I know nothing more depressing than waiting for this evil to possess me, totally powerless to avert it. Every prisoner knows this tightening of the heart, this profound insecurity, this constant sense of helpless vulnerability to whatever might be thrown at you, from the small inconvenience of a few days in solitary confinement right up to death itself. There is nothing you can do but turn your back, to become as small as possible..."*

At the same time, for Gramsci, the prison memoirs were a distraction from what he knew he should be reading about. The very immediacy and depth of connection between him and the prison memoirist should have aroused his suspicions. They were indications that they were too alike, that their present conditions had too much in common to offer any kind of useful enlightenment, genuine abstraction or of course actual escape. He read widely and voraciously throughout this period, from the surprisingly well stocked prison library but also books and journals he was able to order from Sperling and Kupfers in Milan, courtesy of the ever faithful Piero Sraffa, and those he had brought into prison with him. The journals and reviews were drawn from an extensive European literary culture which thrived in the 1920s and '30s, and provided an invaluable guide for the intelligent reader in this first age of mass literacy. Gramsci read as many as he could get his hands on, even those sponsored by the Catholic Church and the Fascist State, and ordered books which looked especially interesting or received favourable reviews. But it was all a bit too random and aimless, a bit too much like reading for leisure and pleasure than for any clear political or even intellectual purpose. He felt, he wrote to Tanya, that he was "...just devouring books one after another" like some kind of literary glutton.

* * *

> ***"Something which concerns every man in prison: how can you avoid wasting time and carry on studying? First you have to get rid of every 'scholastic' attitude and not dream of attending regular, systematic classes. The best you can hope for is settled, undisturbed solitary study. One of the most rewarding things to study in prison is modern languages. You need only a grammar, which can be found for very little at a second-hand bookstall. Even though you don't learn to speak***

the language correctly, you can learn to read it. This is important because it will give you access to another culture and civil society, even if you have little prospect of ever actually going there.

Furthermore, many prisoners underestimate their prison library. No doubt all prison libraries are inconsistent. Books are thrown together haphazardly, whether gifts from ex-prisoners or from patrons who can get hold of publisher's remainders. There are always some prayer books and bad novels, but a political prisoner ought to be capable of extracting blood from a stone. The trick is to have some aim in mind while you're reading and take notes. That is, if you have permission to write.

Let me give you an example. In Milan, I read lots of different books – above all, popular novels – until the director of the prison library let me go in alone and select what I wanted from the books not yet on display. I also helped myself to others which, because of their political or moral tendencies, were not available to everybody. Well, I found Eugene Sue, Montepin, Ponson du Terrail etc., which sufficed if one looked at them from the following angle: why are these books always the most read and the most frequently published? What needs do they satisfy and what aspirations do they fulfil? What emotions and attitudes emerge in this squalid literature to have such wide appeal?"

That winter Gramsci's health deteriorated again, with recurrent kidney infections that made it hard to stand and move around his cell. He had to remain seated during much of the exercise periods, or be helped to stand and walk by other prisoners. In December 1928 Tatiana Schucht – still not fully recovered from her own illnesses and neurasthenia – made the long and arduous cross-country journey from Milan to Turi, and took a room for a couple of weeks in an inn near the prison. She was able to visit

Antonio almost every day. Now it was his turn to be truculent, and hers to be perplexed. He was plainly ill and immobile, and he had not seen any of his family for many months. This provided some explanation if not excuse, but nonetheless she struggled to cope with his ill temper. This was a side of his personality she had only previously glimpsed, in sarcastic remarks or especially aggrieved passages of his letters, or in passing comments from her sisters, but which for now seemed to be entirely dominant.

He chided her about things he had asked for and not received, such as the American fava beans with which he flavoured his tobacco, or that she had had delivered to the prison, mainly clothes and food, which were simply confiscated under prison regulations before he'd even seen them, and earned him another ticking off from Parmegiani the Prison Director.

"Listen," he told her, within seconds of their opening greetings on her first visit. "I am not allowed anything of my own except books and underwear."

"But I brought you food and clothes in Milan..."

"That was different! I had not yet been convicted! In here I'm not allowed any of my own clothes. I have to wear the prison uniform. Nothing metal either, not even the little Vaseline tin you sent for my chapped lips."

"But surely..."

"No! There are no exceptions! Please don't send me anything I haven't asked for. Really, Tanya, you seem to have no idea what it's like to be in prison!"

He was shouting now. Even the ever-present guard looked perturbed. Tanya looked down at her hands in her lap. She was thinking, *he wouldn't talk to Julka like this,* and not for the first time recalling her mother's remarks about Antonio being rude and moody. How had Julia Grigor'evna put it? He was "like a goat that had lost an eye and just keeps going round in circles!"

Across the scratched wooden prison table, with his stored-up anger released and subsiding, Antonio noticed the marks of Tanya's own recent periods of illness and hospitalisation, allied to the exertions of the journey from north west to south east Italy, and just possibly – his own remorse setting in – the effects of his own tirade. There were whole clumps of grey in the hair on her downcast head. Her features, never too clearly defined at the best of times, had blurred into a permanent look of physical strain, accentuated by new creases and wrinkles, not far away from tears. Parts of her body – her eyelids, her shoulders, the skin on her neck – had begun to droop and sag under the gravity of age. The last vestiges of youth had faded. All Tanya's previous sparkle and effervescence, so evident on their first encounters in Rome, seemed to have dissipated. Now, under the assault of his stern words, she looked childish and old at the same time, and even smaller than ever. Thinking over the visit afterwards in his cell, he imagined – in fact he knew from memory – that neither Julia nor Evgenia would have crumpled under challenge like this. *They would have shouted back; shrieked in Zhenya's case...*

On another of Tanya's visits he brought up the representations she had been making to the Ministry of Prisons, asking that he be transferred to the *Casa Penale Speciale* for sick prisoners in Soriano near Vitorbo, which would be nearer and easier for her to visit. She had claimed, and still did, to be acting on his behalf, but she had not consulted him at all.

"How could you do that without asking me?"

"I just assumed you were in no position to..."

"Please don't make assumptions about my position! I'm just glad they turned you down. Can you imagine the journey in my condition?"

"But surely they'd allow you special conditions for travelling?"

"Why? I've not been granted any 'special conditions' so far! I'm in prison, for God's sake, not on holiday or retired on a pension. Besides, even if they bought me a ticket for a sleeping car I don't want to move. I'm fine here..."

"You don't seem fine to me..."

"I'll be the judge of that! It's me that's in here... I know what it's like to be in prison. I've got the marks of it on my skin! Honestly Tanya, you have no idea..."

"Antonio, I was only trying to make things better for you..."

"But when you do things without asking me it makes me feel like a prisoner twice over, with you ordering my life just as ideas come into your head..."

Then there was Julia's continuing silence, which somehow he seemed to think Tanya could account for. Months had gone by without any kind of communication, not even the hastily scribbled notes enclosed or transcribed in Tanya's letters. The very last of these in the summer of 1928 had been especially confusing, a few short sentences full of effusive declarations of closeness, affection and sympathy – "I feel as if I finally know you!" she wrote, with no obvious cause for this sense of revelation – accompanied by lovely photographs of herself and the children. He wrote back to her, delighted: "Now I am really happy once again." And then nothing.

He wrote to her, as gently as he could manage, about how he longed for contact and for some "immediate, direct, living impression" of her and the children's lives. Without it, he felt that "my life is frozen up and paralysed." He had sent her, via Tanya, the wooden paper knife he had whittled away at for over a month, "and at the end of it my fingers were half worn away too. Have you made use of it?" He asked her how Delio was getting on with the Meccano set he had sent for his fourth birthday and (with a hint of self-conscious provocation) what her father Apollon with his extensive studies of Rousseau and other classical pedagogues – made of the child's development. In conclusion he pleaded, "My darling, write me a long letter." Still no response.

"Do you know," he said to Tanya on the last of her December

visits, "she hasn't written now for nearly four months, while I've written to her twice without reply? I'm not writing again, unless I get some direct news from her..."

"But I've had no news either," she replied. "I just think it's important to maintain contact. Her letters might just have gone missing. Antonio, you really should keep writing..."

"Why? I don't want to sound petty or childish, but I can't help thinking sometimes that if she no longer writes to me it's because she's no longer particularly interested..."

Tanya was not looking at him directly, which was always a bit of a give-away. He convinced himself that there was something he was not being told. He was furious again when he discovered that Delio had not been told that he was in prison, and berated Tanya about it.

"Has no one considered that he might find out about it indirectly? That's the worst way to learn something like that, because the child mistrusts everything he's told and withdraws into himself. He starts making things up for himself, on the basis of his worst fears and fantasies!"

This was just what had happened to him as a child, he said, when his father had been imprisoned, and his mother had gone to elaborate lengths to conceal it from their children and the rest of the family. She told them their father had gone on a long visit to her mother's house in the village of Gaeta, just a few hundred yards from the prison where he was actually being kept.

"A very long visit... five years, eight months and twenty two days!"

Signora Gramsci even used to bring her husband's letters home from prison with her so that they would be postmarked and sent from Ghilarza. Antonio would always remember the atmosphere of shame and subterfuge that hung over the family home for the rest of his childhood.

"In the end she had to tell me the truth anyway," he told Tanya, "because they couldn't afford to keep me in school. I never really forgave her for keeping it from me, or Dad for getting into trouble in the first place. I'm sure that my grievance caused them yet more pain..."

That was why Julia should tell the children where he was now.

"Otherwise, where will they think I am? Just "not there", which is the worst kind of absence, the unexplained, unaccounted for kind, which a child will always blame themselves for...The truth can hurt at first, but they soon get over it."

It just becomes another aspect of everyday reality they have to deal with, which is far healthier than fantasy and fear.

"Children are rational creatures, and they can understand even the most serious matters. In fact it makes them stronger, because they feel trusted and respected rather than disregarded and abandoned."

Tanya sensed his own strength of feeling, and undertook to communicate it to Julia; "I'll try..."

"Why do adults forget they were once children?" he continued, "and what that felt like? I remember so clearly finding out the truth for myself, and realising I couldn't rely on anyone else to tell me. By the time I was ten I'd become a real trial to my mother because I insisted on absolute frankness about everything, even the most trivial daily routines, because otherwise I always imagined the worst, and this caused endless rows and scandals..."

Even now, his mother had never fully acknowledged what had happened back then, or realised that he (and his brothers and sisters) had worked it out for themselves. This had simply added to the practical and emotional burdens she had had to carry throughout her life.

"No wonder she used to creep out to church at night swaddled in her black shawl, to pray on her own and weep for hours on end... Julia really must tell the children where I am, not least because she herself does not have my mother's fortitude."

* * *

Men in Prison: the title of one of the Frenchman's several as yet unpublished novels, based on his years before the war in a Paris prison for juvenile delinquency. If I had his imagination and boundless good will towards his fellows, and his universalist conviction that all lives and societies are equally complex and worthwhile, I might attempt a novel on the same theme. Mine would no doubt be darker and less engaged, reflecting my very different temperament and circumstances, and my very much lower opinion of men than his.

In my view, one of the most interesting things about men is that their own personal concerns are just not that interesting. There is this huge disparity between their view of themselves and of their own worth on the one hand – with enormous strength of will and character required to maintain that inflated self-regard – and on the other, any objective measure of the worthwhile contribution they make towards history and humanity. It amounts to a kind of arrogance and vanity, all-consuming from the inside and utterly pathetic from the outside.

Of course in prison everything is reduced and exacerbated, so you see the folly of men in its most condensed, rawest, extreme form. Prison brings out their primal competitive nature, their lust for status, largely because there is so much less to compete for, hierarchies are flatter, and the advantages of superiority so much less marked and substantial. Prisoners' intense focus on immediate gratification – food and drink, defecation and urination, above all sex – simply brings to the surface what most men really and most deeply and frequently think about.

Men in prison, and men in the prison of their own desires and inadequacies, spend much of their time in banal longing for the sight and sound and smell of women, and for recip-

rocal female desire, admiration and blessing. Even the most restrained and intelligent men can be reduced to Neanderthals – tongues lolling, knuckles trailing, hips and appendages thrusting forward uncontrollably – by the mere hint of a female presence. A word or a scent or a picture can do it; or a glance across a communal prison visiting hall, stored up for later rumination and imaginative elaboration. For the most part it is a longing which can never be satisfied, which simply makes it all the more banal. Attempts to satisfy it by oneself offer momentary relief, but the longing soon returns redoubled. For myself, I am surprised by how easily I can turn it off. I am well aware that in the process I am turning off some essential part of myself, but it feels like civilisation, and a peculiarly modern kind of liberation. Even the blessed Freud accepts that sexual repression is crucial for the exercise of reason, for artistic creativity, for mutual tolerance and social solidarity. I am living inside my own head, at growing distance from my body. In so many ways I am glad to say goodbye, especially to a body as stunted and ugly and untrustworthy as mine.

All this explains why I will never write a novel; the Frenchman once told me that he couldn't go more than a couple of days without sex. It seems that what the English call "moral incontinence" is essential to literary production.

In February 1929, about seven months after his arrival at Turi, and nearly two years after his first, unsuccessful application, Gramsci finally received permission to write in his cell. This meant he could take notes on his reading, and impose a structure, order and purpose onto his reflections they had so far lacked. What had been a diverting pastime could become a programme of study and research, with some kind of written product as outcome. This was, for him, a moment of profound release, a massive improvement in his conditions of existence.

His brother Carlo had again helped out by engaging a lawyer to petition the prison authorities.

With distinct improvements in his health as winter turned to spring, Gramsci faced the new year with fresh vigour and enthusiasm. He wrote to his mother on 24th February that: "The tonics I have been taking have helped me enormously. The weather here has been better than elsewhere. It has rained and snowed but there have been sunny spells. I've suffered much less this winter than in Milan, let alone the winter 1926/7, which I spent travelling lightly clad in prison vans that had stood the whole night in the snow." These early months of 1929 found him in much better spirits, he assured her. He might just be able to wring something worthwhile out of all this miserable time in confined isolation. That same month he wrote to Tanya: "Do you realize? I am actually writing in my cell. For the time being I am only doing translations to get back into practice; meanwhile I am putting my thoughts into order."

He even received a note – relatively long and expansive by her standards – from Julia in May, with news of the children, their development and daily routines. Delio was now nearly five and going to school. He was over a metre tall, and weighed twenty five kilos. Apollon had observed that the boy was very outgoing and expressive, "…like an engineer or an aviator, destined to survey the world and make his mark upon it, and serve the great cause of socialist construction like his father and grandfather." Giuliano, who would be three in August, seemed much more introspective by comparison, "…deep in his own thoughts and sensations, and taking unusual care over his responses to other people and things. Perhaps he has a more artistic bent, like his mother and maternal great grandfather."

Antonio wrote back to Julia, thanking her for her news and her father's evocative descriptions of the children. He had pondered on them for several days, "…like a naturalist who finds a tooth or a small tail bone in some prehistoric cave and from it tries to reconstruct an extinct animal the size of a whale." He described his own current state of mind as "passive and apathetic." This might seem paradoxical to her, especially in the light of his improved physical health, but he considered it a good sign of his adjustment to prison life and his overcoming "the fear of death which is at the root of all the psychological phenomena I observe in here. Prisoners are terrified that they will die before release. For most of them imprisonment itself is a kind of slow, inexorable death. They can be deeply degraded by the realisation that they are caught in the vice and can't get away"; or they can reconcile themselves to their fate and draw quiet strength – as he felt he was now doing – from this reconciliation. He was "becoming a real fakir; soon I'll be able to swallow swords and stroll barefoot over Gillette razor blades..."

"So now I am absolutely calm, and not even the prolonged lack of news can cause me anxiety, although I know this could be avoided with a modicum of good will on your part... But I don't mean to reproach you! During the last few days I've reread all the notes you've sent me over the last year, and I felt your love all over again. When I write to you, I sometimes feel I'm too dry and dour, while you write to me so freely and naturally, as if it was just part of your busy daily life. It makes me feel like I did those few times when I made you cry, especially that first time (do you remember? In our room at the Lux?) when I was really bad with you, and on purpose too."

In his first separate letter to Delio, enclosed with this letter to Julia, Gramsci asked his son to write him letters of his own as soon as he could, even if he had to dictate them to the grown-ups. "I know that you like making aeroplanes and trains, and that you're taking an active part in the industrialisation of the country. But do these aeroplanes really fly, and do the trains really run? If I were there with you, I'd put my cigarette in the funnel, so that at any rate we'd have a bit of smoke!"

Then in late June and early July there was another flurry of letters and photographs from Julia; "Two in a fortnight!" he told Tanya exultantly. Julia told him of an altercation between the boys, when Giuliano had damaged a paper hat made from folded newspaper Delio had brought home from school. Delio had set to fixing it with great determination, and a practical streak which she couldn't imagine came from either her or him, their father, "with your literary and philosophical tendencies."

Antonio wrote back that: "On the contrary, as a child I was an intrepid and deeply practical pioneer. I never left the house without grains of wheat in my pocket and matches wrapped in little scraps of oil cloth, just in case I was cast away on a desert island. I was also a gallant builder of ships and handcarts, and knew all the names and types of naval vessels from A to Z and back again. My greatest success was when a village character asked me to make a paper model of a double-decker schooner so he could reproduce it in tin!"

Julia's next letter, which reached him just a week or so later, included a new photograph of the children. He wrote back: "It made me very happy... Apart from anything else, it pleased me so much to see that they have bodies and legs. For three years I've seen nothing but their heads, and I was beginning to suspect they'd turned into cherubs, minus the little wings behind their ears. Delio looks like he understands the need to pose for the camera, takes himself very seriously but is impatient to get on with something else. Giuliano, on the other hand, is staring at that mysterious object, not at all sure there isn't some nasty surprise behind it. An angry cat might spring out at any moment, or a magnificent peacock. Why else would they have asked him to look in that direction and not move?"

He asked for more photos of her, "...at least once a year... otherwise all sorts of daft ideas enter my head. I start imagining that you have grown much older and weaker, with lots of white hairs and so on! I'd also like to see you in a group with the children, because a group gives a more vivid picture. You get an idea of relationships between people, which you can elaborate into other groupings and episodes of real life, leaving the photographer and his carefully aimed camera behind, with his cats and peacocks!"

He fretted that he had never clearly expressed his appreciation of her, of how strong she had had to be in bearing "the heaviest burdens of our union", in both their brief periods together and their much longer separations. Part of the explanation for his reticence was her deference towards him, which made him feel like "a farmer appraising a beast of burden." They were still struggling, nearly thirty years into this new century, with traditional notions of how men and women should treat each other. He was supposed to be strong and authoritative, "which in all honesty I rarely feel", while she was supposed to be weak and submissive, "which I know you not to be." But they could not simply shrug off the burdens of history and social convention. The "new man" and "new woman" of Socialism would be a long time coming yet.

What's more – he had acknowledged to himself for some time, but was only now confident enough in Julia's understanding to share – he was foolishly jealous of her intimacy with the children and deeply resentful that he could play no active part in their upbringing. On every level – emotional, intellectual, even pedagogical – he would have loved to have been intimately involved in caring for them and helping them to develop. Apart from anything else, he would have been able to counter the influence of Rousseau which the Schuchts had picked up on their travels around cosmopolitan Europe, all that "hopelessly Bohemian" nonsense about letting a child grow up "naturally and spontaneously and without direction... But perhaps I'm annoying you with the mention of Rousseau which once before (do you remember? In the apartment on Via Vesalio?) made you so angry. Or that time a couple of years ago when I had the temerity to recommend via Tanya that you read *The Constant*

Nymph by Margaret Kennedy, that rather silly but immensely popular English novel about a musical family headed by a wayward patriarch, "children of nature" wandering the "deserts of Bohemia" in a most peculiar ideological atmosphere, and where to cap it all the pubescent heroine appears to die of growing pains!"

Then it all went quiet again. In the whole year from July 1929 to July 1930, Gramsci received just one letter from Julia, in late December. It was brief and cursory, a few random jottings about the children between other obviously more important tasks. Delio had got lost in the apartment block; Giuliano liked to help with the washing up; both had been out playing in the snow. Her previous letters had felt like engaging communiqués from within her daily life; this came over as a burdensome duty, a reluctant chore on a par with peeling potatoes or mopping the floor.

He wondered more than once whether his growing frankness about her and his disclosures about himself had somehow offended her, or put her off in some other unspecified way. Was it perhaps, yet again, his disparaging remarks about Rousseau? Or the implied comparison between the Schuchts and the Sanger family in *The Constant Nymph*? He wrote back to her about another worsening in his health and mood over the winter, caused in part by her lack of communication and the growing sense that he was losing touch with his family, the children in particular:

> *"I know almost nothing of their development, but from what you say Delio seems very backward for his age. At five and a half he cannot find his own way around the apartment block. At less than five, I could freely move around my village and the surrounding area. Without ever having travelled more than a couple of kilometres in either direction, I could point out where I lived on a map, as well as the big cities of Italy. I don't think I was that unusual. A very young child absorbs an amazing amount of information which guides him*

in that initial period of logical thought as he learns to speak.

At the risk of making you angry, I have to bring up Rousseau again. The problem is that your own conception of child development (and that of other members of your family) is too metaphysical. It presupposes that the whole man is already latent in the child, and that you just have to help it emerge, letting the spontaneous forces of nature do their work and so on. I believe a child has to be consciously formed and directed by the norms and standards of his own social circumstances and historical era; otherwise he is not equipped to play a full and useful part in them. He will pick up bad habits and his personality will develop quite haphazardly.

The idea of education as unwinding a pre-existing thread was useful in countering the harmful indoctrination of the Jesuits, and the oppressive effects of rote-learning, but it's now quite out of date itself. Education can be systematic and rigorous without suppressing natural curiosity and love of learning, assisting the child to engage with the world around him rather than leaving him to his own devices while he is buffeted with extraneous sensation. Strangely, it may be that Freudian psychoanalysis is reviving the idea of the noble savage, corrupted by society and history, in some new and even more insidious form..."

Gramsci conceded in conclusion that he may be extrapolating far too much from the very little information he had to work with from Julia's sporadic notes and Tanya's second-hand reports. Recalling his naturalist analogy, he recognised the danger "of starting with a piece of a mouse's tail and ending up with a sea-serpent! I embrace you lovingly." As he handed over the letter to the prison secretary, enclosed in a shorter note to Tanya for forwarding, he felt a brief pang of anxiety about the likely effects on Julia of what he had earlier acknowledged as his "tendency to lecture, or worse to preach." Should he have kept his criticisms to himself, at least till his irritability had subsided? Should he take his lead from Julia, and remain largely silent for the time being? How do you maintain contact with a loved one thousands of kilometres away, in a life and a society so different that it might be on another planet?

Tanya actually moved to Turi in December 1929, so that she could visit Gramsci more easily and regularly. It caught him by surprise, and somewhat perplexed him. It would of course be helpful and handy to have her close by, but why exactly had she moved here? She could visit him more frequently, and bring things with her to prison, but the system they had established for ordering and delivering books, supplies and provisions to the prison was actually quite efficient and reliable, so long as Tanya stuck to the rules. It was always good to see her smiling face in the visiting hall, but the conversation always seemed to falter after the opening pleasantries, especially now that she herself was losing touch with the larger world beyond Turi di Bari and had little of note to report. With each visit, he felt the pleasure of their initial contact subside, and his irritability rise. She also made a convenient focus for his bewilderment over Julia, her sister.

He wrote to Tanya about Julia's almost total silence on 13th January 1930: "Don't think I'm angry; I'm actually past caring... I don't want to feel sour with rage again or go through more weeks of migraine, agonizing and punishing myself for something – I know not what! – I might have said to cause this stand-off. I must ask you not even to mention this subject again when you visit or write to me. Let me have whatever news you receive, but don't exhort me and don't preach at me." He went on to tell her about a collection of letters and writings he had been reading by Silvio Spaventa, an Italian patriot imprisoned for his involvement in the Neapolitan Parliament in 1848. Gramsci was struck by the similarity in Spaventa's account, "in the somewhat romantic language of his day", of his time in prison to "certain states of mind I frequently experience." Spaventa wrote to his father in 1853:

> *"It is two months since I have had news from you; four months or more since I heard from my sisters... Don't you believe that for a person like me, who is finely attuned to his feelings, this privation is bound to be extremely painful? I do not believe that I am loved less by my family than I always was, but misfortune tends to have a dual effect. People cease to care for the unfortunate, and he ceases to care for them. I'm less worried about the former than the latter. Cut off as I am from every human and loving exchange, beset by the intense boredom of long imprisonment and the fear of being forgotten, my heart is slowly becoming bitter and sterile."*

Gramsci continued: "What I did not foresee about my own imprisonment was the other prison added to the first, which consists of being cut off not only from other people in general but also from one's own family. I anticipated the blows of my enemies, but not from my loved ones..." Finally, he acknowledged Tanya's efforts on his behalf, and the sacrifices they required of her: "But there's always you, you're bound to say. It's true, you are very good, and I love you greatly. Only there are some things for which one person can never take another's place." For that other person he still felt "a great upsurge of tenderness which would be best expressed in a loving embrace, but only clumsily in words."

In August 1930, Palmiro Togliatti wrote from Paris in an internal memorandum for the *PCd'I* leadership in exile that "…Antonio must be demoralised about certain family matters, whose substance we do not grasp." Attempts might be made in Moscow to "see Antonio's wife and clear things up... It seems incredible to me that there should be people around him who create so much muddle. Apparently his wife sends her letters to Gramsci via some office, which then has to forward the letters. This office has held the letters for six months! Couldn't someone teach this blessed woman that in modern cities (and in villages too) there are rectangular boxes with a slit at the top and that when letters are put in them one can be sure that they reach their destination with reasonable speed?"

* * *

Work, work, work: the only answer to anxiety and depression. In fact, the most efficient outlet for all that negative nervous energy, sanctuary from your feelings on the higher level of abstract thought. The best advice I can offer the prisoner wishing to do something worthwhile with his time? Use your misery...

Gramsci wrote his notes, excerpts and translations in ruled school-type exercise books ordered from *Laterza e Figli*, the booksellers and stationers in Bari. The first notebooks contained fifty sheets, one hundred pages with twenty two lines on each side. They had red and black marbled covers made of stiff card. On the front was an oblong space where the Prison Director Parmegiani wrote Gramsci's prison number and his own signature of authorisation. Upon completion each sheet was examined to ensure that no prison regulations had been violated, and stamped with the prison seal in the top right-hand corner. In the same spirit of petty bureaucratic scrutiny, he was not allowed all his notebooks to hand in his cell. As he filled them up, they were deposited in a storeroom, and he could only take out a few at a time.

Gramsci wrote in a small, precise, right-leaning copperplate, with the headings singly or doubly underlined according to their function and importance. Notes which had been revised and rewritten elsewhere were crossed out (but still legible) with neatly ruled, cross-hatched lines. If they were meant to be disregarded altogether, they were crossed through (but again still legible) with a single horizontal line. Each letter was written clearly and precisely, with capitals – especially A-s, T-s, S-s and Fs – stately and almost ornate, betraying long hours of calligraphy practice in childhood and a lingering commitment to appearance and legibility.

As he told Tanya, his very first prison writings were translations, mostly from German and Russian, with the aim of improving his facility in those languages but also just getting used to studying systematically again. His first translation was Franz Nicolaus Finck's *Die Sprachstamme des Erdkreises*, a short but authoritative catalogue of world languages published in 1923, which reminded Gramsci of his student love of linguistics and philology. He also understood and wrote in French, which was customary among Italian intellectuals of the time, and some of the later notes were written in or translated from French. At this early, preparatory stage, he even tried his hand at English translation. He did not understand much of the language, so his exercises were simply isolated phrases such as "last not least", "Hard Times" or (one he especially enjoyed disentangling, not least for its resonance with the prison mentality) "I can find fantasies where none is." When soon afterwards he began making notes of his own, they were mostly short fragments, quotations or commentary on other writers he was reading or could remember from the last twenty years. They were thrown together scatter-gun style as he recalled an event or an observation, or was reminded of something else altogether; at this stage, little more than references, pointers and *aides-memoires*. He was looking for a way into history, along quite definite lines of enquiry: the formation of intellectuals, the influence of religion, the practice and theory of politics, developments in philosophy and ideology, the interests of social classes and how parties sought to represent them, the overriding importance in Italy of the north-south split and the limitations of national unification. Some of these Gramsci set out on the very first page of the first notebook, dated 8th February 1929, in the sixteen-point programme of study he would pursue tenaciously over the next five years. The only one of those sixteen points he did not undertake or even begin was the only vaguely autobiographical one, number 8, "Experiences of Prison Life".

Gramsci's early prison studies were focussed around a single overriding theme, dictated by his own recent experiences of political defeat and imprisonment, agitating his mind like a grain of sand inside the shell of an oyster: the mystery of Italy. Day after day, week after week, month after month, through the last year of the 1920s and into the fretful, uncertain 1930s, he sat – or more often stood and paced around his cell, reflecting on his last note and composing the next one – wondering how on earth had it come to this? How had he ended up here, imprisoned for the crime of political persuasion in the cause of social progress, with that cause trashed in the name of a half-baked ideology of reaction which itself claimed to be "progressive" or even "revolutionary"? Only that question was gradually honed into more political, impersonal, historical shape. And at the heart of this enquiry was an even simpler question: why was the country he had been born and grown up in, albeit on its outermost periphery, with its proud antecedence in classical civilization, so fundamentally silly and half-formed? How could he explain "the paradox of a country that is simultaneously very young and very old", puerile *and* senile?

How could it throw up such philosophical peculiarities as *Lorianismo,* named after the influential writer and prestigious academic Achille Loria (1857-1943), a self-professed "historical economist" who claimed to have "surpassed Marx"? When he wasn't composing overblown poetry along the lines of his *Ode to my Walking Cane,* Loria specialised in such absurd predictions as a solution to world hunger and class exploitation involving huge aeroplanes with glue on their wings and fuselages which would catch birds as they flew around the world. He foresaw the decline of the occupation of doorman and other "ground-level servants" because of the danger of death by binoculars dropped from the high-rise buildings where everyone would be living. This would soon be followed by social revolution instigated by these unemployed servants.

Juvenile delinquents could be effectively rehabilitated in prisons on high mountains or even on yet more immense aeroplanes, because there was a direct "scientifically established" correlation between morality and altitude. According to Loria, people behaved better in thin air. Pain could be overcome by sleeping outdoors because it "thickened the skin". War could be overcome through the curing of syphilis, the cause of the widespread intemperance and despotism found amongst the ruling classes. Italy could level its troublesome, obstructive mountains and transport the soil to its Libyan colony to fertilise the desert.

How could such nonsense find a hearing in any self-respecting national culture? Part of the answer was Italy's failure to create its own "national intellectuals". Instead, they were formed either by the progressive currents of French and German culture or the reactionary perspectives of the Roman Catholic Church. They were thus either free-floating pan-Europeans or agents of the Vatican, but never primarily Italian. Either way, they were "cosmopolitan not national", and left space for all sorts of local oddities in between. Italy had no settled, constructive, mature intellectual life of its own, which meant that preening charlatans like Loria or more recently the posturing "idealists" clustered around Mussolini could rise to the top and gain great prestige and influence.

Public life was characterised by bluster and gesture, with a tradition of "say one thing, do another" government. Reality was obscured by rhetoric; rank careerism and opportunism by supposedly grand principle. A seam of prolix oratory ran deep through Italian politics, from the ineffectual unifiers and scheming cliques of the *Risorgimento,* through the windy demagogy of the maximalist Socialists, to the "stupid gladiatorial posing", "martial pomp" and "fawning philosophy of pure action" of the Fascists. This latest outburst was all the more ridiculous for its glorification of "the innate genius of the Italian race" and other pieces of populist flattery that had no basis in the historical record. The single most notable feature of Italian politics was the weakness of the central state and its remoteness from most people's everyday lives.

This lack of a mature national politics and an effective state accounted for successive Italian governments' adventures in what Gramsci called "half-arsed, castle-in-the-air imperialism", based on the "mirage of exploitable colonial lands" and the vacuous slogan "Italy goes it alone". This was backed up and enforced by incompetent and occasionally disastrous military campaigns against native populations usually armed with little more than sticks. What this meant in practice was grabbing a few dusty scraps of land no one else much wanted, dumping on them those mostly Southern surplus peasants who didn't want to emigrate to the USA or South America, and by and large leaving them to get on with it. Or not, because the Italian colonies amounted to very little without the investment capital, technology, resources and skilled labour the country could not (unlike other more "successful" empires) afford to export.

This was why Italy was never taken entirely seriously abroad, and why the menace and the brutality of its own local version of paramilitary reaction were so often underestimated and so rarely understood. Foreigners saw only the comic opera of Italian Fascism, with its beautifully tailored uniforms, its highly choreographed ceremonies and posturing, its overblown oratory; easily mimicked and, from a safe distance, enjoyed. They did not see its very real and threatened violence and its systematic reorganisation of politics and the state. Italian Fascism was an iron fist inside a velvet glove puppet, and they were amused or even charmed by it. They fawned and swooned, this endless parade of holidaying dignitaries, political grand tourists, personalities and literati come to marvel at "the glory of Rome" and the delights of Mussolini's patronage.

Beneath all of this was the curious childishness of the Italian people, most purely represented in its petty bourgeoisie, and a determined refusal to grow up. You could see it in any gathering of Italians away from home, Gramsci observed, which "...soon forms into giggling, nudging, fearful cliques, worried about contagion and abandonment, and what these foreigners might be talking about in their strange guttural barking languages." Then they start looking round for Daddy, or any other figure of authority who might tell them what to do and where to go.

It was like some strange folk-memory of the latter days of the Roman Empire, when most of its citizens were still living well and peaceably but increasingly fretful about the encroachments of the barbarian hordes. The modern Italian popular masses were just too comfortable – with their tasty food and light entertainments, their mostly temperate climate and their just about adequate housing – in their craven subordination to the prevailing order of the ruling elite. Upon these silly people Gramsci turned his harsh "social moralism", which he contrasted to the populist indulgence of the Fascists and the unsympathetic paternalism of the northern industrialists and their "scientific" apologists.

The Italian petty bourgeoisie were like the Bandar Log "monkey people" in Kipling's *Jungle Book*, Gramsci wrote, "...who sing every minute of every hour... but do not act, who claim to be the wisest, cleverest, most clear-sighted people on earth; you'll see just what we're capable of... tomorrow." Or they took after the seventeenth century popular-theatrical character Stentorello, "talkative, vain, hollow... howling, bawling and preening like smug academics. They eulogise the virtues of their race and the wisdom of their ancestors, while they themselves do no work or produce anything of any note or value." They are "pensioners of economic history... absolutely parasitic classes, living off their ancestral patrimony... leftover people in their cities of silence, all those beautiful but pointless mediaeval centres, urban clusters without industry but with centuries of accumulated wealth to swaddle them against the upheavals of global capitalism." The Fascists had flattered these people by calling them "producers of savings", when all they ever produced were rents on land and property they were largely absent from.

Around these small-town *signori* and provincial gentry were ranged various grumbling sub-types: the primitive share cropper who pays his rent with a portion of his harvest, owns some tools and a yoke of oxen and a small house he has built himself with extra earnings in the mines or the *carabinieri*, "in other words by 'contriving' and saving... He hates 'the bureaucrats' because they impose taxes for state services he does not personally receive or understand"; then, agricultural day-labourers, who are "drunkards and spendthrifts, incapable of sustained work, physically deficient because of chronic malnutrition or simple stupidity... semi-beggars with a makeshift life on the margins of the rural underworld"; finally, the "petty intellectual starvelings... a famished threadbare rabble hoping for minor municipal postings as clerks and messengers, jostling for political favours and merging with the career criminal underworld." All of these types see themselves as "subversive" of the established order, but with no clear political purpose or social identity, they are available to the highest bidder but always finally on the side of reaction.

Not surprisingly, when it came to the way in which the country was governed, "...between the normal political poles of consent and coercion stands corruption and fraud... there has never existed a 'rule of law' but only a politics of arbitrary power and personal cliques." The most recent example was the change in electoral law, adopted in parliament in May 1928 and approved in a plebiscite in March 1929. This stipulated that a single list of four hundred candidates, selected by the Fascist Grand Council from a thousand names submitted by the state employers' and workers' confederations, would be presented for approval to the electorate. At the same time, three million people in places and social groups with a tradition of anti-Fascist politics were removed from the electoral roll. At a stroke, parliamentary democracy was absorbed within the Fascist state.

This also meant deep and persistent contempt for legality and moral order in public affairs, widespread tax evasion and opportunistic criminality. This in turn engendered fascination with violent crime, reflected in the popularity of serial novels and lurid press coverage at one extreme and at the other the explosion in the academic subject of criminology. In its most positivist guises this new "science" explained criminality by national or regional stereotypes. This was a step forward from the Inquisition. Its new more humane methods of incarceration and rehabilitation were an improvement on torture and summary execution, but it still rested on a notion of "innate good and evil", albeit geographically rather than morally distributed. Certain settings produced bad people, supposedly, especially in the South. "They are not bad people," proclaimed this new scientific criminology, "they just come from bad places." This line of thinking removed whole social subgroups from their cultures and their histories, from their real places of work and residence. They were "excused for their wrong-doing" – with just as much condescension as the absolution of the Catholic confessional – but in the process rendered "subhuman", almost animalistic. More than once Gramsci had heard Sardinians like himself referred to as "monkeys" by northern mainlanders.

This antiquated, fragmented Italy, whose classical culture lay at the foundation of western civilisation, was little more now than a collection of squabbling, self-interested, petty-fogging cliques, gathered around the fountains and statues in the village square, arguing the relative merits of their own local wine or cheese or *Signor* Big Man. Nothing was wrong or right, because there was no common law, just a stream of declarations and instructions from the centre which were met with indifference or contempt in the localities. A weak central state went hand in hand with the mythology of the outlaw, whose forms and secondary expressions Gramsci could see daily all around him, even in this obscure provincial penitentiary for sick prisoners. Most of them, even some of the politicos, carried about them a kind of subversive glamour, as though their petty thefts and gestures of defiance automatically possessed some larger political purpose, a noble fight between some ill-defined "us" against an even vaguer "them". *Utterly pathetic...* but it was always worthy of close study.

This was why Gramsci spent more time alone in his cell, and frequently turned down the chance to exercise. He had to figure it all out, and he only had so much time before release or – the more likely outcome, he already suspected – death. He preferred to continue reading and writing on his own, rather than mill about with the same old deadbeats and losers, playground bullies and self-styled "kings of the wing." "Life in company kills me," he wrote to Tanya, "irritating my nervous system to the point of convulsions." Even his own personal pursuits and interests became more confined to his cell, more "focused and organised" as he put it, as his studies went ever deeper.

Tanya had brought him a small rose cutting and some herbs and flower seeds on the last of her visits in December 1928, "for a taste and smell of life on the outside!" she wrote on the attached card. He set about cultivating them in his designated patch of the prison courtyard, a square metre beside the wall, as far as the limited sunlight and fluctuating temperatures allowed. In late April he reported to her that:

"...the rose has gone down with terrible sunstroke; all its leaves are burnt and blackened. It looks desolate but amazingly it's putting out fresh buds. The sunstroke was inevitable, because all I could shade it

with was a piece of paper, which the wind blew away. In any case it's still alive, and the prognosis is favourable. I'm afraid the seeds have been very slow to emerge; most of them seem to want to remain in hiding! They were rather old and moth-eaten; perhaps the gardener who sold them to you as good seeds meant they were good to eat. What has come up looks more like parsley and onions than flowers. Every day I'm tempted to pull them up gently to help them grow, but I can't decide whether to follow Rousseau and let nature take its course or intervene with an 'authoritarian' hand. The two ideologies are fighting it out in my head! The six chicory plants are doing well enough by themselves, and should provide seeds for my next crop, but there's no sign of the dahlias and the bamboo."

In early June, he was able to "draw up a final balance sheet on the flower situation. All the seeds have failed except one. I'm not sure what it is, except that it's probably a flower and not a weed. The chicory is blooming away, and the bamboo has put out a leaf as large as a hand, with another on the way. The rose is budding well, and recovered from its sunstroke; but will it cope with the summer heat ahead? I suspect it's too weak and sickly to come to much, but time will tell." In fact, by early July the rose had "completely recovered... From 3rd June to the 15th it started putting out leaves till it was green again. Now its branches are fifteen centimetres long. It even tried to put out a tiny bud, but it withered and turned yellow. Anyway it's taken root, and I wouldn't be surprised if this tiny timid rose will flower next year." It would not have the chance to, because new prison regulations forbade such recreation. The flowerbeds were ripped up and their contents destroyed.

* * *

When does the political prisoner cease to be especially political, and become just like any other prisoner? In my

> ***experience, about three or four years into his sentence, when political society recedes into his own distant memory, a new set of political issues and protagonists has taken the stage, and his own daily prison routines have superseded his political engagements and concerns at the forefront of his conscious mind. The mass of latent stimuli that each man carries away from his former activities begins to be snuffed out. There remains only the gleam of the old will, which exhausts itself in grandiose plans and fantasies that will never be realised. The prisoner stretches out on his bed and passes his time spitting at the ceiling and dreaming impossible dreams. At that point, the politico should be considered "out of action", "non-combatant" or "withdrawn from the trenches", and left alone to the company of his own thoughts.***

On 16th June 1930, Gramsci received a visit from his older brother Gennaro, the only person from outside Italy who could legally get to see him. The visit was entirely unexpected and unannounced. Gramsci was simply summoned from his cell at the appointed time in the early afternoon and told he had a visitor. It couldn't be Tanya, because she had been just a couple of days ago and did not plan to come again till the following week. She was again unwell, so even that was uncertain. The only other visitor he ever had at Turi was his younger brother Carlo, who had to make prior arrangements to travel from Sardinia and wouldn't just turn up like this. Piero Sraffa, Gramsci's friend from Turin, had promised to come during one of his trips to Italy from England, where he was a lecturer in Economics at Cambridge and a close colleague of John Maynard Keynes. But so far Sraffa had not received permission because he was not an immediate family member.

"My goodness, Nannaro! What a pleasant surprise! It must be..."

Antonio felt the sudden jolt he always felt on contact with the outside world, plucked out of his cocoon of quiet contemplation, but this time multiplied many times over by this unheralded encounter with his elder brother. He thought back frantically to when he had last seen him. It must have been some time before he left for Moscow in May 1922; Gennaro then left for Paris in December of that momentous year. They were both still living in Turin then, both working on the communist press but not having much to do with each other outside work. They had always been closer to each other than to other members of the Gramsci family, mainly in their shared political outlook and engagement, but there was still ill feeling between them from their forced, impoverished years together in Cagliari and Turin, not to mention the irritability and antipathy of siblings some years apart in age. Then there was their mutual and never discussed attachment to Pia Carena, who had helped Gennaro flee to France when the Fascists mistook him for Antonio, and the business about Gennaro drawing his brother's salary while he was away.

"... over eight years ago. The *L'Ordine Nuovo* days, before you were attacked..."

Gennaro smiled ruefully and held up his right hand. The index finger was missing just above the knuckle. All that remained was a perfectly healed small stump, which wiggled involuntarily on the upturned hand. He held it to his nose, so that it looked like the missing finger was delving deep into his left nostril. Antonio laughed with a sharp snort, and said, "Ever the practical joker!" The prison guard who had escorted Gennaro into the prison, a relatively friendly Sardinian from Paulilatino, a village near Ghilarza, looked on in some distaste.

"How are you doing, little one?" Gennaro asked. He sat back in his hard chair, intertwined his deformed hand in the other one, and rested them both on his substantial paunch. He was now, Antonio calculated, forty seven, eight years older than himself. Corpulent and balding, well dressed in a carelessly middle class and confidently male way, he looked for all the world like a French shopkeeper or provincial town clerk, comfortable in prosperous middle age. But then Nannaro always had looked middle-aged, even when he was a youth and Nino was a small child; looking at him now, Antonio concluded that the years since they'd last met had been kinder to his older brother than to him. He could imagine him in a large white apron, serving up a half kilo of cheese or an armful of baguettes, along with some snippet of local gossip or banter, or presiding benignly over the registration of marriages, births and deaths. Perhaps Nannaro really did have some of that "talent for business" his father and other brothers had always gone on about.

"I'm fine right now," replied Antonio, "but I've not been too well at times. All the old ailments, plus a few new ones brought on by this place. You're looking very well yourself..."

"Yes, I'm glad I went to Paris. There's plenty of printing work, and I've got a good woman and a nice apartment in the 5th *Arrondissement*, near the *Jardin des Plantes*. Life is good, and certainly a lot better and freer than here..."

"I've never been to Paris," said Antonio, "though I'd very much like to." He was keeping a close eye on his older brother, and wondering why he was here.

Gennaro said he had been to see Tanya before coming to the prison. "She seems nice enough, and she obviously cares deeply for you. Your sister-in-law, I gather. She told me all about her complicated family..."

"Yes, I met her sisters in Russia, Evgenia and my wife Julia. Tanya had stayed in Italy when the family left in 1917, and I looked her up when I settled in Rome."

"There's not much to her, little scrap of a thing. I took her out to lunch and she barely touched her food..."

"It seems to run in the family," said Antonio. "I used to call them my little birds. I've never seen any of the Schucht sisters eat a hearty meal. Not even Julia when she was pregnant..."

"Well, Tanya doesn't look too well on it. I'm not sure I've ever seen anyone so pale and drawn, at least not since the war. You'd never think she'd spent most of her life in our Italian warmth and sunshine."

"She's retained Soviet citizenship, as well as the Russian complexion!"

Tanya had shown Gennaro the latest photographs of the children, "fine looking little boys. Honestly Nino, you little pipsqueak, I never thought you had it in you!"

"Well, I clearly did!" said Antonio with a laugh, and finally brought the opening pleasantries to a close. "So what's brought you here?"

Gennaro sat upright and, with a glance towards the Sardinian guard who made a point of looking away, leaned forward in his chair.

"Well, it's delicate..."

He had been approached by "Ercoli" (Palmiro Togliatti's party codename) in Paris. The party wanted Gennaro to visit Antonio, in order to determine his attitude towards "the latest developments in the movement..." The fierce struggles at the top of the Russian Communist Party, and hence in the Comintern, had finally come to a climax, with Stalin installed as the undisputed successor to Lenin. Having vanquished Trotsky and the "Left opposition" in 1927, he had then taken on the "Right opposition" around Bukharin, Rykov and Tomsky. They had all been removed from their posts in the party and the Comintern and finally expelled from the party. Antonio was familiar with this part of the story – indeed he had anticipated just such damaging splits in his letter to the Comintern in 1926, which had been intercepted and suppressed by Togliatti – but more recent developments surprised and shocked him.

Stalin's latest factional manoeuvres necessitated the "left turn" of 1929, when the Bolsheviks had renounced all aspects of bourgeois democracy and political collaboration with the social democrats of the mass Socialist Parties. They were now vilifying these former comrades and allies as "social fascists" or the "left wing of the bourgeoisie", the "useful fools" of reaction.

"Or was it 'tools?'" pondered Gennaro, who had never joined the *PCd'I*, and whose own politics and circle of friends were closer to the left-wing social democrats. "Whatever... some stupid dogmatic formula..."

They were even blaming the social democrats for the failure of the botched German revolution of October 1923, perhaps the single most disastrous and largely self-inflicted setback the movement had ever suffered. The Comintern's own sober, measured reflections on the catastrophe, under Lenin's clear-eyed if faltering guidance, seemed now to have been entirely forgotten. More broadly the communists had decided that the final crisis of capitalism, long ago predicted by Marx as the global economic system tottered under the weight of its own contradictions, was not just inevitable but imminent. Communists should agitate and prepare for the international dictatorship of the proletariat, led by the vanguard parties of the Communist International, without any kind of intermediary stage or "transition" through parliamentary democracy and political legality.

"But that's ridiculous!" exclaimed Antonio. "Especially here in Italy. We have to get rid of the Fascists first, and there's no sign of that..."

Gennaro regarded his younger brother balefully. "That's as may be, little fellow..." He sighed and resumed his account. Any opposition to this new line within the Communist International was being condemned as "opportunism" and "deviationism". Resistance or even doubt was being dealt with by large-scale expulsions, as the new line was driven through every national Communist Party.

"You must have heard that Angelo Tasca was expelled in late 1928," said Gennaro.

"Yes, I did. A shame, but Angelo was asking for it. He was never really a communist... should probably have been expelled a long time ago..."

"And they've finally got round to expelling Amadeo Bordiga."

"That's no great surprise either..."

"Well, now they've expelled Leonetti, Ravazzoli and Tresso..."

"That's a very different matter! They are good loyal comrades... Leonetti joined us in Turin during the war, and helped found the *PCd'I*. You'll be aware he married Pia Carena..."

"Indeed. I see them occasionally in Paris. They've got two lovely little children."

"Did I ever tell you...? Oh, never mind. Tresso was a protégé of mine, intellectually limited but thoroughly sound. And Ravazzoli was never any kind of threat, just a bit too cosy with the trade unions. I really don't know what to think about all this. I understand that this new line was imposed by the Comintern, but I can't help but feel that Ercoli agreed to it too readily..."

The guard nodded towards them to indicate that the visiting time was nearly over.

Gennaro concluded with: "I'll leave it with you to mull over before I report anything back. I'll come and see you again later in the month, and you can tell me what you want me to say. In the meantime I'm going to spend a couple of weeks in Ghilarza. I'll tell them you're fine, and that you send your love. Okay?"

The atmosphere at Gennaro's next visit, a fortnight later, was very different. In the meantime he had been under heavy surveillance because the police had realised he was up to something and sent a whole detachment of plain-clothes men to follow him around the country. When he met Tanya again, prior to visiting Antonio at the prison, she told him she had got quite used to being watched, even when she was back up north. She was regularly called in for questioning, and her rooms searched; "Every time it feels like a violation," she said, and necessitated frequent moves. Here in Turi, they were aware of being watched from every corner of the restaurant, and overheard by one particular fellow who insisted on being seated at the very next table and even moving with them when they asked to be seated somewhere else.

At the prison Gennaro was met and accompanied by the prison secretary, who had been "…expressly instructed by Signor Parmegiani the Prison Director to enforce the prohibition on political discussion during visits to Special Tribunal prisoners." In the visiting room itself, this fussy little man insisted on sitting at the table with Antonio and Gennaro, listening intently and waving a finely manicured index finger whenever their discussion strayed anywhere near the real purpose of the visit.

"What about the three?" was the nearest Gennaro could get to it.

Antonio, exasperated on a number of fronts, simply responded, "Nannaro, you're my older brother! Just do what you think best..."

Otherwise their conversation was confined to family matters. Their mother had been ill earlier in the year, but seemed to be on the mend. Nannaro's daughter Edmea was growing into a fine girl, pretty and intelligent. Recalling seeing her now to Antonio, Nannaro was close to tears, not least because he had had to keep his distance for fear of upsetting the child and the carefully maintained silence about her parentage.

"She looks so much like her mother..." was all he could manage.

Antonio understood that he wasn't the only member of his family undergoing the pain of separation. Gennaro changed the subject and lightened the atmosphere by describing how delighted Tanya had been to hear of some of Antonio's childhood ambitions, "…and not just the Admiral and air-pilot stuff either... Do you remember when you were six and declared you wanted to become a Trappist monk?"

Even the prison secretary smiled at that one.

* * *

Christmas is as special a time in prison as elsewhere; perhaps even more so, because nowhere else are the twin pillars of Christianity – celebration and suffering – quite so starkly illustrated. And of course the secular basis of Christmas, a chance for families to be together, is just as starkly absent; all the prisoner has for comfort is his memories of family Christmases past, invariably enhanced by sentimental longing. What you notice in prison, for the whole week leading up to Christmas, is a steady build-up of excitement and vitality, childlike in its simplicity, which is as much to do with the anticipated break in prison routine as the religious or even secular purpose of the holiday. For many prisoners, especially those without much outside contact, the highlight is a portion of spaghetti and a quarter litre of wine, which the administration issues three times a year instead of the usual soup.

Don't think for a moment that I'm amused by this, though I might have been so before my own imprisonment. I've seen too many moving scenes of prisoners eating their meagre bowl of pasta with religious scrupulousness, mopping up with a small piece of bread even the faintest hint of grease that might still cling to the earthenware bowl! The slightest disappointment can puncture this atmosphere of celebration. On Ustica I saw an ordinary prisoner weeping inconsolably because he had lost his Christmas spaghetti gambling. He had been in jail for many years and the thrice-yearly pasta had become his life-blood, a staple of his miserable existence. It is quite understandable why the reference to daily bread is included in the Our Father.

When Antonio Gramsci was eleven and just finishing at elementary school, he was asked by the parish priest if he had "a vocation". What did this mean? Had he heard "a calling from God?" said the old fellow. Still Antonio looked puzzled. Finally losing patience, the priest spelt it out to the nonplussed little boy: did he want to be a priest? "Er, I'm not sure..." was all he could think of to say, both flattered and embarrassed by the suggestion. As far as he knew, he was the only one of his classmates to have been approached. For once, his distinction – this ever watchful, sharp-tongued, malformed cripple with a father in prison – was a source of prestige rather than stigma and shame. Several times in his childhood, teachers (and rather more sardonically, his brothers and sisters) had said he would make "a good little Jesuit", with his enquiring mind and way with words and his serious expression. Actually Gennaro regularly called him a "nosy little po-faced blabbermouth", especially when Nino spied him chatting up one of the village girls, but it amounted to the same thing really.

Antonio always had something of the cleric about him. He would accompany his mother to Sunday mass and to confession the previous evening. There he would confess the same innocuous childish "sins" of disobedience and bad language, receive the same penance in return – two Hail Marys and three Our Fathers, sometimes three Hail Marys and two Our Fathers for a bit of variety – and emerge feeling cleansed and refreshed for a further week of mental enquiring and looking serious. He approached his Catechism classes, in preparation for his confirmation at the age of eight, with the same earnest devotion and appetite for learning that he brought to *Robinson Crusoe* or observation of foraging hedgehogs.

Antonio ceased to believe in God at around twelve or thirteen, as soon as he could properly think it through for himself. In a world explained and governed by science and reason, and a new century offering endless giddy mechanised human progress, there was no place for some distant, immaterial "supreme being" who demanded total obedience and blind faith and in return offered little more than suffering and loneliness. With his father in prison, and Sardinia in deep and persistent economic depression, both God and humanity seemed to have given up on each other, at least in these parts on the outer edge of the modern world. At best, he would later write, "God is only a metaphor for an ensemble of men organised for mutual assistance." But he remained fascinated by religion and its institutions, and the hold they seemed to have over the thoughts and feelings of otherwise rational, sober people, not to mention their global reach and power.

He witnessed the consolation it gave his mother and other family members during times of trial and hardship, and the sense of purpose it endowed on otherwise mundane lives. It offered a badge of belonging to these people of the periphery which no other agency – the state, the ruling or opposition parties, the monarchy and the nobility, the press, public culture and the arts – could be bothered with. Their lives had religious if not civil meaning and purpose. These were the building blocks of "mass faith", cemented by a subtly mixed mortar of coercion and consent, and forming a secure and durable pyramid with the "community of the faithful" on the lower levels, the several upper layers of the clergy in their own strict hierarchy, and the Pope at the very top.

Above all, he appreciated the historic, universal standing of the Roman Catholic Church. All across the western world an eleven year old boy could confess the same sins and receive the same penance, and be asked the same question about a "vocation" by a more or less kindly parish priest. There was a set script and a moral calculus fixed in Rome and rigorously enforced everywhere. This was the most effective and durable global movement there had ever been, at least until the emergence of communism. It touched the everyday lives and deepest thoughts of half of humanity, and in some way conditioned the existence of all the rest. Without armed forces of its own or much by way of economic power, at least since the late middle ages, the Church was still able to dictate the policies and actions of states and governments all over the world.

The Lateran Pact of 1929 between the Pope and Mussolini was the latest example, securing the operational autonomy and moral sway of the Vatican within Italy while consolidating – literally blessing – the Fascists' grip on secular power. Apart from anything else, it had a massive economic impact on the country by transferring huge funds from the state to the church, to "compensate" for the surrender of any claim to temporal, territorial sovereignty over the country beyond the Vatican City itself. This in itself had boosted the real local power of the church and the attractiveness of the priesthood, which had been suffering a collapse in recruitment for at least the previous fifty years. All of a sudden, a "vocation" had become a much more attractive proposition, especially in a period of persistent high unemployment. The Pact might be derided in the left wing press as "a concordat of tinpot dictatorships", but this was to underestimate its historical significance, its economic and political benefits to both Church and State, and its negative impact on any prospect of a revival in progressive politics.

Even at moments of steep decline, under the combined assaults of industrial capitalism and positivist science, and the shallow materialism and popular scepticism they jointly engendered, the Church was capable of adapting and renewing itself, and maintaining its influence alongside the global empires of the great nation-states. Just how did this ideology, based ultimately on obscure mythology and doctrinal obfuscation, retain its preeminence? How to explain the subtlety of its morality and the complexity of its theology, alongside the mumbo-jumbo of its liturgy and the hollow ritual of its ceremony? Or the glaring contrast between its magnificent buildings and ornaments and vestments and the grinding poverty of most of its adherents, its aptly known "flock"? Or the depth of popular faith in a religion which conducted its proceedings in an obscure classical language unspoken elsewhere for centuries, so that (as Gramsci observed) "...the people watch religious rites and hear exhortatory sermons, but have no real idea what's going on. They cannot follow discussions and ideological developments, which are the monopoly of a caste."

This was a religion, a body of belief, which seemed to allow its believers to take from it an infinite variety of influences. How could this tradition simultaneously inspire Dante's Inferno and a cult based on a relic reputed to be the penis of an angel? How, Gramsci wondered in one of his earliest prison notes, could a popular and reputable Catholic novelist produce a book – plucked off the shelves of the Turi di Bari prison library in a well-thumbed, yellowing edition – which "...seeks to enlist our pity for a priest who has raped over thirty young girls, because he is bound by the vow of chastity?"

Part of the answer lay in the social origin and location of the clergy, all those clever and talented sons of respectable but impecunious families like his own. They were drawn from real communities all across Italy, unlike the cliques and castes who dominated the political parties, cultural and intellectual life, and public administration. Once ordained, literally "indoctrinated", their deployment closely corresponded to the organisation and structure of the Italian state, and in many places far surpassed it. They respected and adapted to the prevailing mores of different parts of the country, sometimes in flagrant defiance of the official church doctrine. These relatively educated individuals had a "presence" in the smallest habitations, usually benign and occasionally disciplinary, representing both God and their congregations to each other, interceding between the divine and the lay. When Gramsci thought again of his own family in distant Ghilarza, they and all their neighbours would always approach the parish priest for help and advice before any public official.

These were the "organic intellectuals" of the Universal Church, drawn from the key intermediary classes of feudal and then bourgeois society, with suitable local adaptations. So, in the north they were drawn from among the artisans and peasants, whereas in the south they tended to come from the land-owning gentry. There they often owned land and extracted rents on their own and also the Church's behalf, a sub-section of the feudal ruling class. Some even took a wife, stretching the tolerance of the church's moral code and the "community of the faithful" to its very limits. But as long as they came from the town or area where they preached and prayed, and performed the ceremonial and pastoral functions of the priesthood reasonably competently, they were accepted by the locals as "one of ours".

This contrasted sharply with schoolteachers who, with the rapid expansion of elementary schooling in the later nineteenth and early twentieth centuries, were dispatched from training colleges in the big cities to the outlying towns and villages where most of the people still lived. Even if they stayed at their posts, which many didn't as soon as they saw where they'd been sent, they were regarded as alien invaders, bringing a very young and shallow "civilisation" to the natives. Popular literature was full of stories where some upstart young teacher was seen off or tamed by a wise old priest.

The accommodation between church and people worked both ways. At least in the rural South and for usually good practical reasons, the supposedly strict moral codes of Roman Catholicism were surprisingly flexible in their application. Childless marriages could be dissolved for a fee, and in other cases matrimony took place only after conception, once its "fruit-fulness" had been tested and proven. In the era of widening, ultimately universal suffrage, the Church had also developed its own political capacity and organisation, through such agencies as Catholic Action and the Popular Party, with a socially progressive or even left wing veneer over a conservative or downright reactionary politics. The Church had organised and sponsored a whole host of popular cultural initiatives, including novels and plays by writers Gramsci called "Father Bresciani's progeny", after a nineteenth century Catholic novelist who specialised in sentimental homilies. They had very little literary merit, but they sold in vast quantities, and plainly touched a common chord. This was a kind of literary "Lorianism", peculiar to Italy, which said as much about its audience as its creators. In an era of growing literacy, within strictly defined intellectual and political limits, it kept the Church deep inside people's hearts and minds.

But at the same time, the Church was losing whatever grip it ever really had on the "faith" of lay intellectuals, who were drawn towards the new "sciences" of positivism and materialism, in the process becoming ever more detached from the popular masses who persisted in their religious faith. Part of the explanation for the failure of Italian Socialism was its rabid and shallow anti-clericalism, which Gramsci had described in a 1918 newspaper article as "nothing more than the peevishness of a child who believes that his mother gives larger bowls of soup to his eldest brother." Even his own *PCd'I* had failed to appreciate the deep historical roots of this new social Catholicism and its popular agencies. Hundreds of thousands of peasants were drawn towards these detached, arms-length sub-sections of the Church and had even organised strikes and cooperatives through them. They had been amongst the first targets of the Fascist "upsurge" in the countryside, because Mussolini at least understood the challenge they posed to his "revolution". One of the key provisions of the Lateran Pact of 1929 was to bring Catholic Action within the political orbit of the state, thereby neutralising its progressive potential.

From the top down, successive Popes had tried hard to "modernise", particularly Leo XIII with his encyclical *Rerum Novarum,* which recognised the plight and interests of the emerging, late 19th century industrial working class. Leo had promoted a scholastic "Thomist" philosophy (Gramsci noted) "...not as a narrow, static and exclusive frame of knowledge but as an organism of living thought." This helped to disguise the fact that at least since the French Revolution, the church had grown increasingly out of touch with the emergent creeds of economic liberalism, moral individualism and political democracy. There remained within it deep currents of resistance to any form of "modernism". In those countries which had embraced the Reformation, and which not coincidentally played a key role in the industrial revolution, Roman Catholics had become a marginal, persecuted sect. Across the world, the reassertion of the authority of the clergy had suppressed the "community of the faithful" and delimited lay involvement in church affairs. The Church was slowly losing the historical initiative, the hegemony of "mass faith", reacting to rather than shaping social development.

Its internal politics had always been complicated: "It is noteworthy," Gramsci wrote in December 1931, "that all the innovations within the church, unless they come from the leadership, contain something heretical. These heretical elements become more explicit and strident until the centre reacts forcefully, throws the innovators into disarray, reabsorbs the waverers and casts out the recalcitrants. The church has never gone in for self-criticism, despite its self-proclaimed attachment to the masses of the faithful... The historical development of the church has come about through faction-fighting; the various religious congregations are really factions that have been absorbed and regulated in the form of religious orders. Ultimately, innovations have always been imposed rather than proposed, and accepted only by compulsion."

The Church sought to impose its own institutional prerogatives on life, rather than emerging organically from within it. At least since the Counter-reformation, it had been dangerous to think, write and speak openly and honestly within the Church. Being a Catholic had become simultaneously very easy for most people and very difficult for some. It was easy to believe in general terms and to have respect for the Church, its personnel and institutions; there was very little in practical terms to distinguish this popular faith from Protestantism or Orthodoxy. But it was very difficult to be an "active Catholic intellectual," Gramsci observed, because "one is expected to embrace a whole slew of notions on encyclicals, counter-encyclicals, papal briefs, apostolic letters etc., and the historical deviations from the Church's line have been so numerous and so subtle that it is extremely easy to fall into heresy or semi-heresy or a quarter-heresy. Sincere religious sentiment has been desiccated; one must be a doctrinaire to write in an orthodox way."

These were for the moment jottings and isolated fragments, to be worked up into fuller accounts at some later stage. But Gramsci applied himself to his studies of Catholicism with a dedication he admitted to Tanya bordered on obsession. It was becoming, with reference to the young Torinese worker who looked at everything through the prism of "What will Japan do?"— his very own personal Japan. He would already have been acutely aware of the parallels between the Catholic faith he had been born into and the Socialist one he had adopted in his youth, their similar trajectories of rise and decline and patchy attempted renewal, the waves of change and reaction which buffeted millions of people around in their sealed chambers, drowning many and raising select others to the surface. In particular, there were glaring parallels between the reactionary Catholicism and the Stalinised Bolshevism of the early 1930s, both seeking to impose their prerogatives from above, impatient of dissent or "deviation", ruthless towards organised "opposition", indulgent towards obedience and "loyalty". What was Stalin if not the newly-anointed Pope of world communism, surrounded by fawning, nodding courtiers and dogma-spouting, heresy-hunting cardinals? The seminary-trained Josif Vissiaronovitch even adopted the *faux*-humility of St. Peter's successors, simultaneously fostering and disowning his own personality cult, an "ordinary man" who just happened to be infallible. What was the emergent creed of Stalinism if not a kind of Counter-reformation within the historical dialectic of Socialism?

And while it was becoming easier to be an "ordinary" communist – with millions accepted into party membership on significant anniversaries and with each new wave of orchestrated political upheaval, and subject to minimal "political education" beyond the mouthing of a few basic dogmas and obligations, the "catechism" of codified, authorised Marxism-Leninism – it was becoming ever harder to be an "active communist intellectual". Indeed, if the latest reports and rumours from Russia were to be believed, it was becoming positively dangerous. But for the moment, in his own deepening isolation, Antonio Gramsci kept his doubts to himself and shied away from their dispiriting conclusions. Under the keen eye of the prison censor, not to mention the ones in Moscow and inside his own head, these glaring parallels between Communism and Catholicism could not yet be made explicit.

* * *

"The great Victorian historian Macaulay attributes the ease with which even the most cultured Athenians were blinded by the most puerile sophism to the very great influence of live and spoken discourse in Greek life and education. The habit of conversation generates a certain aptitude for showy argument that renders the adversary momentarily speechless.

The same observation can also be made about certain classes in modern life, as an explanation of their weakness (workers) or distrust (peasants). The subaltern classes are

> ***easily and immediately impressed by the verbose oratory and long words of the gentry and the high bourgeoisie. Upon ruminating on the things they have heard, initially impressed by their glitter, they discover their deficiency and superficiality. In the end they become habitually apathetic, cynical and distrustful. When one is removed by one's circumstances from the normal channels of ordinary human interaction, for example by illness or imprisonment, one also begins to see just how facile most conversation actually is. There are good reasons why chatter is commonly called idle. Most talk really is small."***

Tanya Schucht's visit to Antonio Gramsci at Turi di Bari Penitentiary for Sick Prisoners in July 1930 would be her last for two and a half years. She had been staying at Turi for six months, in a small rented room above a pharmacy on the edge of town, in order to be able to visit Antonio more frequently, supply him with books and provisions, and support him during his bouts of illness and low spirits. But her own fragile health had taken another turn for the worse. She had, Antonio wrote to his brother Carlo, been "leading a monk's life, isolated from the entire world"; even more so than himself, "if that's possible." She suffered a prolonged and very painful bout of phlebitis that came on in the spring. It confined her to bed for whole days at a time and otherwise left her hobbling around like an old cripple. She had expected it to ease with the onset of summer and the warmer and drier weather, but if anything it had got worse. She was still wearing the tight bandages that contained the swelling on her legs.

"Here, look!" she said, raising up her exposed lower leg for Antonio to examine, as if he needed convincing by the physical evidence. The guard in attendance, a rather gormless lanky youth from Palermo, looked on, startled. Antonio, not quite so surprised by the exposed ankle, could see him trying to decide whether some prison regulation was being infringed. It prompted a rare smile.

Tanya said she had consulted her doctors in Rome, and been told that on top of her established nervous debility and physical ailments, she was now exhibiting the symptoms of a type of neurasthenia known by the German word *angst*.

"Goodness me!" said Antonio.

Tanya tried to allay Antonio's concern with a funny story about how the Italian doctors had struggled to pronounce the word. They had settled on the Italian word *angustia,* which meant something quite different, "the condition of poverty".

"Oh dear!" replied Antonio, always amused by examples of linguistic confusion.

"Yes," said Tanya, turning serious, "but funnily enough I am quite broke!"

Her savings, built up over many years of working as a nurse, a teacher and more recently as a clerk, were now pretty much exhausted. She had come to rely on a small monthly remittance sent to her by her father Apollon in Russia, but he was increasingly inclined to impose conditions and restrictions in return, even hinting that his own funds were now dangerously depleted. He was constantly reminding her in the postcards he enclosed with the rest of the family's letters that he had a wife and several unattached daughters and dependants to support.

"Including Julia and of course his two beautiful grandsons," Tanya remarked pointedly.

"But she still won't accept the pitiful amounts I can send her!" said Antonio, seizing the hint.

"Well, that's another matter," she said. "Of which there is more to be said..."

The upshot of all this was that for the first time in his life, Apollon was now "feeling the pinch." He was trying to sell off various scattered family assets, including a small farm near Geneva which had stood empty and unused for so long it was no longer clear who legally owned it. In his letters to her, Apollon had begun to question the value and purpose of Tanya's "way of life" and choice of residence, and to suggest that she might rejoin the rest of the family in Russia for the sake of her own health, to resume paid employment and help support and care for "...the people you are actually related to."

"Well, that might be for the best..."

"But Antonio, I really don't want to! Or abandon you here."

But without Apollon's financial support, which he had signalled would shortly be withdrawn, she would at the very least have to return to Rome and seek paid work. Tanya had also gathered from Evgenia that their father's standing in the Communist Party as a founder member, respected intellectual and old Bolshevik was also in some jeopardy. If anything, in this new post-Lenin era in Soviet Russia – when the Party's priorities were rapid industrialisation and the collectivisation of agriculture, and the rising stars of its first Five Year plan were compliant technocrats and untainted proletarians – Apollon's aristocratic manner and background and the substantial legacy it had conferred were proving a positive handicap.

His post of Librarian at the Electronic Institute, which he had held since 1924 and which conferred a small honorarium, had recently been given to a younger man deemed "...more in tune with the latest scientific and technological developments". More than once, Evgenia told Tanya and Tanya now told Antonio, Apollon had been challenged in party meetings on his own record of paid work, which amounted to little more than a few terms teaching Russian to army officers in Rome before the war. His old haughty bluster in response, about how he had been "...too busy organising the revolution to take on a regular job", had simply made things worse. The comrades had simply dismissed "all that talk about the old times" as irrelevant to the new era.

He had also been included on a list of "high-born Bolsheviks" denounced for their "Europeanism" in a magazine article, which argued that Russia was more Asiatic than Western, and that the value of Bolshevism was in "stirring up" the Russian people and enhancing the international prestige and power of the country. Apollon was cited as an example of the "cosmopolitan intelligentsia of old Europe", who had "corrupted the soul of Mother Russia." There were not so subtle hints of anti-Semitism in references to "elements of the old order" who had swapped one set of "Talmudic tablets" for another or (as in Apollon's case) married into "alien traditions." The people who produced the magazine were outright nationalists, who even expressed sympathy for Fascism. One or two had proclaimed themselves Russian Fascists. But the most worrying thing of all was that they and their vile publication were being tolerated by the Soviet authorities, while old Bolsheviks and lifelong revolutionaries were being rounded up and sent to Siberia or abroad.

"At least there's no immediate danger of that in our case," said Tanya. "Father takes great care to avoid any suspicion of disloyalty..."

"So what are these conditions and restrictions of his?"

"Well, Antonio, this is where it gets awkward, and painful..."

Apollon, with the vociferous support of Evgenia and the silent acquiescence of Julia, had told Tanya that he thought it would be for the best if the Schuchts had nothing more to do with Antonio. There might not be what Apollon called "political advantage" in maintaining contact; he had "heard things" which he would not or perhaps could not specify. And after all, none of them – not even Julia – had spent much time with Antonio or ever really got to know him. He remained, to all intents and purposes, "a distant stranger with," Evgenia alleged, "no interest in his family." Even the two boys had very little idea who their father was.

"That's true enough. As far as they are concerned, I might as well be the Flying Dutchman or the man in the moon! Have they even been told where I am yet?"

"Well, Delio heard about it from another child at school and asked his teacher what prison was..."

"What a way to find out!"

"But his mothers managed to persuade him it wasn't true..."

"As if that's any better!"Apollon had declared that they might as well be told anyway, because Antonio would be imprisoned far away for the foreseeable future, quite incapable of contributing to the family's affairs and fortunes. They hadn't actually got round to it yet, Tanya thought, because they were concerned not to upset the child's "nervous disposition."

"So he's just been left to stew on it!"

"Well, so it seems..."

"And despite my limited time with them, I have after all upset the physical health, emotional equilibrium and life chances of at least three of Apollon's precious daughters ..." Antonio exclaimed, with some considerable bitterness, not to say *angst*.

"That's another thing..." said Tanya. "I think it's time you knew, especially with me leaving Turi, the full extent of Julka's illness..."

The diagnosis of epilepsy which she had received in 1927 was only part of it. Julia had been seriously disturbed for at least three years now, "on occasions quite deranged." She had given up her job with the NKVD some time ago, and they had just recently got round to stopping her salary, which added to the strain on the family finances. She was largely confined to bed at home, with periods of hospitalisation along the way.

"And we're not talking about the sanatorium at Serebranyi Bor where you stayed, Antonio, and met Zhenya and Julka and the rest of the family. As you know, facilities like that are reserved for high-ranking state and party officials. With Father's declining fortunes, Julia has been treated in the clinics and asylums for ordinary citizens. These are not nice places..."

"No," said Antonio. "I can imagine. And I can't say I'm wholly surprised by the news..."

After a short, uncomfortable silence, he continued: "Well, at least this would explain the silences and the scribbled notes and their strange dissociated tone... but I can't understand why you and the others have waited three whole years to tell me this."

The silence continued. Even the gormless guard looked uncomfortable, shuffling from one foot to another. Gramsci broke it in a flat, angry monotone directed at the ceiling.

"The same sort of reason the children haven't been told where I am, I suppose..."

Turning back to Tanya, and letting out a deep sigh, Antonio said, "I'm going to tell you a story... As a child I was a tireless hunter of lizards and snakes, which I fed to a beautiful hawk that I had tamed and kept on a long leash. On three or four of my expeditions into the countryside around Ghilarza I came across a creature very similar to the common grass snake, except that it had four small feet, two at the front near the head and two at the back near the tail. It was sixty to seventy centimetres long, very wide and fat, with the girth of a grass snake but half the length."

He raised his hands in the air, and demonstrated the creature's rough shape and size.

"It slid or rather waddled along very slowly and clumsily in short abrupt jerks, without much assistance from its pathetic little legs. They just kind of flapped about and got in the way..."

With his right hand he mimicked the creature's lolloping gait.

"In my village this reptile is called a *scurzone*, a Sardinian dialect word which means 'foreshortened.' Back at school I asked the teacher, who was actually a retired engineer and not a qualified teacher at all, what the *scurzone* was called in Italian. He laughed at my description and told me it was an imaginary animal, usually referred to in mythology as an asp or basilisk, and that he knew of no real creature like the one I had described. Even when the boys from another village chipped in and said they called it a *coloru*, he insisted that these were all country superstitions and that grass snakes with feet did not exist."

Antonio now had Tanya's, and the guard's, full attention.

There was an undercurrent of quiet anger in his voice, and a determined look on his face.

"This teacher wasn't stupid – he did a lot of research into natural history, and had built up quite a collection of fossils and rocks – but he couldn't believe that the *scurzone* or *coloru* could be real and not have poisonous breath and burning eyes. I can still remember my anger at being told I was wrong when I knew I was right, and at being laughed at for being superstitious. I have always reacted badly against authority based on smugness and stupidity. It is in my experience typical of minor patriarchs used to lording it over people around them who are smaller and weaker than they are..."

Tanya was looking down at her lap, in further uncomfortable silence. Antonio waited for the implications of his story to sink in, then exhaled and let himself relax into a small laugh.

"In fact, I looked it up just recently in the *Larousse* table of reptiles, and found a grass snake with four feet called the *seps*. It's found in Spain and southern France, so it's entirely plausible that there should be a variety on Sardinia. The beautiful *Larousse* illustration doesn't look much like the *scurzone*, which is an ugly thing, with a large head and a conical tail. The front legs are too close to the head, and its feet are white and stunted and of very little practical use. It's quite unlike other lizards and snakes, which may be frightening but are basically elegant and graceful. But I have to say I am strangely fond of the *scurzone*, this ugly deformed Sardinian creature which is not supposed to exist and spends most of its life hidden under rocks, but which I have seen with my own eyes at least half a dozen times. I might even say I identify with it..."

* * *

Any philosophy of substantial value and integrity should provide a viable personal ethos as well as a collective

outlook on life and the world. It must feel true to the individual in his daily life and personal relationships, and enable him to make sense of what is going on around him. It combines theoretical rigour with practical relevance, common sense with good sense, as well as providing a rational and logically coherent account of the place of people and episodes in history. This holds true for any philosophy which achieves widespread currency at any given moment. Thus the "Philosophy of Praxis" expounded by Marx has become the prism through which the most progressive elements of humanity view the world but also experience their own lives and immediate surroundings. It "makes sense" of their raw, mediated or unmediated, daily experience.

What is the central attitude of this latest hegemonic philosophy? It is a certain organised or "compassionate" sarcasm. In the face of popular "illusions" – belief in justice, equality, fraternity; the various elements of "the religion of humanity" that emerged in the aftermath of bourgeois revolution – Marx expresses himself with a compassionately "positive" sarcasm. That is, he mocks not the most intimate feeling of those illusions but their contingent form in a particular perishable world, the cadaverous smell that leaks from behind their painted façade.

This contrasts with "right wing" sarcasm, which is rarely compassionate but is always "negative", purely destructive not only of the contingent form but of the human content of those sentiments. It is arrogant and disrespectful and unhesitatingly cruel. Marx always seeks to stand alongside people, rather than over them, even if he doesn't always succeed. Even in his own time, Marx's "sense of the masses" took him beyond the politics of clubs and secret societies which the mid-nineteenth century radical left largely consisted of.

Compassionate sarcasm should also be distinguished from scepticism, which is a necessarily passive, vegetable-like outlook. If the sceptic intervenes in everyday life, it means he believes he can convince others. In other words he is no longer a sceptic but stands for a specific positive opinion. These "sceptical" standpoints are generally useless, and can only triumph if people are persuaded that other opinions are even worse.

What is the basic method of our compassionate sarcasm, theorised in the philosophy of praxis, and how is it to be applied to any event or subject of study? It is "absolute historicism", which seeks to locate everything in the ebb and flow of history. Where does this person or people or episode fit, and how have they come to be? In the search for story and meaning and understanding we place ourselves at the heart of our common humanity, and connect with each other across time and space.

History, that is our common human experience, is the only "absolute" value. It stands above God or reason or even the philosophy of praxis itself, which may in fact prove specific to the historical epoch within which it has emerged. The question should always be: how did this happen? What is the story here? And we should continue to pose those questions until we feel properly satisfied in our understanding. From there we can proceed to pass judgement and plot the best way ahead, the most promising course of action.

In late 1930, a new group of Communist prisoners arrived at Turi. They had all exhibited various types and levels of ill health, and were brought together from prisons across the country for transfer to this "Special" penitentiary for sick prisoners. Gramsci had already been holding informal political discussions in the exercise yard, and with this influx of new comrades proposed a more structured programme of study and discussion. They would talk about some of the themes he had been pursuing in his own studies, such as the role of intellectuals in Italian history or developments in popular culture, but also the issues facing the Communist Party in the struggle against Fascism and for proletarian revolution. If it went well, he reasoned to himself, it would animate and enrich his own studies, just as dialogue and debate had always done when he was a free man, as well as improving the political understanding and judgement of his incarcerated comrades.

From the beginning the discussions did not proceed smoothly or well. This was, Gramsci soon realised, a new generation of communists, somehow harder and more impatient with each other than he was used to. They were quite different from the thoughtful, open-minded, curious and collaborative comrades he had lived and worked with through the latter days of the war, the Factory Councils and the occupations of the red years in Turin, then the breakaway from the Socialist Party and the formation of the *PCd'I*, or even the first years of Fascism.

Back then workers, intellectuals and even peasants had mucked along together in the great cause of socialist revolution, largely oblivious to their personal, regional or even class differences, or at least prepared to work together to overcome them. In meetings and less formal gatherings, and on long walks around the night-time streets of Turin and Rome, the talk would roam freely over any topic anyone cared to mention, but always come back to the central question posed by Lenin in the very first years of the century: *What is to be done?* They could argue ferociously, and disagree profoundly, but they never lost their sense of a common bond and a unitary purpose, and their determination to act together to make a better world.

This lot were nothing like that. They were tetchy and unpleasant with each other, bridling at the slightest insult just like ordinary prisoners, disinclined to listen but all too inclined to hector. They didn't seem able to concentrate or pay attention to anyone else for longer than five minutes, and while Gramsci introduced the classes they would talk amongst themselves or even stand up and wander off. They would interrupt his introductions, and challenge the relevance of the topics he had chosen.

"All this stuff about intellectuals is all well and good, Comrade Gramsci..."

Was there a trace of sarcasm – real, hard-bitten sarcasm – in that "Comrade"?

"... but what we really need to know is how to install the dictatorship of the proletariat!"

Or: "Less of the bloody Croce, Comrade Gramsci, and more of Comrade Stalin!"

Do they not understand that Benedetto Croce, the Italian high priest of Hegelian anti-positivism, has already contributed more to the elucidation of Marxism than Josif Vissiaronovitch ("Who?" said one of them) *ever would?*

"It's not books we need. It's weapons training!"

Gramsci wrote in a note in December 1930, with the latest bruising exercise yard encounter fresh in his mind, that "...this kind of intelligence, also often called 'talent', revels in superficial polemic. It aims to appear independent, challenge every authority and pick away at fundamental truths with objections to minor details... It is in fact a kind of facetiousness, trying to keep a straight face but always inclined to smirk, in reality based on intellectual clumsiness and narrow-minded provincialism."

For his part, Gramsci realised that all this time in isolation and quiet contemplation had rendered him remote and cool. Perhaps his studies and what he called his "lines of enquiry" had taken him too deep inside himself and into territory which did not actually interest anyone else. He just could not seem to engage or charm people the way he used to, and get them to perceive the remarkable brain at work atop his stunted, ungainly body.

He found it hard to deal with the new comrades' interruptions, or any kind of deviation from the notes he had prepared, other than by asserting his authority or simply shouting them down, whereas in the old days he would have welcomed and used them to develop another line of argument; the creative whirr and buzz of the dialectic. He was, he feared above all else, turning into the kind of pedantic, flustered old fool he had sneered at as a university student and young activist. And he was just as incapable of reaching these mostly younger hotheads as the most obscurantist professor or pompous party official had been of reaching him and his friends in Turin.

They would parrot dogmas and formulas without any clear idea what lay behind them, or even what they meant, but simply to declare their allegiance to the cause, *or worse* (Gramsci thought) *to whoever happens to be in charge at the moment.* Most of these men had joined the party since the 1926 crackdown or just before, and been arrested for clandestine agitation in the streets and factories. They had very little experience of open mass politics or, from what he could gather, the daily lives of the ordinary people they claimed to represent and (even more absurdly) lead.

None of them had ever met or worked with Gramsci before. They showed little deference or even respect for this funny little Sardinian hunchback, who used to be something in the old days but by his own admission had been "out of the struggle" for some years now and unable to say anything very useful about it. They had all embraced the *svolta* or "turn" to the new line imposed by the Comintern, with its perspective of the imminent collapse of Fascism, the historical redundancy of bourgeois democracy, the social democrats being "social fascists", and the rapid transition to proletarian dictatorship under the impulse of deep and widespread economic immiseration. Unemployment and malnutrition would expose the bankruptcy of capitalism and hasten the advent of socialism.

"Starving peasants have no option but to throw in their lot with the workers! And if we need to starve a few more to get them to see sense, so what?"

Gramsci tried chipping away at their blind certainties – "Misery and hunger can provoke uprisings and revolts, which may even shatter the prevailing social order. However, that does not equate to a revolutionary strategy for building socialism or in itself destroy capitalism" – but even this simple restatement of the basic tenets of historical materialism was met with scoffs and sneers. He'd try another tack: "Fascism has profoundly disorientated the popular masses. They need a restoration of democracy to recover their balance and their sense of historic mission"; hadn't Marx himself said that political democracy was a prerequisite for the social and economic democracy of socialism?

The cockiest of them, a young printer from Bologna, pointed out that this was not what *PCd'I* General Secretary Comrade Palmiro Togliatti had told the Comintern Sixth Congress the previous year: "We are now in the period of preparation for the proletarian revolution, not the restoration of bourgeois democracy. There will be no so-called transitional phase..." Their defiant stares and tight-lipped silence dared Gramsci to disagree with the current leadership of the party and the Comintern line. His own silence indicated that he did, but thought it better not to say so.

Another older comrade, who had been here as long as Gramsci but had dutifully adapted to the Comintern line and thrown in his lot with the new arrivals, said he was "confused". Had not he heard Gramsci himself describe the social democrats in 1926 as "the left wing of the bourgeoisie"? What's more, he had heard though the clandestine party network that Gramsci had communicated his assent to the *svolta,* and the "inevitable and very necessary" expulsions of Tasca and the other oppositionists, yet here he was disagreeing with it. How could this be?

So that's what Nannaro decided was for the best...

To the one or two sympathetic comrades he would complain privately that "...the party has been infected by maximalism... There is a fear of any and every idea that can't be found in the old maximalist dictionary of clichés. Any tactic which does not correspond to this dream world is considered an error and a deviation. You end up unable to adapt to changing historical circumstances, preferring words to political action or confusing one with the other, and capable of nothing but abstract schemes and fixes. We've gone backwards! We're as bad as the maximalist windbags of the old Socialist Party..."

Instead, he would lay out how he saw the basic facts of the situation: "Even under the most favourable conditions, the Party cannot count on more than a few thousand activists in Italy. The working classes are demoralised and disorganised, and Fascism is stronger than ever. We need allies, not sectarian isolation, and that requires compromise and concessions to other social classes, mainly the peasantry and the lower middle classes who resent the destruction of their freedoms by Fascism. A popular, broad-based anti-Fascist movement is the only way forward..." At best, his audience would respond with sullen acquiescence, but more often disperse around the prison in muttering huddles.

Gramsci's educational programme lasted just a few weeks of November and December 1930. He proposed a fortnight's break to mull things over, and hopefully take the heat out of the situation. But if anything this just made things worse. Opinions hardened into factional differences and sectarian outbursts, and criticism became more personal. Gramsci had become a social democrat, they were saying, a gradualist not a revolutionary, and was no longer a communist. Hadn't his old *L'Ordine Nuovo* comrade and friend Angelo Tasca been expelled in 1928 for just such right-wing deviationism? His admiration for Croce and other bourgeois intellectuals indicated opportunism and disloyalty, while his line on Fascism and bourgeois democracy flew in the face of the Comintern and *PCd'I* strategy, and recklessly flouted the properly Leninist "democratic centralism" its implementation required. Hadn't "the three" been thrown out more recently for just such heresy?

There was even talk of writing to the Party leadership in exile to denounce Gramsci's disruptive influence, of excluding him from the communist group at Turi and refusing him their company in the exercise yard. One day, after a heavy snowfall, the prisoners threw snowballs at each other. Standing alone in the corner of the yard to avoid being hit, Gramsci felt a snowball whistle past his ear and hit the wall. A large stone fell to the ground. When he looked around to see who might have thrown it, all he could see was scornful eyes upon him. One of them, a volatile young man from Florence whose politics were nearer anarchism than communism, broke into a smirk and indicated with a finger that the stone had fallen off the roof, while his immediate circle of hangers-on burst into laughter.

Finally, when Gramsci tried to resolve a confrontation between some of the new comrades and the prison warders – "They don't make the rules! And they have to enforce them to keep their jobs..." – he was accused of excessive regard for legality, and of "being afraid to lose your privileges, *Comrade* Gramsci, like being able to write in your cell and receive books and special food from outside." He tried to explain that he had fought hard for these concessions, with letters and petitions to every level of the prison service "right up to Mussolini", but this only seemed to increase the suspicion and animosity.

"Bloody hell," said the Florentine anarchist, "he's even in correspondence with *Il Duce*!"

Gramsci didn't disclose the subject of his latest appeal to Mussolini, which "His Excellency" had been good enough to approve in November after it was rejected all the way up the prison system: to be allowed to read the autobiography of the disgraced Leon Davidovitch Trotsky. Nor did he point out that his so-called "privileges" did not seem to include the right to a decent night's sleep, because repeated requests to be moved from his cell, the very first on the first corridor, had been turned down. There was constant coming and going past his cell to the infirmary and other parts of the prison, and the more brutal guards were not averse to banging on his door in the middle of the night "just for the sheer hell of it," he wrote to Tanya.

> *"The upshot is that in the whole month of October, I slept for an average of less than two and a half hours per night. I even drew up a statistical table and a graph to prove it! It helped to kill some of the time when I wasn't sleeping... As they say in Sardinia, I walk up and down the cell like a fly that doesn't know where to go and die."*

In March 1931 Gramsci wrote to his brother Carlo: "In order to stick rigidly to my absolutely correct behaviour in accordance with the necessities of prison life, I've come into conflict with some other prisoners and been forced to break off personal relationships."

When the *PCd'I* held its Fourth Congress in Germany in April/May 1931, and repeated the call for immediate insurrection and proletarian revolution, it was duly relayed back to the imprisoned politicos. Gramsci reiterated his private view that Italy would first have to pass through a democratic phase, focussed on the struggle for some kind of constituent assembly. This brought further grumbles and suspicious looks around the exercise yard. Painfully aware of his isolation, he withdrew into his cell and his studies, effectively ostracised. He took comfort in new intellectual insights and skills, including a greater facility at reading English, which "I find much easier than German," he wrote to Tanya. "I read an extract from *The Economist* on the Five Year Plan in two or three days, and don't think a single word escaped me."

Meanwhile, rumours continued to circulate among the party networks in Italy and in exile about his dissent from the new line. No attempts were made to seek clarification from him directly, and for the time being his name disappeared completely from the party press.

* * *

What does prison smell like? Completely different from the outside world. For this reason it is impossible for the prisoner to describe it, because he becomes so used to it that he ceases to notice. It seeps into his very being, and he is absorbed into it like an instrument in an orchestra or a drop of water in a cloth. Indeed, insofar as he is a part of it, he can no more describe it than he could tell you about his own character or what his soul looks like. He can only know that it is different by the expressions and demeanour of visitors from outside, who can be relied upon to spend the first few minutes of visiting time with their mouths upturned, their nostrils flaring and a look of sheer disgust and panic in their eyes. Unless he asks outright, which would be considered rude and vulgar by all social classes and types, even the lowliest in the hierarchy of prison society, the prisoner can only surmise what prison smells like to the outsider by deduction and speculation. And for that he must rely on his own observations of the prison environment and routine, what elements they contribute to the general odour of incarceration.

Mould from damp cellars, and the wretched prisoners confined to them for punishment, safety or convenience; the admixture of spilt blood and rusty iron from antique manacles and shackles biting into bare wrists and ankles, one and the same chemical element, Fe, the former animal and the latter mineral; vegetables boiled into mush in bubbling vats in the prison kitchens, augmented with a few scraps of gristly meat on the turn and the bones of beasts boiled up so often they are quite bleached of colour, taste or nutritional value; urine and faeces in standing buckets, emptied on the ground around the prison to simultaneously scorch and enrich the soil, but slopping over the sides on every step of their journey

from the cells, down the landings and corridors, through the communal and reception areas and out through the iron gates; the full range of other male secretions, from the sweat of honest toil in the workshops, kitchens and laundry, to the semen spilled in anger or consolation, in loneliness or perversion; and over it all, sporadic and mostly vain attempts to mask every other smell with crude chemical disinfectant, which by eliminating the least repulsive only succeeds in highlighting whichever is the strongest and most disgusting.

That, all of that, is the smell of prison. Or so I imagine, because after all I am now so thoroughly part of it.

In the absence of much company inside the prison or visits from outside, the closest Antonio Gramsci came to everyday ordinary human contact over the next two and a half years – from the summer of 1930 to the beginning of 1933 – were the photographs he had collected of his family and loved ones, augmented by the new, latest ones he regularly pleaded for in his letters to them. He kept the photos in a shoebox under his bed, neatly sorted by subject and in chronological order. He would sit studying them for hours on end, like the Bedouin on Ustica, for signs of change in their subjects or their circumstances, or comparisons between different individuals or branches of the family. He set them out in a row on his bed like stills from a film, so that at least in his imagination he could bring them to life over time, moving through their own lives like real human beings. *Or perhaps*, he sometimes thought when studying their fixed poses and smiles, *actors*. These moments of quiet solitary contemplation, with his gallery of photographs laid out before him or picked out for closer scrutiny, were almost the only time in these barren years he allowed himself the luxury of feeling.

The various children were especially fascinating, not just for their endearing looks and rapid development, but also for their similarities to each other and their echoes of previous generations. They offered proof of his own place in family history, reminders of his own childhood and, in their expressions of determined optimism, of his own sterling efforts to imbue the squalor of its circumstances with purpose, honour and dignity. To his sister Teresina he wrote that:

> *"Your kids are lovely-looking, and strong and healthy. I'm really amazed to see how much more robust Franco seems. Some time ago you sent me a photograph of him looking thin and delicate, but this one shows as clear as day that he's not only strong but sunny and lively too. I'd be grateful if you would send a copy of the same photo to Tanya, who will send it on to Julia. I sent her a few of the other photographs myself, though from a technical point of view they were rather poor; the Russians notice these things! She wrote to me that Delio and Giuliano were very interested in them and were asking lots of questions about their Italian cousins."*

To his mother he wrote rather more frankly, with a touch of mischief, that:

> *"I don't think Franco and Delio, roughly the same age, are like one another in the least, though Delio is very like Nannaro's child Edmea. Franco's hair isn't curly, and I think it must be dark brown. Anyway, Delio is certainly much more handsome. I was struck by how little Franco resembles our family. I suppose he's much more like his father Paolo, with his Campidano stock. Or might he even be a little Moorish? Their daughter Mimi is very like Edmea when she was a baby. For the most part, it's marvellous how all these children have the Gramsci family features. So do Delio and Giuliano, very much so. They make me think of faces seen long ago, faces which suddenly surface in my memory after so many years of oblivion. The last picture of Delio was like seeing Mario when he was eight years old. Giuliano's features make me think of Nannaro, and even more of Uncle Alfredo."*

To his mother Gramsci wrote again, about two small blurred photos of her that Gennaro had brought him:

> *"It seems to me that in spite of your years, and all you have put up with, you've kept youthful and strong. You can't have more than a few white hairs, probably a lot fewer than me. And unlike me, I'm sure you've still got at least some of your teeth! Your expression is very lively, even though it's – how shall I put it, mamma? – a little matronly. I'll bet that you'll live to see your great grandchildren, and see them growing up too! One day in the years to come we'll get a big family photograph taken. All the generations will be in it, and yourself in the middle to keep us all in order!"*

Naturally he took the closest interest in the photos of his own two small sons, and tried hard to construct from them some sense of how they might be living and growing up. Each new photograph would add a detail or a development to the story, some new cause for delight or concern. But towards the end of 1930, it was a group photograph of Julia, Delio and Giuliano that made the deepest impression. The boys looked well enough – Delio as usual a little dreamy, Giuliano slightly annoyed and anxious to be off and doing something else – but Julia's expression was vacant and distracted, inclined to anger, almost "warlike" he observed. He could not help but compare it to his favourite picture of her, right at the bottom of the pile in the shoebox. It was a group photo taken in Ivanovo in July 1922, in those far off days a couple of months before they met. Somehow the photographer seemed to have drawn her out of herself and presented her confident public face, the young music teacher and member of the Ivanovo Arts Education Committee. The contrast with this latest photo was stark. Her hair was unkempt and falling over her face. She was trying to smile for the camera, or rather for the photographer slightly off to the right. But her thin stretched lips just made her look ill, and their forced smile conflicted with the sad, mirthless look in her eyes. She seemed to be saying to her husband, "Here am I with your two children. They are all I have left of you. I am struggling to care for them, and holding them close because I fear that I will lose them just as I've lost you, and that without them I will disappear. Even with them I do not know who I am or why I am here. They are your children. You are their father. Why are you not here with them and me?"

Julia, Julia, Julia...

* * *

> ***"Resistance stretched over an unusually long period of time in a besieged location has in itself a demoralising effect. It comprises suffering, exertion, lack of rest and the constant presence, not of acute danger which fortifies, but of that chronic danger which breaks men down."***
>
> ***Karl Marx, 'Events in the Crimea', 14th September 1855, noted by Antonio Gramsci, 21st May 1931.***

If Antonio Gramsci's relationship with his two small children was conducted through photographs on his side and scraps of overheard adult conversation on theirs, his relationship with his wife now consisted of garbled hints about her from others, and worried or exasperated outbursts from him. All of it was conducted in writing via second or third parties over great distances, with several layers of possible or actual censorship to pass through. Julia now hardly ever wrote directly to him herself. Her news was more often transmitted through letters from Tanya, who was settled back in Rome, unable or unwilling (*or,* Antonio sometimes wondered, *forbidden?)* to travel to Turi. She enclosed the odd scribbled note from Julia or postcard from Apollon, almost (Antonio surmised) as supporting evidence for her own vague allusions to things going wrong. Tanya regularly apologised for not feeling able to tell him more. His own responses to the scraps from Moscow came in increasingly reluctant and terse messages relayed via Tanya in Rome, which he admitted to her were becoming increasingly "dishevelled".

He complained to Julia on 6th October 1930 that: "When I look back on our correspondence, such as it is, and the hopes I had when I was arrested that you, my wife, would be my primary point of contact with the outside world, I cannot help but feel bitter disappointment. You write to me, your husband, as you would a stranger. We have never succeeded in getting a dialogue going, only ever a series of monologues." He spent many hours wondering why this might be, what had gone wrong or never been right in the first place, and what his own part in the failure of their marriage might be. Were there any "extenuating circumstances", as a lawyer might put it, some excuse or at least explanation in their personal backgrounds, social place and historical setting? Was there still, against all the odds and from the depths of their own isolation and misery, something they could actually do to save themselves and each other? Was there even any point in trying?

Without any clear statement from Julia or hard information from anyone else, he lost himself in speculation, clutching at straws, turning every little molehill of fact into a mountain of supposition. He lurched between anguished self-pity at one extreme and the "disinterested" chill of his notebooks at the other, from *fur mich* to *fur ewig*. A fortnight later in October he observed in a letter to Tanya that, from what little he could gather of the real situation, "Julia is gradually approaching the state that Zhenya reached in 1919, in that she refuses to adopt a regular rhythm of living. What was understandable in 1919, with all that everyone had recently gone through, is nothing but absurd romanticism in the more settled conditions of 1930." Conscious that "...you forward all my letters to Julia, even personal ones addressed to you", he shared a hypothesis derived from his recent reading and reflection, "...in the sincere hope that it might be of some practical help in illuminating the way ahead."

All mental disturbance had its basis in history, he argued, and varied over time according to the change in historical developments and circumstances. Every epoch generated its own form of madness, a complex interplay of social stresses and personal confusion. The complexity of each era's favoured or even "fashionable" mental illness directly reflected the complexity of the society and political economy in which it arose. Whereas the post-war epidemic of neurasthenia was a direct result of famine, disease, revolution, injury and death on a mass scale, and the simple exhaustion of living through such turbulent times – as such, an easily understandable human response to social catastrophe and upheaval – personal breakdown now had much less obvious causes in the organisation of everyday life at work and in the home. "Nervous debility" had been domesticated or privatised by the turn from war to peace, from privation to plenty, from social conflict to social stability. To make matters worse, it doubled back on itself in the form of personal shame and social disgrace at having survived what had destroyed so many others. Previously, "society" was to blame; now, it was the fault of the "individual", a graphic example of the restoration of bourgeois hegemony over the way in which people saw themselves and each other.

These "psychological disorders" seemed to be increasingly common across the industrialised world. Julia's disturbance was "…no isolated phenomenon, as evident in the scientific publications concerning the new industrial work systems introduced from America. In the regulation of every aspect of their workforces' lives, Ford and his cohorts are putting their workers' physical and mental health under enormous strain... Unless we are able to make the necessary adjustments in mentality and way of life, mechanization crushes us. And I'm taking mechanisation in the broad sense, to include the scientific organization of brain work, such as you and I have been professionally engaged in. Its disciplines and demands are unyielding, relentless, occasionally overwhelming."

This was the psychological or "spiritual" manifestation of what Gramsci referred to in his own writings as "Americanism... the basis for any modern form of planned economy." At least in America – but also in economies as diverse as Italy and the Soviet Union if its "scientific" advocates had their way (most notably Trotsky, who in 1924 had called for an "Americanized Bolshevism") – it meant relatively high wages in return for strictly regulated performance on automated production lines. Each task was separated and allocated to a "specialist" worker, who was required to repeat it consistently and endlessly. Every moment of the working day was subject to "Taylorist" methods of "time and motion" study, efficiency and quality improvement.

Outside work, if there was really any such place under this new managerial regime, Ford "...employs inspectors who supervise the private life of his employees, their food, their beds, the size of their rooms, their rest hours, their physical and mental health, even their sex lives. If the workers don't conform they're dismissed." Europeans might bridle at such methods, "but this was because of those aspects of Americanism that subvert the stagnant European society. We think we can live as we please... We're absurdly romantic, and in our efforts not to be bourgeois we fall into Bohemianism, which is in fact the most typical form of bourgeois behaviour."

His "hypothesis" on the socio-economic basis of Julia's psychological disturbance, and his somewhat muddled suggestion that it was a consequence of both American-style "mechanisation" *and* European "romantic Bohemianism", unsurprisingly elicited no direct response from her or anyone else. His own curt summary of her condition – as "an inferiority complex" in which she "suffers from unreal problems" – was similarly ignored. In his own deepening isolation, he took stock. After three years of silence or deception following his arrest, he had learnt the full extent of Julia's illness. Or so he had been led to believe. He realised now that he had still not actually got from anyone a coherent account of what was wrong, just scattered and inconsistent signals from her of her mental illness and reports from others – all transmitted through Tanya – of the various vague diagnoses and "wonder cures" she was being subjected to. These latter ranged from full-blown Freudian psychoanalysis – *that should be interesting*, he thought to himself – to a "rest-cure" with the children in the Crimean resort town of Sochi; this last the final, hard-won fruit of Apollon's dwindling prestige.

None of them seemed to do much good. A manically cheerful and resolute note from Julia about her latest "self-discovery" or treatment – enabling her to "rebuild my psyche... and attain a development of my personality that I did not have when we were together, when I always felt like your little girl" – would be followed by months of aching silence, then a message from Tanya that things were back to square one. His own letters back to Julia, by turns chiding and tender, began to seem to him as confused and contradictory as hers. And in their confusion, there was the ever-present risk that some throwaway remark or "hypothesis" would come over as clumsy and seriously hurtful. It was like walking on eggshells. How could it be otherwise, given how little he knew of the real situation, and how unused he was becoming to dealing with other people in normal circumstances? How could he, in his externally imposed isolation, hope to understand what Julia was going through in her self-imposed isolation? His words to her really were shots in the dark. He was casting his love into a void, expressing nothing so much as fear or contempt towards his own feelings. He was hiding in his mind from his heart; or rather behind his heart, where the ancients located the soul, observing his own feelings clinically and dispassionately but quite unable to do anything about or with them. More and more, he fell back into what he himself described to Tanya and Julia as "pedantic lectures", apologising frequently and profusely for his seeming inability to strike any more human or sympathetic note.

After one of Tanya's most downbeat accounts of Julia's condition, he declared to his wife in November 1930 that "all is revealed". She was undergoing, he suggested, a "…psychological crisis which was bound to have a physiological basis" in her many years of irregular hours and habits and inadequate diet. When Tanya had told him that Julia was undergoing psychoanalysis, this had prompted him to "…reread your letters from a psychoanalytical point of view." He could now detect in them "…ruptures between form and content, for the purposes of disguise and distraction." Perhaps this reflected something "permanent in your personality" which had now surfaced "against the background of a social environment which permanently demands an extremely strong tension of the will." He understood and accepted her recourse to psychoanalysis, as "…a response to the growing moral pressure exerted on individuals by the apparatus of State and society and the mental illnesses this pressure produces." This was, he had gleaned from his reading, the basis of the latest and most advanced "scientific" approaches to psychiatry, though one should be as wary of it as of any "formulae for living" which promise much but at best "…translate half-formulated desires into conscious aims."

Freudism was a useful tool in "…the passage from the old economic individualism to the planned economy." It could help you find your own way through life, so long as you set aside such eccentricities as its apparent advocacy of sexual relations between fathers and children and its overriding preoccupation with the feminine personality. But perhaps a properly "historicist" psychoanalysis could best be done alone, "dialectically and with intellectual objectivity... You can thereby become your own doctor." He wondered whether she might not be better served by hard and purposeful work. In other words, in this most intimate and interior form of medicine, she should seek to "heal thyself."

To this end he set her the task of researching for him a debate recently conducted at Oxford University between Benedetto Croce and the Russian intellectual and Soviet official Anatoly Lunacharsky on the tenets and veracity of historical materialism. The wily old Italian liberal philosopher's intimate knowledge of Marxism had clearly taken the Bolshevik luminary and recently displaced Soviet Minister of Education by surprise, and revealed in him a surprising ignorance of the main currents of Italian cultural and intellectual life. In particular, Lunacharsky had struggled to refute Croce's critique of "the hidden God in the economic base" posited by Marxism, the notion that economics determined every other aspect of life. Against this, Croce set his own master concept of "ethico-political action", conscious planning and strategic intervention, as the primary factor in the course of history. Antonio wrote to Julia that he would be interested in any "special essay" Croce had composed after the debate.

In the same spirit of "healing through work", he further suggested that she might propose a Russian translation of a new edition of *Ancient Capitalism: A History of the Roman Economy* by Giuseppe Salvioli, which he had been reading and was much impressed by. "It requires a Russian translator with a very good knowledge of Italian, who can understand and correct the distortions of syntax and the rather clumsy grammar in the Moscow edition published after the author's death." He understood that the Soviet state publishing house paid for proposals for translations which were published, and suggested this might help the Schuchts' straitened finances. They were, according to Tanya, worse off than him here in prison, with his daily allowance and the money sent to him via Carlo from the *PCd'I* in exile, which sustained a prison "account" of several hundred lire, or even the Gramscis back in Ghilarza, where several working-age adults enabled the family to employ a maid. This, Tanya explained pointedly, had been beyond the Schuchts for some years. On a lighter note, Antonio shared with Julia a curious coincidence he had come across in his own notes on the military campaign for *Risorgimento*, Italian unity, in the 1870s. An article he had read in the *Nuova Antologia* had addressed the question of whether "a victorious offensive on the *Giulia* front (in north east Italy) would have carried the war into the Slavic countries."

"Just think," he wrote to his own Julia, "I seem to have written this down without making the connection with you, at least not on any kind of 'conscious' level! I wonder what your Professor Freud would have to say about that!" Whatever Julia felt or decided to do, he pleaded with her "to write to me with utter frankness" and – as tactfully as he could manage, in the light of the scatter-brained nature of much of her previous correspondence – "with a greater love of system." In response, in one of her sporadic, pained attempts at an ordinary letter, on 9th February 1931, she confessed that "when I think of writing – which I do every day – I think of what makes me remain silent. I remember that my weakness is new to you." He duly responded, in a similarly clumsy, halting attempt at endearment and sympathy:

> *"I have always known that you were weak, and indeed at times very weak. I knew in short that you were a living, breathing woman, my darling Julka... In the circumstances it's hardly surprising that you're a little harassed mentally, and that I feel powerless to do anything about it. When I think about our life, I cannot but conclude that we never really had a chance. We were together too briefly, always in abnormal circumstances, and cut off from the concrete reality of everyday life... All we can do now is try to salvage the little joy we had and that lives on in our children. I want to be a real father to them, and not just a memory in an ever-receding past. Who are you? What is this family I am supposed to be a part of? Who is Julka + Delio + Giuliano? And how can I add myself, your Nino, to that beautiful 'personal equation', the rather delightful term astronomers use for corrections to their calculations of the movements of the stars?"*

The matter of the children's upbringing and education continued to provoke distant conflict. Antonio had been forbidden to write directly to them, having written once to Delio and had the letter returned unopened and unread, because of fears that it might upset the child's "sensitive nervous system." *My God,* he thought, *another one!* At first he wondered whether the Schuchts were still keeping his imprisonment a secret, or at least a family taboo, and were worried that the child might ask awkward questions about the prison stamp on the letter and the envelope. It turned out that Delio had not yet learnt to read and write, because (Tanya wrote) "...the doctors don't want him to go in for brain work too early."

In April 1931, Tanya forwarded two photos and a sheet of paper with Delio's scrawled attempts at handwriting. Antonio wrote back to her:

> *"I couldn't make head or tail of it, or of why he should start writing right to left, and not left to right. I am however glad he writes with his hands; that's something anyway, better than writing with his feet! Since the Arabs, Persians, and the Turks who've not yet accepted Westernisation, and perhaps other people too, write from right to left, it doesn't seem to me terribly serious or dangerous. Once Delio has learnt Persian, Turkish and Arabic, writing from right to left will be of great advantage. But why not take this logic further? Wouldn't it have been better to leave his personality free to develop on its own in other ways too? Why was he forced to dress like other people? Why not leave his clothes scattered around the room and let him choose spontaneously: socks on his head, shoes on his hands, gloves on his feet?"*

Tanya chose, perhaps wisely, not to share this letter with her Russian relatives. She had recently met with Antonio's brother Carlo, who had visited Moscow to discuss Antonio's situation with officials in the Comintern, and taken the opportunity of meeting his in-laws. They were, he reported to Tanya when he returned to Rome, turning the children against Antonio because they believed he was not a dutiful father. They were even considering making a complaint to the authorities about his failure to support his wife and children financially, apparently oblivious of his repeated attempts to get Julia to accept gifts and money, because they had been advised that this would entitle them to state support. In turn Tanya chose not to tell Antonio what Carlo had told her, but forwarded a message from Apollon that "…Julia does not refuse to write because she is sick, but because she finds it very painful under the conditions she is obliged to do it in." *What a strange thing to say,* thought Antonio, confused and conflicted again between his feelings towards the Schuchts of concern and contempt. *What could these "conditions" be?*

In fact, Julia wrote again to Antonio in early May 1931, in an apparently upbeat mood. She was feeling very much better, conveyed news of the children and her own wishes for the future, even some observations on the spectacular achievements of the first Five Year Plan. Was this permanent, or another false dawn? He wrote to Tanya that "…Julia seems to have recovered a certain confidence in herself and her own strength." Perhaps, he speculated, she "has escaped from the deep sea to the shore" Her recovery owed a lot, she had said, to the new scientific methods being pioneered in the Soviet Union for the treatment of mental disorder. This was, Antonio wrote to Tanya with more than a hint of his customary irony, "…a touching example of the Soviets' great faith in science, of an almost religious character, in stark contrast to the corresponding loss of faith in science in the West." And what did this latest wonder treatment amount to? Apparently, someone had suggested to Julia that she should "unravel herself", whatever that might mean, *as if she hasn't done more than enough of that already...*

On 1st June 1931 Antonio finally received a properly legible letter, or rather what he described to Tanya as an "epistle", from

Delio, in which the child expressed his "love of Pushkin's stories." Antonio wrote back to Julia: was the sentiment genuine? He also wondered to himself whether the letter had been composed or even written by the child. In response, he transcribed a folk-tale from Sardinia which he asked Julia to recite to the children:

> *"A child is sleeping. Nearby there's a big cup of milk ready for when he wakes up. A rat drinks the milk. The child, waking to find the milk gone, screams. The mother screams too. The rat bangs his head on the wall in desperation, but realises that won't achieve anything, so he rushes to a goat for some milk. The goat says she'll give him some milk if he gets her some grass to eat. The rat goes to the country for grass, but the parched land begs for water. The rat goes to the fountain, but the fountain has been ruined in a war and needs stones to plug the holes. The rat goes to the mountain for stones, but it has been so devastated by logging that all the stones have rolled down and broken into tiny pieces.*
>
> *The rat tells the mountain the whole story so far, and promises that when the child grows up he will replant the trees on the mountain. In return the mountain tells the rat where he can find stones still intact. The rat takes the stones to the fountain, the water to the land, the grass to the goat and the milk to the child, who has so much he can even bathe in it! He grows up strong and tall, and plants the trees which attract new soil and regular rain to the mountain, which prevents flooding in the plains. In other words the rat conceives and executes nothing less than a piatilietka, a proper Five Year Plan (especially welcome in Sardinia, where coal mining has caused almost total deforestation)! And even the smallest creatures are capable of the greatest acts!"*

In July 1931, Gramsci received permission to write weekly rather than fortnightly letters, an easing of conditions following on from a slight reduction in his sentence (by one year, four months and five days; *490 nights...)* the previous year. These were, he realised, small acts of government mercy that actually meant the Fascists were feeling even more secure. As for the increased entitlement to letters, he confessed in a letter to Tanya that he was surprisingly unmoved by this substantial increase in what had been his most enjoyable and purposeful activity. Now he found it increasingly onerous and disruptive of his personal routines. He frequently forgot things he'd previously been informed of or even written himself, which created regular misunderstandings with his correspondents. Awaiting their responses became a fresh trial, especially when they were delayed by tardiness, mishap or the censors. He felt "...less desire to write than ever... every day another thread tying me to the past breaks."

When she wrote back asking him what he meant, he replied that from their silence and the lack of visits: "I can only conclude that the people I love have grown used to the idea of my being in prison." Previously he had been glad to leave the past behind. These "broken threads" were a mark of his independence and personal progress: "I was almost proud to be isolated. But today I realise the squalor and sterility of a life directed solely by one's own will... I no longer have a real programme of study and work. I'm no longer curious about anything, daunted by the scale of the tasks I set myself and the limits of my own resources."

When he finally brought himself to write directly to Julia again, he reiterated that:

"...when I was arrested I believed that you would help me keep in touch with the outside world, or at least your and the children's lives. At the risk of hurting you greatly, I have to say that you've done just the opposite. You have aggravated my isolation and made me feel it even more painfully... I know next to nothing about you, not even if you've gone back to work. Your letters are extremely vague. I can't succeed in imagining any of your life. I've tried so many times to start a real dialogue with you, I've asked you so many

> *questions and indicated the kinds of things it would interest me to know. All this has produced nothing. So I have fallen back into this crab-like state of mind, which makes it very hard and painful for me to write to you at all. Try as I might, and though I hate myself for it, I just cannot find within me the sympathy and understanding to reach out to you and offer you the support you undoubtedly need. I am simply too cut off, too deep down inside myself. In these circumstances, expecting me to have anything truly worthwhile to say about your own depression is like asking a drowning man to show you how to walk. This letter is one more attempt to make contact. I hope it is still possible, and that we may still be in time."*

At the very end of July, with the approach of the children's birthdays, he wrote to her again:

> *"In a few days Delio will be seven years old, and at the end of the month Giuliano will be five. This birthday is especially important for Delio, because the age of seven is widely considered an important point in the development of a personality. The Catholic Church, undoubtedly the global institution with the greatest body of organisational and propaganda experience, has fairly recently set the first communion at seven. This represents a solemn entry into the community of the faith, and endows upon the young child an ideological formation that should stay with them for life. I don't know whether you're planning to celebrate this birthday in any special way. Perhaps this is the moment to explain to Delio that I am in prison and why, though I appreciate you may still want to keep it from Giuliano. Such an explanation, together with the sense of trust and respect it conveys, especially if he is required for the time being to keep it from his younger brother, would I'm sure make a great impression upon him and mark an important point in his development."*

* * *

The most persistent and widespread medical condition in prison is hypochondria. Communications from outside should avoid any mention of medical problems or treatments, as much as practicably possible, because prisoners will immediately imagine they have them. I have seen people driven close to suicide for fear of illnesses and sufferings caused by mysterious diseases whose existence the medical profession out of sheer malice refuses to acknowledge.

There is so much time to brood in prison. Boredom is the worst enemy; a special kind of boredom which doesn't spring from idleness, because in prison there is always some function to perform, but from the limited contact allowed the prisoner with the outside world. Saints and hermits were also tormented by it. They called it the "midday devil" because towards noon they were seized by a longing for change, for the world, for the novelty of other people. They thought it was the devil tempting them when it was simply the acute boredom of monotony and solitude. When medicine has replaced God as the cause and solution of every misfortune, the prisoner seeks solace in medical diagnoses and treatments.

Prisoners avidly read articles about illness and send for pamphlets and books of the 'Every Man his own Doctor' and 'Emergency Treatment of the Sick' variety. They end up discovering that they have at least three or four hundred ailments and detect in themselves the symptoms of all of them. There are some here, even amongst the political prisoners, who swallow all the pills and medicines their mates refuse to take, convinced that these medicines cannot fail to do them good, or at least alleviate ailments they don't yet know they have.

These fixations sometimes reach the heights of arrant absurdity. I knew a political prisoner who sent for a treatise on obstetrics. He said he had once assisted with an emergency birth, and since he'd been in prison he'd fretted that he might

not have done things properly. If he should ever again find himself in the position of assisting at a birth (in prison?!), he wanted to be sure he knew what to do! Such are the morbid digressions taken by otherwise intelligent people who for any amount of time are steeped in the prison mentality. In reality, there is nothing much wrong with anybody in prison which cannot be cured by rest and good sleep, a change of diet, regular exercise, and if absolutely necessary proprietary medicines readily available from the prison dispensary or a local town pharmacy.

In early August 1931, Antonio Gramsci suffered his most serious medical crisis yet. On the morning of Monday 3rd, he suddenly started coughing up blood. In response to his cries for help, the guards sauntered along from the guardroom next door. When they saw the blood on his bed and his clothes, and in large splashes on the stone floor, they panicked and sent out for the prison doctor. Doctor Cisternino was, they were told and they told Gramsci, out at lunch and would then be attending to other patients in the town. But he would come to the prison as soon as he had finished with them. In the meantime he had told them to keep an eye on him.

"And a fat lot of good that'll do me," he said, through anxious gurgles and racking breaths.

Gramsci's coughing fit went on till four in the afternoon, by which time he had brought up – by his own reckoning – over half a pint of blood.

"It wasn't anything like a continuous haemorrhage," he told Dr. Cisternino when he finally showed up in the early evening, "more like a gurgle in my breathing to begin with, like you get from catarrh. An abrupt cough followed, and my mouth filled with blood."

Cisternino was sitting on the very end of Gramsci's bed, with his customary, barely disguised sneer of haughty contempt.

Gramsci continued, anxious to get the detail and the sequence of the symptoms right, and in the process perhaps quell the terror he still felt some hours after the onset of the attack. Cisternino's manner did nothing to calm him, but then he wouldn't expect anything else from this pompous Fascist fool.

"The coughing wasn't especially violent, or even pronounced. It was exactly the sort of coughing you get when you've got something in your throat, just isolated bursts..."

"Can you show me now?"

Gramsci coughed, apprehensively, and spat out the product into his handkerchief.

"May I see?"

Cisternino examined the contents of Gramsci's handkerchief, with no more disgust on his face than previously. Gramsci found this display of professional indifference oddly reassuring, almost impressive. It was mostly catarrh, with streaks of heavy dark blood.

"Mmmm..." said the doctor.

"It was all blood before," said Gramsci hopefully. "This looks much more normal..."

"Well, we shall just have to see how you get on. In the meantime I shall prescribe calcium chloride with a trace of adrenalin."

He did not say what this was supposed to achieve or alleviate, or what he thought the basic problem might be, and Gramsci did not feel inclined to ask. Cisternino returned two days later on 5th August, and made a thorough examination with a stethoscope. He was at least able to rule out any bronchial infection, and suggested that the blood had come from the intestines, "…which given your medical history, Signor Gramsci, of digestive problems, would not be entirely surprising... In the meantime you might consider smoking rather less."

Gramsci resisted the temptation to light up a Macedonian there and then, but simply looked back at Cisternino with an expression that said, "And what would be the point of that?" In fact he did try to reduce his smoking, as much for reasons of thrift as health, by making three small cigarettes with the tobacco that would previously have made one. But the effects on his concentration – "I read little and think less" – made him reluctant to give up altogether. Instead he tried to eke out his tobacco, getting through one packet every five days.

The coughing eased over the next few days, and there was no more blood in the catarrh. But in the meantime, Gramsci's left side was covered in a rash of red spots. *It could be anything,* he decided, and no worse than similar rashes he'd suffered previously. It had been unusually hot recently, even for August, and he had been sweating profusely on many nights in recent weeks. But from feeling his forehead he could tell that he was also feverish, especially in the couple of nights before and after the blood-coughing fit. He chose not to call Cisternino back to examine the rash or consider the fever. The initial examinations and prescriptions had cost enough, a large chunk out of his prison account, and he was loathe to give Cisternino any more business than was strictly necessary. Besides, he would not want the doctor to think he was weak, or a malingerer. In the meantime he made frequent, sometimes obsessive, use of a thermometer he had had Tanya purchase and send him, noting the slightest variation in his temperature, especially before and after eating.

Antonio wrote to Tanya, describing the whole incident in precisely the same details he had given Cisternino, and trying to reassure her that "…there's nothing very worrying about it." In response to her concerns about his meagre diet, and what it might have contributed to his intestinal problems, he told her, "You mustn't think that I go without anything I can buy to supplement my prison rations; the problem is there's not much to buy. This year fruit has been on sale just a few times, and fresh cheese not for a long time. The canteen only sells stuff I can't eat;

even ham has been forbidden me by the doctor, not least because of the state of my teeth. I keep strictly to what he orders, and eat nothing much but eggs, milk and rice cooked with butter. Even so, I can't seem to sort out my insides." Various dietary "cures" – going for days on nothing but milk, or grapes, or even lemonade – might briefly calm his stomach, but mainly because they passed right through him without troubling his digestive system.

Medicine didn't seem to make much difference either. The stuff Cisternino prescribed just made Gramsci feel drowsy and constipated, and the various remedies and "compounds" Tanya sent or ordered from the local pharmacy did little lasting good. He made meticulous notes of their ingredients and their effects on his temperature, weight and well-being, and duly reported them to Tanya for her to consult with her medical friends; all to little effect Rather, he thought prison conditions were much more significant. Frequent disturbances and wakefulness in the night made his condition noticeably worse, whereas better sleep made it much better. To that end he wrote several letters to the Prison Director Parmegiani to protest against the continuing noisiness around his cell at night, without result beyond official acknowledgement of the receipt of his complaints. If anything, his complaint that "the observance of regulations becomes an object of trafficking between the guards and prisoners" – packets of tobacco and quarter litres of wine exchanged for "special consideration" during inspections – made the "nightly rackets" even worse. He spent his days in a dull torpor, and his nights tossing and turning. The best use of his time at any hour was to read or write in his notebooks, his own preferred therapeutic work. It did not require physical health; if anything, deep thought offered a way to rise above illness, spurred on by the sense of urgency induced by failing powers.

Throughout 1931 and 1932, Gramsci continued to study intensively and for long hours, to consult and order a wide range of books and periodicals, which were sent to him by Tanya, his brother Carlo or direct from the bookshop in Milan where Piero Sraffa kept an open account for him. They were, he observed to guards or fellow prisoners who noticed the piles of well-thumbed journals and rows of heavily annotated books in every spare corner of his cell, his "lifeblood" or more frivolously his "menagerie." He was especially proud of the books and periodicals he had to fight to read, like his treasured volumes of Marx, and which he knew were now lifetime companions.

Through these years he was translating a small anthology of Marx's writings from German into Italian, to help him through those periods when he didn't feel capable of original thought. He also undertook a highly original study of *Canto X* of Dante's *Inferno*, which offered some light relief, taking up where he had left off as a student before the war. But even this had a serious aim: to "demolish" more conventional interpretations such as one he had just come across by a certain "Rastignac", and "…to demonstrate that the representatives of a subaltern social group can give short shrift to intellectual pimps like Rastignac in matters of science and artistic taste." Gramsci's reading of Dante had an added but unstated personal purpose, to focus attention on the anguish of the character Cavalcante over the fate of his son Guido; it was a beautiful and moving portrayal of a worried, grieving father.

When he had finished with books and periodicals, he sent them to Tanya or Carlo for safe-keeping or disposal, or donated them to the prison library. He was quite meticulous in their cataloguing and storage, with lists of publication and location details worthy of any library, and in overseeing their further usage. He instructed Carlo "…not to lend them to people outside the family circle... I don't see why my books should help entertain people who are indirectly responsible for my being in prison." Rather, he hoped they might form the basis of a family library for his brothers and sisters and nephews and nieces "…and who knows? Perhaps one day my own children..."

Alongside his reading he made new notes, revised and rearranged old ones, gradually filling up the marbled exercise books with his spidery writing, and bringing his reflections on history, philosophy and political economy into focus. For months at a time, he went back over his several years' collection of journals and reviews, sorting out what he wanted to keep from what he would send to Tanya for storage or disposal. It took so long because he couldn't resist using select quotations or responses of his own as a stepping-off point into original reflections. Some of these – "monographs" as he called them – were beginning to take on the shape of fully formed outlines of his central themes, the role of intellectuals in Italian and European history in particular, which he allowed himself to imagine being published somewhere, some day. His only problem, he wrote to Tanya, was that "I am too often plagued by serious headaches that do not permit the necessary concentration." For most of this time he was entirely alone, cut off from his family in Russia, Rome and Sardinia and from his party in exile and in Italy, and even from most of his fellow prisoners at Turi di Bari. They might glimpse him through the bars of his cell, standing in his customary position at a high desk covered in books and papers, pacing around and in between the stacks on the floor as he cleared his thoughts, or sitting in the sun when he ventured out into the yard during exercise periods, usually with a lit Macedonian cigarette in his hand or his mouth. By and large he kept himself to himself, politely but cursorily answering enquiries into his health and welfare, or exchanging comments on the weather. He showed no interest in the frequently loud and feverish disputes among the other political prisoners.

His own mood was a kind of serene fatalism, a sardonic peace with himself, a settled melancholy, chiding himself only (he wrote to Tanya) for "...the weakness of not having dared to remain alone, of permitting myself ties of love, obligations and close relationships." Those he had formed in his years of freedom, he now felt, had brought him nothing but trouble. If only he could insulate himself altogether from other people and the outside world, "I might convince myself not to ponder any more, to resist any external stimulus, and to put aside any letters I may receive without reading them." This was, he argued, a highly desirable and productive kind of "emotional continence" which was "decidedly out of fashion, but in my circumstances – stuck in here but hard at work – represents by far the most psychologically healthy and intellectually productive mode."

He sought to allay Tanya's continuing anxiety about his physical health, which had prompted her to write to his brother Carlo and even the prison doctor Cisternino, by insisting that he had made "a fair recovery" from the blood-coughing episode in August, and relaying a story from his childhood:

> *"When I was four I suffered haemorrhages and convulsions for three days in a row. I was deathly white, and the doctors gave up on me. My aunt insisted that I only came back to life when she bathed my feet in the oil of a lamp dedicated to a statue of the Madonna. Until around 1914, when I was twenty three, my mother kept the little coffin and the special shroud they were going to bury me in. As you know, I've never been especially robust, but since then I've never suffered a serious illness apart from neurasthenia and dyspepsia. I am as sceptical of medicine as any sensible person should be of any 'science' which makes such grand claims for itself, but I do respect and listen to doctors, even our good Doctor Cisternino. I have even greater respect for vets, because animals can't describe their own symptoms, which means vets have to be accurate in their diagnoses. After all, animals cost money, whereas most of humanity is a dead loss."*

Antonio was now making systematic if sometimes perfunctory use of his new entitlement to one letter out per week, spreading them roughly equally between his birth-family in Sardinia and, via Tanya, his new family in Russia. But their responses were still sporadic. Whole weeks or even months would go by without a word, which left him feeling irritable and resentful at their apparent failure to understand the "...importance which correspondence assumes in prison," as he wrote soon after his illness to his mother, who had been strangely quiet: "It fills up the blank days, and gives some savour to life."Even his brother Carlo, previously so diligent in his communications and representations, had made only sporadic recent contact through Tanya, despite having moved to Milan with Piero Sraffa's help to be within easier reach of his brother. There were hints that he was in some unspecified difficulty over the money he received from the *PCd'I* in exile; with the Italian authorities, the party or the Comintern, or even with his own personal expenditure and accounting, Antonio knew not what, though he was aware that Carlo had been in and out of work. The job Sraffa had helped him get, with the textile company Snia Viscosa, had not lasted more than a few months.

He found the long silences from Sardinia as hard to bear as Julia's, especially when his brother and sisters' most recent letters had made much of their mother's worsening health. Signora Peppina was now in her seventies, and feeling the effects of a lifetime of hardship and personal sacrifice. Because of pains in her hands she was unable to write, and only able to communicate with Antonio by dictating letters to others. He detected in this a certain historical justice, because she had taught all her seven children to read and write, and could now make use of them to ease the strain on her own hand. All of them, he assured her, remembered her strength, kindness and tenderness towards them when they were young: "You are now and always have been in the only real paradise that exists, which for a mother must be in the hearts of her own children."

It turned out that Signora Gramsci and the family, and much of their village of Ghilarza, had been struck down with malaria in the summer of 1931. With the onset of autumn and cooler weather, they were all now feeling much better. Antonio responded in some relief to the news by recommending that they petition the local council for the construction of sewers, "…just as their predecessors had the foresight to construct an aqueduct. An aqueduct minus sewers means malaria as sure as night follows day. The women of Ghilarza used to be fat and ugly because of the bad water; nowadays it must be because of the malaria! The village men no doubt will be going in for an intensive wine cure..."

He gathered from the renewed correspondence that his nieces and nephews had been asking about him, and complaining that their Uncle Nino never wrote or sent gifts to them. He asked that someone explain to them that not being able to do what you want when you want is precisely what being in prison involves. "Tell them I've got a very big cell, bigger even than any of the rooms in their houses. The only trouble is that I can't leave it." To his mother he concluded: "I am more serene than ever, though I'm getting older in prison. I've lost all my teeth and can't chew, which is especially annoying because soon there'll be lamb for sale in the canteen."

In contrast there was no better news from Moscow. From what he could glean from Julia's scribbled notes enclosed with Tanya's fuller letters, his wife's psychological condition was now worse than ever. From his great distance, Antonio struggled to understand and to help, all too obviously (at least in his own mind) failing, not least because he was discouraged from communicating directly, but had to address his wife through Tanya, the other Schuchts or whoever else might be reading these letters. His tone was by turns hectoring, pedantic or simply exasperated. He routinely interspersed his "lectures" with apologies for them, then proceeded with another one, apologising again for his "intellectual formation" and "inadequacy in matters of the mind and heart."

Julia was now placing "inordinate faith" in psychoanalysis, it seemed to him, with all "its phantasmagorical and witch-doctorish elements, harking back through dreams and fantasies to some kind of innate 'human nature' which actually derives from previous and entirely different historical epochs. By taking her deeper inside herself, it is simply taking her further away from her own real life in the present day and the outside world." If it had any value, it was as a means of understanding and treating what Dostoyevsky called "the insulted and the injured", unfortunate and unusually sensitive individuals who find themselves trapped between "the iron contrasts of modern life." They were quite incapable of reconciling their own internal desires with the external demands of work, family and community, and all those other "social forces which bind us together but at the same time can tear us apart", including the love of those around them.

The resulting conflict was "disastrous for exceptionally refined and sensitive temperaments" like Julia's, but psycho-analysis offered only limited insight and very little practical help. She had to seek her own resolution to her personal crisis rather than some kind of ready-made formula from elsewhere. It did no good, for example, for her to disown her artistic and musical skills and wish she could do something "more useful", as she had recently taken to doing. This "metaphysical error" simply cut off an important source of personal pleasure and expression, and a crucial outlet for her personality, not to mention one of her few remaining occupational options. Julia had to find a way of reconciling herself to the world around her, but could not hope to achieve this by simply denying herself, her personal background and formation and family history.

This latest "lecture" went down especially badly with the Schuchts. Julia communicated via Tanya her displeasure at being called "injured and insulted", which she (and, she pointed out, Dostoyevsky) took to mean the most decadent members of the lower social orders. Another possible translation of the original Russian into Italian was "humiliated and offended", which conveyed much more accurately the way Antonio's "insinuations" had left Julia feeling. In one of her most recent "morbid outbursts", with an added undertow of suspicion and jealousy, Julia had even urged Tanya to "break off your relationship" with Gramsci and return to the family in Russia. Tanya also transcribed the brief, gruff postcards Apollon enclosed with the latest correspondence from Moscow, expressing his paternal displeasure at the upset "the Italian" continued to cause his family and asking Tanya to pass it on. It was especially hard, he pointed out, on his wife, mother Julia Grigor'evna, who was herself in failing health and "feels the slights against her family acutely."

Antonio tried to explain himself more clearly, with reference to the debilitating contrasts between the ideal and the real, the personal and the public, the individual and the collective, especially at historical moments of crisis and stress: "We are all of us, including myself, subject to social forces and cultural leftovers that we cannot individually control." Various personal responses were available: vulgar scepticism, social hypocrisy, absolute conformism, or (and this is what he would advocate, and attempted to apply to his own troubles) "thinking historically, dialectically, and identifying one's own problems and solutions – what I gather Freud calls the 'work' of psychoanalysis – with intellectual dispassion... Again, one must be one's own doctor." He sent off this further clarification, more in hope than expectation, and more aware than ever of his limitations as a husband and the fragility of his bond with his faraway wife. He tried to set aside the feeling, strongest in the hours of darkness, that the entire Schucht family had it in for him.

His reading, especially the lighter popular fiction he used to wind down towards sleep, began to resonate with his personal preoccupations. Whole paragraphs or even chapters would leap out at him and illuminate his own miserable predicament. So, in December 1931, he read *Villa Beatrice: Storia di una donna* by the Florentine Catholic writer Bruno Cicognani, in which the personality of its protagonist was laid bare like "some natural phenomenon", as Gramsci wrote in his latest notebook. "Beatrice is the personification and typification of emotional coldness, incapable of loving anyone else, in part because of a heart ailment... Naturally Beatrice is unaware that her psychic existence is determined by her physiological condition." Cicognani's account was "hackneyed" and "inconsistent" and "lacking in artistic representation", but Gramsci could not ignore the parallels with Julia's personality and his own increasingly detached attitude towards her, "an anatomical specimen not a woman."

In another note that same dark month, he recalled the play *La Morte Civile* by the popular 19th century playwright Paolo Giacometti, about "a man serving a life sentence in prison who manages to escape, and discovers that his wife and daughter have been able to rebuild their lives successfully in his absence. Rather than disturb their happiness, he kills himself."

* * *

Prison is a kind of ideal society, a form of Utopia. Its isolation allows for the application of strict regulation, the imposition of sudden and total change in social order, and the wilful dismissal of all previous experience and knowledge; in other words, it displays all the traditional features of Utopian or "experimental" communities.

This is one of the major ways in which prison differs from outside society, and helps to explain why it is one of the most law-abiding places in society; and why – most curiously of all – the most law-abiding prisoners are often those who have most seriously offended against the laws of the outside.

> ***I once witnessed a group of murderers – bound together by the length of their sentences, the nature of their offences, and the cultural codes that lend a kind of honour and glamour to the forcible termination of human life – take to task a young thief who had been helping himself to more than his fair share of bread in the prison canteen.***
>
> ***"Where would we be," said their acknowledged "capo", a scarred pock-marked Sicilian who had killed dozens of rival gangsters for control of the alleyways of Palermo over a ten-year period, "if we all just did as the fancy took us?"***

There was also in this period growing discord in Antonio's communications with Tanya. What started out as mild teasing and mock scolding – with jokey threats to break off correspondence – began to turn serious. She made careless mistakes in ordering books for him: "Instead of sending me a German grammar for Italians, you sent me an Italian grammar for Germans (and that's a fact)." She sent him some new glasses, which he acknowledged went some way towards alleviating his headaches, but she had spent at least four times more than necessary by choosing such fancy frames. More seriously, she had taken it upon herself to write letters on his behalf to the lawyers who had been involved in his trial and subsequent fruitless appeals, or to the prison authorities, the government and even Mussolini about his conditions and his sentence; all without consulting him. They entered into a long convoluted dispute over whether they should seek an independent medical examination to get to the bottom of his various ailments. Tanya, with her own medical knowledge and connections, thought the prison medical service wholly inadequate. Antonio could not see the point of going to "the considerable expense of an examination by a doctor of our own choice" to tell him what he already knew.

Could she not see how it undermined what little power and

dignity he had left, he wrote to her, this wilful interference in the only areas of his life he felt he had some control over? Such special pleading represented for him "a form of suicide." He wrote in his notebook at around the same time about the 19th century anti-Austrian rebel Count Confalonieri, who had written to the emperor "...like a broken man, pleading for mercy and compassion... His imploring words betray a violation of the spirit a hundred times more humiliating than a death sentence; they are the groan of defeat by a shattered will."

She continued to send things to him that were denied under prison regulations: items of food which did not meet his dietary restrictions; a Thermos flask for coffee which was deemed a "potential security risk"; live yoghurt which went off in the post; books he hadn't ordered, and which would in any case only be allowed in the prison if they had been sent by the bookshop in Milan. These were all "useless gestures", especially the clothes she sent: "I have enough sweaters to last me several years, four or five, and two of them I've not even touched yet." It wouldn't be so bad if she was able to care properly for herself, since he needed above all for her to be well and strong: "I had to laugh at your remark that you are 'always hungry' as if this was an illness and not a sign of good health. It reminded me of the Neapolitan comic figure Monsignor Perrelli who tried to cure his horses of the disease of hunger by starving them to death. But at least he didn't apply his strictures to himself!"

During Tanya's six month stay in Turi in 1930, Antonio grew even tetchier with her at visits or in letters. Just as frequently, he apologised. He was not used to such intimate personal contact, he reasoned. Her proximity reminded him of the family life he was missing and his effective estrangement from her sister, his wife. Her meekness, combined with the obvious effects of her own deteriorating health, just made him more irritable and impatient, then guilty for the way he had treated her. Reporting sardonically that his "mother calls you a saintly creature", he began to openly question her motives in caring for him, and coming all this way to be near him: "I think you've lost the desire to live for yourself, and live only for others." He noted her poor health and inadequate diet, which confined her to bed in her small room in Turi for days on end, and wondered whether she might be better off back in Rome or Milan, or even – as Apollon was now openly urging – back in Moscow with her own family.

In March he accused her of living "in an intellectual miasma" when she told him she "quite enjoyed the feeling of not knowing what to do with my life", and of "wishful thinking and childish daydreams" about travelling around Italy. "I assure you," he wrote, "the 'Grand Tour' is as outmoded as the Romantic poetry and idealised landscape painting it gave rise to." He repeated his earlier accusations that really she had no clear understanding of his life in prison, which was utterly devoid of any kind of heroism or nobility: "In your eyes I am a kind of new Gandhi... you still think of prison as a boarding school for little aristocratic orphan girls under the patronage of queen mothers." And as for the central issue of Julia's illness, Tanya had shown "merciless cruelty" in concealing it for more than three years.

Again, in subsequent letters and visits he apologised profusely and tried to explain why he sometimes seemed to create conflict for the sake of it: "I have to create a dialogue." His whole temperament, not just his political outlook and principles, was governed by the dialectic. What she took to be ill temper on his part was just his own personal manifestation of the "compassionate sarcasm" inherent in Marxism. Or so he said; the tone of their correspondence improved markedly when Tanya moved back to Rome in June 1930. She regularly wrote that she was making plans to visit him soon; when they came to nothing, he was saddened and exasperated, but once his irritation had died down, relieved. She should spare herself the expense and the strain on her health of the long and arduous journey across half the country.

As he had done before, he used his personal troubles and worries as a spur to work. His master-concept of hegemony was coming into plain view, "the essential ingredient of the most modern philosophy of praxis", as he wrote to Tanya, "eliminating the mechanistic, fatalistic conceptions of economic determinism" which had dominated Marxism in the "revisionist" social democracy of the Second International, but also superseding the later "historical idealism" of Benedetto Croce. It took the best of Lenin's conception of political action, and broadened it out into a theoretical exposition of how any society is governed.

Though Gramsci had made regular use of the term previously, in its conventional sense of national superiority or domination by force, it began now to take on much richer, deeper meaning and broader explanatory power, mainly in answer to two questions. Firstly, why do popular masses consent to their own subordination, when it is so plainly not in their own historical, material or moral interests? There is an element of coercion in the process, with any half-competent state not hesitating to deploy its own police and security forces against them for the purposes of repression, but brute force is only half the answer.

For the most part state force is held in reserve, always visible as a deterrent but rarely used, for the simple reason that no state could resist a concerted or permanent internal siege. Instead, popular consent is continuously won through a complex process of political persuasion, economic negotiation and cultural influence. A "common sense" of "ordinary daily life" emerges, a kind of "subaltern mentality" which the vast majority readily espouse because it enables them and their families to lead their lives in relative comfort and peace, "getting by" and "making do", "making the best of a bad job" in the hope of some small amelioration. "With a bit of luck" the standing and wealth of their families and communities will improve over generations, with each set of sons and daughters slightly better off than their parents. In the meantime, "Subaltern classes are subject to the initiatives of the dominant class. Even when they rebel against them, they are in a state of anxious defence."

There is a kind of infantilization at work in the assertion of hegemony in a class society. The "subaltern classes" surrender their dignity and autonomy in return for relief from the burdens of power and responsibility, which are retained and exercised over every aspect of public life by the dominant class. In this condition of lifelong childhood, "ordinary people" never get to run anything beyond their own personal lives and immediate families – "private spheres" which are themselves subject to increasing restriction and control under the "Fordist" disciplines of industrial society – so they lack the experience, skills and self-confidence to take control of broader society. They routinely defer to their superiors. These subaltern classes form a kind of shield, or "historical bloc" to use the old French syndicalist George Sorel's term, around the ruling group, protecting, dignifying and disguising the raw "corporate self-interest" of their rule. Alliances of social classes and subgroups are negotiated through manoeuvre and concession, and come to identify their own subaltern corporate self-interests with the status quo. At its simplest this is represented by the acceptance of the terms and conditions of waged labour; at its most complex it takes the form of compliance with the precepts of parliamentary democracy.

In this process the role of "intellectuals", by which Gramsci meant so much more than "great thinkers" or academics, is absolutely crucial. "Traditional intellectuals" – teachers, clerics, lawyers etc. – sustain the established order through the institutions of civil and political society and the state which employ them. But they are not much good at promoting change, in part because they have their own "corporate interest" in the established order, but mainly because of the lack of a close "organic" relationship or "connectedness" with the masses of "ordinary people" or "general public", from whom they maintain a fastidious distance and sense of superiority. In this situation of social stasis, "the people feel but do not understand or know, while the intellectuals know but do not understand or above all feel." Their function is "purely bureaucratic" or formal, and they remain "a caste or a priesthood" within the settled hegemony.

"Organic intellectuals" have very different roles and characteristics. They emerge from within specific social classes to organise any necessary adaptations to the established order through the political parties, civil and spiritual associations, the arts and the media. These adaptations could be relatively minor, with the aim of absorbing critical ideas or oppositional groups into the historical bloc around the ruling elite. This kind of piecemeal change or accommodation is typical of the process of "transformism", whereby opposition elites are bought off, or of periods of "passive revolution" when radical change is imposed from above. Or the organic intellectuals could be revolutionary, aiming to overthrow the ruling elite and construct a new historical bloc around a new leadership drawn from a rising social class.

This gave rise to Gramsci's second central question: how are those intellectual strata formed in any specific historical period and situation? And more to the point, how can some new "potentially hegemonic" social class like the industrial proletariat cultivate its own "organic intellectuals" to assist in the revolutionary process and the construction of socialism? This was already happening as a consequence of industrial development, the expansion of civil society and the widening of the vote – all those "autodidacts" and popular library subscribers, hungry for "enlightenment" and culture – but they still had to be forged into a coherent, constructive force.

This is never easy: "The revolutionary class is always intellectually weak. It struggles to give itself a culture and to give force to a conscious and responsible cultured class of its own. What's more, all the malcontent and redundant members of other classes throw themselves on its side in order to regain a position for themselves." What all too often you end up with, passing themselves off as "opinion formers" or the "cultured elite", is a shifting rabble of castes and cliques adding a bit of spice and flavour to the bland stale stew of bourgeois society. This was evident in the intellectual and cultural life of most advanced industrial countries.

There was a further complicating distinction among the "organic intellectuals", between "the cultural intellectuals" who form artistic avant-gardes and assist in the winning of hegemony but are then cast aside by the newly hegemonic class, and the "technical intellectuals" who are then favoured and brought forward to consolidate the new hegemony. This process was evident in the history of bourgeois revolutions, always presaged through art and ideas but solidified through science and technology, though it was nothing like as clear how proletarian revolution would manage it.

This was clearly an undercurrent within the continuing struggle in the Soviet Union between Stalin and the old Bolshevik opposition, whose cultural formation had been mainly literary and artistic, ill-suited for the technical tasks of industrial development and national planning. The political conflict in Russia was represented in the intellectual sphere by the engineers and planners of economic and technological development on one side, the foot-soldiers of the Five Year Plan, and the constructivists and futurists in art and literature on the other, all those wild-eyed paint-spattered "geniuses" building giant flowers and declaiming blank verse in the salons and market squares of Moscow and Leningrad. But for the moment Gramsci did not feel able to spell it out in those terms. Besides, in the very early 1930s the outcome of this conflict – technology or art? – was not at all clear.

But, Gramsci believed, he had at least glimpsed the process whereby the organic intellectuals of the revolutionary proletariat came forward, learnt their craft and helped to mount a serious challenge to the prevailing hegemony, in the "constructive resistance" of the Turin Factory Councils and the early years of the Soviet Union, which had contested the dominant ways of doing and thinking in every aspect of human experience. This in turn held out some prospect of an effective revolutionary party for the circumstances of contemporary, developed, liberal-democratic capitalism. This new kind of party would form, in an updating of Niccolo Machiavelli's exquisite study of the art of government in the sixteenth century, a "Modern Prince" for the twentieth century.

* * *

Illness in prison takes on a wholly different character and function to illness on the outside. Someone in here is always ill, so illness becomes a running theme of prison life, not least because everyone worries about catching it. News of some new contagion spreads more rapidly than the contagion itself: What are the symptoms? Who has got it, and how did they get it? How serious is it? Is there any treatment available?

But the biggest difference is that inside there is no real incentive to get better. If anything, because illness provides a handy, unquestionable excuse to avoid work or chores, it can come as a positive blessing, a generally accepted justification for all that staring into space and spitting at the ceiling. If it involves a fever or even loss of consciousness, so much the better, because that may bring delusions or dreams which are in themselves an interesting break from prison tedium.

We do not have to earn our living, because our livelihoods have been taken away from us. So why resist illness? In fact some prisoners seem to actively seek it out, partly for the privilege of indolence but also for the interesting experience of subjecting their bodies to some new pestilence. You hear stories, for example, of an underground trade in "smallpox

blankets". In the absence of anything much else to do, day after endless day, a good rash or cough or discharge can provide hours of diverting entertainment.

During their occasional consultations, the Fascist Doctor Cisternino would try to engage the Communist prisoner 7047 Gramsci A. in political discussion. As he took his pulse, calculated his blood pressure, wrote out a prescription, or even while he listened to Gramsci's laboured breathing through a cold steel stethoscope on various parts of his pasty pigeon chest, Cisternino would ask what his esteemed patient-prisoner thought of the latest developments in "public affairs", or of "our great government's latest achievements" in some sphere of industry or agriculture.

Gramsci was always wary of some kind of police trick, aimed at gathering evidence against him or his erstwhile comrades, ever since his encounters with 'Dante Romani' and Corrado Melani in Milan prison back in 1927. But here in Turi the Doctor genuinely seemed to want to talk politics, or rather to probe and bait this ex-MP and party leader who claimed to have had contact with *Il Duce* himself, now fastidiously referred to as "the head of government." Cisternino was especially fascinated by stories Gramsci could relay about his personal dealings with what the doctor usually called "His Excellency" Mussolini.

They had corresponded before the war as fellow Socialist Party activists and journalists, and followed each other's progress in regional and national politics, with Mussolini always several steps and years ahead. Gramsci had submitted articles to the newspapers Mussolini had edited, "…some of these articles, I have to confess, sympathetic to Mussolini's own political positions, which caused me some considerable discomfort later on. I even supported his argument for 'active and operative neutrality' at the beginning of the war, though I parted company when he started openly advocating Italian intervention..."

Some time after the foundation of the Fascist Party, "...this would have been in 1921..." Gramsci submitted an article to Mussolini's *Il Popolo d'Italia,* which was of course rejected. "Thankfully... Again, that would have been used against me..." Then there was the apocryphal meeting in the bar of the Parliament building after Gramsci's maiden speech as an MP, with the spurned handshake and the deadpan look, which he now (smiling to himself) refused to confirm or deny to Cisternino: "Oh, it makes a good story..."

Even now, all these years after those turbulent times, Gramsci was able to write directly to "His Excellency" at the final stage of one of his tortuous, nit-picking campaigns to improve his prison conditions or his access to restricted literature, and appeal to some kind of shared intellectual heritage and principle, ending his petitions with "Thank you and respects." He could be sure of a moment of "M"'s attention and a scrawled initial across the bottom of the letter, amidst the torrent of paperwork which famously consumed much of *Il Duce's* working day (and night). More often than not the communist prisoner actually won Mussolini's approval, communicated with a big bold black tick of his large fountain pen (Gramsci was especially proud of winning the right to read Leon Trotsky's autobiography, slipped in at the end of a long list of innocuous requests in September 1930). This writing implement was itself the subject of more than one poetic paean or ballad, with ludicrous analogies to a "worker's tools" or a "gladiator's sword", published in the popular Fascist press, and recited or sung enthusiastically at black-shirt rallies and *squadristi* nights out. Mussolini's scrawl of consent to Gramsci's latest request would send a ripple of quiet fury back down the chain of prison and state officials whose long legalistic objections had been cursorily overruled.

At the base of that pyramid, Cisternino sat salivating, erect and alert, almost physically aroused, as Gramsci answered his questions. "Tell me, Signor Gramsci, what were your overall impressions of our leader when you faced him across the parliamentary benches?.... What was he like as a young man?... Was he wearing his military uniform on that occasion, or stripped to the waist? .... When would you say his magnetic appeal to women first became apparent?" Gramsci would indulge and lead on the Doctor – *where's the harm in it?* – with comparisons to Julius Caesar or Napoleon Bonaparte, made-up quips and ripostes ("All the speeches in parliament are not worth one breath of a chanting Fascist!"), detailed and entirely fabricated descriptions of Mussolini's attire ("On that occasion I believe he wore a blue shirt, with gold trimmings around the collar and cuffs, and a plaited brocade between the epaulette and the second button..."), and the rumoured dimensions of His Excellency's genitalia.

"As a young man, I can tell you from memories as fresh as yesterday, Benito was brimming with vim and vigour! And I tell you now, he has the todger of a stallion! Or so I heard tell from a comrade who shared a urinal... But I actually believe that what women see in him first and foremost is his eyes. Yes, Doctor Cisternino, his enormous eyes..."

Gramsci might even sit upright or stand, if he was capable of it, and offer the provincial doctor an impression of the strutting, pouting, declaiming young orator and rising star of the pre-war Socialist Party, all bulging eyes and thrusting pelvis, windy maximalist rhetoric and choreographed hand gestures. Cisternino would look on in awed silence, quite oblivious to the camp excess in Gramsci's performance. But the conversation between the communist political prisoner and the provincial Fascist functionary, such as it was, would always come down to one simple conclusion. This was the comparison between the treatment Gramsci was receiving here in the Special Penitentiary for Sick Prisoners at Turi di Bari, as the new order of Fascist Italy approached the tenth anniversary of the March on Rome and Mussolini's accession to power – "Ten years..." Cisternino would say, with a smug smile, a fond sigh and a knowing nod of the head – and what he could have expected if he had ended up in a prison camp in "your precious communist utopia" of the Soviet Union.

"Here you get the considerable benefit of my medical expertise, the humane pastoral care of the prison guards and officials, a prison uniform regularly laundered and mended..."

"Ah!" interrupted Gramsci with a quote from his most recent reading of prison memoir, looking down at his faded cotton jacket. "This species of ignoble pyjamas!"

Cisternino continued regardless. "... A diet especially suited to your gastric requirements, a government allowance to purchase extra food and other supplies, even..." – and here he would sweep his free hand around the prison cell – "... all the books and journals you could wish for... And what do we ask in return, Signor Gramsci? Sixteen hours a day, seven days a week slave labour in some Siberian forest or salt mine? With filthy rags to wear and a wooden board in an unheated hut to sleep on? The crammed bodies of your lousy deadbeat neighbours your only source of warmth? A contrived confession extracted by torture of your leading role in some outlandish conspiracy to overthrow the state and replace it with some foreign dictatorship? Blind obedience to the official ideology of our glorious nation-state?"

Cisternino would pause for effect, as he packed away his stethoscope, or scribbled his signature on Gramsci's latest prescription.

"No, *comrade*, all we ask is that you serve your time, refrain from any further subversive activity against the state, and treat your guards and fellow prisoners with politeness and respect. No comparison, wouldn't you say?" The doctor had a point. Gramsci might try to argue, as he did to begin with, that repression or even imprisonment and summary execution in the young Soviet Union had served the greater cause of international proletarian revolution, especially in the very early days of capitalist encirclement and White counter-revolution. As such, the proletarian discipline of Bolshevism had far firmer historical justification than the reactionary authoritarianism of the Fascists, with the historical materialism of Marxism as its legacy and guide, the support of all serious "progressive opinion" across the world as its buttress, and the noble cause of international communism as its ultimate aim. But now, fifteen years after the glorious October revolution, with the Soviet Union largely safe from external interference, firmly established economically, diplomatically and administratively, rapidly emerging as a global powerhouse and earning fulsome or grudging praise from right across the political spectrum, "Red terror" was far harder to justify, especially when turned against its own people or even high functionaries.

The news from the Soviet Union was ever more troubling, even when allowing for the distortions of the pro-capitalist press and the rabid anti-communism of most western governments. To be sure, the wonderful achievements of the first Five Year Plan, the electrification of whole swathes of the country and the rapid industrialisation of the economy, were being hailed even in America as a model of planned and managed development. But they were offset by rumours of famine in the Ukraine and elsewhere, with dispossessed and "collectivised" peasants dying in their millions, all in the cause of the "elimination of the kulaks as a class." Whole ethnic or national groups were being uprooted and forcibly resettled thousands of kilometres away from their historic homelands.

Stalin had ruthlessly out-manoeuvred and crushed any and all opposition, including many of the old Bolshevik revolutionaries Gramsci had met and worked with in Moscow and Vienna. Just about everyone he had known there was dead, imprisoned, expelled or in exile, or forced into a deadening and anxious acquiescence to Stalin's latest dictates. Even old Apollon Schucht, according to heavy hints in Tanya's recent letters, was deeply worried for himself and his family, while feeling forced into ever more abject public displays of fawning loyalty. At a recent party meeting, he had beaten himself so hard on the chest in exculpation for his class background that he had collapsed unconscious on the floor.

Gramsci was all too aware, during these years of ostracism within the *PCd'I* and by extension the Communist International, that his own name offered no protection. In fact it was not just a diminishing asset but a potentially deadly burden. He might be imprisoned in Italy, but Julia and the children were effectively stranded in the Soviet Union, hostages to his own ill-fortune. The families of disgraced Bolsheviks were suffering for the alleged crimes of the "enemies of the people" they happened to be related to. Why should his family be any different? If he needed one, this was yet another reason to consider himself "out of action", to keep his head down and concern himself only with matters of grand historical or theoretical significance rather than the tortuous and, from his distance, incomprehensible tactical twists and turns of the "inner-party struggle." *Another kind of "subaltern" deference...*

But what of the greater cause of international proletarian revolution he had devoted his pre-prison life to? He could not help reflecting to himself and one or two confidantes among his prison comrades over how it had degenerated into a maelstrom of terror and purge; a "Thermidor" far worse than anything the first revolution of the modern era in France had thrown up. The defeats in Europe and Asia, and the failure to make much headway in the Americas or the African and Asian colonies, helped to explain the retreat at Stalin's insistence towards "socialism in one country" and the arrant subordination of revolutionary prospects across the world to the Russians' *raisons d'etat* and foreign policies. "We have a country to run," as Gramsci had heard the great Lenin himself say to the Fourth Comintern Congress all those years ago, admonishing the rabble of "left oppositionists" who could not even run their own tiny marginal parties with any semblance of unity, purpose or efficiency, including the young *PCd'I* led by Amadeo Bordiga. But this did not justify it, or offer any real insight into why Soviet Bolshevism had turned out so brutal and crude, and so utterly unsuited for export to other more advanced "democratic" societies.

To answer that conundrum – and this, rather than the horrified squeamishness of many western intellectuals at the latest reports of terror and famine and the vanquishing of oppositionists, was the approach Gramsci favoured; or rather was inexorably drawn towards by every element of his intellectual and political formation – you had to look deeper into history. In particular, you had to tease out the historical differences between the societies and economies of the east, with their cultural and social simplicities and the brutal uncompromising state machines which had made them relatively easy to run but also topple, and the much more sophisticated, malleable, established and popularly accepted ruling orders of the west.

The revolutionary strategies they called forth were also profoundly different. In military terms, the struggle in the east was a "war of manoeuvre", with mobile forces making sudden assaults on easily identifiable points of weakness in the enemy's defences. That was how the Bolsheviks were able to take over the Russian state in October 1917, when "power fell into the streets" in Trotsky's memorable phrase. The weak Provisional Government of Oleg Kerensky could simply be pushed aside by a small organised band of *putschisti*, arrested over their soup and pheasant at a marble table in the Winter Palace. But that was when the real revolutionary war began, with the civil war and the struggle against bourgeois subversion and foreign intervention that was not decisively won for a further decade or so. The Socialist Eden of liberty, equality and fraternity remained a very distant prospect, for all Stalin's outlandish claims. The worry was, as "the Frenchman" Victor Serge had argued years before, that one autocracy had simply been exchanged for another.In the west, revolution was a very different matter, a "war of position", of gradual attrition across a wide front against an enemy that was well dug in and could call upon several layers of defence all along the line. The new emergent power had to engage the old enemy in every sphere of modern life – popular culture and the arts, the press and public opinion, the organisation of the economy, industry and agriculture, education and social services, the endless "battle of ideas" – with the aim of assuming responsibility and control in every one of them, not as some single bold and decisive, one-off "balance tipping" intervention *but in the process of* taking more formal political and state power. By that stage, the war would be largely won, and the aftermath of revolution would thankfully be far less destructive than it had necessarily been in the east. Any other political strategy, such as the call for immediate insurrection that Stalin continued to foist on the Communist International, and that Gramsci heard loud and clear whenever he ventured into the Turi prison exercise yard, was just a dangerous, counter-productive dream.

In the meantime, Gramsci wrote in his notes, with a clear eye on Fascism and the emerging National Socialism in Germany and Austria, but with a sneaking suspicion that this might also apply to the ruthlessly re-stabilised, decidedly post-revolutionary Soviet Union under Stalin, the global class war had reached a precarious stalemate. "The so-called crisis of authority consists precisely in the fact that the old is dying and the new cannot be born. In this interregnum, morbid phenomena of the most varied kind can emerge. If the ruling class has lost consensus, or failed to achieve it in the first place – that is, if it no longer 'leads' but only 'rules' through sheer coercive power – this actually means that the great masses have become detached from traditional ideologies, they no longer believe what they used to."

Instead, apathy and cynicism prevail. There are no guarantees of "historical progress." The "motor" that had driven social and economic development for the last hundred years had stalled. It can even appear to go backwards, and only get going forward again by concerted, broad-based political and cultural action. Or – and this was clearly what was happening in Italy and Germany and, Gramsci feared, Russia – a "strong man" could impose authority and order without regard for democracy, legality or justice, or genuine consensus and unity; a "Caesar" or "Bonaparte" figure prepared to sweep aside all internal opposition for the sake of a semblance of security and stability.

In early 1932, Gramsci found out about a programme of prisoner exchanges between the Soviet government and the Vatican, now constituted as an independent state under the terms of the 1929 Lateran Pact. The Pope had been able to secure the release of communist prisoners in Italy in return for a Russian archbishop who had been condemned to death in 1923. Ever since, both sides had kept lists of prisoners they might swap. Gramsci's name had been included in the latest discussions. The deputy Foreign Minister of the Vatican even visited Turi prison. He was unable to see Gramsci but left him a card: "Mons. Giuseppe Pizzardo, Deputy to the Secretary of State to His Holiness, Regards." In the meantime, Tanya Schucht had heard from someone in the Soviet Embassy in Rome that their Foreign Secretary Litvinov had made contact with the Italian ambassador in Moscow about the possibility of Gramsci's release. She relayed the information to Carlo Gramsci, who in turn (during one of the very few visits Antonio received at Turi in this entire period) excitedly told his brother.

Nothing came of any of it, even if it had any truth or mileage in the first place. Soviet foreign policy at that moment was directed towards good relations with Italy, with the aim of pre-empting an alliance between Italian Fascism and German National Socialism. In the spirit of Realpolitik, the Soviets were keen to avoid even the appearance of interference in Italian internal affairs, which would include whom the state chose to imprison. Besides, what real value was there in this ex-leader of one of the smallest parties in the Comintern, notoriously truculent and non-collaborative, out of action for over five years now and rotting away in an obscure provincial jail in the remote Italian south? If the stories from within the *PCd'I* itself were to be believed, there was some doubt over whether this fellow – *what's his name again? Gramshky? Grumschkov?* – was still or ever really had been a loyal communist anyhow.

* * *

An interesting essay could be written on the mutations which news undergoes in prison, when it is passed through the filter of the prisoners' own personal desires. For example, rumours often circulate about pardons and amnesties the government is all set to announce any day now. Yes, we're all going to be set free, with only minor restrictions on our movement, place of residence, contacts and activities; even they may have been lifted in some of these accounts.

It turns out that someone has spotted a forthcoming anniversary of some significant Fascist political action or state measure, or detected a softening of tone in official rhetoric, or heard that some international solidarity campaign has received some new declaration of support or famous signatory. Sometimes all three of these preconditions occur. As the news travels around the prison, it dries and hardens like glue, until we are all stuck to it, hanging on to it for dear life. The timetable for release becomes ever shorter, so that "perhaps next year" becomes "six months", then "the next few weeks" and finally "imminent".

Political prisoners like me are especially prone to these bouts of wishful thinking and Chinese whispers (curious phrase, that) because of course we know, even more than the

ordinary criminals, that we shouldn't be here in the first place. We have committed no crime, under any normal legal jurisdiction, and can be safely expected not to commit any normal crime upon release. Oh no, we're much too high and mighty for any of that. So, we declare to each other upon hearing of the latest "amnesty", it's no more than we are due.

Visiting relatives are often the source of these false hopes, I have observed, reassuring the prisoners that they have ultra-reliable sources of information, 100 per cent authentic. They enter into a conspiracy of mutual delusion, and before you know it they're planning their next birthday or Christmas at home. When it all turns out to be a tissue of lies, all hope comes crashing down and we fall back into the prevailing prison atmosphere of torpor and despondency.

Antonio Gramsci now felt entirely abandoned by everyone and everything he had ever belonged to: the *PCd'I* and the international movement it was a minor part of; his family in Sardinia, who corresponded fitfully and half-heartedly, and (Carlo aside) never even thought of visiting him; his family in Moscow, who sent him the occasional scribbled note or message translated by Tanya from the Russian and attached to one of her letters, but otherwise showed dwindling interest. Even Tanya for one reason or another – distance, ill-health, inconvenience, work obligations, Gramsci's own concerns that a return to Turi would simply end with her in the local hospital; some vague inhibition that was never clearly spelt out but which Antonio suspected came from Apollon Alexandrovich, or a rather more direct injunction from Evgenia – stayed away from Turi for the two and a half years between June 1930 and January 1933.

She maintained her end of their correspondence dully and dutifully, with long and painful periods of silence explained by other, obviously more important matters to attend to, in letters largely devoted to general reflections on the state of the world, the daily news and her latest reading. Misunderstandings and personal disagreements proliferated, requiring long and tortuous clarifications. In the autumn of 1931 Tanya and Antonio got involved in a strange protracted exchange, prompted by a popular film she had seen, about the notion that Jews and Gentiles lived in "two worlds", quite separate, different and self-contained. He pointed out in response that this was historically wrong, essentially anti-Semitic, and very odd coming from her with her partly Jewish ancestry. In lending this idea of *due mondi* credence, Tanya was subscribing to "a way of thinking worthy of the Black Hundreds, the Ku Klux Klan or the Nazis." Perhaps she was revealing her Russian heritage: "Many Cossacks used to believe as an article of faith that Jews had tails!"

For her part, Tanya resented his implication that she was anti-Semitic and might, as she put it, "take part in a pogrom". All she had done was make a passing reference to a film she'd seen. He had seized upon it "...to try to back me into a corner, and play word games like the journalist you once were." He wrote back that he too found her remarks "positively offensive." He had never been "the kind of jobbing journalist who sells his pen to the highest bidder, and for whom an ability to lie is an occupational necessity." He had always stuck to his principles, told the truth as he saw it, and never been anybody's yes-man. As for this "two worlds" nonsense, he regretted ever taking the matter seriously in the first place. He should have shrugged it off with some joke about cultural stereotypes "...of English reserve, French pomposity, German organisation, Spanish arrogance, Italian flair and finally Slav mysticism, all the caricatures used by popular novelists and scriptwriters." She responded that racial differences were real, and could be acknowledged without blame or prejudice. She cited a number of historical and contemporary examples, including her own family, where her parents' "differences in temperament, due in turn to their difference in race" had caused unhappiness which had undoubtedly and adversely affected "the condition of us children".

Piero Sraffa felt moved to intervene, by pointing out various recent changes in the law and in public opinion which revealed the growing force of anti-Semitism, prompting real fear amongst Italy's small and previously integrated and secularised Jewish population. Antonio, secluded in prison and working with the "universalist" attitudes of a much earlier era, could not be expected to have kept up with these developments. Sraffa was also involved in further discord between Antonio and Tanya, when he sought Antonio's advice for his own work on Croce. Tanya passed it off in her letters as help with a fictional book review she herself was writing, but Antonio's long and detailed responses over the course of six letters were interpreted by the censor as an attempt to get his writings published abroad. He was interrogated and his cell was searched, and new restrictions placed on the subjects he could write about and the publications he could consult.

More productively, Antonio's own letters to Tanya outlined his latest reading and writing – on literature, religion, intellectuals in Italian history, developments in Marxist philosophy – interspersed with bulletins on his health and moods. He was working hard on getting his notes in order and conducting fresh research. Though he never said so, and she never pointed it out, it was apparent to both of them that his studies – systematic, fruitful and profound as they were – were both driven by and a diversion from his personal troubles. His own deepest conscious thoughts began to feel like a safe haven from both a cold uncaring outside world and the dull debilitating routine of prison life, not to mention the ghosts and demons of his own mental undergrowth. He fought hard and with mixed results against the personal feelings his sense of abandonment provoked: self-pity, resentment, vindictive ill-temper, exacerbated by continuing illness and insomnia. His irritability towards anyone and everyone even raised eyebrows among the prison guards. One or two would ask, with genuine concern, "How are you doing?" "Fine, fine, fine..." he would respond, clearly irritated by the break in his concentration. Then, guilty at his discourtesy, he would force a smile and say more fully, "I'm fine, really. Thanks for asking..." For all his efforts to maintain a calm and cheerful demeanour, the best he could achieve was a kind of emotional neutrality or numbness.

Try as he might, he could not prevent his worse feelings surfacing in the opening or final paragraphs of his letters; or more to the point, souring them. The "two worlds" business was the least of it. He chastised both Tanya and Carlo for their small part in the abortive prisoner exchange, mainly for not keeping him adequately informed or enabling him to contribute to the process. Tanya continued to write to the authorities – all the way up the "Head of Government" himself – about Antonio's declining health, and to ask for outside medical examination and treatment, but without telling him much about it. Worried as he was by his own deteriorating physical condition, he deeply resented her undermining his position as "master of my own life." His customary concluding "tender embrace" often jarred violently with the preceding tirade.

Spurred on by the thought that he might never leave prison alive, he made endless complex calculations of how long he had left to serve under the permutations of various amnesties and appeals. This prompted further rancour with Tanya over the slightest deviation from his instructions. His brother Carlo's interventions were well-intentioned but often clumsy and counter-productive. When the government announced a limited amnesty for political prisoners on the tenth anniversary of the March on Rome in October 1932, Carlo sent Antonio a telegram intimating that he might soon be released, and looking forward to "coming to Turi to embrace you as a free man." For some hours he dared to believe it, before being disabused by a curt remark from the Prison Director passing his cell. It subsequently turned out that his mother, sick and frail herself, had actually been told that he'd been set free. He thought back to his own few hours of delusion, and the gut-wrenching disappointment that brought it crashing to an end, and multiplied it a hundred times to imagine the effect on her.

He wrote furiously to Tanya and his sister Teresina about the muddle and what he saw as their part in it, and declared that "after the fiasco with the telegram" he wanted nothing more to do with his brother . He regretted and resented his dependence on Carlo as the conduit for funds, when he had proved so "immature" and "unmanly". To them all, he tried desperately to convey a clearer sense of the state of mind that prison had reduced him to: "I've grown insensitive to other people's feelings, yet sometimes I have the impression that I am being skinned alive. The weeks, the hours, even minutes weigh on me; it's as if someone were filing away my nerves. Ideally, I would wish to be left alone, to forget the world and live like a beast in a den." In December 1932 he wrote to Tanya that, after the first phase of his arrest and conviction, and the second of his most tolerable and productive time at Turi, "a third phase of my life as a prisoner has begun."

In the same spirit of "sharp cleavage", he proposed through Tanya that he and Julia should consider themselves formally separated and free of their obligations to each other. It was ridiculous, after all these years of separation and with no prospect of reuniting, that they should maintain the pretence and keep their lives on hold; especially Julia, who might not enjoy the best of health but still had her freedom and much of her life left to live. He had long ago accepted that he no longer (if ever he did) embodied any kind of romantic dream she might have of a Prince Charming figure. But it may be that he made her condition worse. Someone else, nearer and stronger and physically available to her, might make it better.

However, in the summer of 1932 Julia's mental health actually seemed to be on the mend, enough for her to write directly and coherently to him. She was now saying she hadn't much use for her doctors, and that she was determined – as Antonio had been urging – to "stand on my own two feet." She was even considering going back to work, and pursuing his suggestion that she might propose or even attempt Russian/Italian translations. In response he expressed his delight: "Why should we let ourselves be crushed by the lives we've led up to now?"

He was especially pleased that she had got over her "...fixation with a psychoanalytic cure, thoroughly steeped as it is in charlatanry." As for her plan to go back to work: "It would make me extremely happy to see you apply yourself systematically and reach a high level of specialisation" in technical translation. This would surely make her feel "practically useful" to the great Soviet cause of constructing Socialism. He also urged her "to dedicate part of your time to music", which she had given up in an "act of spiritual amputation" because she considered it incompatible with her immediate practical responsibilities: "I have always believed that only artistic activity brought you fully to life." From Tanya he received the first photographs of Julia in some time, which he found delightful, "...though it's clear that she has suffered a great deal." Nonetheless, he wrote back: "We can say with some certainty that she is through the worst of it and is beginning a new life." For a while longer he and Julia corresponded freely and openly. He asked for more photos of her and the boys, and added as a joke a reference to his time on Ustica: "You don't want me thinking of you as the Bedouin's wife, do you?" He even felt able, in the light of her apparent recovery, to give a full and frank account of his life in prison, "...empty, terribly and depressingly empty... I barely live at all, but hang on grimly to the outskirts of animal, or rather vegetable existence." The tedium was only relieved by her letters, which: "I read and re-read constantly; they give me a few hours of serenity and happiness." He even dared to suggest that Julia and the children might come to Italy to see him.

But again nothing came of it. Julia went quiet again. Perhaps she had decided to accept his earlier offer of formal separation, but hadn't got round to telling him. Without any word for months on end, how would he know? Perhaps his own encouragements, chastisements and suggestions for therapeutic work had provoked some new crisis. In his darkest moments, he questioned the whole basis of their relationship. It had always seemed to him that she had drifted into it, without much conscious choice of her own, and that she had allowed herself to be influenced and guided, and on occasions turned against him, by other members of her family. Could it be even worse than this? One particular thought would nag away at him through the long prison nights, a thought Victor Serge had come perilously close to articulating in Vienna when they were sharing their troubled emotional histories. Had Julia been somehow assigned to him, as part of her job for the NKVD? He dismissed it as soon as it emerged. It was too preposterous; it vastly overrated his importance in the Comintern, as well as poisoning the memories of their precious few months of genuine togetherness, not to mention the lives of their two small children. *But still...* Even if it was not literally true, he began to think of his wife as one of the "sentencers" who had stood in judgement over him, albeit "unconsciously", and condemned him to imprisonment for what was beginning to feel like the rest of his life.

He felt a desperate need for clarity and order, a settling of accounts, and offered again via Tanya to end the marriage. It was simply too late for him and Julia; there was now no realistic chance of making anything of their relationship. Perhaps the life of a full-time communist militant was in any case incompatible with personal intimacy and family responsibilities. Isn't that what the most hardened and effective revolutionaries had always discovered, to their own massive emotional and psychological cost? Was there any such thing as a "happy marriage" in

Jacobinism or Bolshevism? In this he saw a terrible and destructive "egotism, where one's own philosophy of life and political ambitions prevent real attachment to the people around you. You're so busy trying to save the world, you can't save yourself or the individuals you love."

He was now too old, ill and isolated to change, and stuck in prison for the foreseeable future. But Julia was only thirty six, and hopefully returning to full health. She still had it in her to make a new life for herself: "Why should a living being remain tied to someone as good as dead? I accept that my gesture may appear romantic, a kind of emotional blackmail – you'll be so overwhelmed by my magnanimity that you'll feel compelled to refuse – but I am quite serious and resolute. I don't doubt that it would be difficult and painful for everyone, but I am convinced that it would ultimately be for the best."

All of this was conveyed to Tanya in Rome, in the hope that she might find an appropriate way to communicate it directly to Julia, "...reflecting coolly and calmly on what I have been saying, and thinking primarily of Julia's life and future." Tanya, perhaps understandably, prevaricated, and the matter became – towards the end of 1932 – yet another issue of distant altercation between her and Antonio. He wrote in exasperation: "Just answer me one thing: are you willing to act as go-between with Julia or not? A yes or no, that's all I want. I will be very annoyed by any further evasions, which will simply prolong the agony. It has to be like a surgical operation or decapitation, and can only be justified if done firmly with one clean cut." Unbeknown to him, Piero Sraffa urged Julia via Tanya to visit "Nino as soon as possible in order to save the marriage", but received no direct response.

In the round of amnesties that commemorated ten years of Fascist rule in October 1932, Gramsci's sentence was reduced to twelve years and four months, which meant that he had a further eight years to serve. Piero Sraffa petitioned the government, through his uncle who was a senior judge in the Italian Appeal

Court, for conditional release for Gramsci in the light of his worsening health. This would, they argued, prevent him from undertaking any kind of political activity or even normal daily life, so he couldn't possibly pose any kind of threat. The government did not dismiss the petition, but made clear that they required a formal plea for clemency from Gramsci himself. He refused, on the basis that this would represent an admission of guilt and as such a kind of "suicide" for a political prisoner like himself. In his notebooks he made several further references to Confalonieri and his grovelling pleas to the Austrian emperor. For some weeks afterwards, Gramsci and the other politicos at Turi were placed in strict solitary confinement to absorb this latest demonstration of Fascist power and their own weakness.

Later that month, on 30th December 1932, Gramsci's mother died in Ghilarza. His family decided not to tell him, because they feared the effects of the shock on his own ill health. Carlo, the only brother in regular contact with Antonio, was also still feeling some remorse over his own role in the "telegram fiasco" a couple of months before, and the upset this had caused their mother. For several years after Signora Peppina's death, Antonio was still writing to the family expressing his concern over her health and asking for news. He even wrote directly to her, wishing her all the best for Easter and her birthday. He was dismayed but not entirely surprised to receive no reply. 1932 had been, Gramsci wrote to Tanya on the second day of the new year:

"...the worst of my years in prison. Nor does the new one look particularly enticing. If '32 was bad, '33 is almost bound to be worse. I'm very run down and the load I have to drag along gets heavier all the time. The balance between my personal resources and the efforts I have to make gets more and more unfavourable. I am not demoralised though. On the contrary, I gain strength from realistic analysis of my situation and my determination to resist."

* * *

There is nowhere more "private" than prison. The prisoner is confined to his own company for long stretches of every day, month and year he spends inside. He is necessarily denied the chance encounters with other people which constitute "public" life, especially in our great cities with their essential oils of enforced company, fleeting exchange and anonymous courtesy.

But prisons are also "public institutions", established and maintained for the reassurance and sometimes entertainment of the "public" on the outside, fidgeting in their anxious liberty. The prisoner, for all his privations, is actually on show for his entire prison sentence, a living example of the consequences of wrong-doing, a mixed message of safety to the law-abiding and of deterrent to the criminal.

Nowhere is this contradiction more apparent than in the prisoner's correspondence with his loved ones. His most private thoughts and feelings must pass through the "public" screen of censorship and administrative routine, several layers of it, before they reach their intended "private" recipients. This gives rise to a certain "prison style" of writing, which is artificially restrained, painfully self-conscious and necessarily insincere. The "codes" which all prisoners adopt in their correspondence – for people, places, intimate reminiscences – are only the first layer of subterfuge; the last is made up of the feelings they conceal from themselves.

Tanya Schucht returned to live in Turi in January 1933, and resumed regular visits to Antonio at the prison. With her own health for the moment restored, she felt able to come back south. Her savings had been replenished by her earned income and the very favourable terms on which she had been renting a room from Nilde Perilli in Rome. And though she never spelt it out to Antonio, an ailing Apollon was confined to a sanatorium and unable or disinclined to impose his will on the family (he would die in May, and be buried at Novodevic cemetery; again, this was kept from his son-in-law in Italy for several years). Evgenia was now putting it about that Gramsci had become a Trotskyite and would bring further catastrophe upon the family. She had raised predictable objections to Tanya rejoining Antonio. But without the authorisation of their invalid father, Tanya could disregard them (in the interests of family harmony, she chose not to tell Gramsci about them either). She could take up again what she was beginning to think and speak of quite openly, if sometimes ruefully, as her "life's work" of caring for her brother-in-law.

"Goodness knows," she would say to anyone who cared to listen, "he needs it..."

As if to underline her own growing confidence and their renewed intimacy, she began to refer to him in person and in writing as "Nino". In February she wrote to Piero Sraffa her impressions of his condition and appearance after their two and a half years of separation: "Nino looks like a little child, a baby, he has lost so much weight. He's very pale and drawn." He had described to her a bout of "several weeks of true neurasthenic frenzy, of continued and spasmodic obsession that did not give me a moment's peace." In early March, she wrote to his sister Teresina: "I think it is vitally important that I visit him as often as possible, for he is without doubt going through a very bad time just now, so bad that it really frightens me."

On 7th March 1933, Antonio Gramsci suffered a further bout of acute illness and partial paralysis. As he was getting out of bed he fell to the ground and couldn't get up again. He was helped back to bed, where he remained for several days, weak and feverish. At times he was delirious and hallucinating. He found out later that for hours on end he held forth quite lucidly on the futility of religion, interspersed with long tirades in Sardinian dialect. He reasoned in a letter to Tanya that he must have thought he was going to die, and did not want to be attended to by a priest. He recalled with horror the experience of Jean Barois, the central character in a popular pre-war French novel, who receives the religious sacraments before dying. His wife later discovers his will, which stipulates, "…lest old age and sickness weaken me so much that I will fear death and fall for the comforts of religion, I state now that I do not believe in a substantial and immortal soul. I know that my personality is a mass of atoms whose dissolution entails total death. I believe in universal determinism..." In the novel, the will is thrown into the fire.

"At least I did not suffer that indignity," Gramsci wrote to Tanya afterwards, "so my ranting and raving must have had some effect! My audience was a worker from Grossetto, nodding off in exhaustion, who I'm quite sure thought I was going round the bend...The windows and walls of my cell were covered in figures and faces, not frightening, rather the opposite: smiling, in all sorts of poses. These were not people I knew, or at least could remember, but they did not wish me ill. I can only imagine that I thought I was being attended to by the popular masses! Every so often I would struggle to sit upright, only for the air to solidify and fall on me, pushing me back on the bed with a thud. My eyes kept superimposing new images on top of old ones, a tumble of faces and bodies and buildings and fields. I kept hearing things too, voices saying very clearly, "Are you there?" or "Are you asleep?" or other odd words. Again I have no idea who these voices belonged to, but they were not hostile. It had the quality of a film, and what I gather is referred to as a dream sequence..."

Doctor Cisternino was called, and eventually arrived, to offer a diagnosis of cerebral anaemia, a disruption of the flow of blood to the brain, which might account for the blackout but not for its severity and duration. On 18th March, Tanya wrote to Piero Sraffa that "Antonio's condition seems hopeless." Two weeks later Gramsci was visited by another doctor from outside, in long delayed response to Tanya's letter to Mussolini in the autumn. Professor Umberto Arcangeli, a friend of hers from Rome, diagnosed "Pott's disease, a form of tuberculosis of the spine; he also has tubercular lesions in the upper lobe of the right lung which have caused two discharges of blood; one of these discharges was copious, and accompanied by fever lasting several days. He is also suffering from arterio-sclerosis, with hypertension of the arteries. He has suffered collapses, with loss of consciousness and partial aphasia lasting several days. Since October 1932, he has lost seven kilos in weight. He suffers from amnesia, and is unable to write as he used to." Professor Arcangeli concluded that: "Gramsci cannot survive long under present conditions. I consider his transfer to a hospital or clinic to be necessary; that is, if it is not considered possible to grant him conditional liberty."

There was no immediate response from the prison authorities. Gramsci remained in his cell for the next few months, into the summer of 1933. He was largely confined to bed, sometimes feeling better, sometimes feeling worse, usually drifting along on a tide of semi-conscious memories and speculations. The veins in his feet swelled up, which made it extremely uncomfortable to wear shoes or even socks. He now had eleven teeth left, most of them loose, which made eating well nigh impossible. One week he complained in a note to Tanya: "I have nothing to say to you or anyone else. I'm completely finished." The following week he wrote to apologise for having hurt her feelings. "I've become half-mad from the pain in my head, and the spasms in my hands are getting worse. I am hoping for a transfer to a modern prison infirmary. All that matters is to get out of this hell where I am slowly dying."

He was at least transferred to another cell in the basement of the prison, well away from the noisy guardroom. It was damp and dark, normally used for punishment, but much quieter. He was also allocated a permanent cell-mate to keep an eye on him, Gustavo Trombetti, the "worker from Grossetto" who had attended to him in March. As Gramsci's symptoms eased, he began reading and writing again, only to have permission temporarily revoked while the prison authorities pored over his notebooks to see if they might provide the basis for some kind of forbidden communications or conspiracy between Gramsci, Trombetti and the other communist prisoners at Turi. This prohibition caused him as much pain and annoyance as his physical ailments, desperate as he was to get his scattered notes in proper order while he still could. His correspondence began to prepare people for some kind of end: to Tanya he wrote "I am emptied out", and to his sister Teresina "Don't be surprised if I don't write much from now on."

In the summer of 1933, an international campaign was established in Paris for the liberation of victims of Fascism, including Antonio Gramsci and other prominent Italian communists and socialists. The writer Romain Rolland, from whom Gramsci had taken the motto "Pessimism of the intellect, optimism of the will", published a pamphlet *Ceux Qui Meurent Dans Les Prisons de Mussolini* with Gramsci's face prominent on the cover, looming over a posturing Mussolini. The propaganda bulletin *Azione Antifascista* devoted most of its June issue to Gramsci, as part of a campaign for political prisoners of all persuasions. It was an overture by the Comintern to other political forces, and signalled some easing of the sectarianism and dogmatism of the "Third Period" and a move towards a "Popular Front" strategy. It was also belated recognition of the counter-productiveness of its denunciations of bourgeois democracy and "social fascism", which had plainly assisted the rise of actual Fascism, most notably in Germany, where Hitler and the National Socialists had just come to power and proceeded to quash the divided communist and social democrat opposition. Now the watchword was "left unity." One of the earliest, and somewhat embarrassing, responses to this new more open Comintern line came from the French Trotskyists, who launched their own appeal for Gramsci's release.

After almost two years of silence, the *PCd'I* underground and émigré press began referring to Gramsci again in his official capacity of General Secretary, and urging action to "Save Our Leader!" Illegal leaflets appeared in Italy referring to "Gramsci, the greatest Italian of the age, leader of the Italian workers." Professor Arcangeli's medical report was published by the French Communist daily *L'Humanité* in May and elsewhere in succeeding months. This time the headlines "Gramsci is dying!" did not seem far-fetched, though the accompanying allegations of "torture" and "assassination" might have been. There was a report in the French press that Gramsci had actually died, which was quickly corrected, and further talk of high level contacts between the Soviet and Italian governments, but nothing concrete.

The international campaign did at least cause the Italian government some diplomatic discomfort. They rejected the claim that the Amnesty decree of November 1932 entitled Gramsci to immediate freedom, but in the face of the medical evidence began to relent on whether Turi was a suitable place of confinement. In October 1933 authorization was granted for Gramsci to leave Turi prison and an official request circulated around local authorities across the country for a clinic "suitable for an important political prisoner suffering from tuberculosis and other serious diseases needing special treatment. The location chosen must be easily watched and guarded."

A clinic was identified in Formia, a small town near Gaeta, half-way between Rome and Naples. Antonio Gramsci left Turi di Bari Penitentiary for Sick Prisoners on 19th November 1933, aged 42, after almost five years there. During that time he had lost his health, all his teeth and most of his contacts and reputation in the outside world, and composed the bulk of the notes and letters which would establish his posthumous fame. Before Gramsci left Turi, Gustavo Trombetti managed to hide the eighteen notebooks among the personal possessions in Gramsci's trunk, while Antonio kept the guard talking in the prison storeroom. He stopped for eighteen days in the prison infirmary at Civitavecchia, while his new room in Formia was fitted with iron bars at the windows and transformed into a cell. On the way to Civitavecchia, he saw himself in a mirror for the first time in five years, and returned in shock and haste to his police escort. During his stay, he recognised a number of his former closest comrades in the prison halls and corridors, but they chose not to make contact.

1933/37: Cusumano Clinic, Formia/Quisisana Clinic, Rome

Incapacity forms an entirely separate category of human experience. When every movement, however slight, must be planned in advance, and when you can no longer rely upon your body to follow your instructions, conscious or involuntary, it induces an outlook of stealth and suspicion. You look out upon the world as an expanse of hazards, out to the furthest horizon, which are best avoided by staying put. This means you actually retreat ever further inside yourself, ever more useless in your corporeal existence, ever more inclined to isolation and self-pity and even greater incapacity. This is how you disappear, and it must be fought with the tenacity of a tiger.

Gramsci finally arrived at the clinic in Formia run by Professor Giuseppe Cusumano on 7th December 1933. He was still a prisoner, formally "in a state of detention", with a round-the-clock police guard on his room and regular police patrols of the clinic gardens and surrounding area. Tatiana Schucht visited him weekly from Rome where she had relocated, back in her room at Nilde Perilli's. She now routinely called him "Nino". On several occasions he mistook her for Julka as she entered his room or gently shook him awake. He was also visited by his brother Carlo and by Piero Sraffa. All three were followed by the police and routinely reported on. In Formia, Gramsci resumed work on his notebooks, revising and reordering old notes and composing some new ones. In the summer of 1934 he was examined by another independent doctor and friend of Tanya's, Professor Vittorio Puccinelli from the Quisisana Clinic in Rome.

Puccinelli was not impressed with the conditions and standards of care at the Cusumano Clinic, which charged 120 lire a day for its "special treatment" of prisoners like Gramsci. This money had to be raised by his relatives in Sardinia and Russia, and topped up by clandestine funds from the *PCd'I* in exile. Puccinelli relayed his concerns to Tanya, who reported to Piero Sraffa "a lack of edible bread and of hot water for bathing, and medical care that is desultory and often incompetent."

In early October 1934 Gramsci submitted a petition for conditional freedom, based on clauses in the penal code on the rights of sick prisoners. On 25th October his conditional freedom was granted, in return for an assurance that he "would not use this new provision to make propaganda in Italy or abroad". He was even allowed a few brief outings with Tanya, Carlo or Piero Sraffa in the gardens of the clinic and nearby streets, on foot or by carriage. But he remained confined to the clinic, under even closer surveillance by the police, who suspected an escape plan "aided by anti-Fascist elements in New York." Gramsci's name continued to feature in anti-Fascist propaganda, but the "escape plan" had no basis in reality. Tanya visited him at least weekly, talking or sitting quietly in his room while he rested or slept. For the next eighteen months he wrote hardly any personal letters. The only substantial one was to his dead mother on her name-day in March 1934. Tanya wrote to his sister Teresina in April that he "lacks the strength to write, and you can easily imagine how much suffering this causes Julia, who has not had any direct news from Nino in more than a year."

In June 1935 Gramsci suffered another breakdown and asked to leave the Cusumano clinic, which was ill-equipped to deal with his mounting health problems. This included, he said in his application to the Inspector General of the Formia police, an attack of gout "due to medical negligence, since for more than a month I had drawn their attention to muscular pains and swollen ankles", and the beginnings of a hernia caused in part "by an inappropriate diet and poor hygiene (flies and ants in the food, fingermarks on the dishes etc.)" It was also noisy, not least because the small building housed the living quarters of the large Cusumano family. He complained that he could hear "continuous to and fro from five in the morning till midnight".

On 24th August, Gramsci travelled with Professor Puccinelli to the Quisisana Clinic in Rome. He made much sardonic play of the fact that the name of the clinic was "Here Heal Yourself" in Latin, explaining to the Professor that this had been his own prescription for his wife's psychological troubles.

"Ah," said the Professor. "Not my area of expertise, I'm afraid, but I'm not sure that would be the clinically recommended approach..."

"No," said Gramsci. "And more to the point, it never seemed to work!"

At the Quisisana, Tanya visited almost every day, work permitting, and frequently stayed into the evening. Carlo and Piero Sraffa also continued visiting when they could, still with a police escort at a not so discreet distance, and twelve armed guards stationed around the clinic. According to Tanya, writing to Sraffa in September 1935, "Antonio never leaves his room, except to stand out on the balcony." This was not entirely accurate. A fellow patient, Lina Corigliano, later recalled, "I was the only patient with a radio in my room, and when Mussolini was due to give an important speech announcing the foundation of the African empire, everyone at the clinic crowded in to listen. I knew that in the next room there was an important personality under constant guard, and I sent him a message asking if he too wanted to listen to *Il Duce*. The answer came back, "Thank you, I'm not interested." Instead we arranged for him to come the next day to listen to a broadcast of Bizet's *Carmen*."

Into 1936, Gramsci began corresponding again with Julia and his sons in Moscow, after a silence of some years. Addressing her once again as "Julka", he tried to reassure her: "My dear, I have always waited for you, and you have always been one of the essential elements of my life." He commended her on her apparently improved mood – "I can't remember when you last wrote so gaily, and with so few mistakes!" – and several times suggested in vain that she might come to see him. Her family and especially Evgenia were vehemently opposed to the idea. Besides, this was not so much a reconciliation with Julia/Julka, whom he thought of even more clearly as one of his "sentencers", as with his steady decline. For all of that year and into the next, he was largely confined to bed, growing weaker, still able to read but unable to write without enormous effort. His letters were now mostly short missives to his sons, wishing them well on birthdays and other special occasions, telling them to behave themselves and work hard at school, commending or criticizing their own letters and enclosed drawings, and recalling childhood experiences of his own. He proposed that at a set time every day they and "mother Julka" should observe "Papa's five minutes" when they should think and talk about him, while he did the same in Italy. For their twelfth and tenth birthdays in August 1936, he sent them both watches as gifts, procured for him by Tanya at a watchmaker's in Rome. It only occurred to him afterwards to wonder whether they had been taught to tell the time.

He understood that he knew next to nothing about his sons. What he did find out – about Delio's flights of fancy or Giuliano's slow development, the concerns of their teachers, above all the "false, cloying artificial atmosphere" in which they were growing up with Julia and their "little mother" Evgenia – continued to displease and sometimes disturbed him. He made frequent unfavourable comparisons with his own childhood capabilities and interests, surprisingly oblivious to the massive historical, geographical and social differences between growing up in remote rural Sardinia in the late 19th century and in a major industrial metropolis in the mid-20th, or indeed to the fact that to these Young Pioneers he was a distant stranger.

To Delio he begged for longer letters, and chided him gently for the oddly formal tone the boy tended to adopt: "You've written me four lines which sound like they're from a phrasebook for foreigners. 'The parrot is well.' 'Give him my heartiest congratulations and best wishes!' 'What's the weather like?' 'We're having good weather here' etc..." When Julia wrote that this gentle rebuke had annoyed Delio, Gramsci wrote back to him: "Why didn't you tell me yourself? If you don't like anything in my letters, you really should say so. I love you so much, and the last thing I want to do is hurt you. I'm so very far away, and I can't take you in my arms and kiss you, but I so wish I could."

To Giuliano he wrote: "I know you only from your letters, which were few and far between. The boy's interest perked up when he saw an enormous picture of his father in a display of prominent communist political prisoners in Gorky Park in Moscow. He found out from a neighbour that he'd been in prison for some years, and wanted to know all about him. With Delio and "Mamma Zhenya" he met Romain Rolland, and got a taste of impending political celebrity, with stirring speeches, photographs taken for the anti-fascist press, pats on the cheek and ruffled hair.

Antonio was touched and amused. He made tentative and sometimes clumsy attempts to communicate with this child he had never met, about trips to the country and the seaside, or how he was getting on at the "special school" the Schuchts had decided to send him to. It was a boarding school near Sochi , for "children of a nervous disposition." The boy would otherwise, Tanya told him, have been kept behind for at least a year at the school he had been attending in Moscow. He wasn't happy at this new school either, she intimated, and kept getting into trouble. It brought back to Gramsci his own feelings when he had been sent away to complete his elementary schooling. He encouraged the boy to "face events with courage and calm."

He continued to berate Tanya about her poor diet and its effects on her health. It was nothing to do with her appetite –

"I've seen you eat a whole boiled chicken for breakfast, followed by lamb and potatoes for dinner!" – so it must be something to do with her lack of routine. Carlo would chime in on joint visits, and Antonio or Tanya would report on the latest set-to with Julia or Evgenia, or worries about the boys' education. It was something like family normality. In late 1936 they finally acknowledged that Signora Peppina Gramsci and Apollon Alexandrovich Schucht had died some years before. Antonio said that he had suspected as much all along, but could not be bothered to make a fuss about yet more bad news being kept from him, supposedly for his own protection. They talked no more of it. As for his general outlook on life, he achieved a certain intellectual serenity bordering on political maturity. Accusing Julia yet again of "a certain superficial and bohemian slackness", he said he preferred the humdrum rigours of "a *Corporal's Manual* to Valles' *Resisters*", the record of glorious defeat of the 1871 Paris Commune, and confessed to a burgeoning "gradualism" in his personal manner and perspective.

On 21st April 1937 his sentence formally expired, but he was not well enough to leave the Quisisana. He had planned to return to live with his family in Sardinia. A room had been rented for him in the village of Santulussurgiu near Ghilarza, where he had attended elementary school, but his final wish – stated to Piero Sraffa on a visit from England – was to join Julia and their children in the USSR. Before any of these plans could be finalised or implemented, he suffered a cerebral haemorrhage on the evening of 25th April, lay unconscious throughout the 26th, and died early the next morning, 27th April 1937, aged 46. On 12th May, Tatiana Schucht wrote from Rome to Sraffa at King's College Cambridge:

"Dear Friend,

I'm sorry for the delay in replying to your letter. It has taken me some time to gather the strength to describe our great misfortune in detail. Firstly, can you tell me whether you are in a position to put Nino's writings in order? I managed to get the notebooks out of the clinic, among Nino's clothes and other personal possessions, with the help of an orderly who distracted the guards. For the moment they are safe in the vaults of the Banco Commerciale, thanks to the kindness of the Director Raffaele Mattioli who remembers Nino fondly, but they can't stay there forever. Nino did ask that everything be sent to Julia until other instructions came to light – whatever they might be – but I thought I'd better consult with you first.

The cremation has already taken place, after an arduous journey across Rome in a sudden thunderstorm. It was difficult to get permission to proceed with the funeral from the police, who put all kinds of legalistic and bureaucratic obstacles in the way, but Carlo and I finally succeeded. Before we left Quisisana, I arranged for a photograph of the corpse and for a death mask to be made. I intend to have the mask cast in bronze, along with the right hand. I also have some photos taken at Formia in 1935, when Nino received his conditional liberty. They are quite precious, not least for the look of satisfactione – even the hint of a smile – on his face.

The days before he died, Nino didn't seem to feel any worse than usual. In fact he was a lot more serene than he had been. I arrived at the clinic as usual at around 5.30pm on the 25th. As we always did, we talked about that day's news. When I took out my books for a French literature lesson I had later that evening, Nino objected and insisted that we carry on talking. In any case, he said with a laugh, I shouldn't have taken a job that demanded specialised knowledge and would exhaust me! How would I be able to continue looking after him?

Even so, we looked up some words together in the Larousse. Then we talked until dinnertime, when he ate the usual minestrone, fruit compote and a piece of sponge cake. He left the room to go to the toilet, but was brought back on a chair carried by several orderlies. He had collapsed there, lost control of his whole left side but managed to crawl to the door and cry for help. When he was back in bed, Nino asked for a tonic to drink, but the Doctor refused until it was clear what was wrong. They brought Nino a hot water bottle for his feet; he said it was too hot, but that the left foot didn't feel very much at all.

At about 9pm Professor Puccinelli finally arrived and conducted an examination. He asked Nino to move his lower limbs, and kept repeating Nino's own words, 'The left leg is weak, yes, it's weak.' He ordered that Nino be bled, and be kept absolutely still. Nino struggled to get comfortable, grasping the bars of the bed with his right hand, and almost toppling out of bed. Over the next hour he vomited several times. He tried to blow his nose, which was blocked up with food, and continued breathing with some difficulty. Another doctor examined him and advised that his condition was extremely serious. At this point the nursing sisters brought in the priest. I objected strongly and insisted that they leave. After some argument, during which the priest questioned my authority, they left. Throughout the next day, the 26th, Nino lay still and barely conscious.

Very early the next morning the vomiting began again, and Nino's breathing became terribly painful. I kept watch over him, wetting his lips, reminding him to breathe when he seemed to have stopped. But then he took a last deep breath and fell back into silence. I called the doctor, who confirmed that it was all over. It was 4.10am on 27th April. At 5.15 the nurses carried the body to the mortuary. Later that morning Carlo came. Together we arranged for the photographer and the man who would make the death mask to come and do their work. It wasn't easy; we had to make all kinds of written declarations about who we were and what we were doing. Later in the afternoon Carlo asked to see his brother one more time, but he was refused, supposedly on orders from the Ministry.

Carlo and I were the only people present at the cremation, apart from a large escort of police guards. The ashes have been deposited in a zinc box laid inside a wooden one, and stored at the Verano

Cemetery, where they can stay for up to ten years without payment. The news of Gramsci's death was broadcast by the Italian state radio and published in the newspapers. All of them called him a political criminal and communist subversive, and one of them called him 'the maddest, most fanatical of all.' It's obscene; I don't know how to go about protesting. Best regards, T."

Part Three: From Behind the Heart

"Gramsci lived a defeat for most of his adult life, from 1920 until his death in 1937." Quintin Hoare, Introduction to A. Gramsci, Selections from Political Writings 1921-1926

"And he died of an illness, not of a bullet like the communist generals, diplomats and leaders of Russia, when they disagree – even a little – with Stalin, and as would have happened to Gramsci himself had he gone to Moscow." Benito Mussolini, Il Popolo d'Italia, 31st December 1937

"Gramsci surprisingly does not seem to have concerned himself seriously with the full range of issues under discussion within the Russian party, or – despite his long stay in the Soviet Union and command of the Russian language – to have reflected critically, at least prior to his arrest, on the overall development of the Russian revolution." Quintin Hoare

"No political leader has suffered a persecution such as I have lived through." Silvio Berlusconi, 27th November 2013

"Avanti o popolo, a la riscossa! Bandiera rossa, bandiera rossa! Avanti o popolo, a la riscossa! Bandiera rossa triomphera! E viva comunismo e la liberta!" Italian Communist anthem Bandiera Rossa (Red Flag)

1937: Rome

My Dear Tanya,

What a great relief it is to be settled in my lovely new room! Thank you so much for helping me move and settle in. With the curtains drawn apart and the windows thrown open, the light and the air high up on this Roman hill can flood my eyes and lungs, restoring me to life after all these years of gloom and foetid prison atmospheres. I am much recovered, thank you very much for asking. I float high above the aches and pains which had become as much a part of my existence as words or feelings. I can honestly say that I have not a care in the world! The excruciating blockages in my arteries and intestines and thoughts and senses have been thoroughly dispelled by the heat and the glare of the parched high summer in this city of eternities.

From where I sit, I can clearly see the stone walls and roof tiles of the ancient imperial *urbs*, with trees and shrubs in full green leaf seeming to occupy every available space between them; together they form a patchwork of rock, terracotta, timber and foliage. Occasional figures scurry about, with the hurry and vigilance of dogs, but otherwise it's a scene mercifully free of people, with their devious ways and constant chatter about nothing. I hear them now, trampling through my memory and imagination, complaining about the heat and the stillness I glory in. And I block them all out, as if by dial or switch, as is now my right and privilege as one of the departed.

If I peer closely enough through the summer haze, I can also just about make out the glassy surfaces and frothing spouts of the dozens of public fountains in this dry desert of a town. Above them rise the sharp, sky-piercing points of church towers and spires, in this least observant city at the heart of the Catholic universe. And around them, I see the squat statues and obelisks of the spacious piazzas where the real moral business of Rome is conducted. If I allow my gaze to meander further through the gates and porticoes, into and through the galleries and *palazzi* which occupy every second building, I can gaze at priceless paintings and frescoes that here just seem ordinary and everyday. I remind myself that I am contemplating masterpieces of the ages.

At the very furthest point of my vista, I can just about make out the inexplicable ancient mound of broken pottery that marks out the plebeian district of Testaccio. Scholars have speculated that it has some kind of sacramental purpose, but I think it's just where they dumped stuff! On the opposite, wrong side of the winding River Tiber from all the patrician magnificence, stands similarly grubby Trastevere. A haze of steam and smoke, with its own distinctive tinges of brown and yellow and purple, rises above the river from the collective labours of *Testacciani* kiln-stokers and lathe-tenders, *Trasteveriani* engine-tuners and metal-bashers. Their toil continues, oblivious to changes of ministers, hair-raising crime and scandal, talk of some new vainglorious imperial adventure; the so-called affairs of the day. The centre of these districts, in death if not in life, and in spirit if not exact location, is the green and grey patchwork of the *Cimitero Anti-Cattolica*, otherwise known as the English or Protestant cemetery after the various Romantic wanderers and Republican agitators who have ended up there.

This, dear Tanya, is where my own ashes will eventually reside, relocated from the dusty shelf at Verano cemetery where you first stored them for safekeeping. Within a year you will arrange for them to be moved to the English Cemetery and placed in a little pale grey stone box on its own small patch of hallowed ground purchased by your father during your family's joyous sojourn in Rome in the early 1900s. As with all aspects of my care, you will pride yourself on your diligence and devotion, and just as carefully avoid reflection on your deeper motives, recording your achievement in a small square photograph of yourself in plump late middle age. There they will rest, these flakes of incinerated flesh and bone, while world war rages and dictators are mostly toppled, not far from the grave of the cockney poet John Keats with his matchless inscription: "Here lies one whose name is writ in water", falling just the right side of pathos and self-pity.

A decade and a half later, another Romantic poet for a rather different, cinematic age, Pier Paolo Pasolini, will sit at the site of my ashes and compose an ode to me in a similar fit of longing and despair at mindless consumption and the tyranny of economic necessity. In that same year, 1954, the author of this novel about my life and loves will be born at the furthest edge of the old Roman Empire, up near the wall constructed by the Emperor Hadrian to hold back the bearded, barbarian Scots. He will take his turn at my grave in the Papal Jubilee year of 2000, and compose his own elegy to his intellectual hero, with a heavy nod to Pasolini: "Far better to choose desire than the fantasies of Fascists, to consume ourselves in fire and live on in flasks of ashes", while his eight year old daughter sits on a nearby bench swinging her legs and demanding *un gelato*. If anyone should come looking, this is where they will find my mortal remains.

* * *

In this, my final and (by my reckoning) roughly 250th letter to you since my arrest all those years ago (in response to your over 600 letters and postcards), I feel the need to make some kind of settlement, dear Tanya, to reach some kind of conclusion. I apologise in advance if you find anything I have to say hurtful, but if a person cannot speak freely and truthfully at the very end of his life, then what is the use of freedom and truth? Besides, you know that everything I say to you is tempered by my boundless affection and gratitude for all you have done for me during my incarceration and long decline, without much by way of complaint on your part or genuine entitlement on mine.

I suppose that is where I have to start. Try as I might, and accepting that in my weak physical condition I am not capable of the full intellectual rigour I have always demanded of myself, I cannot form any clear idea of just why you have attended to me so assiduously. Tell me, Tatiana Schucht, daughter of Apollon (as all your certificates and papers insist on adding), why have you devoted most of the last ten years of your life – the most settled and productive of your middle years – to looking after me, with intervals due only to your own ill health and poverty or family obligations and prohibitions? I just don't understand why a capable, independent, educated and cultured woman, fluent in at least four languages and conversant in several others, *au fait* with the latest cultural trends and scientific developments, would willingly choose such an arid way of life.

After all, we have no formal relationship or mutual responsibility beyond sister and brother in law. That itself is based on the flimsy foundation of my few brief periods of cohabitation with your sister Julia, legally formalised in a cursory wedding ceremony in Moscow in late 1923 before I left for Vienna, and then endorsed in a similarly brief bureaucratic flurry of vows and declarations and signatures at the Registry Office in Rome before Julia returned to Moscow in 1926. My marriage passed by in a flash, and now in my mind has all the allusiveness of a dream. A dream of a dream, a dream of a dream of a dream...

I have sometimes had occasion to wonder whether it actually took place at all. Given our sporadic correspondence, you her sister remained the only tangible, recognisable proof to me of Julia's existence. That Schucht family likeness, much commented on by others and causing me regular confusions of identity, was all I had left of her. But you were not Julia. For long stretches of time, this was the single uppermost impression I had of you. Like her but not her, that's who you were, a chiaroscuro silhouette or a photographic negative, reminding me through your presence of her absence. But, several years older, a constant reminder of how much she would have aged since I last saw her, grown older and further away from me. Forgive me again, but I can now see that this was the primary source of my regular bouts of irritability with you.

Talking to other men about their wives and marriages, their habits and expressions and hard-won compromises, I long ago concluded that mine just did not amount to the same thing. If marriage is above all a shared life, then mine and Julia's might just as well never have happened. My own feelings towards her – grievance, yearning, resentment, bewilderment – are far more prominent in my mind than anything she might have done or we might have done together; a sure test of the failure of our relationship to get far beyond our initial courtship and infatuation.

On a strictly emotional and psychological level, that places my relationship with you, the sister of my "wife", on an even less substantial footing. But then what has been the nature of our relationship? Can it even be described as a relationship, this odd merger of unstated desire and barely understood need, under circumstances of such restricted choice and personal dislocation? Were we brother and sister? Mother and child? Or, as I am sure Julia suspected, unconsummated lovers? Celibate romantics, inhibited by decorum and shyness in our early days of acquaintance; then later, when it would have caused no upset or inconvenience to anyone, even (I suspect) Julia, kept apart by ill health and prison conditions? Were we patient and nurse (and don't think for a moment that I never noticed your fascination with illness)? Or litigant and advocate, negotiating together the tangled mess of Fascist legality and the even more tangled mess of my own sense of wounded dignity and guarded autonomy?

My confusion becomes plain when I try to picture your face, which in your absence I have never actually been able to do. Even five minutes after your departure I just see a blur of features, an odd amalgam of all your sisters, with added touches of resemblance to your parents, but never you distinctly and clearly. I know I see *something*, and I can describe and catalogue its components: a small rounded forehead, greying hair pulled back tightly from the face and occasionally released in a brief spasm of shaken freedom, high cheekbones housing limpid blue eyes, a narrow pursed mouth slow to smile but when it does, lifting and lighting up the whole face.

In other words, I see the face of a middle-aged woman of mixed European and Slavic descent, the face of millions of women across this ancient, fractured, troubled continent, holding themselves and their families and communities together and getting precious little thanks in return. If I have been parsimonious or grudging in my own gratitude for all you have done for me, it has been out of my own failure to understand just who you are and why you have been here with me for much of the last ten years of my life. And my bewilderment matches that of millions of other men, let out to play with each other – sometimes happily and collaboratively, sometimes cruelly and violently – while their women sacrifice themselves to drudgery and misery, including patching their men up and raising a rag to their lips and foreheads when they come home bruised and bleeding. You are in my mind a kind of everywoman, familiar but uninteresting, a blur of roles and features and suppressed desires and disregarded terrors.

Again, please forgive my casual brutality. I do not have the energy or skill to dress my thoughts in softening devices, so I am speaking as I see it, "from behind the heart" as Marx once put it when asked to identify the source of his "compassionate sarcasm." When any initial offence has passed, you will see the genuine love and curiosity behind my questions, and the real practical value I place on your routine ministrations. And – in further defence of my high-handedness – you know from our many previous conversations that I have always been bewildered by *all* other people, while always endeavouring to understand my bewilderment as the consequence of my own physical separation and individuality. We are all, as far as each other is concerned, "others", with all the uncertainty and suspicion that implies. A supreme effort of will and reflection is required to bridge that gulf, and I do not always succeed.

There I go again, pontificating! And, as you once said when I came out with something similar years ago, in a similar tone of isolation and dejection, that's some conclusion for a so-called Marxist! But you know, Marx ended up feeling pretty much the same way. We identify ourselves as much *against* other people as with them. Perhaps we can attribute it to the competitive individualism of capitalism. When we are fated to scramble against each other for the slightest material and social advantage, we end up living as well as being born and dying alone.

Finally, my darling Tanya, I have to thank you for taking such great care of my notebooks, my only conscious legacy and concrete achievement, the final proof of my worthwhile existence. They will be spirited out of Italy by Vincenzo Bianco (the faithful emissary of my failed attempts to remit some scraps of my prison income to Julka and the children) in the Soviet diplomatic post next year, 1938. In Moscow they will be stored and studied under Ercoli's supervision, placed in order by theme and date of composition, making use of (but also correcting) the basic labelling system you devised and stuck to their front covers. Eventually they will be returned to Italy, edited and published after a great triumphant war against Nazism and Fascism, in which the communists will provide the most serious and steadfast internal resistance.

Ercoli, now properly known as Palmiro Togliatti and leader of the largest and most effective mass democratic Communist Party ever, *Il Partito Comunista Italiano,* will use my posthumous prestige as the source of the party's moral authority, and carefully selected fragments of my often cryptic notes to guide its post-war political strategy. This will be based on the themes of national unity, broad social alliance of progressive forces, respect for parliamentary democracy and free debate, economic reconstruction and cultural renewal, with the clear and overt aims of proletarian hegemony, popular democracy and socialist transformation of our society. All this will be more than adequate replacement for the death mask and the cast of my right hand which you went to such lengths to commission, but which will be lost in the chaos of protracted worldwide war.

Please don't ask how I know all this – I simply ask you to trust me – or that you will return to your family in Russia a year or so after my death, but not before being photographed beside my urn with that look of humble defiance. You will live with them there, forming a particular vigilantly protective attachment to my unmet son Giuliano, and in a condition of incipient domestic and ideological conflict with your sister Evgenia and my other son Delio, whom she continues to consider and treat as her own baby. Julka will maintain her demeanour of *not being quite all there*, not least because for long stretches of time she won't be, away at some sanatorium or psychiatric institution.

Please don't ask me either how I know that you will be evacuated with your mother and sisters on the outbreak of war to Frunze in Kyrghizia. There you will contract *tifo addominale* complicated by *pellagra* (vitamin deficiency due to malnutrition) and die a year after your mother Julia Grigor'evna in September 1943, aged (if you don't mind me mentioning it!) just 55. Together, Tanya, our lifetimes will amount to just over a century; and what a century it has been!

A tender hug for you my dear, from your Nino.

* * *

Dear Ercoli,

I am aware that this is our first direct communication since my arrest in late 1926, and that our very final communications – over my infamous letter to the Comintern – were somewhat terse. I cannot say that over these last ten years we have occupied a prominent or frequent place in each other's thoughts. For our own quite separate reasons, we have both kept a fastidious distance, in our own minds as well as our personal relations. I have regarded myself as increasingly "out of action", a prisoner of war with nothing of much use to contribute to the ongoing daily struggle. You have in contrast been entirely immersed in that daily struggle, with the close attention to detail and incident which derives from your personality and professional formation as a lawyer. Perhaps, as you were always prone to, you have not seen the larger historical picture which, to my great regret and loss, is all I have had to contemplate.

For each of us these very different perspectives have undoubtedly required a careful calculus of success, defeat and compromise, with not a little subterfuge over what we were up to. On occasions that has amounted to outright deceit of our colleagues, companions and families. The loss to ourselves has arguably been just as grievous as the loss to others. We have sacrificed our own integrity and well-being, for the sake of a greater cause which has sometimes seemed tantalisingly close, more often far away and receding even further. We have both arrived at conclusions and actions we would previously have regarded as unpalatable, our very own compromises with history. We have both made enemies among our comrades, some of whom we would also have regarded as friends.

Watching our party fragment into warring cliques, I have sometimes wondered whether the deliberate distance between us two amounts to that kind of implacable antipathy. If so, that would be especially unfortunate. After all, we are fellow Sardinians, whose lives have converged on a number of crucial occasions, from our both winning scholarships to Turin University in the same year, 1911, to working together as eager young Socialists to shake up the party old guard in its northern city bastions, setting up *L'Ordine Nuovo* in 1919 and agitating for the Factory Councils, and finally founding the Communist Party in 1921 and steering it through the difficult early years and into some kind of settled place in Italian politics.

I was the Party's leader for a couple of those years, by default more than ambition, when all the comrades more prominent than me were arrested. You and I worked together closely, on the party's last political statement as a free, legal entity, the Theses presented to the Lyons Party Congress of 1926. You succeeded me, when the dust had settled after my arrest. You will remain leader for many years to come, somehow – and this is testimony to your skills and instincts, rather than any kind of slur on your moral probity – surviving purge, war and political upheaval. They will call you "a wily old fox", and marvel as you trim and tack on the rough seas of international communism, doing the bidding of your Comintern masters, all the while preserving the democratic temper of the Italian party and its national-popular strategy and practice, carefully keeping apart what the International was designed and determined to align, using my name and notebooks as a primary source of unsullied, unimpeachable moral and intellectual authority.

So, Ercoli, I write to you as a comrade and a friend, as well as guide and mentor, albeit from a very different position to the one you find yourself in. I lie here rotting away, notionally free but even less capable of free movement than I was in prison, more dead than alive in fact, while you live and work in exile in Paris, one of the most beautiful cities of the world. You are able to wander its *jardins* and *boulevards* as the fancy takes you and meet whoever may wish to meet you. But from what I surmise about your political situation, I suspect I may have more intellectual freedom in physical confinement and bodily decay than you have in the prime of life and with the entire world available to you. So I intend to be candid, much more than you are used to or may seem wise in the anterooms and corridors of the world proletarian revolution (are we still calling it that?), but which here on my deathbed seems entirely fitting. I am much too tired, ill and desperate to engage in euphemism, subterfuge or elaborate dissimulation. Let me start with the USSR. I read a report of the 14th Congress of the Communist Party of the Soviet Union in an Italian newspaper in December 1934. I have it here with me now, amongst my jottings and snippets. It seems reasonably measured and accurate, partly reproduced from *Pravda* (I recognise the tone and some of the terminology) and reflecting the markedly improved relations between the countries' governments at that time. The report pointed out that Stalin didn't even bother to give a speech at the end of the Congress. He simply said that "...the discussion at this congress has revealed the complete unity of the views of our Party leaders on all questions of Party policy... The question arises: Is there any need, after this, for me to reply to the discussion? I do not think there is. Permit me therefore to refrain from making any concluding remarks." There then followed a stormy ovation. All the delegates rose to their feet. There were thunderous shouts of "Hurrah!" and "Long live Stalin!" The delegates, all standing, sang the *Internationale*, after which the standing ovation resumed.

Stalin not bothering with a concluding speech was, the newspaper said, the final measure of his complete ascendancy, "as eloquent in its own way as our own dear *Duce's* finest, and rather longer, perorations." Is this what happened? Were you there? Is this what the revolution has come to? The movement blessed by its leader's presence, rather than guided by his strategic vision? I cannot help wondering what would Lenin have thought. Vladimir Ilyich, who wrote in his last testament that Stalin could not be trusted, and whose last testament Stalin proceeded to suppress. Vladimir Ilyich, who I once overheard airing the common despair among Russian intellectuals at the prospect of a revolution conducted by "...a people who are two hundred years behind the rest of Europe and who so far can't even manage to do up their own fly-buttons properly." Vladimir Ilyich, whose last major speech to the Comintern, which I had the privilege to hear and see, argued that its previous resolutions and programmes had been just "…too Russian, imbued with the Russian spirit... if some foreigner somehow manages to understand them, he wouldn't be in any position to implement them. I agree with all of them, but we have not learned how to present our Russian experience to foreigners in a way they could apply to their own situations." That, dear Ercoli, is true revolutionary modesty, not the "immodest modesty" of Vladimir Ilyich's successor, who finds himself so securely supreme he can't even be bothered to respond to debate.

And what of the opposition? Or rather Opposition, as it always rather pompously styled itself. Well, I recall Victor Serge pointing out that a very similar "leadership cult" was being constructed around Stalin's oldest and most venerable adversary, Leon Davidovitch Trotsky, with very little attempt at "immodest modesty". There had been two strands of Communist opposition, Serge told me, "…for the great majority, including us two my friend, resistance to totalitarianism in the name of the democratic ideals expressed at the beginning of the Revolution. For a number of our Old Bolshevik leaders it meant, on the contrary, the defence of doctrinal orthodoxy which was authoritarian through and through. These two mingled strains had, between 1923 and 1928, converged upon and imbued Trotsky's vigorous personality with a tremendous aura."

The old man brought the same manic energy to opposition that he'd used to power his dashes around Russia in his legendary armoured train in the civil war. When he was defeated and cast out, it was still not too late. If in exile from the USSR he had promoted a renewed Socialism, critical in outlook and fearing dogmatism more than diversity, he might have attained true greatness. But he was the prisoner of his own orthodoxy, especially since his occasional lapses into creative unorthodoxy were being denounced as treason. He sought to carry into the world a movement which was not only Russian but extinct in Russia itself, killed twice over, both by the bullets of its executioners and by changes in popular mentality. Tell me, Ercoli, what do you say to that? Would you agree with Serge (who will learn of my death from a leaflet handed to him on a march in support of the Popular Front government in France) that Trotsky and Stalin are but two sides of the same debased coin? Would you now accept that my warning in 1926 – in the letter I was asked to write on behalf of our own party, and which you intercepted and withheld from the Comintern, about the tone and conduct of the debate inside the Russian party and the poison it would spread across the whole international movement – has been proven horribly correct?

And would this account for a report Serge received from his sister in law in Moscow that her young son frequently wakes in the night from dreams that "...the whole country is suddenly crawling with all kinds of invisible and therefore especially dangerous reptiles, snakes and scorpions with such terrible names as 'wrecker', 'opportunist' or 'Trotskyite'?" Or what she herself has noticed, that "...people have started to avoid each other, not just because of the fear of informers or denunciation, but from a kind of numbness or lethargy. What is there to talk about when everything has already been observed, explained and decided by the higher-ups?" After twenty years of revolution, she says, people are exhausted, and seeking nothing but their own private peace and consolation wherever they may find them. This is why they tolerate the decay of the revolution, their revolution, because they are tired of it. There are many forms of hegemony, some of them based on weakness and defeat...

Let us now, perhaps in search of some light relief, move on to Italy, our beloved, bewildering, benighted native country (if we

Sards, that is, are ever really regarded or regard ourselves as proper Italians). Why did it take us so long to recognise Fascism for what it was? Not "a circus of buffoonery" or even "a pathetic petty bourgeois swoon before the strutting figure of Mussolini" as I recall you describing it in the mid-twenties, but what you called more recently and entirely correctly "a reactionary mass regime"? Why, as another comrade has asked, did we spend "all those years discussing 'What is Fascism?' like someone who has been hit on the head by a falling roof tile and totters about wondering what the tile is made of?" All the while, the Fascists were making a finely calibrated and immensely successful appeal to the worst instincts of the Italian people; that same Italian people who we thought we heard clamouring for proletarian dictatorship in the name of historical progress.

It is clear, at least to me on my elevated "disinterested" perch, up here *fur ewig*, that while we communists waded around in dogma and trimmed our arguments and policies according to the latest Russian fashion, Fascism was digging itself deep into every aspect of Italian society and culture, its "soul of iron and stone" (Mussolini's flattery again) that on closer inspection turns out to be tin and concrete. Our confusion and delay contributed directly to the depth and longevity of Fascist rule. By the time we were recognising the stark reality, and taking such forlorn sidesteps as your 1935 call for "an opposition born within the Fascist regime itself", it was far too late. The years of reaction, roughly 1920 to 1929, had been superseded by the years of consent, roughly 1929 to 1936. Our time of ascendancy, the fifty "progressive" years between *Risorgimento* and the defeat of the Turin Factory Councils, was well and truly over.

We could by then see all around us, all too plainly, myriad signs of the restoration of self-confidence of the high bourgeoisie. The gossip columns were full of their daily doings and facile sayings. They mounted exhibitions of their latest artistic acquisitions, which were always described in the reviews as "sumptuous", as though that was the ultimate measure of artistic value. The *kitsch* decorative styles of Art Nouveau and Art Deco were passed off as artistic schools or even movements. Experimental theatre declined and disappeared, displaced by revived traditional genres like farce and melodrama. Even the revolutionary new medium of cinema turned back to tried and trusted settings, subjects and narratives.

Following the economic crash of 1929, capitalism shook itself down and free of its grudgingly conceded social obligations, re-established market discipline, and resolved its various crises at the expense of the weakest masses. Wages in Italy were cut by ten to twenty per cent in October 1927, by eight per cent all round in December 1930, and by seven per cent all round in May 1934. Artificially high prices impoverished the diet and stunted the growth of the people; little Italians indeed. The poor were herded into crowded slums on the outskirts of the big cities, the infamous *borgate*. Trades unions and other civil associations were smashed, or turned into Fascist corporations and absorbed into the state apparatus. The press were reduced to the role of cheer-leaders and sneering cynics on behalf of the prevailing order. The universities and great cultural institutions, even our one intellectual of true global standing Benedetto Croce, were cowed into submission or acquiescence. From then on, the Fascists were able unimpeded to guide the country towards its small but significant part in global disaster. Punchinello grew up into Caesar, and swapped his truncheon for a squadron of dive-bombers.

"Ha, ha!" went the world. "Look at the funny Eye-ties!"

"Yes!" we said, in our places of exile, Paris and Moscow. "Aren't they ridiculous!" All the while forgetting that for the rest of the world, our French and Russian hosts included, we were "funny Eye-ties" too. And that Italian cudgels, bullets and bombs can do just as much damage as German ones.

Of course we were right to point out the diabolical comedy of Mussolini's regime, which would remain the abiding motif of its international reputation, in a vain attempt to prick its pomposity and self-aggrandisement. But in the process we laughed off its dark brutality, which crushed our own popular revolution in the very early 1920s in a storm of blood and fire, but thereafter was always only ever as ferocious as it needed to be. This relative restraint in turn helped the regime to establish its international legitimacy – "You don't have to like Mussolini, but at least he's made the trains run on time", which was never actually true – especially when other more blatant and persistently brutal forms of reaction came along in Germany and Spain. But without Mussolini and his preening foppish *squadristi,* there would have been no Hitler and National Socialism, no Franco with his Phalanges. Italian Fascism provided the template for *Kristallnacht* and Guernica. It was only comical insofar as the country it lorded it over, silly little old Italy, was so much less powerful and internationally competitive than Germany or even Spain.

But, you will argue quite rightly, we communists at least maintained some kind of presence inside the country under Fascism, while the rest of the "opposition" went into cosseted exile in the smarter suburbs of the self-styled democracies, trading on their martyrdom for a place at the literary salons and diplomatic receptions of Paris, London and Geneva, and returning unharmed to their positions of command in the post-war Italian state, Christian and Social Democrats of the new, CIA-sponsored Europe. True enough; we communists deserve credit for simply being there, surviving, not least because it provided the core of the Resistance and of your post-war mass democratic party of national reconstruction.

But what if we had realised what we were up against and promoted anti-Fascist alliance right from the very start? What if we had worked alongside the Socialist Party and the trades unions, even as a separate party ourselves but calm and sensible and constructive, and above all realistic about our own limited capabilities and influence? What if we had placed ourselves truly alongside the people, embedding our politics and practice inside their daily lives and experiences, their intellectual and cultural pursuits, their collective identities and activities, their hearts and souls, so that we could grow and learn with them, not as some kind of alien presence foisted upon them? There are so many "What ifs", old friend. Sometimes they are all we are left with, but they may just prompt more effective solutions from future generations than we were capable of.

Well, Ercoli/Palmiro, there we go, a dream of a dream indeed... I should finish by thanking you for preserving my letters and notebooks and arranging for their publication, however mixed your motives may be. Under your guidance the first book of commemoration will appear in 1938, a set of recollections simply called *Gramsci*. It will be predictably subjected to Stalinist critique of my record, focusing on my early support for intervention in the war and my alleged Bergsonian "voluntarism" and social-democratic "reformism", then my critically appreciative studies of the "liberal idealist" Benedetto Croce and of course my 1926 letter to the Comintern. You will have to acknowledge publicly that these dullards and sycophants have a point, though in your heart you know it's nonsense. "Comrade Gramsci was not always in full possession of the facts," you will say to them, well aware that I knew all I needed to know to spot cant and hypocrisy when I saw it. You will say to yourself, in the slightest whisper and with the full "organised sarcasm" you know I would have brought to the situation, that "Mussolini got Antonio before Stalin could."

Finally after another world war, now as a government minister, you will create of me a communist "martyr saint" – a propaganda device I would thoroughly loathe on a personal basis, but whose ideological force I would just as thoroughly appreciate – to guide the Italian people towards a kinder, gentler, more constructive socialism than ever attempted or achieved anywhere else. Like all grand historical projects, it will fall far short of its objectives, not least because we consistently underestimate the adaptive skills of the bourgeoisie in preserving their hegemony, both nationally and globally (I see a crooning, toupéed, perma-tanned, come-again *Duce* for a more indolent post-industrial age...), but at least we tried our best.

You and I will be personally commemorated in a thousand squares and street-signs, train and tram stations; entire estates of hurriedly thrown-up and shoddily built tower blocks of workers' flats on the bleak outskirts of the major Italian cities, modern *borgate*; and even in your case a whole grimy factory town in the Soviet Union. Could we ever have imagined *that*, my friend, as callow youths at the University of Turin in 1911, fresh off the boat from Sardinia? We will leave our mark, Palmiro, and hope that future revolutionaries will take up where we left off.

We Italian communists were always honourable and honest, even if we were often found wanting for a sense of art or fun or sport or humour, and therefore lacked the most intimate contact with all those puerile, senile Italians. And, we have to admit, old student friend and fellow Sardinian, we had some fun of our own along the way! Even if we never got round to "throwing the mainlanders into the sea", as I advocated in that famous schoolboy essay regularly thrown back at me as evidence of my incorrigible deviationism...

Your comrade and always faithful friend, Antonio.

* * *

Dear Mamma,

I had planned to come home to Sardinia upon my final and unconditional release. I understand a comfortable room had been rented for me in the village of Santulussurgiu, which I remember well from attending secondary school there. I was looking forward to seeing how much the place had changed in the intervening thirty five years, and whether any of my old schoolmates were still there. Perhaps we could have gone hunting *scurzoni* in the hills, to feed our pet hawks! Or simply sat sipping coffee in the village square we used to run around after school, rousing the village elders from their midday slumbers. But it looks as though all our plans were in vain. It would just be too physically challenging and politically complicated to make the long sea journey and resettle on our simple island. Alas! Instead I have made arrangements to rejoin my wife and children in Russia, where I can at least hope for the medical treatment and nursing care I will need, and finally make the full acquaintance of the two sons I have hardly known or, in the case of young Giuliano, even met.

All these deliberations over what will almost certainly be my final resting place have caused me to reflect on what it actually means to refer to somewhere as "home". Is it the place where we were born, over which we have no choice or control? Is it any of the places we pass through in adolescence and young adulthood, those busy years which connect our childhood and adult selves and which are commonly regarded as formative of our characters and careers? Or is it the place we finally settle in, either because it feels like a "home of our own" or because we lack the gumption, energy, inclination or personal resources to move on anywhere else?

I suppose I pose these questions in these terms because I have never really felt "at home" in any of the places I have found myself in. At the end of my life I am presented with a choice of residence which is not obvious but in fact troublesome. Having made my "home" for the last ten years in various squalid prisons and clinical, anonymous hospitals, I have absolutely no idea where to go next. Believe me, I would much rather one place over any others was able to lay claim to what remains of me. But like many long-term prisoners and invalids, I would actually prefer – and I baulk at what this reveals I have been reduced to by "prisonitis" and physical decay and collapse – to remain where I am, guarded and nursed for the rest of my days, held but safe, secured *and* secure. Perhaps if I try hard enough I will be too sick to move!

The fact that there is no "home" for me after these forty six years of life represents a triple failure. Firstly and most importantly, Mamma, I have failed to find my own place in the world. This is hardly surprising, given my adult career of revolutionary agitation, with the dissatisfied temperament and revulsion at the world as it is which that automatically implies. Then this final chapter of enforced isolation and captivity in places of the state's choosing. Nonetheless it feels like a personal failure, not least because without some kind of foothold in the real existing world, beset as it is with misery and strife, greed and oppression, and without some kind of stake in the lives of other real living human beings, with all their quirks and foibles, you can never hope to understand the small part of the world you inhabit let alone capture the rest of it. If one believes as a matter of principle, as I do, that all lives are equally complex and valuable – the main difference being in how hard and well we work to lay bare our complexities and realise our value – then being cut off from the lives of others, and seeing only their simplest and most superficial outlines, is the hardest deprivation of all. Only in our relationships with others do we become truly ourselves. In prison these last ten years, I have seen and felt the world slip away.

We only have one life to live, in the time and place we are born into, and one lifespan to make that time and place somehow our own. I never managed that. I have spent my entire life in other people's places, on other people's time. On that basis alone, Mamma, I judge myself a failure. My second "home", with my wife and children, has proved as elusive and chimerical as anywhere else. I only ever spent months with them, so how could we have possibly accumulated the ragbag of triumphs and tragedies, chores and routines, quarrels and reconciliations which come to constitute a marriage and a family life? Our family estate – those objects and experiences we can truly call our own – would barely fill a hat box let alone a home.

Julia and I were only ever passing strangers, who happened to find ourselves sharing time and living quarters for brief periods in this tumultuous era. We reached out and touched each other, tenderly and gingerly, as if we might break a bone or pass our hands entirely through if we pressed too hard. For both of us these brief spells of joy and happiness came to feel like burdens in our memory, casting the rest of our troubled lonely lives into sharp, dark relief. We have lived our lives in the shadows, our own shadows as much as anyone or anything else's. That is no place to make a home for ourselves or – as I am too well aware from the circumstances of my own childhood – our children.

Finally, what of my home with you, in Ghilarza, which I left for good in 1911 aged twenty and hardly ever thereafter returned to, with at least part of my motivation an urgent need to escape from you and your clutches? For many of those intervening years I was wholly out of touch. Even when imprisonment presented the time and opportunity to resume our correspondence, as well as welcome relief from prison tedium – how I would look forward to those Monday afternoons of letter-writing! – many months would go by without word back from you. You finally went wholly quiet, through 1933 and beyond, the worst of my prison years, when "pessimism of the intellect" finally overwhelmed "optimism of the will".

At other times, usually through some misunderstanding or pig-headed resentment on my part, I would go "on strike" – as pointlessly and self-destructively as that most blunt of political-economic instruments usually is – and refuse to write to you or anyone else at all. But, stripping away all the niceties and formalities of sentiment and decorum – what you once resentfully called my "dutiful son act" when I turned up unannounced for a good meal and a change of clothes from secondary school – I feel no sense of belonging or even much affection for my Sardinian "home" with you.

In all honesty, it ceased to feel like any kind of home to me as soon as Father was imprisoned and the family was plunged into poverty and shame. His disgrace, and the atmosphere of silent taboo in which the family conspired to deal with it, soured my childhood and destroyed forever any basic trust I might have had in other people. I could never feel that I could rely upon them, even to tell me the truth of what was happening. After that, I assumed a certain cast of mind which bore me through all the subsequent deceptions – blaming the clumsy housemaid for my deformity when it was the first sign of spinal tuberculosis, the disease of shameful poverty; Edmea's unacknowledged parentage; the reality of your and Apollon Schucht's deaths; the details of Julia's mental breakdown and the concealment of my incarceration from my own children – but blighted my whole life, even when contrived for my own supposed protection. Even you, with the best of intentions, are guilty of this most mundane but treacherous deception. I am sure you recall me pestering you throughout my later childhood for the full details of even the most trivial incident or contact. I had learnt that I had to remain vigilant at all times, to compensate for my childish lack of power with an attitude of constant alertness. Otherwise the world could end without warning.

I know full well that you tried your very best to bear our family's decline and loss, alone and unaided even by your own birth family, quite literally working your fingers to the bone to keep it going and together. One of my clearest early memories is of you sitting by the cold hearth long into the night, with a single candle for illumination, sewing other families' torn and threadbare linen till your fingers bled and your hands went into spasm, just as mine have tended to in my final years. I study them closely as they twitch and clench, so similar to yours in shape and size, and wonder whether I should regard this affliction as your final gift or vengeance, caress or slap.

As soon as they could stitch and darn, my sisters were enlisted in the family business, pouting and grumbling at the time thereby lost to play and friendship. I used to think that growing up amongst women had given me some special insight into feminine ways. Well, I certainly know what it's like to find myself among hard-pressed women. Perhaps that familiarity is what drew me towards the similarly troubled Schucht sisters, and why I felt so "at home" amongst them, watching them stab and mutter at their embroidery. And I see all too clearly the effects on my masculinity of constantly feeling that I was somehow out of favour and in the way, without the faintest idea how or why. It is so hard to maintain the normal range of male feelings towards women – curiosity, respect, affection, desire – when one's closest female companions seem to be in a semi-permanent state of irritation or outright hostility towards you.

Mamma, I am so sorry for my cruelty, and well aware that you bear very little of the primary responsibility for our family's hardships and misfortunes. With seven children to raise alone, you did your very best to make up for our handicaps and raise us well. The fact that we have all made more or less worthwhile lives of our own is your final achievement; even if we Gramsci brothers and sisters have not been especially kind or close to each other. Above all, you communicated to us your love of books and stories, and taught all of us the precious skills of reading and writing which had set you apart from almost all the local girls of your generation (and provided another small source of income in the hard times, "writing other women's love letters" as you used to put it).

Of all my brothers and sisters I was the one who took up those skills most diligently and enthusiastically, perhaps because of the physical disadvantages and disabilities I suffered. I wasn't going very far with my puny body, so I'd better make the most of what you called "the brains in that big head of yours." Another childhood memory: me at the family dinner table doing my homework or drawing meticulously detailed pictures, while my brothers and sisters scoffed or complimented me over my shoulder. Growing up with you I was often cold or hungry or in pain, but this was more than made up for by the precious gift of literacy, the key to the door out of our own little personal worlds and into the great big historical world outside. You gave me the means to make a life for myself (if not necessarily a "home") far away from the squalor and destitution of Sardinia. You gave me somewhere I couldn't wait to escape from, but also the means with which to make my escape. And for that I am eternally grateful.

Mamma, I know you died in late 1932, nearly five years ago now. It was kept from me, but I suspected it all along. When I wrote my last letter to you in 1934 (in fact my only surviving letter to anyone from that miserable year) and told you "how much I care for you, but how little I know about how you are", I was hoping that it would elicit some definite news, if not from you then at least from those who were physically close to you. I already had an inkling that you were dead, and that I was casting my love and regards to you into a dark hole far deeper than the one which much of my childhood has come to seem to me. I was never actually told when and how you had died. It just became one of those cold facts that we all understood and acknowledged but made no explicit reference to. When Tanya finally let it slip last year, in 1936, we just let it sit there between us, smiling gently at the exposure of yet another convenient deception.

I wonder how many families across the world deal with their tragedies like this, not with weeping and wailing but with cold, silent resignation. And who's to say, in the cold light of human history, that one is any better than the other? There are many different ways to skin a cat, as I recall you saying when I was very small, marvelling at the casual cruelty of the expression without having any idea what it meant. I also seem to remember wondering whether you yourself had ever skinned a cat! Now I know for sure, and from the absence of direct communication from you for nearly five years, that you are long dead and gone. So, soon, shall I be.

Your ever loving son, Nino.

* * *

My darling Julka,

I asked you to come and see me and you never came. I asked if I might come and stay with you and you fobbed me off. There were always unspecified "practical obstacles" in the way, and "potential disturbances" to avoid. I asked you to write to me and you rarely wrote. Even when you did, they were usually scraps attached to longer, fuller letters from Tanya. I asked you to put more care and thought, more of yourself, into your few notes, but by and large you restricted yourself to banalities and trivialities. I asked for more detailed descriptions of the children's lives, and you replied that: "To write a report about the children's lives would be to destroy the essence of them." When I replied that I am not a policeman, and asked only for your subjective impressions, you said this was placing "intolerable pressure" on you. Or worse, you got your father or sisters to tell me to lay off, because I risked provoking some new crisis.

Your more substantial personal thoughts so often sounded like they had been dictated to you by someone else. Or they had that worked-through finality, neither inviting nor even permitting any natural response, closing down rather than sustaining dialogue, which I could only imagine derived from your psychoanalysis. Then I realised that I was being drawn into the circle of your therapy, seduced into treating you as a subject of study or analysis of my own. Your notes to me became evidence, so that I read and reread them, pored over them, trying to guess how you were the day you wrote them. I found myself examining the handwriting for clues, to see how firm your hand was and so on, trying to extract every possible sign and meaning from these few scratched lines.

From there I would proceed in my prison cell to even more abstract musings. What is it about our time that wears people out? How and why are our societies and economies organised in such a way that certain nervous types, "the insulted and the injured", find the strain intolerable and break apart? In the absence of any account from you beyond the vaguest allusions to your childhood, this was all I had to go on. Then you accused me of "over-analysing", and of forgetting that I was your husband and not your doctor. Again I sensed someone else protecting their position through you, hiding behind you, using you as a shield.

You said that you found my description of you as "injured and insulted" itself injuring and insulting, and again I heard another's voice advising you what to write. It seemed to me that we were spinning around each other in ever widening circles, or being spun by forces beyond our control. All the while we were seizing hold of each other ever more tightly yet somehow escaping each other's grasp and hurtling ever further away from each other into cold space, taking with us bleeding and broken scraps of each other's torn-off flesh and bone.

I tried to make allowances, to quell my natural tendency to think ill of people. I tried not to be quite so "subaltern" or "Sardinian", retreating to what you once called – making me laugh out loud – my "island fastness". I convinced myself that you were doing your best to keep in touch. I told myself that the notes relayed by Tanya were giving me true sketches of your daily existence, perhaps without you even knowing it yourself. I would take great heart from the odd glimpses of your old – or should I say young? – self, which I took as reaffirmations of your continuing concern and affection. But then you would go quiet for months or even years. I would realise I'd lost you again, and probably for good. Rereading your old notes, I would see that they were merely dashed-off scribbles from a spare five minutes, mistaken by a lonely prisoner for the ordinary life of someone he once lived with. Someone he thought he loved, someone he thought loved him.

There were a few startling exceptions, about every couple of years – I can say that because I kept a meticulous record in my head, a mental list of dated excerpts – when apparently without meaning to, you came out with something quite profound and heartfelt. Thus, you wrote in 1929 that "…our misunderstandings have served to bring us closer together, by forcing us to reach out towards each other and clarify what we really mean". Then in 1931, that "…if we were together today, I would not seek to defend myself against your intellectual and moral influence like I used to, and for that reason I feel close to you."

But these rare declarations of feeling usually just left me perplexed and agonising for weeks on end. Over-analysing again perhaps, but without further explanation from you, what else could I do? So I would ask myself what did you actually mean by them? Were you making some genuine effort to reach me, or at least to captivate me like you did at Serebranyi Bor? Was I still capable – and believe me, I tried, from the depths of my prison squalor – of the imaginative leap required to make contact with you? Or were these odd kind words of yours just isolated sparks in the darkness?

Putting it as bluntly to myself as I dared, were they moments of sincere lucidity in the midst of your madness, or just more scraps of madness? And did it make any real difference either way? Was this all I could expect, given the hints I was receiving from other people about your condition? Madness turns everyone into strangers. I've come close enough to it myself to recognise its essential ingredient of separation. We withdraw deeper inside ourselves in an attempt at self-protection – your defending yourself, for example, against my "intellectual and moral influence" – which is itself deeply damaging. When Tanya finally got round to telling me the full extent of your nervous breakdown, with the added complications of suspected epilepsy, it was some three or four years after its onset shortly after we parted and you returned to Russia. What hurt me most was not that I had been kept in the dark for so long, but that I had been totally excluded from caring for you. I was never even given the chance to be a proper husband to you. I saw at last that we had become, perhaps always were, perfect strangers.

And, I have finally decided, it could never have been otherwise. The fact is that for the last ten years we have been physically apart, not just from each other but from almost every other free human contact. Here was I, in my prison cell or hospital bed, behind barred windows and under constant armed guard. There you were in your sanatorium or asylum, or allowed back in the family home only under close medical and psychiatric supervision. Our most intimate communications were supervised at both ends: the prison censors at mine, and at yours the "office" which Togliatti scoffed at and your father tried to explain made it impossible for you to write unguardedly. What possible chance did we have of keeping in touch? How on earth could we reach across thousands of kilometres and the most profound and hostile ideological divide of our age, when we were both being forcibly kept out of touch with anything but our own immediate surroundings of walls and functional furniture? Even when I tried hard to bridge that divide, addressing you as a comrade and fellow communist, I thoughtlessly assumed a shared theoretical understanding and political perspective, above all a capacity for analytical objectivity which you did not possess. I simply ended up re-emphasising our temperamental differences. I thought I was tuning you, like one of your violin strings, only to find that I was stretching you to breaking point.

What remains unclear to me is whether I was always a

stranger to you, even in those moments when we were free and together and you were apparently happy. Were you only ever, as I often suspected, just going along with things? Looking back, I wish I had pushed you for some clearer statement of your true position while you were briefly still capable of it in the months after we first met. But I was always aware of your "finer feelings", your brittle fragility, and worried that by speaking too bluntly I might somehow break you. Or worse, at least from my point of view, lose you.

As it is, I fear that I harmed you irreparably by simply meeting and getting to know you. I was as "unsuitable" for you – as Evgenia never failed to point out – as you were for me. Given your frailty and my doggedness, our starkly contrasting temperaments, this would always be a mutually destructive encounter. While drawing me towards you, you were fending me off. You hated your beauty, but hated its appeal to me even more. I wanted to get to know you, oblivious of the fact that what you feared above all else was knowing yourself, so that every new realisation on my part was another blow to your psychic integrity. I was trying to pin you down, through our conversations and our letters, like a rare and precious butterfly. I carried on prodding and piercing, with my criticisms and speculations and suggested "projects", blithely unaware that the very act of identification and description would kill you. And that I, the blundering "scientific" fool, would be left disconsolate and bereft.

I ask you now, my dear doomed Julka, daughter of Apollon Alexandrovich and Julia Grigor'evna, sister of Evgenia and Tanya and Anna and Nadia and Victor, mother of Delio and Giuliano, wife of Antonio, who are you? Who have you ever been, apart from the sum of your tenuous relationships with other people? What are the basic features of your personality and outlook on life? After all these years of examination and analysis, I have no clearer idea than when I first set eyes on you and froze in your gaze, that late summer afternoon in your sister's room at Serebranyi Bor in 1922. I am just as puzzled over my effect on you. How did it feel to receive my letters? Apart from bulletins on the weather or my own state of physical and mental health, what did you ever get from me? The best I could muster were suggestions for therapy or work, and they were mostly shots in the dark, based on my own limited experience or superficial research. Predictably they were poorly aimed and clumsily delivered, little more than admonishments and barked instructions to "pull yourself together" or "find your own way through". In their lack of sympathy and understanding, I suspect they represented a madness of my own, separation from above rather than below, haughty abstraction rather than subaltern withdrawal. Perhaps intellectual condescension is preferable to peasant resentment, but there were probably residual elements of the latter in my manner towards you, the loveliest daughter of a Russian aristocrat, as well as large preening dollops of the former. When I played at being husband to you or father to our children, with comments about your psychoanalysis or their reading and schooling, I was simply demonstrating my ignorance and distance.

Finally, in the fear and remorse of my dying years, I tried to come back to you. I strained against all my pride and dignity to communicate to you my vulnerability and self-loathing. I knew, and tried to tell you, that these overwhelming negative feelings could only be assuaged by the tender concern and loving embrace of another human being. I sought some reassurance that if I was not worth much to myself I was at least worth something to someone else. This cry for help, this act of self-abasement brought me some wisdom and self-awareness, even if only that you were and would always remain my one true love and the mother of my children. But even this was hard to maintain on the rack of my final days. Our marriage came to seem like a hollow fiction, something I might have just imagined rather than experienced. There were just not enough real fleshy physical memories to call upon in my death throes, as guide through the darkness, and proof that we were ever really truly together.

Dear darling Julka, we should probably have remained "just friends", as I remained – and I know you sometimes doubted this – with your sister Tanya. Our struggle to maintain emotional intimacy, the closeness of feeling that is supposed to characterise the "companionable marriage" of the twentieth century, brought upon us little more than pain and confusion. Our love, which we had found such a thrilling surprise at the start, was in fact a murderer jumping out on us from a dark alley. The fact that we lay together a few dozen times, and produced our two beautiful babies in the process, cannot possibly prove that we were "meant for each other" or that this was "the love of our lives", or any other such romantic flummery.

With me now as good as dead, you must try to rediscover your own way, to live the life you would have led if we had never met. I know you won't, that you will live out your days under the spell of "Mamma Zhenya"; as "maiden aunt" to your own children. You will undergo long periods of psychiatric disorder, hospitalisation and "treatment" at the hands of the Soviet health care system. This system will grow increasingly impatient with its own deviants, as it deviates further from its humanistic founding principles. The psychoanalysis which you embraced and I derided in the early years of your illness will come to seem like the gentle holding of hands when compared to the push-and-pull, shove-and-heave of "scientific" pharmaceutical, electro-convulsive and behavioural psychiatry.

In the years of "thaw" during the 1960s, you will settle with your sister and lifelong companion Evgenia in Peredelkino, Stalin's "colony" for favoured artists and intellectuals. The two of you will be installed at a sanatorium for veterans of the Communist Party of the Soviet Union, where you will both remain till you die. You will share a large airy room, and spend your days reading books and journals, writing letters to public and literary figures, and taking a particular interest in the activities and publications of Soviet youth organisations. Evgenia – irony of ironies – will help to edit and translate the first Russian (and highly selective) edition of my *Prison Letters,* a task from which she will undoubtedly extract a measure of consolation bordering on retribution. You will both remain fiercely loyalist to the end, dismissing any internal or external criticism of the Soviet Union as capitalist propaganda, including the mildest murmurs of dissent from our son Giuliano. In old age you will be bedridden and immobile from disease and paralysis in your legs, reduced to the condition in which I first encountered Evgenia. Thankfully your epilepsy will be brought under control by improved medication and more enlightened treatment. A book published in the 1970s, about love amongst revolutionaries, will compare you to *Ophelia* in Hamlet.

You will die aged 84 in 1980, eight years after Evgenia's death has given you a brief taste in old age of semi-contented independence and an unmediated relationship with our sons. Delio and Giuliano, the noble savage and the late developer, will make their own separate ways as a Soviet naval officer and a professional violinist. Their memories of me will be vaguer than of your father, old Apollon, who died four years before me but at least got to know his grandsons. They learnt from him how to ice-skate and will remember it every time they lace up their ice-skates and make light of the Russian winter. All they have of my paternal instruction in sportsmanship is a desire in one of my letters, never realised, to teach them how to skim stones across still water.

Even my surname will prove a dubious inheritance. Delio was named Schucht-Gramsci soon after birth, but Giuliano simply Schucht because (you will eventually tell the Soviet authorities by way of explanation) "his father was detained in Italy by the Fascist government." After my death, conferring upon me a rehabilitation the other communist fatalities of 1937 will have to wait decades for, they will start inscribing their schoolbooks *Gramsci*. By the end of the Great Patriotic War they will re-name themselves Gramsci for public purposes too, because of the shame attached to your Germanic surname. You will petition the Soviet state repeatedly for formal recognition, which will finally be granted in the late 1950s, so that my sons will be known henceforth as Delio and Giuliano Gramsci. They will spend much of the rest of their lives explaining where it came from and how it is spelt and pronounced, and warming their cold Russian hands on my borrowed Italian prestige.

As for you, always a junior "Mamma" after Mamma Zhenya, your only personal asset and legacy to our children and grandchildren will be your tenuous association with me, especially after I have been rediscovered and internationally acclaimed in the leaden years of the 1970s as Marxism's foremost "theorist of defeat". There, for us and our bitter entanglement, is some final triumph. I wish I could, but always knew I couldn't, stroke away your troubles...Nino.

* * *

And I see you coming towards me, along Via Siccardi in Turin, in your black silk dress and your shoes with patent leather and silver buckles, accompanied by your sister Tatiana. You are both talking and laughing at the same time, the very picture of sisterly companionship. It is the late summer of 1916, you are twenty. She is some years older but several inches shorter, a pleasing but less striking version of yourself. In an act of characteristic strong-mindedness, you have told your family that you will not be accompanying them back to Russia, but will stay here in Italy with your "sympatica" older sister. You are, you have told your blustering father Apollon in no uncertain terms, old enough to make your own decisions now. If he wants to swap a settled, comfortable and fulfilling life in lively, liberal, democratic, warm Italy for the uncertainties of starving, servile, autocratic, cold Russia, well, that's his look-out. But you won't be joining him there.

Instead you have secured a place in the Music Conservatory of the University of Turin, due to begin with the new university term in the autumn. The professors were so impressed with your virtuosity with the violin, and assured handling of your difficult signature-piece, Wienawski's Legende Opus 17, that they have offered you a generous scholarship to cover your tuition fees and living expenses. You took great pleasure in conveying the news to your father, along with the money-order he had sent you, and which you told him gleefully, "would not be needed now!"

You took just as much pleasure in reading your letter to him aloud to Tanya before you stuck it in the letter box at the main Post Office in Via Cavour, and in her laughing delight at the glorious cheek of it. That'll show him! In these days of wartime upheaval, of female emancipation and imminent workers revolution, he can't continue to throw his weight around and expect everyone to bow down before his patriarchal authority. Back in your room at the university, where Tanya is staying on this visit from Rome, you offered each other your best impressions of an apoplectic Apollon, all puffed-out checks and held-in breath to induce a furious reddening of the face underneath his bushy beard, which he thinks makes him look like Tolstoy. "Methuselah, more like!" you tell a giggling Tanya.

You have already been turning heads around the university. You turned mine at a meeting of the Young Socialists I had been asked to address about the latest nonsense coming from the noisy gang of interventionists and self-styled "idealists" gathered for shelter under the flailing arms and bulging eyes and barrel chest of Benito Mussolini. My own impression of old Benito made everybody roar with laughter, and exposed his little clique of "national socialists" as the vain buffoons they are. I caught you looking up at me from the front row, your deep-set blue eyes in your high cheekbones, and

I struggled for the breath to keep my words coming out. When you stood up and asked me a question – something about the "wilful slaughter of old Europe's young manhood" – I struggled for an answer, not because I didn't know what you were saying but because anything I might say paled into insignificance when compared to your beautiful face.

Afterwards I made straight for you, catching your eye and sitting myself on the edge of the small stage so that our heads were at the same level. I complimented you on the quality of your contribution, which you shyly dismissed as what was "uppermost in everyone's minds". We made an arrangement to meet for coffee the next day. Before I knew it we were sharing a bed and my very first experience of physical love with a woman. In wartime, you said, the normal rules and time-scales of courtship did not apply. Then you squatted over me and we did it again.

You were with me in your black silk dress at the head of the workers' demonstrations for peace and bread and freedom. You were with me when we took control of the factories and government offices, and showed that we could make a better fist of it than the toffs and ninnies of bourgeois hegemony. You were with me when we proved the practical efficacy of socialism over capitalism, you and me and all the other millions of provincial nonentities, people of the periphery, the sons and daughters of toil at long last taking centre-stage in history, making our own history rather than being made by it.

We began in the most advanced societies, economies and cultures of Western Europe, including our own brave and delightful Italy, then spread like a wildfire across the more backward countries of Asia, Africa, Australasia and the Americas. Even the rotten old feudalism of Tsarist Russia was eventually swept aside, almost as an afterthought, when their own small local middle-class intelligentsia realised they were being left behind in the race towards modernity and the triumph of reason in human affairs.

We have taken over the world, Julka, and made it a happy,

peaceful, safe place for the people of the present and the future, including the babies we shall raise into healthy, collaborative, creative and expressive citizens of the new order. There is no sign of your mental fragility, no sign of my physical frailty, no sign of Stalinism or Labourism or Fascism or Nazism, no sign of failure and defeat, of double rations and half-measures, of sectarian intrigue and personality cults. There is only the slow steady march of proletarian hegemony across every sphere of human life in this whole beautiful world of ours. The workers and peasants and soldiers, the nobodies and everybodies of the earth, have become "the people" in this new age of worldwide equality, individual liberty, political democracy and social solidarity. This is the end, beautiful friend, the one I see in the bright sunlight outside my room in Rome as I draw my very last breath.

Acknowledgements

This is a work of historical fiction; necessarily so, because of the many gaps in our knowledge of how Antonio Gramsci passed his short life. His final fifteen years, from his trip to Moscow as a Comintern delegate in 1922 to his death as a Fascist captive in Rome in 1937, are the most obscure of all, despite being by far the most significant and productive. The lives of the Schucht family, with whom Antonio's feelings and fortunes were inextricably linked throughout this period, are if anything even more obscure, largely because they were spent in the spreading darkness of Stalinist Russia. This makes the novel form the best, perhaps the only way to understand what this extraordinary man went through during those years of retreat and reflection.

Having said that, I have tried hard to stick to the established facts, and only turned to creative speculation when it seemed essential to deepen understanding or further the story or fill in those pesky gaps. The historian in me hopes it's obvious where fiction departs from fact; the novelist that it's not. Straddling that contradiction is the occupational hazard of these enterprises. As Anthony Burgess put it: "The virtue of a historical novel is its vice – the flat-footed affirmation of possibility as fact." The most obvious example of this quandary here is Gramsci's observations on prison life in Part Two. Those not in quotation marks are made up by me, usually on the basis of a much briefer comment by Gramsci himself (for example, his extraordinary note on prison tears); those that are come directly from the letters or notebooks themselves.

I have been hugely assisted by Derek Boothman, who has not only shared his own research into Gramsci's life and thought, culminating in his beautifully translated, just-published edition of the *Pre-Prison Letters,* but pointed out the other available pertinent sources. Some of these are only just emerging from

Russian and Italian archives. Perhaps the single most valuable is the family history compiled and published in Italian a few years ago by Antonio Gramsci Jr., the son of Giuliano (the son Antonio Gramsci Sr. never met), which put right a lot of inaccuracies in the accepted record. I hope my rudimentary Italian has enabled me to incorporate Antonio Jr.'s most important corrections and revelations.

Until then, all we really had was Giuseppe Fiori's magnificent biography, brilliantly translated into English by Tom Nairn, but published long ago in 1970, and Paolo Spriano's authoritative histories of the *Partito Comunista Italiano*, only some translated. The Russian archives were at that point largely inaccessible, and the Italian archives under the political control of the *PCI*. While the Italians were by far the most open and honest of all Communists, and went to great lengths to make their own history available to reputable academic scrutiny, there was inevitably an overlay of political purpose, especially in their treatment of their founder/martyr Antonio Gramsci. This also tended to make the histories rather too reverential, bordering on the kind of "Lives of the Saints" hagiography which Gramsci himself detested.

I have made much use of Fiori and Spriano's work, but brought it up to date where new facts or insights have emerged. My other main sources have been the two selections from Gramsci's prison letters, by Hamish Henderson (London 1988) and Lynn Lawner (London 1979). Both are superseded now by Frank Rosengarten and Raymond Rosenthal's complete 2011 collection,which I've also consulted and, now available in paperback, unreservedly recommend.. Beyond Gramsci, I have made much use of three other writers for a sense of period and place: the extraordinary social historian of the Soviet Union Sheila Fitzpatrick; and that pair of errant geniuses, Victor Serge and Mikhail Bulgakov, almost exact contemporaries (and in the former case, known acquaintance) of Gramsci. Exhibitions of the work of other contemporaries, the German constructivist/ collagist Hannah Hoch and the painter Paul Klee, provided artistic inspiration (if only the work of the *Kommunistische Partei Deutschlands* had been up to their standard!). For my attitude of friendly cheek towards old Nino himself, my primary influence was Pier Paolo Pasolini's wonderful poem *Gramsci's Ashes*, which I was directed to in turn by Scott Walker's extraordinary song "Farmer in the City".

For background (and the occasional startling discovery), I have waded through the 2011 Columbia University edition of Gramsci's entire prison notebooks, diligently translated, edited and annotated by Joseph Buttigieg. This likewise takes our understanding of Gramsci a long way beyond the more famous *Selections from Prison Notebooks*, translated and edited by Quintin Hoare and Geoffrey Nowell Smith and first published in 1971. The *Selections* was itself a brilliant piece of scholarship, largely responsible for introducing Gramsci to the English-speaking world, but its masterly collation of fragments necessarily left a lot out, and in the process skewed our sense of Gramsci's own preoccupations. You would never have guessed, for example, quite how obsessed he was with the ideology and organisation of the Catholic Church – the depth and durability of its hegemony, and how international communism might emulate it – or that for most of his prison years he was far more interested in culture than politics. To be fair, Geoffrey Nowell Smith (in interview with me) now acknowledges this imbalance.

Nonetheless, if my humble fiction has spurred you to read Gramsci himself, you can do a lot worse than start with the *Selections*, kept in print all these years by the ex-CPGB publisher Lawrence and Wishart, who also published my own heavily 'Gramscian' study of *The Politics of New Labour* in 2011. Writing and researching that book was what really got me back into Gramsci, and convinced me that if there is any way through the quandaries of political agency and historical explanation that confront us in the 21st century, it's to be found in the life and thought of this funny little Sardinian hunchback, this "person of the periphery" (to use the late great Stuart Hall's delightful epithet for his own intellectual hero). My final acknowledgement is to Stuart, who died while I was writing this novel, and in an unforgettable session at the Communist University of London in 1976 first alerted me to the truth and wisdom and humanity to be found in the "open, libertarian and always democratic Marxism" of Antonio Gramsci.

Andrew Pearmain, Norwich, England, 2014.

TOP HAT
BOOKS

Historical fiction that lives.

We publish fiction that captures the contrasts, the achievements, the optimism and the radicalism of ordinary and extraordinary times across the world.

We're open to all time periods and we strive to go beyond the narrow, foggy slums of Victorian London. Where are the tales of the people of fifteenth century Australasia? The stories of eighth century India? The voices from Africa, Arabia, cities and forests, deserts and towns? Our books thrill, excite, delight and inspire.

The genres will be broad but clear. Whether we're publishing romance, thrillers, crime, or something else entirely, the unifying themes are timescale and enthusiasm. These books will be a celebration of the chaotic power of the human spirit in difficult times. The reader, when they finish, will snap the book closed with a satisfied smile.